WITNESS
8

STEVE CAVANAGH

WITNESS 8

HEADLINE

First published in Great Britain in 2024 by
HEADLINE PUBLISHING GROUP

1

Cataloguing in Publication Data is available from the British Library

Hardback ISBN 978 1 0354 0820 7
Trade paperback ISBN 978 1 0354 0821 4
Waterstones ISBN 978 1 0354 2112 1

Typeset in 12.76/16.82 pt Adobe Garamond Pro by Jouve (UK), Milton Keynes

Printed and bound in Great Britain by Clays Ltd, Elcograf S.p.A.

HEADLINE PUBLISHING GROUP
An Hachette UK Company
Carmelite House
50 Victoria Embankment
London EC4Y 0DZ

www.headline.co.uk
www.hachette.co.uk

For Jon Wood.
Legend.

'The strength of a family, like the strength of an army, lies in its loyalty to each other.'

– Mario Puzo

Prologue
Ruby

There's something wrong with Ruby Johnson.

That's what her grandma used to say.

These days, Ruby often thought about what her grandmother had said. She wasn't a little girl any more. She was twenty-two now. Older, definitely wiser and perhaps more self-aware. It often occurred to Ruby that she was not like other people. It happened in moments such as this.

It was coming up on midnight. Ruby was at the counter, stirring a cup of coffee, in a kitchen almost twice the size of her apartment. The kitchen belonged to a thirty-five-million-dollar townhouse on the Upper West Side of Manhattan. Chad and Lara Puller were due to return any time now. They were one of Ruby's newer clients. She'd been sitting for them for just a few months. Upstairs, Clara, six, and Zara, recently turned three, were fast asleep in their large and expensively decorated bedrooms. Babysitting made up about forty percent of Ruby's little enterprise. Mostly, she worked as a maid and/or cleaner for most of the high-class residents of West 74th Street. To buy a house here you had to be seriously rich. Throw a nickel in any direction and you'll hit a successful Broadway producer, a plastic surgeon, a CEO of a high-end tech company or anyone on the board of a Fortune 500 behemoth. At any time, there could be between twelve and thirty million dollars' worth of cars parked by the curbs.

The long-term residents grew up here. Old money from New York real estate, not the two-bit slum lords who pretended to be millionaires – these people were rich.

Crazy rich.

And what allowed Ruby into their homes to look after their children, clean their floors and do their laundry was that some of them remembered that Ruby was *one of them*.

Or at least she *used to be*.

She wasn't an outsider. She was *their* kind of people.

Or so they thought.

Ruby's family had money, once.

Or that was what her father would have had people believe.

Ruby certainly thought that she belonged with these people.

Only Ruby's grandma knew different.

Ruby stirred the coffee and gazed into the dark liquid, her reflection lost in a swirling spiral of foam crema in the center of the cup.

She thought about her grandmother.

As a young child, Ruby would sit on the cold tiles in the grand hallway of her grandparents' house and eavesdrop as the adults talked in the lounge.

'There is something wrong with Ruby,' said her grandmother. Smart lady.

'What do you mean? She's quiet. Shy, maybe. But there's nothing *wrong* with her,' said her mother.

Even as she spoke, Ruby could detect the tone of denial in her mother's voice. A slight quiver in the throat. Ruby knew, deep down, at the age of ten, that Grandma's statement hit a lot deeper than her mother would ever reveal. Ruby's memories of her grandmother were probably all mixed up by her youthful gaze and innocent perspective, but they were still clear enough. Grandma always wore fine gold chains that got caught in the sagging folds of skin that hung around her neck. She always dressed in black, as if in mourning for someone, somewhere, all the time. Her false teeth were loose, giving a clacking, hissing and sometimes gummy sound to her words.

But her eyes . . .

Grandma had huge blue eyes that seemed to take up most of her face. They were misty with age, as if they gazed out behind a thick fog, but those eyes saw everything. And they always seemed to fix on Ruby whenever she entered her grandma's living room. Those old, dusty sapphire eyes came to life for Ruby. There was no affection in that stare. No curiosity. No love. It was more like – watchfulness. As someone might look upon a stray coyote that had wandered into your back yard.

There's something wrong with Ruby.

Ruby knew, even then, her grandma was right.

The sound of the front door opening brought Ruby's mind back to the present.

She took the spoon from the coffee cup, quickly opened the dishwasher and dropped it into the cutlery rack, then closed it and spun round just as Chad and Lara walked in. She flashed a smile.

'Hi, how was your evening?' asked Ruby brightly.

'Insufferable. Bad food, too much small talk. These galas are all the same. But it's for a good cause,' said Lara as she held on to the door frame and slipped off her Jimmy Choo heels.

Ruby took a moment to admire Lara's dress. Sleek, black, cut to fit her slim frame while accentuating everything that could bear it.

'How are the kids?' asked Chad, as he took off his bow tie and popped open the top button on his dress shirt.

'Sound asleep. They're little angels. I just made you some coffee. You two are always bang on time,' she said, handing Chad the cup. 'Lara, can I get you a nightcap?'

'Just water would be fine. I don't know how the hell Chad can drink coffee at this hour and still sleep like a log.'

'Good genes, I guess,' said Chad.

Ruby got some ice from the dispenser and poured a ten-dollar bottle of Icelandic water into a glass for Lara.

'Okilly dokilly, well, if that's everything, I'll just take off,' said Ruby.

'Our driver can take you home,' said Lara.

'No, it's fine. Thank you, Lara. It's a nice evening. I'm only ten blocks.'

'Ruby, parts of your neighborhood . . .' but Lara didn't finish the sentence. She wanted to say that Ruby lived in a dangerous area. But it would've been an unkind reminder that Ruby no longer enjoyed West 74th Street as her address. The Pullers, like everyone else on Ruby's client list, knew she had once been a resident. Before something bad had happened.

Still, she was one of them. From money. Trustworthy. Reliable.

'Don't worry. I'm fine. I'm free tomorrow if you need anything. I do love spending time with those little perfect peach fairies upstairs. They're sooooo adorable,' Ruby said.

'The kids are all good for tomorrow. Chad's taking them to the park. Just text me and let me know how much for tonight and I'll send it,' said Lara.

'Great, goodnight, you two. Don't let the beddy bugs bite,' she said.

As the thick mahogany front door closed behind Ruby, the bubbly expression slid from her face. She skipped down the steps to the street.

Chad wouldn't be taking the kids anywhere tomorrow.

Ruby took out her phone, pulled up her photo files. She had shots of the diaries of all her clients. Most of them just put the calendars on their fridge, some had them in little notebooks on the hall table, others synced their diaries to their Google Home Hubs or Amazon Echos, which made them easy to access.

Tomorrow, Lara had a nail appointment at eleven, then lunch with the girls.

Chad had racquetball with Jeff at eight thirty in the morning, then he was taking the kids out.

The slow-acting emetic that Ruby had added to his coffee would have Chad puking his guts out within a few hours. She expected to get a text from Lara around nine, saying Chad was ill in bed, and could she take the kids for the day?

Ruby charged extra on Saturdays, and she needed the money.

This little trick could only be pulled once or twice. Chad would blame the food at the gala. Last spring, Ruby had managed to work every Saturday for a month, dosing both parents of four different households. An outbreak of Norovirus in one of the kid's schools provided great cover.

She stood on the sidewalk and gazed up at the houses lining the street. She knew these people. She had spent time in their homes, unobserved. She knew their bathroom medicine cabinets, their underwear drawers, their email passwords, their internet search history, their diaries and, in some cases, their text messages. She knew their innermost thoughts . . .

Their secrets.

To Ruby, knowledge was power. Something else she had learned from her grandmother. Yet, with all that she knew of the residents and their lives, that knowledge could not seem to help her solve the biggest problem of all.

Ruby was in trouble. She had spent months worrying, thinking, tearing her mind apart at three in the morning, trying desperately to think of a solution.

She'd had various ideas. None of them seemed to suit her purpose. And every night as she paced her little room, unable to sleep, she hated the residents of West 74th Street even more. Yet walking seemed to help. It always did when Ruby was worried. The small effort of physical movement at least gave her the illusion she was getting somewhere.

She inhaled, took in the smell of fresh spring rain on the midnight streets of Manhattan, and took off toward home, letting her mind wander with her feet. As she passed the houses, she glanced up at the bay windows of these old brownstones and counted off her clientele one by one.

Out of all the homes on the street, Ruby worked for almost half. The homes that had not yet sampled her services either had live-in nannies for the kids or used a commercial maid service. But they would come round, eventually. Neighbors talk. There was even a private neighborhood WhatsApp group that included most of the homes and people she worked for. She had been recommended so many times that a friendly client had added her to the chat.

Ruby had walked this street more times than she could remember. When she was young, she'd felt at home here. This was *her* street, with *her* people, even though back then she didn't know all of them. But, still, she *belonged* here. Those were the early days. The good times.

She also remembered the bad times. That's what her mother called them.

One night, she had sat Ruby down and told her there would be some changes to their lives. That money was now a problem. Her father had made a mistake. Ruby, like children in most rich families, had never had to think about money. It was always there, like water from the faucet, and there was no reason to question it. In the days and weeks following that conversation, Ruby had walked this same street with a different feeling. She'd gazed through the same windows, wondering why their lives were now so different. What did it feel like to have so much money? What would you do if you didn't have to worry about money, ever? What would it feel like to be free?

Tonight, the homes on Ruby's side of the street were in darkness. Only four homes on the opposite side had lights on.

Peter and Petra Schwartzman were having a party. They often held parties, always for residents only, with exceptions made for celebrities. Ruby could hear tasteful jazz and the low buzz of a house filled with people drinking and probably talking about their third and fourth homes, their cars, their boats and their favorite vineyards. Ruby saw that the front door of the Schwarztman's home was slightly ajar. A narrow strip of light spilled onto the street along with the music. For a second, Ruby longed to be inside that home, rubbing elbows with the neighbors. She wondered what would happen if she walked in through the open door. She knew almost everyone in there.

But she wasn't *one of them* any more. Not really. There would be strange looks, perhaps. Questions asked. And the Schwarztmans would be milling around, telling people that Ruby had most definitely *not* been invited.

Everyone who was anyone in the street was probably there. The Pullers couldn't have gone because they were at a gala. The only other residents who were not in attendance probably weren't invited.

The Colchesters had a lamp on in one of the bedrooms, casting a warm red glow from the window. Once the residents had discovered that they'd made a campaign donation to a president who was unpopular in this city, they'd stopped speaking to the Colchesters. Next door's open-plan lounge area was bathed in cold blue light from the underlit refrigerator and low-level LED strip lighting hitting their black kitchen tiles. Just because the Satrianis were rich didn't mean that they had any taste, not when it came to interior design, at least. They were seen as a tacky couple. The Satrianis made their money from selling mattresses. Not the kind of people who were invited to the Schwarztmans' parties.

There were probably one or two other families in the street who weren't partying with the Schwarztmans that night. But their homes were in darkness.

The last illuminated home belonged to Margaret and Alan Blakemore. They had lived in the street for a long time. More than thirty years at least. In their fifties, married but no kids, Margaret had enjoyed a twenty-year career as a model. Alan didn't need to work. As a young man he had enjoyed his trust fund, traveling the world. That's when he'd developed a talent for photography and decided that this would be his career. He'd met Maggs, as she liked to be called, on a shoot for *Vogue*, and when she learned he was a billionaire the rather plain-looking Alan suddenly became more attractive. Their marriage was happy at first, but soon Maggs embarked on a series of scandalous affairs with musicians, actors and other models, and the couple had grown apart. But she always came back to Alan's money.

Maggs was definitely not invited to the Schwarztmans. Not after the rumors. Maggs had been romantically linked to a number of men in the street. Some of them married. And Maggs liked to flirt with men who had nine-figure checking accounts. None of the rich wives could stand Maggs. She was not welcome at these kinds of soirées. Perhaps because Maggs was something of an outsider to the reserved residents of the street, she had found a kindred spirit in Ruby. After Ruby cleaned her house, Maggs took the time to sit with her, have some coffee, ask about her life. Get the gossip. It was a small thing, but Ruby had always appreciated and liked Maggs for this kindness. To the rest of the street, Ruby was all but invisible. Maggs tipped well, but giving Ruby her time meant a lot more. Even though she was always entangled with more than one man, Ruby felt Maggs was haunted by a loneliness no affair could banish.

The chandelier in Maggs's lounge was lit. A harsh, bright, white light. Maggs hated the thing. She lit her living room by antique brass lamps with colored glass shades that she had imported from Hong Kong. Ruby was told to be extra careful when dusting these. Ruby thought it must've been Alan who was up late, because Maggs preferred soft lighting now that she was in her fifties, but still carried the vanity of a catwalk queen.

Ruby was wrong.

As she got closer, she saw Maggs from across the street. She had her back to the window and her hands outstretched, palms upwards. Ruby watched Maggs shake her dyed chestnut hair, as if saying 'no' or pleading with someone. Then she saw who Maggs was talking to.

It wasn't Alan. It was another resident. She knew his face. Knew his name.

He pointed a gun at Maggs. She was backing away.

Ruby's breath caught in her throat and she ducked down behind the hood of a large SUV with gold-plated rims.

She heard the shot, but only just. It was muted, somehow. Maggs disappeared from view – thrown to the floor by the kinetic force of the bullet.

The man pointed the weapon to the floor. Ruby could no longer see Maggs, only the upper half of the man's body from her position behind the SUV across the street.

He fired twice more, turned and left her view.

The front door to the Blakemore house opened and the man, dressed in black, gun in hand, leapt down the steps to the street. Ruby ducked as he looked left and then right. He walked back up the street in the direction Ruby had just come from. Stopped for a second, then moved on, running now.

Ruby crouched low, holding her breath for fear he would see her.

He ran back to the open front door to the Schwartzman's party. They were all probably too drunk to notice him leaving and then coming back in.

Ruby could feel her heartbeat in her throat. Still crouched, she moved round the hood of the car, then crossed the street.

The man was gone. The street empty.

There hadn't been a huge amount of noise from the gun. It must've been silenced, but Ruby had definitely heard the crack from that pistol. Like somebody splintering wood.

She gazed up at the house. The front door was wide open.

She quickly moved up the steps, into the hallway and turned left into the living space.

Maggs was dead on the floor. Blood on her face and pooling behind her head. The feeling in Ruby's stomach reminded her of being on a rollercoaster – it felt as if her insides were doing somersaults and she found it hard to breathe.

She recognized the sensation.

It wasn't fear.

It wasn't revulsion.

It wasn't shock.

It was *excitement*.

Quickly and quietly, Ruby left the house and followed the path of the killer back up the street.

He had stopped around halfway, she remembered.

Why had he stopped?

Ruby saw a pile of garbage bags leaning against a lamp post. One of the bags was ripped at the side. She peeled back the rip in the bag, saw the matt-black butt of a gun. The gun and the bag would be taken in six hours, heaved into a garbage truck at dawn and lost forever.

Pulling the sleeve of her coat over her hand, Ruby reached into the bag and retrieved the gun, then slipped it into her purse.

There was no one else on the street. No sirens from police cars. No paramedics. She watched the windows of the houses. No one peering out.

Ruby turned back the way she'd come, made her way past the Blakemore's home, and kept on walking.

She didn't call the cops. Just walked the ten blocks home on a warm night, her mind alive with possibilities.

Ruby knew who had shot and killed Maggs.

Knowledge is power. She could hear her grandmother saying it now, her watchful eyes mooning at young Ruby from her throne.

The only question on Ruby's mind was what she was going to do with that power. She was used to keeping secrets. For the years she had worked for the rich families of West 74th Street, knowing their minds, their secret affairs, their hopes and fears, and their crimes . . .

She hated them. She hated the fathers, the mothers and even some of the children.

Now was her chance.

A possible way out of the deep trouble that had agonized her thoughts for the past months.

A chance for a new life.

While thoughts of her terrible situation had kept her from sleep, her choices had not. Ruby had hurt people. She knew that she would have to hurt a lot more of them before the end. She did what she had to do without fear, without mercy, without a second thought for those she would destroy.

Suddenly, Ruby had the solution. It was right there, in her purse. Still warm from firing three rounds into a woman she had fondly known all of her life.

Ruby felt nothing for Maggs. No sadness. If anything, she was glad. She could now see a way out.

West 74th Street would wake in the morning to the shocking murder of one of their own.

It would not be the last.

Because, right now, Ruby Johnson had a plan.

PART ONE

I

Eddie

In the beginning, and in the end, it all comes down to money.

New York City runs on the stuff like no other place on earth. Everything is about the green. What you can make. How you can get over. Kickbacks and greenbacks. Everything. And everyone.

All the damn time.

Before I became a lawyer, I was a con artist. When I worked the bars, the hotels, the businesses, seeking out my targets for short-cons, I looked for men who wanted to make a fast buck and didn't care who they hurt in the process. I went after those who had taken a wrong turn in life and never looked back. As a lawyer, I was on the lookout for the same kind of people.

Once you realize that cash is king in this city, things get a lot easier and much clearer.

The case in front of me right now had to be looked at through the lens of this city. My client Jayden Carter and his pal Smokehouse had been driving through the Bronx late one night in Jayden's brand-new Lexus. Unsurprisingly, they hadn't gotten very far before they saw the flashing berries and cherries of a cop car behind them. A single whoop of the siren was all it took for Jayden to pull over. The cops said the rear of his Lexus was dirty, obscuring the license plate. A valid reason for a stop. Jayden had washed the car that morning. Far as he was concerned, this was bullshit.

Officers Ben Gray and Linton Coffee, already pissed off that they were on the lobster shift at their precinct, searched the vehicle and found an unlicensed firearm in Jayden's car. He was arrested, charged and, after being stupid enough to carry an illegal weapon, even if it was just for protection, he made the *right* decision.

He called me.

That was six weeks ago.

Jayden sat beside me at the defense table in a brand-new navy suit, white button-down shirt and a navy tie. He was twenty-six. Single. Ran his own business – a furniture store in East Tremont. Smoke-house, Jayden's childhood friend, sat in the gallery beside my assistant, and secretary, Denise. He wore his best Canadian tuxedo – a baggy denim jacket and matching oversized blue jeans with a white tee beneath. His real name was Philip Martin, but he preferred Smoke-house, on account of his burgeoning hip-hop career. Both Jayden and Smokehouse were college graduates, well read, smart. And they had both done the right thing during the traffic stop – they complied with the NYPD instructions and let their lawyer do the fighting later.

Denise was in her black pant suit and white blouse. She dressed up whenever I needed her to come help me in court. Always professional, smarter than me and most lawyers.

'Mr. Flynn, you have a motion before the court?' said the judge.

His Honor Judge Leonard Hightower was one of the best judges in the city. He wasn't a genius. He didn't even have a particularly brilliant mind. The respect he had among the defense attorneys of the New York legal profession stemmed from two factors.

His interpretation of the law was accurate.

He wasn't biased in favor of the district attorney.

Not much to ask from a judge, really. But the fact that he fulfilled these basic requirements put Judge Hightower in the top rank of the judiciary in New York City.

'I do have a motion, Your Honor,' I said, getting to my feet.

At this point, the assistant district attorney, Thomas Baker, broke from the prosecution table and came over to see me.

'If we could have just one moment, please, Your Honor,' he said.

Baker was a young, hungry ADA, with three years in the office and a thousand convictions under his belt. His fresh face and brassy blues eyes were zeroed in on a senior position.

He didn't want to try this case. Didn't want me to make this motion. Baker wanted to settle.

'Last chance, Flynn,' he whispered. 'Two-hundred-dollar fine, two years' parole, no jail time.'

Criminal possession of a firearm without a license is a felony in New York. If Jayden was convicted, he would go to prison. This was a sweet deal. The last offer I got from Baker was a five-hundred-dollar fine, ninety days' prison time and two years' parole, but this was the best deal I'd ever been offered by a prosecutor.

A small fine. No prison time. Two years' parole.

It wasn't a get-out-of-jail-free card, but it was the next best thing. Baker had two cops waiting in the wings to testify that the license plate was muddy, obscuring some of the lettering. If they could prove the stop was legal, Jayden was going to jail.

Easy. Two veteran cops. Their word against the word of Jayden and Smokehouse who said the plate was clean. You didn't need to be a legal expert to know which way this was going to play out.

Only problem was the offer.

Baker didn't want this case to settle. He *really* wanted it to settle.

That was what made me uneasy about the case right away. My suspicions were confirmed once I'd gotten all the paperwork from Jayden – his arrest sheet and all the legal docs that come with it – property seizure of the firearm and towing receipt.

That was all I needed.

'Hey, man,' said Jayden, 'that's not a bad deal. No jail time?'

'It's your call,' I said. I looked over at Baker. He was talking to his first witness. Officer Ben Gray. Only, he was no longer patrolman Gray. The three blue stripes on the arm of his uniform meant he had gone up in the world since this stop.

That clinched it.

'If you want my advice, we fight. You won't do time with this deal, but you'll be a convicted felon. That brings a ton of shit that you have to carry around. You can't ever legally possess a firearm, you won't get a loan or credit card, you won't get a mortgage, you'll lose your driver's license and that's just the beginning.'

He nodded, said, 'I hear you, man, but this white judge is never going to believe that license plate was clean. Not when there's two white cops saying my plate was dirty.'

'I agree,' I said.

'You what?'

'You're right. He won't believe you over two white cops.'

'So why are we fighting this?'

'Because I'm not going to call you as a witness to testify that your license plate was clean. We're going to get one of the cops to do it for us.'

Jayden looked at me like I'd just told him I'd bought the Brooklyn Bridge for a nickel.

I asked him to trust me. He nodded.

'Mr. Baker, Mr. Flynn,' said the judge. 'Are you ready to proceed?'

'I am, Your Honor, Mr. Baker has agreed to call Officer Ben Gray to speak to the single issue in this case. I will have questions for the officer afterwards.'

'Proceed,' said Judge Hightower.

The tall cop in the new sergeant's stripes came forward, took the oath, sat down and gave fast, clean answers to Baker's questions. Gray and his partner were on the night shift, they saw a Lexus drive past with mud on the license plate, obscuring the lettering. They stopped the car, informed the driver why he'd been pulled over. Got his license and registration and ran a check on both.

'During the stop, Sergeant Gray, was there anything else suspicious about Mr. Carter or his vehicle?' asked Baker.

'Yes, I could smell marijuana. It was a pungent smell coming out of the car. While it's legal to carry it for personal use, I suspected, given how strong the smell was, that there may be a large quantity of marijuana in the vehicle – enough for illegal distribution of narcotics.'

Since the legalization of marijuana, cops looking for an excuse to search a vehicle will either say they thought they saw a gun on the back seat, or say they caught an immensely strong smell of dope from the car. Needless to say, there were no drugs in Jayden's car. Didn't matter that they didn't find any – they *did* find a gun.

'I see, and having formed a reasonable suspicion, did you then search the vehicle?'

'We both did. I found the pistol in the glove box. Mr. Carter did not have a license to carry that firearm and he was given his rights and arrested. I called in the arrest, arranged for a truck to tow the defendant's vehicle.'

'Thank you, Sergeant Gray. Mr. Flynn will have some questions.'

I could have a dozen questions now. The truth is I already knew exactly what had happened.

Gray and Coffee had made a racially motivated traffic stop. Simple as that. There was no mud on the license plate when they stopped the car, but while Gray talked to Jayden, I guessed his partner could smear all the mud and dirt he wanted onto the license plate. There was no smell of drugs. They were looking for a reason to arrest Jayden. If they hadn't found a gun, I suspected both cops would've gotten physical with him and said Jayden struggled, then he would've been arrested for resisting a police officer.

Street cops live and die by their arrest record. They need to keep those numbers high. And what started as racial profiling quickly turned into an opportunity to make some money. There are five tow companies who have contracts with the city. Once the cops arrest a driver at a traffic stop the car can't be left on the street – it has to be towed. There's a randomizer on their cruiser's computer – so once they input that a car needs a tow, the program randomly selects one of the five towing companies. That's who they're supposed to call for the tow. Only some cops forget to press the button, or ignore the result. They call their guy in the towing company who will kick back fifty bucks to the cop for the call-out – usually, the same company who keeps a lot in Long Island, or Jamaica, or Bed Stuy, so they can charge the extra mileage for towing and are likely to keep the car longer because it will make it hard for the owner to get a ride out there.

Greenbacks and kickbacks.

Even those sergeant's stripes.

The officers who are under investigation, or have a large number of citizen complaints against them, normally get a promotion instead of booted off the force. The police commission and the union don't want cops prosecuted nor any successful complaints from the public, because they hate cops getting fired. Gives the boys in blue a bad name. Instead, it's easier to take problematic cops off the street by putting them behind a sergeant's desk. A rotten NYPD cop is far more likely to get a promotion, and the pay rise and pension benefits that come with it, than get fired.

I wasn't going to ask Sergeant Gray about any of this. Not the complaints against him, not the promotion.

I was going to focus on the illegal stop and tow.

I had no proof of any of Gray's criminal activity, other than his promotion, and the fact that on the face of it this was a slam dunk case for a prosecutor, but Baker didn't want to be in court. He was offering me the shirt off his back just to plead this case out.

I guessed he suspected I knew what had really happened.

And they *knew* I must've had a good reason to throw away the plea deal of a lifetime. Baker suspected I had evidence that would blow them away.

I stood, picked up a folder off the desk and took out the thick wad of documents inside. About a hundred pages. Stapled together. I flicked through them, studying the pages, then found what I was looking for, ran my finger along a line of text, then gave Sergeant Gray a big smile.

'Sergeant, when you make an arrest from a traffic stop and the vehicle has to be towed, what is standard NYPD protocol?'

'You secure the vehicle, hit the randomizer on the cruiser and call the tow company that comes up onscreen. Then I make sure the vehicle is transferred into their custody.'

I turned, nodded to Denise. She got up, left the court. I could have done this sooner, but I wanted to make sure Sergeant Gray saw me signal to Denise. And that he saw Denise leave.

'So the tow company who comes to collect the vehicle, that's always chosen at random by the computer?'

'Not necessarily. We have a duty to convey the suspect to central booking as soon as possible. If we happen to see an unloaded tow truck passing by, we can flag it down.'

'Does that happen often?'

'Sometimes.'

The courtroom doors opened and Denise led in four men. Two wore dirt- and grease-strained gray overalls. The other two blue overalls were in roughly the same state. All four wore work boots, their hands dark with traces of oil, and were between forty and fifty years old. They could all have been from the same industrial rock band, but a distinctive individual logo on their overalls, and the same logo on a ball cap that one of them wore, spelled out exactly where they were from – they wore the insignia of the other four city-approved towing companies.

'Is there a record of the randomizer results?'

'Mr. Flynn, is this relevant to your client's case?' asked the judge. Hightower was listening, but he liked things to move swiftly in court.

'If you allow me a few more questions, I believe this will be crucial.'

'Go on, but bring this to a point soon,' said the judge.

'Sergeant Gray, is there a record of the randomizer results?'

Gray, keeping his lips tight, smiled and locked his fingers together before saying, 'There are no records of randomizer results.'

'But we do have your arrest records,' I said, holding up the heavy bundle of documents in my right hand. I reached over, took another pile of pages from the table with my left, held those up too, and said, 'And we have the towing records for the other four towing companies approved by the city. What would happen if we matched up those records, Sergeant Gray?'

I couldn't resist glancing behind me at the gallery. One of the men in overalls was smiling and nodding. All four of them stared intensely at Gray – like he was juicy prime rib and they were getting ready to devour him.

'I'm not sure what you mean,' said Gray, his eyes furtively moving between the bundle of documents in my hand and the four tow-truck drivers in the gallery beside Denise. He sat up in his chair and his eyes grew wider as I let the silence, and his anxiety, build.

'I mean, what are the odds the randomizer gives you the name of the same tow company for every single one of your arrests?'

Sergeant Gray grew very pale. Then his skin color changed again. He looked almost green, like he was about to throw up.

'Before we get into these records in detail, Sergeant Gray, I'm going to ask you once more, and *for the final time* – is it possible that my client's license plate was a little dirty, but that the plate numbers were not fully obscured?'

I could hear the pine bench creaking as all four men in overalls leaned forward. Their gaze locked on Gray.

Sweat broke out on his forehead. He started chewing on his lip, then swallowed, took a sip of water. I was giving him a way out. A path that would cause some immediate embarrassment, but it was better than facing another internal-affairs investigation.

'Now that I think of it,' he said, and then coughed and sat up straighter in his chair. 'Now that I have had time to properly consider it, maybe my recollection of that license plate was not one hundred percent accurate.'

'What?' asked Judge Hightower. 'Speak clearly, Sergeant. Was the defendant's license plate obscured by dirt or not?'

'I can't be sure any longer,' said Gray, shaking his head.

Judge Hightower leaned back in his seat and stared at me.

'Mr. Flynn, I have no idea what just happened, but this officer has just confirmed your client was illegally stopped. That means the search of your client's vehicle was also illegal and any items recovered from that search were unlawfully obtained. This prosecution is dismissed,' said Judge Hightower, and he stood up and left the court.

By the time Sergeant Gray was on his feet, the DA had already angrily stuffed his papers into his faux leather briefcase and was stomping out of the courtroom. Gray looked unsteady on his feet. He joined his partner, they whispered together then followed the DA out of court.

I felt Jayden's arms round me. They were shaking.

'It was luck,' I said. 'I know you've got that weapon for protection, but it's gone now. Trust me – you're safer without it.'

'I know. I'm sorry, Eddie. Thank you for this.'

We hugged it out, and then Jayden and Smokehouse bounced out of the back doors.

I met Denise and our four tow truckers in the lobby.

'Good job,' I said, and gave each of them a hundred bucks.

'Do we get to keep the overalls?' said Bugs.

Bugs wore one of the gray uniforms. Denise said her sewing skills weren't what they used to be, and the badge on this pair of overalls was crooked, with black threads trailing from it.

'Sure. Keep the overalls and the boots. Just don't go pretending to be tow-truck drivers. And take off the badges.'

Bugs, Karl, Johnny and Little Sacks pulled the badges off the overalls I'd bought on eBay last week. I'd represented Bugs some years back on a breaking-and-entering charge. One in a long line of missteps. He promised if he got another chance he would change. I got him off, didn't charge him a cent and we became friends. I helped out Bugs and his pals whenever I could. Usually Bugs and the guys hung out at the Bowery Mission in Tribeca, a homeless shelter that was fast becoming a regular home.

'If you want lunch, you know my tab is always open at Lexi's Deli on 10th.'

'I think we might stretch to a grilled cheese today, if that's alright, Eddie?'

'Whatever you guys need.'

Being homeless in any city is tough. In New York, it's hell. But Bugs was proud. Even though I told him he and his pals could eat every day at the deli, on me, they only went occasionally. Didn't want to exploit any kind of generosity – no matter how small.

'Thanks, guys. We couldn't have done it without you,' said Denise.

We watched Bugs and his pals pocket the cash, and leave the court building with something of a spring in their step.

'You're a lousy seamstress,' I said.

'You should try my cooking,' said Denise.

'No, thanks. You brought me leftover meatloaf last month. Do you remember?'

'Not my finest piece of cooking.'

'I disagree. It's great. It's still holding open that heavy door to the office storeroom.'

Denise laughed, punched me in the arm. We started to follow Bugs toward the exit.

'I meant to ask, how did you get Sergeant Gray's arrest records and towing information?' she said.

I opened my leather messenger bag, took out the two bundles of documents.

I held both bundles aloft, then dumped them in a garbage basket as we walked past. 'Two Xeroxed copies of the TV Guide for last December.'

Right then, Denise stopped, reached into her jacket.

Her phone was ringing. Mine was still switched off.

She took the call, listened, hung up and said, 'Kate needs you back at the office right now. She's caught a whale.'

A whale, in legal terms, is a client with extremely deep pockets.

'What's he on the line for? Divorce?'

Denise shook her head, said, 'Murder.'

2

Eddie

We don't get many whales as clients.

Flynn and Brooks, Attorneys at Law, does not have the kind of office that normally attracts high-earning clientele. We're not based on Wall Street. We don't have glass-walled partitions and five-hundred-dollar chairs. We don't have little branded titanium cases full of breath mints in reception, we don't have a logo on free umbrellas, or even a website.

Our law practice is situated in Tribeca, not far from the homeless shelter. We have the upper floor of the building. Below us is a tattoo parlor called Stinkin Ink. Jocko runs the parlor and takes in our mail when we're out of the office. It's not a bad arrangement. The only drawback is having a client conference when Jocko is tattooing some-one's ass. It's an old building and, no matter how tough you are, when you're getting your ass inked there's going to be some screaming.

I dumped my bag in my office and allowed myself a moment to take in the scene in our new conference room, which had a long table in the center of the room, with three chairs on each side. Kate Brooks had a yellow legal pad in front of her, a Muji fine liner in her hand and was scrawling notes across the page. She wore a sober black business suit and her hair was up, with another pen lodged in the knot. Harry Ford, former senior judge and now a consultant at the firm, sat beside her. He wore a charcoal tweed jacket over a red wool cardigan with a blue shirt beneath it. The leather patches over his elbows were doing their job this morning. When Harry was thinking, his fingers had a tendency to move. Even when he laced them tight together over his stomach – those thumbs of his would turn over and over like two tombola barrels. Now, his elbows were on the table, fingers steepled together, the pads of each one of them lightly tapping the other. He was my mentor and my best friend. The gray had now consumed his hair and he was more reliant on his glasses. Two pairs were suspended over his chest on fine gold chains: one for reading, one for driving.

I couldn't see the client's face, nor the face of the man who sat beside him. Only the backs of their necks were visible. Both wore dark suits. Dark hair.

I pushed open the conference-room door.

Clarence, Harry's dog, sat by his feet. Like always. He got up as I entered and nuzzled my legs. I bent down to stroke him.

'Eddie, good to have you,' said Kate. 'This is John Jackson and his lawyer, Al Parish.'

I'd heard of Al Parish. Never met him. His face was lined here and there, defiant against the swelling that was evident from Botox injections around the cheeks and lower forehead. The hair color was a dye job. He wore a navy suit with a thick silk tie that probably cost more than the refit of our conference room. Aging senior partners in old Wall Street firms all looked the same. Too many hours on the golf course. Too much plastic surgery. Too much money and no inclination to do anything but earn more. Three ex-wives hadn't managed to put a dent in his fortune.

'Eddie,' said Parish, and held out a tanned hand with a one-hundred-dollar manicure.

'Pleased to meet you,' I said. He squeezed my hand hard, the way small men do.

'This is my client, John Jackson,' he said.

The man beside him had all the trappings of wealth that Parish had on display. The suit. The shirt. The haircut. And yet none of that seemed to matter to him. He wore the rich clothes lightly. I put him at around thirty-five. Slim. Smelled clean with some hint of chemical alcohol behind the odor. His hand was soft, but his grip was firm. Unlike Parish, he didn't put the effort into the handshake – he just had powerful hands. I couldn't recall meeting someone who worked with their hands and didn't have a single callus.

A familiar look haunted his face. The look of the accused. It's hard to describe. It's not terror. It's not exactly fear – although there would be plenty of that coming down his road. Harry once said being accused of a crime is like having a ghost follow you. You can't see it. Somehow it remains behind you, or just out of your peripheral vision, but you know it's there. And it's always coming for you.

'Kate and Harry have been looking after us very well,' said Parish.

'Well, they're much better at that than me,' I said, and took a seat at the end of the table – Harry and Kate on my right, Parish and Jackson on my left.

'Mr. Jackson has been charged with first-degree murder,' said Kate. 'NYPD picked him up two days ago. Mr. Parish—'

'Please, it's Al,' said Parish, brandishing a smile that displayed the bleach job on his teeth that made them look like they would glow in the dark.

'Al sat in on the police interview and got Mr. Jackson bail,' said Kate.

'Bail for murder one is no easy thing,' I said.

'It gets easier when you can lay down a two-million-dollar bond,' said Al, and shot Jackson an admiring look.

Kate continued to bring me up to speed.

'Victim was a Margaret Blakemore, fifty-nine years old. She lived on the same street as Mr. Jackson. They were neighbors, but they'd never formally met. Mrs. Blakemore was shot dead in her home two weeks ago. Her husband was out of state, solid alibi. The cops ruled him out early. Police did a house-to-house. There was a street party that night and most of the residents were in attendance. The others were all accounted for with alibis. No one heard anything and no one saw anything. Police spoke to Mr. Jackson. On the night of the murder, the rest of the family was away visiting relatives. It was just Mr. Jackson home alone. All night. So no alibi. Things stepped up a gear a couple of days ago. The cops got an anonymous tip that Mr. Jackson was the shooter.'

'An anonymous tip?' I asked.

'They traced the call to a payphone in Midtown. No other information. Whatever was in that tip became enough for a search warrant. Police found a handgun in Mr. Jackson's home. They took that away for testing together with some clothes. No results have been released, but he's been charged,' said Kate with a look.

I knew the look. The cops weren't going to play their hand just yet. Either they had four aces with forensic evidence linking that gun to the murder or they had Jack high and the murder charge was a bluff to get the press off their backs.

'I remember hearing about this on the news,' I said.

Harry nodded, said, 'First murder in a long time on this part of 74th Street.'

'Doesn't the DA live a block away?' I asked.

Harry nodded.

'Cops would've been under pressure to make an arrest. Could be they're bluffing. This charge might go away on its own,' I said.

Soon as I said that, I saw John Jackson's head roll back on his shoulders, his eyes widened and his mouth opened. Like I had just floated the prospect of taking a boulder the size of a Volkswagen off of his chest.

'Could that really happen?' he asked excitedly.

'This is a murder charge,' said Harry. 'Anything is possible.'

Jackson looked at Kate. She nodded, said, 'Harry and Eddie are right. When something bad happens in a good neighborhood, the NYPD makes arrests and ask questions later. There's just one thing.

Neither Al, nor you, have told us about the gun the police found in your home.'

'It's not mine. I don't own a gun. Never touched one in my life,' said Jackson. 'When I was a young resident in Saint Luke's, I saw what guns can do to people. I must've dealt with fifty gunshot wounds. No way in hell I would ever pick up a gun.'

'John is now a brain surgeon at NYU Hospital,' said Al.

That explained the hands.

'So where did the gun come from?' asked Harry.

It was the question I wanted to ask, but it sounded much better coming from Harry. He had a soft tone that made hard questions land like raindrops on a feather pillow.

'I have no idea where it came from. All I know is it's not mine and I have never even seen it before, never mind touched it,' said Jackson.

'This is where you come in, Eddie,' said Al. 'We have a criminal division in our firm, but as you know, I'm a civil litigator and no one in our team has ever tried a murder case. John here deserves the best, so we came to you. No disrespect, but you're a small outfit. John would also like you to make use of our considerable resources. With you and your team leading, of course.'

'And you driving from the back seat?' I asked.

Al raised his palms, said, 'No fear of that, I promise. This is your show, and we've got the manpower to back your every play – that's what we bring to the table. Also, we're going to handle the lawsuit against the city for wrongful arrest. We're just getting ready to file.'

'Don't you think that's a little too soon?' asked Kate. 'We haven't cleared Mr. Jackson yet.'

'Never too soon to start a lawsuit,' said Al, and winked at Kate.

I didn't like it.

I used to practice alone. I had a partner a long time ago, but that was always destined to fail. In recent years, I've loved working with Kate and Harry. She is an incredible lawyer, but more than that, she's utterly fearless. Harry, well, I just like having him around. He keeps me on the straight and narrow both in and out of the law. And there's no one alive who knows more about trial law than Harry Ford, one of the first African American senior judges to grace the benches of Manhattan's courts.

There was one other thing I did like.

John Jackson.

I can usually tell when I see a guilty client. And an innocent one.

'There's one question before we go any further,' I said. 'Mr. Jackson, John, did you kill Margaret Blakemore?'

The question hit him like a bucket of cold water. That's the way it is at the beginning. Those who are accused of a crime they didn't commit, look like they're drowning. Every accusation is another freezing wave that causes them panic, makes them fight to get to the surface. Until their name is cleared, they spend their lives kicking to get their head above water.

'I have never killed anyone in my life,' he said. 'And I never could.'

Al piped up at this point.

'Eddie, a week before Margaret Blakemore was killed, this guy spent forty-two hours in the operating theatre taking a tumor the size of an avocado stone out of a fourteen-year-old kid's brain. He's a goddamn hero.'

Jackson hung his head, hiding the tears on his face. Fighting down the panic and confusion that overwhelms people in his situation.

I looked at Kate and Harry. They nodded.

We don't take cases if we don't believe the client is innocent.

'Well, John,' I said, 'looks like you got yourself some more lawyers. We'll need to do some digging around the case.'

I turned, glanced through the glass window on the back wall of the conference room. I only saw Denise at her desk.

'Where's Bloch?' I asked.

Kate addressed her answer to the room. 'Our investigator, Bloch, is currently assisting another private investigator in the search for Dyani Sandoval.'

'The little girl who was snatched in Saratoga Springs?' asked Al.

'Yes, Bloch texted me this morning. She's been up there all weekend. She thinks they're close to finding her,' said Kate.

'Who is the PI?' I asked.

'Our friend, Gabriel Lake, freshly returned from a trip to London. He said he wanted Bloch for a matter of diplomacy.'

'Diplomacy? Bloch? *Our* Bloch?' I asked.

Kate nodded, said, 'I think his definition of diplomacy is a bit different from ours.'

3
Bloch

Bloch had been in upstate New York for three days.

She didn't like being away from Kate, but right now Dyani Sandoval needed Bloch more than her childhood friend did. Seven days ago, John Sandoval was tending to his horses on his property. His daughter, Dyani, was practicing for the upcoming tryouts for the school cheerleading team about two hundred feet away. He watched her cartwheel and dance in her faded blue jeans. There had never been a school cheerleader of Native American descent on the team before, but John Sandoval just knew his little Dyani was going to make it. She had incredible stamina. The temperature was in the nineties, perspiration had darkened the back of her T-shirt, her dark hair shone with sweat, and still she danced and practiced her cheers. Always moving.

But her movement had brought her further away from the stables, and close to the white picket fence that bordered the road.

John wasn't concerned when he first saw the white van on the road. He became uneasy as it slowed its approach the closer it got to his fence.

When it stopped and the big man got out of the passenger seat, John was already running for the fence. He watched the man grab Dyani round the waist from behind. Saw him lift her up, her legs kicking in the air. Watched him throw her over the fence like a bag of garbage. Saw him pick her up again, throw her in the back of the van and get in with her. The rear doors closed and the van pulled away at speed as John reached the fence.

This is what he had told the police in the initial report. Amber alerts went up statewide and in neighboring New Hampshire, Connecticut, Massachusetts and Vermont. An unfathomable number of Native American children go missing every year. What made Dyani different was her father. John bred racehorses and he had powerful connections. One friend called another, and called another, and Gabriel Lake was tasked with finding Dyani.

He was a former specialist in the FBI, one of the bright stars of the Behavioral Analysis Unit. Until he was forced to retire early. One of Sandoval's friends was an ex-Navy Seal who had gone into the security business. He knew about Lake through his connections with former seals who had joined law enforcement.

There was no one better to find Dyani.

Gabriel Lake was the man who hunted monsters.

Right then, at noon on a hot Monday in upstate New York, Lake was hunting for a piece of paper. Bloch drove the Jeep rental she'd picked up at Albany Airport. Lake had taken the bus upstate ahead of time and met Bloch at the airport. He said he preferred riding shotgun with Bloch. It gave him time to think. And time to organize his paperwork.

Lake had a plastic carrier bag on his lap stuffed to the brim with paper – newspaper clippings, pieces of torn maps, notes, police reports, printouts of pictures, napkins filled with scribblings in blue ink and what seemed like hundreds of small Post-It notes that spilled out of the bag like confetti whenever he shoved his hand inside.

'You find it yet?' asked Bloch.

'It's here. I have a system,' he said.

'You have a mess. That's what you have,' she said.

'Don't bother me when I'm in the system,' he said.

His right leg bounced up and down on the floor of the Jeep. Maybe it was a nervous thing, or maybe Lake was just one of those guys whose motor was always running.

'Got it,' he said, and drew out a napkin.

'Grady Banks,' he said, reading the name that had been scrawled there, tearing the fine paper with the pen nib.

'I've heard that name before,' said Bloch. As well as her private work for Kate and Eddie, Bloch helped out NYPD from time to time with her area of special interest – children who were sex trafficked all over the US. Bloch didn't have kids, but she had a particular hatred for men who exploited women and children. 'I didn't know he operated out here.'

'His gang is involved in everything else that's illegal in these parts, may as well be in for human trafficking too. The name of the bar is . . . wait . . .'

'Can't you read your own handwriting?' asked Bloch.

'The ink has feathered,' he said, and turned the napkin over in his hands. Held it up to the light from the window. 'The Twisted Slipper?'

Bloch punched the name into the car's navigation system.

The predictive program came up with a different name.

'That's the one,' said Lake.

Within forty minutes Bloch pulled into the lot of the Twisted Stripper. A single-story cinderblock building. It was painted gray with a broken neon sign above the double-door entrance. The structure stood alone on a stretch of barren highway.

'Drive around,' said Lake.

Bloch did a loop of the perimeter. She knew Lake wanted to get a feel for the size of the place. She checked the odometer on the dash as she drove around, making her own calculations. The lot was almost empty. Some pick-up trucks, Fords mostly, a few Harleys and a single white panel van. Lake noted the registration.

She stopped the car and they got out. Bloch put on her leather jacket over the Magnum slung underneath her left arm. She checked her Doc Marten boots and tied a lace, folded her black jeans over the top of them.

Lake made an attempt to tuck his shirt into his gray pants, pulled on his black suit jacket to hide the Glock he wore on his hip. The jacket had been balled and thrown in the back seat last night. He tried to smooth out the wrinkles. Harry once described Lake as 'a carefully arranged mess', and the description stuck with Bloch.

'I think you'll meet the dress code,' said Bloch. 'But you could do with a haircut.'

Lake rubbed his hands over his head, to feel the weight of his curly hair. Like he hadn't looked in a mirror in a month. Which was probably true. There was so much going on inside Lake's head that he didn't have time to think about dry cleaning, his appearance or even the mundane everyday tasks like paying bills or grocery shopping. He showered and brushed his teeth. That was about all he could manage.

All of his considerable mental focus pointed outward.

And for the last few days it was entirely focused on finding Dyani Sandoval.

'Something I wanted to ask you,' said Bloch. 'What exactly did you mean when you asked for my diplomatic skills?'

Bloch wasn't being facetious. She spoke little. And rarely more than absolutely necessary. This had caused some interpersonal issues when she was in law enforcement. Her fellow cops found her cold. She wasn't doing it deliberately – Bloch just didn't do people. She had her friends – her childhood buddy Kate, Eddie Flynn, Harry, Denise and now Lake. That small group of people were her family now.

Despite what her superiors in the police called 'poor social skills', Bloch was one of the most popular cops on the force. For two reasons. One, she picked up on little details that everyone else missed. That was her superpower. And that led to cases being closed. Second, Bloch could pretty much kick everyone's ass in her department.

You pissed off Bloch at your peril.

Which is why she was asking Lake what the hell he expected of her in the diplomacy department.

'You have a way of talking to people that's very direct. Plus, I need back-up and I know this kind of case has a personal interest for you.'

Bloch nodded and followed Lake into the building.

Noon on a Monday is not peak time in a strip club. A few rednecks in plaid shirts supped at their beers as they sat around the circular stage with an aluminum pole bolted to the floor. There was no music. No dancing. A few figures were seated further back in the booths, but it was too dark to make out their faces.

Lake made for the bar. Bloch followed.

The bartender wore a sleeveless, stained checkered shirt. It was hard to tell if the shirt was made that way, or if he'd decided to pull the sleeves off one night in a fit of sartorial sabotage. His arms were thick with muscle, fat and faded tattoos. Bloch had started to smell him from six feet away. As she placed her hands on the bar, she steadied herself against the powerful odor of old sweat.

Lake smiled at him. Waited for the bartender to initiate the conversation.

The bartender wiped at his straggly beard with a wet cloth, said nothing.

'I'd like a glass of water, please,' said Lake.

'We don't serve water,' said the bartender.

Bloch sensed movement behind them. Then she heard the scraping of metal chairs on a wooden floor. Behind the multitude of bottles on the shelf of the bar, there was a mirror.

Two men, much bigger than the bartender, who was going on for six foot three, got up off their seats. One of them, the biggest one, made his way into the gloomy section of the bar. The other, the one wearing a Stetson, folded his arms and watched Lake.

Lake pointed to a sink behind the bar, said, 'You've got a faucet. I'd really like glass of water, please.'

The bartender stood back, grabbed his crotch with one hand. 'I've got this, but I ain't letting you drink from that either.'

The redneck guard behind Bloch laughed.

'I don't like you,' said Lake.

The bartender took a step forward, reached under the bar and came up with a pump-action shotgun in his hands. He held it across his chest, said, 'I don't like you either. And now it's time for you to leave.'

The redneck in the mirror didn't even have time to unfold his arms. With one swift movement, Lake reached across the bar, took hold of the barrel of the shotgun in one hand, twisted it and flipped it one eighty out of the bartender's arms and into Lake's. It was all about leverage and speed. Lake pumped five shells onto the floor then set the gun on the ground.

'I think we're going to stay a while. Is that Mr. Grady over there?' He pointed to the man sitting alone in a booth.

The bartender said nothing. His mouth was still hanging open.

'I thought so,' said Lake.

Bloch followed him to the man at the booth. He fitted the description of Grady Banks, owner of this fine establishment. He wore a leather waistcoat over a black T-shirt. Small, greasy hands lay flat on the table beside a shot of whiskey. It was the tattoo of a swastika on his throat that gave him away. Although, in a place like this, Bloch guessed there could be more than one guy with Nazi tattoos.

Another security guard – one who looked like a heavyweight wrestler – sat alone at a small table pushed against the back wall. He was ten feet from Grady. A large, rusted and bullet-ridden interstate sign had been affixed to the wall behind him. It was the kind of thing that passed for interior decoration in this place.

Bloch saw Lake notice the big man seated at the sign. Way too far from his boss to be any kind of effective security.

They exchanged a knowing glance.

'Mr. Banks, my name is Gabriel Lake. I'd like to talk with you.'

Grady didn't move. He looked calm and confident. His reply was laconic, even disinterested.

'You look like cops. Or you used to be cops. We don't like cops around here. What do you want?' he asked.

'You know what we want,' said Lake. 'There's a white panel van parked behind this building. Just like the one used to snatch Dyani Sandoval. This room is one hundred feet long, but the building on this side is a hundred and thirty feet long. Your man over there isn't doing too good a job protecting you from all the way at the back of the room. Bloch here could do some real damage before that guy got his ass off the seat. So he's not protecting you. He's protecting the door hidden behind that old road sign. We'll leave once you give us Dyani. You didn't expect a ton of media attention when you snatched a Native American girl so I figured whoever has her will keep her hidden until the press storm dies down and her face disappears from the TV screens. Then you'd move her on to a buyer. That's not going to happen now. You're going to let her go.'

'Get the fuck out of here before—' Grady began, but Bloch didn't hear the rest. Her phone had buzzed in her pocket. She took it out, read the text message.

'Lake,' she said, 'got a text from Eddie. He needs us. We need to cut this short. Let me try some of that *diplomacy*.'

Bloch moved past Lake, and as she sat down in the booth across the table from Grady, a faint sound was heard in the room. A distinctive one. The noise that's made when steel brushes quickly against leather.

Underneath the table, Bloch pushed the barrel of her handgun into Grady's knee. His expression changed suddenly.

'You know what happens when you get shot in the knee with a small caliber weapon?' she asked.

Grady didn't move. Didn't speak. His eyes locked on Bloch. After another moment, he shook his head.

'After a knee replacement and a year of physiotherapy, you might walk again without a limp. But the real worry is infection. Small fibers from your pants get lodged in the wound. If the surgeon doesn't remove all those little pieces, they fester, and cause infection. That brings the risk of amputation.'

Grady's Adam's apple bobbed up and down inside his scrawny throat.

'I have good news and bad news,' continued Bloch. 'Good news is you don't have to worry about infection. Bad news is I'm holding a Magnum 500 loaded with a four-hundred-and-forty-grain semi-rimmed cartridge that will take your leg clean off at the knee, instantly. Unless you or one of your pals here knows how to clamp the femoral artery that sits behind your kneecap, you'll bleed out in around ninety seconds.'

A thin bead of sweat rolled down Grady's cheek.

'Here's your choice. Listen carefully. Get your man to open the door and bring out Dyani, *unharmed*, and we'll give you an hour and a half before we call the cops. You could make it to the next state by then. That's the deal. The girl and ninety minutes. Or ninety seconds. Think fast.'

In her peripheral vision, Bloch saw Lake tense. He turned and looked back at the bar. She heard boots on the wooden floor behind her.

Lake swept his jacket out of the way of the Glock on his hip, said, 'Go ahead and pick up the shotgun. Load it.'

The other security guy was obviously making a move toward the weapon. Bloch didn't hear any more footsteps. He was having second thoughts.

Lake said, 'Pick it up. I want you to.'

For all his eccentricities, intelligence and quirks, there was another side to Gabriel Lake. And here it was – on display. His face had darkened. His eyes had taken on a dead quality – like a shark. Bloch felt the hairs on the back of her neck stand up. She'd seen this look on Lake's face in the past – right before he shot a man to death. Lake was a gifted investigator, but he was also a killer. Maybe that's why he was so good at catching them.

No one moved.

Bloch pushed the barrel of the handgun into Grady's knee. He picked up the shot glass, drained it, said, 'Butch, get the girl.'

'What the fuck?' said the big security guy seated at the sign. He got up. The man Bloch now knew as Butch was well over three hundred pounds. And very little of it was fat. His arms looked like anchor chains on a battleship.

'Just get the fucking girl, Butch,' said Grady.

Butch banged on the sign with his fist. It slid back. He disappeared into the dark room behind the sign. A moment later he came back out, with Dyani Sandoval in front of him. The girl was filthy, covered in sweat and crying.

Butch placed his huge hand in the small of her back, pushed her forward. She cried out and landed heavily on her left shoulder. Lake went straight to her.

Bloch's eyes flared.

'I said *unharmed*,' said Bloch.

She stood, grabbed a handful of Grady's long, straggly hair and drove his face into the table. A wet crunching sound was followed by Grady's moans.

Bloch moved out of the booth, and did two things with incredible smoothness.

She holstered the Magnum.

She picked up the empty shot glass from Grady's table.

Butch laughed as Bloch walked toward him.

'What the fuck are you going to do, little lady?' he said derisively.

A short time later, Bloch stood in the lot of the strip club and shielded her eyes from the sun as she watched Dyani embrace her father. John Sandoval kneeled down and held his daughter. They wept and held each other tightly. The news vans were starting to arrive and the sheriff's meat wagon was almost full. Grady had been led out with his nose spread over most of his face.

Butch came out on the paramedics' crash trolley.

'Good news,' said Lake. 'I talked to the paramedic. They think they can save Butch's eye – most of the glass stayed out of the eyeball – but his right arm is in bad shape. The guy told me he'd never seen a spiral fracture this bad since a farmhand got his arm caught in crop machinery. They don't think Butch will play the violin again.'

'Did you talk to the sheriff?'

'Sure, Butch isn't going to want to press charges. He's headed for the State Pen and he only has one arm to defend himself now. He's not going to let it get around that he got maimed by a hundred-and-fifty-pound woman from New Jersey.'

'Good. I have to get moving. I'll need your help on this one.'

'What's Eddie into?'

'Kate caught a new case. A wealthy New Yorker on a murder charge. They need some background and photos of the murder scene.'

'So what do you need me for?'

Bloch cracked a smile, said, 'Diplomacy.'

4
Ruby

Ruby opened the knife drawer and gazed inside.

She had quite the selection to choose from. All were Japanese. The very finest handcrafted steel blades with walnut handles. For a second, her eyes flicked across the kitchen island to Tomas. He sat on a stool at the opposite end of the island, reading his Spider-Man comic book. He was dressed in a Spider-Man-themed sweater, blue jeans and little red-and-blue Nikes. He was small for a seven-year-old. Ruby had picked him up from elementary school and taken him to the waiting town car and the family driver, who then drove them back to Tomas's West 74th Street home.

Tomas's gaze never left the comic book as he angled his head and his small, cherry lips searched for the paper straw sticking out of his juice box.

He wasn't tall enough for his feet to reach the footrest on the stool, so he swung his legs idly. His heels tapped the stool legs, banging out a dull beat.

Dum – dum.

Dum – dum.

Ruby looked back at the knife drawer, selected a blade about six inches long and two inches wide. The steel had a blue, mottled look to it. Like it was submerged in fast-flowing water, just a part of the tempering process to harden the steel as it's folded and cooled and sharpened. The tip looked like it could go through anything.

Ruby listened to the beat of Tomas's feet on the stool.

Dum – dum.

The rhythm echoed her heartbeat.

As Tomas sucked at his juice box, his cheeks concaved and Ruby wondered how easily the tip of the knife would slip into the plump, pink, perfect skin around Tomas's neck.

Dum – dum.

She closed the drawer, walked round the kitchen island to stand beside Tomas. He looked up, glanced at the knife and for a second, he was transfixed by its strangeness. He turned back to his comic book as Ruby gripped the handle tighter, bent her elbow and raised the knife into a vertical position, shoulder height.

Dum – dum.

Her elbow extended, pushing the blunt end of the knife over her shoulder. She was winding up her arm. Ready to whip the blade forward with force.

Dum – dum.

Ruby extended her arm, dropped her shoulder – all in milliseconds. The blade flashed toward Tomas.

And down.

Tomas flinched.

His legs were suddenly still.

The apple on the chopping board split in half, the tip of the blade buried in the hardwood board. Ruby smiled, yanked it free and began quartering the fruit.

She placed the apple in a bowl beside Tomas and said, 'Hey, little mini-munch, don't you have homework you should get started on?'

'Not today I don't. Mom gave Mrs. Gordon a note.'

Behind her, Ruby heard the vacuum cleaner firing up in the hallway. Althea, the maid, was finishing off the last part of her shift.

Althea had started with the family a few months ago. Ruby had previously been cleaning for them one morning per week as well as picking up Tomas from school and babysitting him for two hours afterwards. One day, Ruby got an urgent call from the Goldmans, who had to head out of town for two days due to a sick relative. Ruby had to babysit the kids, which meant canceling her morning cleaning session for Tomas's mom, Alison.

The next week, Ruby got a text message to say she would no longer be required to clean for them.

Althea had replaced Ruby. And Althea was great. So good, in fact, that they increased her hours to Monday and Thursday. Ruby had gotten to know her a little, but the young lady, who was Hispanic, didn't say much even though her English was perfect. Althea kept her head down and worked. My God did she *work*. Her clothes were threadbare. That blue summer dress was so thin and worn it looked like lace. To protect what clothes she had, Althea wore an apron when she cleaned. She kept it in the utility cupboard. It was the first thing she did when she got into the house, put on her little canvas apron. The last thing she did before she left was hang it up. A brown stain was now permanent on the neck of that apron – from Althea's sweat. She worked like no one Ruby had ever seen, but, more than that, she made sure Alison saw her work and appreciated it. Althea always wanted more hours. In this regard, she was a real threat to Ruby, who made sure to try to keep Althea and Tomas separate. She didn't want Althea getting to know Tomas. Althea wanted Ruby's job. This wasn't anything personal, purely business, but, even so, she suspected that Althea could sense Ruby's true nature. Some people are like that. They operate on more than one plane.

'Eat your apple, sweety-boo,' said Ruby, and then cast her eyes around the kitchen.

It was, by any stretch, a dream kitchen for almost anyone. Tasteful slate-gray marble worktops, ivory cupboard doors with bright chrome handles to match the faucets. Everything was showroom-clean and tidy. The refrigerator door served as the receptacle for souvenirs, and the only hint that the kitchen was lived in and used by a family. Magnets marking family vacations to Rome, San Francisco and Disney World pinned up hand-scrawled notes to order more oat milk and eggs, postcards from relatives, old Polaroid pictures, the rough plans for renovation work on the house, and some of Tomas's artwork. A white page adorned with his little handprints in bright green and yellow paint, forming the stem and then the head of a flower. She remembered making it with Tomas one afternoon. She remembered Alison's face when she saw it – the pride illuminating her eyes. It had been immediately pinned to the door with a magnet in the shape of the Eiffel Tower.

Ruby walked past the nostalgia-covered refrigerator and peered round the kitchen door. She could see into the hallway and directly opposite was the lounge. Alison, Tomas's mom, was still talking on the phone. Even though Ruby couldn't hear her conversation, she could see Alison, in her white silk blouse and tan pants, sitting on the couch with the phone pressed to her ear. She'd been on the phone all day. Althea faced the front door, just starting to sweep the machine over the carpet.

Ruby looked over her shoulder. Tomas turned the page of his comic book, picked up an apple slice and bit it in half.

There was no one else in the house.

Ruby had a lot of practice at moving silently.

When Ruby was seven years old, she'd been woken one night by a strange sound in the house. She didn't know what it was at first. It sounded bad. Like something heavy falling and breaking downstairs. She sat up in bed, wide awake very quickly, and listened. There was another sound. This time she recognized it. Ruby swept back the comforter, put her feet to the cold floorboards and padded to her bedroom door. Either the spindle on the doorknob or the latch bolt tended to squeak, but only if you turned it normally. She took hold of the knob, pulled down on it, because that helped, and then turned it very slowly until it could turn no more. Smoothly, she pulled open the door just enough for her to squeeze through. The upper hallway was in darkness, but light spilled up the stairs from below.

Ruby had made her way to the top of the stairs, counting the oak floorboards as she moved. Twenty-three boards to the stairs. Seventeen and twenty were loose and would creak if any weight came upon them. She stepped lightly over them as her lips moved silently, counting her steps. She approached the dog-leg staircase, and kept her little feet on the thick carpet that ran up the center of the stairs. She knelt on the landing, and peered down the next set of stairs into the hallway.

The lamp was burning in the living room. She could see shadows thrown onto the polished tile floor of the hallway. There were no voices.

Her father, Josef, came out of the lounge, holding his wrist. He marched into the kitchen and she heard him holler, 'Get me some ice. Look what you've done.'

A few moments later, Mom came out of the lounge holding the side of her face. There was blood on her lips and in her other hand were the shattered remains of her favorite vase. That was the noise that had woken Ruby.

'You see what you've done! I've hurt my wrist,' called her father. 'Hurry up – get the ice. And put some on your face. I don't want any questions from the neighbors.'

As her mom moved unsteadily toward the kitchen, she glanced up the stairs. Ruby moved quickly, hiding in the shadows between the banisters.

Her mom shook her head. A warning.

Don't come downstairs.

Ruby turned and went back to bed as quietly as she could. She closed her bedroom door, then pushed her bookcase in front of it.

Daddy was being bad again. Josef Johnson was born with every advantage and privilege it was possible to enjoy – loving parents, wealth, good looks, intelligence, contacts and power. By the age of twenty-five, Josef had thrown almost all of it away. He had a fire inside him that consumed his better nature, his habits, his mind and everyone around him. The only thing that could calm it down was the thrill of winning a poker hand, or a horse race. But he was not a good gambler. The losses always outweighed the wins. Soon the only thing that gave him peace was strong liquor – and eventually all that did was add flames.

As bad as her father could be, her mother was just as sweet. She protected Ruby from everyone, especially Daddy. She would take the insults, the snide looks, the punches, the kicks, even the burns – anything as long as Ruby was safe.

Ruby had grown up in a house with a sleeping tiger.

They are dangerous if they are woken. And so Ruby learned to keep quiet.

As the vacuum cleaner whined and Althea focused on her work, Ruby's memories faded and she stepped into the hallway, heel toe, heel toe. She meant to move straight upstairs, but found herself pausing in front of the picture on the wall, to her left, just before the staircase.

The picture of the red priest.

She didn't know who had painted it, or how old it was. Pretty old, she guessed. And expensive. A priest sat at a table, his left arm resting beside a goblet of red wine. The wine had stained his mouth, made it shine like a scarlet button on a puffy marshmallow face. Muddy eyes stared out below wisps of white hair. Red robes flowed from his shoulders to pool on the floor. His expression was hard to read. There was something wise yet feral in his look.

A big, fat fly landed on the painting. It buzzed around the curves of the oil hardened on the canvas.

The buzzing noise increased. What began as a hum, a low throb, became a roar, getting louder and louder, until it sounded like a buzz saw in her head. Ruby covered her ears. But it only made it worse. The noise built. Her head became a pressure cooker. The only way to stop her brain from exploding was to take her hands away from her ears, let out the steam.

She didn't want to talk to the red priest today.

Ruby gasped, let her hands fall by her sides.

She heard his voice.

Rubbbeeeee . . .

Rubbeeeeeeeeeee . . .

She didn't need to speak for the priest to hear her. He knew her thoughts already.

I'm here, said Ruby, in her mind.

You should have cut the boy's throat. It's the only way . . . said the red priest.

Ruby shook her head, looked away from the picture and moved quickly onto the stairs. There was no time to talk to the red priest today. She had business. The buzzing noise left her. She was no longer hypnotized by the picture. Only a faint dizziness remained.

She shook it off.

Concentrated.

There were no creaks on these floorboards. No squeals from these stairs. Alison had new stairs and floorboards put in when they first moved to the neighborhood. She liked to spend money on the house. She had a major reconstruction project planned.

Upstairs, Ruby was alone. She opened the door to the main bedroom, then moved to the dressing table and opened the top right drawer. Black silk cloth lined the bottom of these drawers, and in each one of the five drawers an array of fine jewelry was laid out. This one contained Alison's rings and brooches.

Ruby closed the first drawer, opened the second.

Necklaces.

She was looking for the perfect piece. Nothing too expensive. Something that Alison wore regularly. The diamond heart choker was out. Nobody wears a hundred grand of diamonds when they go for morning coffee with their girlfriends. The rose-gold Versace pearl drop was a good choice, but perhaps not important enough.

Pulling the drawer out a little further, Ruby found the silver lace necklace. A beautiful thing. It looked old and fragile. It had been Alison's grandmother's necklace. Passed down to her from her mother. There was a story to this necklace. Alison's grandmother was given the necklace by an aunt as a gift for her eighteenth birthday. A year later, Alison's grandmother hid the necklace in her boot as she was leaving Poland in the summer of 1939.

Ruby stuffed the necklace into the front pocket of her jeans as she closed the drawer.

Althea saw her coming downstairs. She made a point to let Ruby know that she had seen her. Rubbing her hands together, Ruby smiled at Althea, then smoothed her palms on the back of her jeans, as if she'd just used the bathroom upstairs and her hands were still a little damp.

Tomas had finished his apple.

'Let's do some coloring, Tommy-tickles,' said Ruby, in her singsong voice. She gave him a picture of a squirrel and his crayons. Tomas got bored halfway through and Ruby helped him finish the tail.

Her shift was over. She could hear Alison finishing up her call. Althea was upstairs now, vacuuming the carpet.

The front door opened.

Ruby moved to the kitchen door to listen. Then peeked out.

'Honey, I'm so glad you're home,' said Alison, throwing her arms round her handsome husband.

John Jackson hugged his wife, buried his face in her blond hair, like a soldier returning from war. She rubbed his back then they parted and he held her shoulders.

'How did it go with Al? Did he take you to see the other lawyer?'

'He did. And they're gonna take the case.'

Another embrace.

'Oh, honey, this is great news. This is all going to blow over. Everything is going to be just fine. I know it.'

John's gaze flitted to Ruby. It was hard to read his expression. It was as if Ruby had trespassed on an intimate moment.

Tomas brushed past Ruby's legs and ran into the hallway. John scooped him up in a bear hug.

'Hey, little man. How are you?'

He put Tomas down when he didn't get an answer. The boy looked shy at first, then hung his head.

'Hey, what's wrong?' asked John.

'Daddy, did you do a bad thing?' asked Tomas sincerely.

John looked to Alison, the wound from that question landing in his chest, punching the air from his body. As quickly as the hurt registered, John shook it off. He didn't want to worry his little boy, or let him see that his father was deeply upset.

He knelt down to Tomas, 'Why would you ask that?'

'I heard two of the teachers whispering today. They were pointing at me. They didn't think I could hear them, but I listened real hard and I heard every word. They said you did a bad thing and they felt sorry for me.'

John's brow creased. A menacing look flashed over his face. The expression quickly disappeared, and John smiled at his son. He kept his voice low, and as he spoke the light from the hallway lamp caught on the tear forming in the corner of his eye.

'What bad thing did they say I did?'

'They said you killed a nice lady,' said Tomas, and burst into tears.

'No, no, no, I didn't, son. I promise you *I did not*. Some people are confused right now. The police have made a mistake. I didn't hurt *anyone*.'

As John led Tomas into the living room by the hand, Alison turned away. Ruby could only see her back. Alison cupped her hand over her mouth and sobbed, silently, her shoulders heaving. Ruby stepped forward, making her feet loud and purposeful, so Alison would hear her approach and would not be startled when Ruby put her hand on her shoulder and began to comfort her.

'*Oh, Ruby*, thank you. I don't know what we would do without you,' said Alison.

'I'm here for you. For whatever you need. Whenever you need me,' said Ruby.

She gave Alison a napkin to dry her tears. The skin around her eyes was inflamed and swollen. This wasn't the first time Ruby had heard Alison crying today. Ruby had not been present when the police raided the house. She'd been with one of her other clients, laundry day at the McSorley's. The day after the murder, Ruby had been at the Pullers', looking after their rotten kids as Chad puked his guts out upstairs. The detective had asked Ruby where she'd been last night. She told them the truth: she had left the Pullers' after midnight and walked home. She lied when she said she'd not seen anything, and not heard any shots.

Alison wiped her tears. Ruby spent a few more minutes with Alison, calming her. Telling her everything would be alright.

They both heard the sound of a key in the lock and turned to face the front door.

Esther wrestled her key from the lock as she stepped into the hallway. Alison's mother had shocking white hair in a loose curl and brown eyes that always betrayed her true feelings. She wore a tan suit, black patent-leather Christian Louboutin heels and carried a Gucci shopping bag in one hand. In her seventies, but good for it. Plastic surgery, a rich dead husband and very little conscience had kept her looking young.

Ruby didn't like Esther. Because Esther didn't like Ruby. At first, Ruby thought it was a territorial thing. Another young woman, working in her daughter's house. Always around her daughter's handsome brain surgeon husband. Esther had been a player in her younger days. That was the impression Ruby had. And perhaps Esther thought she spotted a fellow grifter in Ruby.

She closed the front door, embraced Alison, said, 'My darling, how is he?'

'He's okay, I think. We got the lawyer we wanted. He's in the living room with Tomas. Give him a minute.'

Esther didn't ask how her daughter was feeling. Ruby noticed that. She got the impression Alison noticed it too.

'Ruby, how are you?' said Esther, and contorted her face into what passed for a smile, but her eyes always let Esther down. The cold look she gave Ruby was unaffected by what the rest of her face was doing. Esther's gaze sometimes reminded her of the way her grandmother used to look at her.

Ruby said she was okay, but Esther had already turned away from her. She shook off her tan jacket and without looking at Ruby held it out for her to hang up.

Ruby hung the jacket on the coat rail on the opposite wall from the priest picture. It began to whisper in its low hiss, as if there were layers of voices inside her head.

Ruubbbeeee . . .

You have to hurry. Get the money. Your mother doesn't have long left . . .

Ruby turned sharply, and in her mind she told the priest to be quiet.

'Do you like that picture?' asked Esther.

Ruby hadn't realized that Esther was standing in the hallway. She'd thought the woman had gone through to the living room. But she was still there, staring at Ruby inquisitively.

'Ah, sure. It's . . .' She was about to say the picture was lovely, but it wasn't. It was ugly and frightening, and it haunted her. 'It looks very old. Is it expensive?'

'It's worth a lot of money, yes. More than *you* could earn in a lifetime,' said Esther.

Ruby's skin began to crawl, as if Esther was looking right through her. Quickly, Ruby said her goodbyes to Alison and said it would be better to leave the family to some private time.

She lifted her backpack and closed the front door softly behind her. She headed across Riverside Drive to the Henry Hudson Parkway, then on to the Empire State Trail on the Hudson River Greenway.

Her feet took her to Pier One. There were few people around, even in summer. Line fishermen and tourists. At the end of the pier, Ruby leaned over the rail and glanced back at Manhattan, the glass towers, the contour of the island, and then returned her eyes to the mud-gray waters of the Hudson.

She took Alison's heirloom necklace from her pocket and weighed it in her hand. It was surprisingly heavy, and durable, even though it looked as light as lace. The workmanship was exquisite. It was unique and quite beautiful. Handed down to Esther by her mother, who had smuggled it out from Nazi-occupied Poland. And who, in turn, had given it to Alison.

It meant a great deal to both of them. Their family. Their survival, even, was bound up with their hearts in the little diamonds studded along the silver lace of this necklace.

It was probably worth north of fifty grand. She could pawn it for ten thousand, easily.

Ruby balled up the necklace and threw it into the river.

Her phone buzzed in her pocket. A text message from one of her West 74th Street clients. It contained a link to a secret chat called 'Neighborhood Watch'. Ruby looked through the messages in the group. The neighbors were going to have a meeting about the Jacksons, and the murder of Maggs.

And they were inviting Ruby to come along.

5

Ben Gray

The All American Diner sat across the street from Gray's precinct. If he wasn't a cop, he wouldn't have gone near the place. The stars and stripes covered almost every available surface, invariably beneath laminate. The table tops. The menus. Even the floor. It was an assault of Americanness. And that's the way some people liked it.

Not Sergeant Ben Gray.

This country hadn't given him or his old man so much as a dime. A flag doesn't put food on the table. Of course, most of his brother cops were patriots. It came with the territory. And Gray learned to keep his true feelings about his country to himself. That kind of talk ended in broken bottles and bar stools flying through the air – most of them in his direction. So he kept his mouth shut. He ate the eggs and drank the coffee in the All American Diner with his fellow officers before their shift, and didn't say shit.

And he had quickly figured out a way to make his own dime. And it wasn't with overtime either.

Gray sat at the counter, the only surface not covered in the Star-Spangled Banner. Same seat. For eighteen years. Staring at the same eggs on his plate. The only other people in the diner were cops, or the odd tourist. The place never got that busy.

The door to the diner opened and a large man in a thick leather jacket and blue jeans walked into the place to a rousing reception. Every cop in the precinct knew Mick Buchanan. Former lieutenant. Retired these past ten years. Gray looked over his shoulder, saw Buchanan's car parked outside – Mercedes S Class. Only a few months old.

And he knew Buchanan hadn't bought that car with his pension.

Buchanan waved, said hello and shook hands with a few cops, then made his way to the vacant stool beside Gray. He was a huge man with a big face, and hands that could make basketballs look small when he held them. The stool groaned as it accepted his weight. To an outsider, he had a genial air about him. To an insider, this was a man that you feared. For the past five years, Buchanan had run New York's Finest – one of the largest criminal organizations in the city. He had a piece of almost every pie, because what criminal doesn't like police protection, and he ran their own independent operations too.

'How's the desk life treatin' you, Ben?' asked Buchanan.

'I'm bored shitless. I got two years left before they can punch my ticket on the pension and then I'm free and clear. Like you.'

'I heard,' said Buchanan, lowering his voice, 'you had some *trouble* the other day.'

Gray's stomach tightened.

'No trouble. I had to let an arrest go. Stupid, really. The lawyer, he had evidence on our friends in the towing company and he had my arrest sheets. He knew all about it. Instead of him bringing all that shit up in open court, I fumbled the arrest. I don't want that shit out in the open.'

'He had evidence?'

'He had a thick file of documents.'

Buchanan nodded. 'You remember what happened with the speeding-ticket thing?'

Gray nodded. Almost thirty cops had lost their jobs over what seemed like a small scam. It had hit Buchanan's organization financially, and some cops went to jail – the cops who'd conveniently lost a speeding ticket for a small payment.

'You remember Sykes and Kovax?' asked Buchanan.

Both of these men were also indicted for the ticket-fraud scheme. But they didn't get to trial because they were also part of New York's Finest.

What Buchanan feared the most was not rival criminal gangs – he feared his friends above all else: the cops who were up to their necks in the organization and knew who ran it from the ground up and how. Because cops can't do time in prison. Didn't matter if they got six months for taking a bribe, or six years. Prison time for an ex-cop is a death sentence. So they make deals, and they rat on their friends. It's survival.

'What happened to Sykes and Kovax was a goddamn tragedy,' said Gray.

'They got . . . *depressed*, you see.'

Sykes and Kovax were officially declared suicides. They ate their own guns. At their homes. On the same night. And their wives collected their pensions. But Gray and other cops in the organization knew better. Buchanan was terrified Sykes or Kovax would make a deal with the FBI and get a new life in witness protection in exchange for testifying against Buchanan and bringing down the whole house of cards. So he made sure they kept their mouths shut.

'I don't like liabilities, you know? You're not feeling depressed, are you?'

'No way. Look, it wasn't just about me. Flynn could have evidence on every one of us who get kickbacks from towing. He was tight with the other tow companies, brought a driver from each one of them to court.'

'Shit. I fuckin' hate defense attorneys,' continued Buchanan. 'This guy, he used to be a conman. That's the word on the street. Eddie Fly they used to call him. I don't want no defense attorney walking around with evidence that could expose our business. The towing don't pay as much as the girls, or the coke, but hey, it don't matter. They got Al Capone on tax fraud. We'll cool the tow trucks, eat a couple of hundred grand in losses. That don't matter to me. I just don't want this fuckin' guy poppin' up in court threatening my cops. When cops are feeling vulnerable, they do *stupid* things. They talk to the wrong people. Then they get . . . depressed.'

He held Gray in his gaze for a long time. Staring him out. Making sure Gray was solid. Gray felt like he was going to throw up, but he held firm. He had no choice.

'We're not just losing money on the tow trucks now. There's not going to be any girls shipping in any time soon. You heard what happened to Grady Banks?'

'He got arrested for kidnapping upstate. I heard some bitch put Butch in the hospital.'

'Do you know what bitch? Her name's Bloch. She *works* for Flynn.'

'No way?'

'Grady was a Nazi fuck, but he kept those girls coming in. We made a hundred thousand on every skirt. This is costing too much money.'

'Flynn threatened us. In open court. We should do something about this guy,' said Gray.

'He's an attorney,' said Buchanan.

'He's dirty. Didn't you say he used to be a conman? There could be all kinds of people he's pissed off. I don't want this asshole coming after us. We should get the bitch, Bloch, too.'

'If you're going to kill a snake, you don't chop it up from the tail – you take the head off first. Job done.'

Buchanan slapped Gray on the back, friendly, but with force.

'I think it's time we sent a message. You come after one of us? We come after you. I'm putting the word out. We can't take chances these days. And I want you to be there, personally, to make sure the message is delivered. You understand?'

6

Eddie

A week after John Jackson left my office, I was standing outside the Manhattan Criminal Court building, waiting for a hot dog at Akash's stand, when I got the call from Al Parish. The call I had been waiting for.

'I just got word from the DA. The gun they took from Jackson's house gives us a big problem. Ballistic testing confirms the slugs found in Mrs. Blakemore's chest and skull were fired from that weapon.'

'That's not good,' I said.

'It gets worse. There's DNA on the pistol grip – it's John's.'

'Didn't he tell the police he'd never seen that gun before?'

'He told them twice. Once when they showed him the gun they found in his closet and again during questioning, even after I'd told him to keep his damn mouth shut.'

'Hold on a second,' I said. 'Extra onions, please, Akash.'

I took my hot dog and soda and sat on the low wall on the east side of the courthouse. I put the phone to my ear and said, 'In a way, this is good news.'

Parish said nothing for a moment. He was looking for my angle, decided he couldn't find it and asked for directions.

'In what possible way is this good news?'

'Oh, it's bad news for John, no doubt. But in my mind either he's the dumbest killer to ever walk the earth, or he's telling the truth. Who shoots a neighbor dead in a wealthy neighborhood and hides the murder weapon in their closet? One thing we know for sure is Jackson isn't dumb. This confirms what I felt all along. John is innocent and he's on the level. If your client tells you the truth, that's half the battle.'

'But the other side of that battle is unwinnable. This just became a rock-solid case for the DA. There's going to be a press conference at four.' Up until now Jackson hadn't made the news. 'District Attorney Castro is about to make the front page and Jackson's life is going to implode.'

'I imagine an indictment from a grand jury is imminent. That gives us some discovery. At least something to work with so we can start building a defense. We'll need to talk to him before the press conference. He'll make it through this,' I said.

'Will he?' asked Parish.

'He'll make it. Even if we have to carry him. Get him to your office in an hour. I'll call Kate and Harry. There might be a way to handle Castro's press conference.'

'Not much we can do. What's the point?'

'We need to deaden the impact of the press conference, for the sake of getting an unbiased jury at least. And for John's sake. I don't want him splashed over the news, not yet. And I don't want Castro riding our client's case for publicity to help his election campaign.'

'What can you do?' asked Parish.

'I'll figure it out.'

I hung up, texted Kate and Harry to tell them about the forensics and arranged to meet them in Parish's office in an hour. Then I took a bite out of the hot dog and popped the tab on my Pepsi.

People think justice is like the buildings that house the system itself. Huge, indelible edifices that look as if they've stood there for five hundred years. Same as the courtrooms themselves. Apart from microphones and the addition of TV monitors, courtrooms haven't changed for more than a century. Not really.

That gives the notion of justice permanence.

Yet it could not be more malleable. What drives the justice system isn't our constitution, or the laws that govern each state, it's the people in power.

Justice is a hammer. You can use it to tap lightly on stone, molding and shaping it over time.

Or you can crack the whole damn rock wide open.

It depends on who is wielding the hammer.

In this instance, District Attorney Rob Castro was going to pick up his hammer and do as much damage with it as possible.

As I contemplated various ways to go after Castro, a long black town car pulled up at the curb. A serious hunk of shiny black metal with blacked-out windows and titanium rims. That car weighed two and a quarter tons, yet the suspension shifted as the driver got out, opened the rear passenger door and looked at me.

The driver was Anthony Lombardi, better known to me and the rest of the criminal fraternity in New York as Tony Two Fucks. He weighed half as much as the car. That sport shirt drawn tight across his chest must've been made from Kevlar, because no other kind of material could take that strain. Tony was a good guy. Sure, he was a getaway driver and peripatetic hitman for the Mafia, but we all had our foibles. Tony had a little speech problem. His mother, Gloria, God rest her soul, first noticed the problem when Tony, good Catholic that he is, was going through his first confession.

The eleven-year-old Tony got into the confessional and said, 'Fuckin' bless me, Father, for I have sinned like a motherfucker.'

His career as an altar boy was cut drastically short and the priest threw him out of the church.

Tony, for reasons best left to science, could not get through a sentence, no matter how short, without a liberal sprinkling of fucks.

Not even without a 'fuckin' A-fuckin'-men' at the end of his 'Our Father'.

'That fuckin' hot dog any fuckin' good?' he asked.

'It's good,' I said.

'I'll fuckin' pick up a bag when I drop you off. Get in the fuckin' car, Eddie. Jimmy wants to see ya.'

There are a lot of Jimmys in this town, but I instantly knew who he was talking about.

My childhood friend, Jimmy the Hat, who ran half of the city from a restaurant. He was head of one of the most powerful Italian crime families in New York, which made him one of the most powerful men in the country.

I finished the hot dog and the Pepsi, threw the napkin and soda can in the trash and got into the front passenger seat beside Tony.

I don't ride in the back. I'm not royalty, I'm not a made guy and I'm not stupid enough to get into the back of a car that can be locked and sealed by the driver up front, no matter how far Jimmy and I go back.

'How's Jimmy?' I asked as Tony pulled into traffic.

'Fuckin' A, that's how fuckin' good he is, the fuck.'

'You sure? No problems?'

Tony shook his head.

Shit.

I didn't wish any ill on Jimmy. He was my friend. But if he wanted to talk about last night's game, or shoot a game of pool, he would've called. This was a summons. This was official. He'd sent a made guy to pick me up.

If Jimmy was good – that meant this was about me.

And it was urgent.

And it was probably bad.

Real bad.

As we drove, I tried to work out why Jimmy had sent a car for me.

Tony didn't help my thought process. It was only a short journey, but Tony liked to talk.

'That gal you got fuckin' working for you. The fuckin' blonde, what's her name?'

'Denise? The office secretary. You met her last year.'

'Fuck, that's it. Fuckin' Denise. Is she married?'

I looked at Tony.

'What do you mean is she married? You *like* Denise?'

'Of course I fuckin' like her, you know. Real fuckin' nice gal. So is she married or what?'

'She's single, I think.'

'Any fuckin' chance you could put in a good fuckin' word for me?'

I recalled Denise and Tony had hit it off last year, after Tony and his pals had done some driving for us.

'You want me to ask her out for you?'

He nodded, said, 'I ain't so fuckin' good at that kind of fuckin' thing.'

I called Denise on my cell.

'You remember Tony, Jimmy's driver, who helped us out last year?'

'Tony Two Fucks? What about him?'

'He wants to know if you're free Saturday night?'

'And he's getting you to ask me out? He doesn't have the balls to ask me himself?'

I glanced over at Tony. He looked like a ten-year-old waiting to see if Santa Claus had come on Christmas morning. Some guys are built like that. They can kick down a door to a bunker in Baghdad, jump out of an airplane, even shoot somebody in the head and chop up their body, all without breaking a sweat. But ask them to visit a sick relative, make up with their mom or ask a girl out on a date and they'll be paralyzed with fear.

Tony was one of those guys.

'He's shy,' I said.

'If Tony Two Fucks wants to date me, he's gonna have to grow a pair and ask me out in person. Until then, tell him to go fuck himself. Twice.'

I pulled the phone away from my ear, turned to Tony and said, 'Denise says pick her up at eight on Saturday.'

She heard me. I killed the call just as she was screaming my name.

It was only then I looked out the window, saw we were passing the courthouse again. Tony was looping Foley Square. Classic counter-surveillance moves. I didn't give it too much thought. Somebody was always keeping tabs on Jimmy's business and associates.

The car pulled up outside Jimmy's restaurant. I got out, looked around the street. Not too much surveillance today. At least none that I could see. Somebody was always watching Jimmy, though. Either the NYPD anti-corruption taskforce, their vice squad, Narcos, robbery homicide or organized crime divisions. And that was just local. The feds, the ATF and even the NSA had been known to keep tabs on Jimmy the Hat Fellini.

And with good reason. He was one of the smartest mob bosses in the last hundred years. The evidence for that was right here in front of me. With so many agencies keeping tabs on him, and Jimmy running his business from the restaurant, there were only so many parking spaces on the street for surveillance vehicles and Jimmy made sure his delivery trucks took those spaces day and night – which meant that law enforcement had to rent premises with a view of the restaurant – either apartments or some of the empty retail spaces.

Jimmy knew this, so he bought all of the buildings with a view of his place.

If three or more government agencies, and thirty NYPD detectives were going to watch him, they had to pay him rent first. The more eyes on Jimmy, the more rent he took from federal and state law enforcement. He thought it was only fair for them to pay for the inconvenience.

Greenbacks and kickbacks.

Jimmy was downstairs in the private section of the restaurant at a table covered in a white cloth. An espresso and five cell phones sat in front of him. He wore his grandfather's flat cap, white shirt, black braces. He rose and we embraced.

'Eddie Fly, you okay, brother?' he asked.

'I'm fine,' I said.

He looked over my shoulder at Tony, asked, 'Any tails?'

'Clear as fuckin' day. I did two full circuits before I fuckin' came in.'

'Sit down, Eddie,' he said.

'What's wrong?' I asked, pulling up a chair. 'You're both skittish. The feds giving you problems?'

'Nah, nothing like that. It's *you* I'm worried about,' he said.

'Me?'

'Eddie, there's no easy way to say this so I'm just going to spit it out. Somebody dropped a ton of paper on your head.'

My gut tightened like I'd just taken a punch.

'How much paper?'

'Fifty Gs,' said Jimmy.

Shit. I put my elbows on the table, sank my head and inhaled.

'Tony, get him a Scotch,' said Jimmy.

'No, it's fine,' I said. 'I'm okay.'

I wasn't okay. Far from it. This morning, all I was worried about was saving John Jackson from life behind bars. Now I had something else to occupy my mind.

Jimmy just told me that someone had taken out a contract on my life. And whoever completed the hit could collect fifty thousand dollars. That's fifty thousand reasons for every junkie, lowlife and hitman in New York to put a bullet in my head.

7
Eddie

'You've got to have some idea who wants you dead that bad,' said Jimmy.

I shook my head.

'Look,' said Jimmy, 'we can buy you some time. Nobody in New York is going to take that contract. Guaranteed. I heard about this last night and we put the word out. That goes for Jersey too. You still got a lot of respect on the street, Fly Man, and the old bosses remember you. If any of their crew take on this paper, I cut their balls off, and then I give the rest of them to the Lizard.'

The Lizard was another mutual friend – one of the most feared hitmen in New York. He worked for Jimmy, and anyone who needed to disappear got a visit from the Lizard and he took them home to meet his pets – twin Komodo dragons named Bert and Ernie who could dispose of a two-hundred-pound body, skeleton and all, in under an hour.

'I talked to all the major crews. Everybody. No one is going to touch you. Not the Koreans, the Albanians, nobody. We're all making money. No one wants to start a war over fifty grand. Trouble is, that kind of dough will attract outside contractors. Guys in Miami, Chicago, even Texas. There's word that Angel is considering the job. He's a sniper. One of the top hitmen in the country. I don't think the juice is good enough for him to get on a plane, but we're keeping ears to the ground. What we need to do is figure out who put out the hit.'

'I told you, I've no id—Wait. You said none of the crews were going to touch it.'

'That's right. I got their word. They don't want trouble with me. Everyone's making too much money to create that kind of noise.'

Right then, I knew exactly who had put out the hit. I suspected Jimmy had a good idea too, and he was just teasing it out of me.

'But there's one crew you didn't talk to,' I said.

He nodded.

'Because they don't play by the rules,' I said. 'I can't think why they'd come after me, but it seems the only logical choice, doesn't it?'

He nodded, said, 'New York's Finest.'

Police in the city are given the moniker of New York's Finest – and you see that emblazoned on the side of their patrol cars. That name also goes with the crew of criminal police officers embedded in the NYPD who, among the city's criminal fraternity, operate under that name too.

'You piss off any cops lately?' he asked.

'I'm a criminal-defense attorney. If cops aren't pissed off, I'm not doing my job.'

'You know what I mean,' he said.

That's when I remembered. Sergeant Ben Gray. The tow-truck scam.

'There was a cop on the DA's No Fly List I came up against recently. Couple of weeks ago I got a gun possession case tossed on an illegal Terry stop. I got the cop to admit the stop was bad – otherwise I was going to interrogate him about kickbacks from towing companies. Cop was Sergeant Gray, and he was dirty, but I figured it was strictly low-level. I can't believe they would come after me for a fifty-buck tow-truck kickback? It just doesn't make any sense.'

'Kickbacks add up. Say eight to ten tows a week. That's, what, five hundred dollars? That's twenty-six grand a year. Say you've got thirty cops on the towing scam. That's nearly eight hundred thousand, and fifty percent of that is handed in to the boss, Buchanan. That's a big operation all of a sudden, but it don't matter. What I've learned is that nothing in the PD is low level. Last year, twenty cops lost their jobs on the fines scandal . . .'

Cops were taking back-handers to lose or toss speeding and parking fines. When you're NYPD, taking a hundred bucks to look the other way is the same as taking a hundred grand of dope and selling it to kindergarten kids. It's all above the red line.

Jimmy continued: 'Two cops died before they went on trial. They were friends of Buchanan's for thirty years. He made it look like suicide, but I know he killed them both. Buchanan is terrified of another internal-affairs investigation – and another twenty cops out of a job or on trial. One of them might know something. New York's Finest are hurting now. I heard one of their suppliers, some piece-of-shit human trafficker upstate, got arrested. They make millions from those poor kids.'

'Jesus, I didn't know they were connected. Bloch took him down, for God's sake.'

'Then that seals it. It's Buchanan that's coming after you. Until you know for sure, stay low. We can put somebody on the front door of your office and your apartment, if you want.'

'Put somebody on my ex-wife, and my daughter. Not close. Within shooting distance. I don't think they would make a play for my family, but you never know. It's not like I'm in hiding. I don't need your guys at my door. I've already got Bloch.'

'Fair enough. What are you going to do?'

'I can't think right now. I've got other things on my mind that are more immediate. The district attorney is holding a press conference this afternoon – and he's about to ruin my client's life and I can't let that happen. Do you know Castro?'

'Never met him. He was offered an introduction. Standard for new DAs. He declined. I got no leverage with this guy. That's not to say he's clean. Nobody is a hundred percent clean in this town.

I figure he's already partnered up the ass with somebody else. And he's got an election on the way.'

Justice is a hammer. Castro had to make sure he went into this election cycle with a big juicy conviction in his back pocket. Jackson was about to become a high-profile case, and Castro would ride that victory all the way to the ballot box. He had a serious challenger for the election in Morgan Montgomery – former chair of the NAACP, gifted civil-rights lawyer and philanthropist.

'I've got to do something to take the heat off this case. Castro is going to try and turn this trial into O. J. Simpson part two.'

'What can you do?'

'I'll think of something.'

'That's what I'm afraid of. When you're using that big brain of yours, don't forget there's a price on it. Somebody, sometime, is gonna try and collect.'

8

Eddie

Before I met the rest of my team, I had Tony swing by my apartment so I could pick up a few personal items.

I didn't want to be caught empty-handed on the street if some hitman from Wyoming tried to stick a .22 in my face. The brass knuckles I kept in the office for emergencies were too damn heavy, but the ceramic pair in my bureau at home were light enough to carry around in my pockets without ruining the lining of my suit. For good measure, I put my switchblade in my sock. That pearl-handled knife had been a gift from Jimmy, way back after I won my first amateur fight. Jimmy was the better boxer, but I was faster. We trained together, grew up together. I was glad to know him.

Tony dropped me off at the foot of a skyscraper on Wall Street. The law offices of Al Parish were a lot different from Flynn and Brooks. Spread over five floors. Views of the river. Everything was polished chrome, mahogany and brass. Filled with lawyers in expensive bespoke suits.

No fear of clients hearing screams coming from the floor below as somebody got *Mama's Boy* tattooed across their ass cheeks.

Harry and Kate were waiting in the reception area.

'Glad you could make it,' said Kate.

'Jackson here yet?' I asked.

'He's in the conference room with Al and half a dozen other people in suits. All of them charging two hundred an hour,' said Harry.

'We got a plan on how to deal with the DA's press conference?' asked Kate.

'I'm getting there. For now, I need you to handle this meeting with John. You need to tell him that he's going to be alright.'

'But he might go to prison for the rest of his life,' said Kate.

'Sure he might. But for now we need him to be fighting. You've got to tell him he's about to walk through hell, but he'll come out alive and a free man.'

'Why me?'

Harry leaned over, said, 'Because when you tell people everything is going to be alright, they'll believe you. You're not selling it. You're just stating a fact.'

I nodded, looked at the empty leather chair beside Harry. Then took a moment to examine my suit. My tie was half done up, shirt collar open. The shirt was out of a packet of three, the black suit came off the rack. Harry always carried an air of elegance, no matter what he wore. Today he sported a red woolen cardigan under his brown tweed blazer. Dark gray pants. Polished shoes, handmade by a famous gentleman's store in London. Kate always looked classy: dark business suit, white blouse, a million pens in her bag and three legal pads. Organized. Utterly professional.

Harry and Kate looked as if they belonged with the lawyers in here. I looked like a defendant.

Reluctantly, I sat in the leather chair and tried not to make the place look untidy.

A lawyer came through the glass doors that separated the reception area from the hive of the law offices.

'We're ready for you now. If you'd like to follow me?' she said.

We got up, and I followed Harry and Kate down a long, timber-lined corridor to an expansive conference room with the same floor space as our entire office. Wall to wall suits. Al Parish sat at the head of the table, Jackson on his left beside his wife. I began counting the young associates and stopped when I got over ten.

John looked pale. His wife, a blond lady with a soft face and sad eyes, yanked a fresh Kleenex from the box in front of her. She dabbed at her eyes.

Parish introduced us to Alison Jackson. Her voice was cracked with emotion, hoarse and filled with fear. She made a point of saying hello to all of us. Harry took her delicate hand in his, placed his palm on her shoulder and said, 'We're going to take good care of John, I promise.'

She forced a smile.

Alison sat back down beside her husband then cast a nervous glance around the crowded room. Kate watched her, then leaned over and whispered to me, 'This place is like an airport lounge on Christmas Eve. It's freaking Alison out. We need to clear some people out of here.'

I nodded, turned to the closest lawyer to me. He was young. Early twenties. Fair hair, blue eyes and a jaw so square and perfect that it looked like it had come out of a catalogue.

'What do you do here?' I asked.

'I'm a junior associate assigned to Mr. Jackson's defense team. Name's Broderick Rothschild,' he said, and stuck out a muscular hand with soft pink skin as smooth as a newborn's.

I shook hands and he flashed me a smile from a toothpaste commercial.

'And you?' I said, to the young lady beside him.

'Veronica Colville-North,' she said. 'Junior associate.'

'Eric Fong,' said another one.

'Porsche Bloomingdale . . .'

'Harrison Washington the Third . . .'

I stopped faking interest when I got to Harrison Washington III. They were all rich kids. Harvard Law grads. Top of the class. The very best young legal minds in the entire country.

Which made them completely useless to me and our client.

Nobody knows less about winning a murder trial than a young, highly educated lawyer. They may as well have majored in plumbing. The trouble is some of them think they know everything and the rest just think they know something – which might be even worse.

Still, at least I had an idea on how to blow up Castro's press conference.

'Al, I need to borrow these fine associates of yours,' I said.

'Be my guest. They've already prepared motions on discovery and have provided briefs on all the relevant case law. Was there something specific you had in mind?'

'Sure, I need them to go home and change.'

Parish looked at me strangely. I turned to the assembled associates, said, 'I need you all to go home and change your clothes. Wear baggy, ripped jeans. Sweatpants. T-shirts. Beanie hats. Whatever is the worst clothing you have in your wardrobe. Put it on and meet me in Foley Square in an hour.'

I turned back to Parish.

'Al, I assume John has paid you a retainer. I need some of it. For legal expenses.'

'Expenses?' asked Parish.

'Sure, expenses. Murder trials cost money. I need twenty-five grand in cash.'

'What on earth for?' asked Al.

Jackson looked puzzled too.

'John, my colleague Kate is going to talk you through the trial. Trust her. Trust me. The money you gave to Al's firm is for your defense. I need twenty-five thousand for part of that defense.'

'What part?' asked John.

'The part that's going to keep your face off the six o'clock news.'

9
Kate

For some lawyers, there are no bad cases. There are only bad clients.

Kate didn't feel that way.

Most of her practice was concerned with carving large, bloody and expensive pounds of flesh from the torsos of men who as CEOs, executives and directors, decided to use their power to harass and manipulate their female junior members of staff into bed. Or worse. And she was very good at it. In the short time she'd been Eddie's partner, Kate had gutted eighteen companies – resulting in five directors fired, seven resigned and three senior executives demoted. She even did such a good job on annihilating one particularly nasty director that his wife instructed Kate to handle her divorce the week after the asshole got canned.

Kate was great at those cases because she didn't need to work to understand her clients. There was no leap of imaginative empathy required. Kate had been one of those women. Leered at. Pawed at. Marginalized. Ridiculed. Powerless. In her old firm, as a junior associate, she was at the bottom rung. Who could she complain to? Who would fight for her? It took Kate time to realize she had to fight for herself. She got out of that firm almost two years ago. Now she was the person women would come to. She'd become the person she wished had existed when she was getting asked about her stockings, where she bought her underwear, whether she found her supervising partner attractive and the unspoken promise that if she slept with certain people that her career would take off.

Well, she took off alright. With a shitload of their money and a criminal conviction against the partner who had viciously harassed her.

Before she was a lawyer, she was a working-class Jersey girl, growing up in Edgewater with her best friend, Bloch, and a view from her bedroom window right across the river. She had a good family. Loving parents. In the evening, her mom would knit in her La-Z-Boy chair in the living room. Kate would listen to the *click, clack* of the needles and stare out of the window. At night, the yellow office lights from the skyscrapers of Manhattan were like fallen stars on the dark waters that separated her from the island. She had always wanted to be one of those women, in the office late at night, working hard. If it got past eleven thirty, and her father had not come home yet, the young Kate couldn't help but notice the increase in the pace of her mom's knitting needles. Her pop's shift as a New York police officer finished at ten thirty. If he wasn't home by eleven thirty, that could mean one of two things. Either he'd hit a bar for a drink with his buddies, or something bad had happened to him. Her mom's fraying nerves were driving those needles at a furious pace by midnight. Kate could even see the Jersey bridge from her room. She watched the headlights of the cars as they drove across and said a silent prayer that one of them was her father's car.

That he was coming home safe.

In the end, he always did come home. Kate would hear the front door banging closed. And then the silence filled with absence of the *click-clack* of the needles. If he was late, there would always be the same joke too.

Her mother would scold him: 'Why didn't you call to say you'd be late? I was worried sick.'

Her father's reply was always the same. 'Darlin', this is a dangerous job. Lots of cops don't make it home to their wives. Sometimes they stay the night in their girlfriend's house.'

Then more reassuring noises would float up the stairs. Kate would hear the creak from the oven door, the clink of cutlery and glasses on their little kitchen table and her parents would sit down to eat at midnight. Kate never went downstairs. She could have. Could've sat on her daddy's lap and he would've held her and tickled her and told her she was a bad girl for staying up so late.

But she let her parents have their time alone. It was enough to know he was home safe.

Now, Kate sat beside Harry at the conference table in Al Parish's lush, million-dollar offices, across the table from a rich man facing life in jail. Kate was still that working-class Jersey girl. They had taken a break when Eddie and the assistants left around a half hour ago. The Jacksons got some refreshments while Al went with Eddie to get the cash from the firm's vault. Now, they were all back in the room. Al at the head of the table, the Jacksons on his left. Kate and Harry pulled up chairs across the desk from the Jacksons.

Where you sit in relation to your client is important. Al Parish knew this as much as any lawyer. Putting himself at the head of the table was a power play.

You are in my house.

This is my office.

My client.

My case.

You're just the help.

But you don't fuck around with Kate Brooks.

It seemed as though Al hadn't yet read that particular memo.

'John, you know Kate. Now, Eddie will be our main courtroom warrior. We needed a battler for this case. Kate will be doing some of the prep work . . .'

Harry raised a finger, opened his mouth as if to object. He knew how good Kate was, and he felt protective of her. Even though Harry was an elder statesman, and former judge, and an utter gentleman who would defend Kate with his life, he also understood Kate didn't need him to fight her battles. He paused. Closed his mouth. Put his hands on the table and smiled at Kate.

She didn't need Harry fighting for her. But it was nice to know he was available should the need arise.

'Can I interrupt, Mr. Parish,' said Kate, then directed her voice to the Jacksons. 'Al is unfamiliar with the precise way that Eddie and I work. I'll be handling the opening statement in the trial, and I'll be cross-examining witnesses alongside my partner. Eddie has a . . . *creative* approach to the law. That's what he's doing right now,' she said, and nodded toward the TV in the corner. It was a live news feed. After Eddie had left along with the associates, one of Parish's assistants had turned on the local news channel.

Castro was going to start his news conference any minute.

'Al, would you mind getting up for a second?' asked Kate.

A look of confusion spread over Parish's features, but he got up.

'I want to sit next to John for a moment,' said Kate as she moved round and took Parish's chair.

Sitting across the desk from a client puts distance between them and you, as well as a physical barrier. If Kate was going to get this man's trust, she wanted to use every available weapon in her arsenal. When Parish sat down beside Harry, and now found himself across the desk from his client and Kate at the head of the table, his confused look soon turned to irritation.

He coughed. Looked at Harry. He had been put firmly in his place by a woman thirty years his junior. Either he would deal with that, or Kate would have to deal with him.

Harry beamed Parish a knowing smile.

Parish didn't smile back.

Kate focused on John. She opened her arms, leaned back in the chair and kept her eyes on his – concentrating, making sure she had his full attention.

'John, this case is going to take some time to come to trial. Thankfully, it won't be too long. District Attorney Castro has an election coming up and he has a serious challenger for the job. Morgan Montgomery is a popular civil-rights lawyer – lot of people in this town will vote for him. If Castro wants to win, he will fast track this case to trial and ride your conviction to an election victory. So you're not going to have to wait for years. That's the first piece of good news. Here's the second – we're not going to let Castro win. You have to trust us to defend you. But that trust goes both ways. We have to trust that you're going to get through this. We need you strong for the trial.'

Jackson hung his head, squeezed his eyes shut. He was physically in great shape. A surgeon has to look after his mind and his body to be able to perform at the peak of his skills. This was not a physique and mind that was made for vanity – it was built for the service of others. Sensing his pain, Alison wrapped both her arms around John, placed her head on his shoulder and whispered to him that it would be alright.

'Listen to Alison, John. Things are going to be okay,' said Harry.

John's head snapped up, his eyes wet and red, and when he spoke his voice was breaking. 'How do you know it's going to be okay? You *can't* know that.'

'We know you're innocent,' said Kate. 'We wouldn't be here otherwise. That's how our practice works. We don't represent the guilty.'

'People think I murdered that woman,' said John, and broke down.

Kate let him cry. Let his wife comfort him.

'John . . .' began Parish, reaching out a hand to him. Kate shot Parish a look. Harry gave him a nudge under the table and then shook his head – telling Parish to shut up.

This was technique. An old lawyer's trick. If the client wants to cry, let them. Say nothing. Let it all come out. Look sympathetic, but professional. Kate didn't have to fake the sympathy – this man's heart was breaking right in front of her. Yet she knew that for his own good, John needed to listen to her. That meant he had to stop crying. If Kate tried to comfort him, it would give him encouragement, relax him, let his emotions run wild. Kate couldn't afford that. Easiest way to stop a client from crying was to sit in front of him in complete silence. It's hard to cry in front of somebody. Even a relative stranger. Soon, the silence from the lawyers would make him uncomfortable. And that discomfort would rapidly overtake his emotional state.

All of this happened in less than thirty seconds. John wiped his face with a Kleenex, apologized to everyone.

'It's okay,' said Kate. 'I have never gone through what you are experiencing right now, but I've sat beside enough people who have and I think I understand it. You feel like you've got a sign around your neck that says you killed somebody . . .'

'Yes,' said John, nodding. 'People look at me on the street, or when I'm in a restaurant having lunch. Friends, neighbors, they all think I killed Margaret.'

'But you didn't kill her. And *you* know that,' said Kate.

'Of course *I* know that – but no one else sees it that way, apart from my family.'

'Everyone will know you're innocent, given time,' said Kate. 'Until then, this sign you've got around your neck, I know it feels heavy, but you're going to have to carry it. Alison, she doesn't see that sign. We don't see it. When you're with us, it disappears. That sign is not in your home. It's not in this office. And when we win your case we're gonna take that thing off your neck and burn it for all the world to see. All we need you to do is hang in there until we get to that day. Can you do that?'

John looked at his wife. Held her hand. Drawing strength from her fingers.

'I can do that.'

'We know you can, John,' said Harry. He was right. To cut into kids' skulls and perform live-saving operations that can take ten hours or more requires a special kind of fortitude.

Harry continued, 'We're going to keep things light today. We just have a few questions. I want you to open your mind, speculate a little. Could someone who has access to your home have planted that gun in your closet?'

'No way. It's just us, and Ruby the nanny, and Althea the maid, and they've been with us for a while. They're just young girls. Ruby is the sweetest girl in the world. She had a terrible upbringing and managed to get through it. Tomas loves her. And Althea, the maid, she just works and works and works. We trust them completely.'

'Okay then, do you have any idea how that gun got into your closet?' asked Kate.

'Sure I do,' said John.

This was new information. Harry leaned forward and Kate drew the top off her pen, held it to the page, ready to make a note.

'The NYPD planted it there,' said John.

Kate and Harry said nothing. Proving that the NYPD planted a gun in his home and then somehow faked the DNA results was a lot for any jury to swallow. Plus, there was no evidence for any of it.

'The police arrested you and searched your home because of a tip. An anonymous phone call. We've asked for the recording in discovery. Tell me, do you have any idea who would have made that call?' asked Kate.

'No clue.'

'Someone with a grudge against you? Maybe a former patient, or their family?'

'I have a great relationship with my patients and their families. I don't hate anyone and, far as I know, nobody has any strong feelings against me. I'm just baffled by the whole thing.'

As he talked, veins stood out on his neck. Alison laced her fingers through his and spoke as John swallowed down the rising emotion.

'John is the kindest, sweetest man I've ever met. I don't know why someone would lie about John. Obviously, they've never met him. They don't know him. If they did, they couldn't lie about him. On our first wedding anniversary, John was a new resident at the hospital. He spent seventeen hours in the theatre with a five-year-old kid from Harlem. He removed a tumor from his brain. John got home exhausted just before midnight, and you know what he did? He cooked dinner for both of us and we ate it in our pajamas on the kitchen floor. We didn't even have furniture. We'd just moved from San Diego. He slept for four hours and then went back to check on the boy. You know what that kid is doing now? He's in college on a basketball scholarship and he's probably going to get drafted next year into the NBA. He writes to John every couple of months. And John writes back. That's who my husband is, Miss Brooks. He's the best man I know.'

Kate and Harry nodded.

And the load they carried felt a little heavier.

Kate understood that being a lawyer meant owing a sacred duty to your client. That you represent them to the very best of your ability. But that's only the oath you take as a new lawyer. If you care about your clients, you carry around their pain inside. Until you can let it go. Representing an innocent person accused of murder adds to the load. Kate had already found herself unable to sleep some nights, thinking about this case, thinking about what might happen if John was convicted. That was the nightmare that kept her awake, that made her get up early and into the office – the weight of that responsibility was sometimes too much to bear. But Kate took it on. She cared. Couldn't help it.

'The press conference is starting,' said Al Parish, breaking the silence.

They all sat back in their chairs, raised their head to look at the screen.

District Attorney Robert Castro stood outside the Manhattan Criminal Court building, wearing a white suit, blue shirt and red tie. His hair slicked back. He was flanked by assistant DAs in dark suits. Castro stood tall, the low afternoon sun in his eyes. The camera angle picked up the battle line of reporters in front of them, their mics held aloft like swords.

'Ladies and gentlemen, thank you for coming,' began Castro.

While he spoke, he patted his jacket.

Both sides.

Like he was looking for something.

Then he unbuttoned the jacket, checked his inside pockets.

Both sides.

He looked over the heads of the journalists, then took a second to get his shit together. Composed himself. He knew it had been a rocky start and the silence that filled the space between him and the microphones was beginning to become awkward.

He coughed, put on that fake professional smile that all politicians wear, as if they all bought it from the same store.

'Ladies and gentlemen,' he began again, 'thank you for coming. I've come straight from the grand jury room and can confirm that we have an indictment against John Jackson for the murder of Margaret Blakemore. This is a first-degree murder case and we intend to speed this case to trial at all—'

Castro's head shot up. Something was happening right in front of him. He narrowed his eyes. The press conference had come to a complete stop. The shot of the courthouse took in some background. Kate could see people moving quickly past Castro, moving toward whatever was going on behind the reporters.

'What the hell is going on?' asked Parish.

Sweat broke out on Castro's top lip. His nose wrinkled, his brow furrowed and his fake smile had died – replaced by a scowl of pure anger. Even his pallor changed – a bright red seeping up from the collar of his shirt.

Harry shook his head, said, 'There's only one man alive that can piss people off that badly.'

10

Eddie

We met outside the now permanently closed Corte Café, on the corner of Lafayette and Duane. While the junior associates were lousy lawyers, they could at least follow basic instructions. They had come in their Sunday-morning-hungover-trip-to-the-convenience-store clothes. Baggy, ripped jeans. Sweatshirts either way too big or way too small. Faded gray T-shirts and stained sneakers. Baseball caps and beanie hats. The kind of outfit you might wear if you were painting the apartment and you didn't mind it getting ruined.

The point was none of them looked like Harvard grads who all happened to work in the same firm.

They had all followed the brief.

Except one.

Harrison Washington III, because I would have a hard time forgetting that name, had come in oversized Dolce & Gabbana jeans, bright white Gucci sneakers and an Alexander McQueen shirt.

I watched him cross the street from Foley Square.

He could sense my disapproval. And it didn't look like he cared too much. He stood in front of me, a defiant look on his face. His outfit must've cost more than ten grand. The denim alone, with what looked like little diamond sequins, must've been seven or eight thousand dollars.

'I'm afraid I don't own any *ripped* jeans,' he said, with a smirk.

I knelt down in front of him, grabbed a handful of his jeans and ran my switchblade through ten inches of denim, opening his pants from his shin to this thigh.

'You do now,' I said.

'Oh. My. God! I—'

'I don't want to hear it,' I said, cutting off Harrison Washington III. He was motionless, staring open-mouthed at his ruined Dolce & Gabbana's.

'You all know what to do. Now go for a walk. I'll see you in ten minutes. And remember, I don't need lawyers – I need lemmings.'

They dispersed, and went in different directions.

Harrison Washington III didn't close his mouth until he'd crossed the street.

All I had to do now was go pick a fight with the DA.

The waiting area in the district attorney's office, just a block over from the Criminal Court building, hadn't changed in years. There was no budget for décor at 10 Hogan Place. Same old worn seats. Same old stained coffee table.

Same old reception staff.

Herb Goldman had been an old man when I'd first stepped into this office. He was now positively ancient. Liver spots covered his face, but he always looked sharp. Black suit. White shirt. Blue necktie. The only indication Herb was getting older was the flap of loose skin that hung over his shirt collar; it kept getting bigger. Three or four district attorneys had come and gone through his office in just the last few years – resigning or getting kicked out on corruption charges.

Herb would outlast them all. I liked Herb.

'How are you still alive?' I asked him.

'Only the good die young, Eddie. Never mind me – I read the news. How the hell are you still alive?'

'I'm like you. The devil is keeping me alive for a higher purpose.'

It had been a rough few years. I had the scars to prove it.

'Do you think I could grab five minutes with Castro?' I asked.

His face darkened at the mention of the DA.

'Have you met him yet?' he asked.

I shook my head.

'I seen a lot of assholes come through these doors,' he said. 'This guy takes some beating. I even put in for retirement.'

'How does Mrs. Goldman feel about that?'

'She's got a nice place picked out in a seniors' retirement facility in Florida. Goddamn Florida. It's like an elephant's graveyard.'

I winced, said, 'Sorry to hear that.'

'I'm praying I'll have a stroke before it comes to that,' he said, then picked up the phone and hit a button. He waited until the call was answered.

'Hi, Maura, Herb here. I got Eddie Flynn with me for the DA.'

He listened in silence. Then put the phone down.

'Now is not a good time,' said Herb. 'Castro is stressed to the balls and he's on the warpath with everybody.'

'Sounds like the perfect time for me to see him,' I said with a smile.

Herb smiled back, said, 'Go on through. If anyone asks, you snuck past me.'

I pushed through the doors to the outer offices. Islands of desks and stacks of paperwork with assistant DAs, secretaries and paralegals moving files, on the phone, or punching the keys on their workstations. It was hot. Men had loosened their shirts and ties, and I noticed bottles of water on every desk. The DA's office was at the end of a narrow corridor that began on the other side of the room. I made my way through the chaos of a busy prosecutor's department, along the corridor and found the DA's door open.

Castro stood in the center of the room, his large desk behind him. He was in his underwear, wearing only underpants with a shirt and tie. Flopping out a pair of white suit pants, he stepped into them and then turned and noticed me.

'What the hell are you doing here?'

'Thought I'd come and straighten a few things out before your press conference.'

It was then that I noticed a pair of black pants folded over his guest chair. Castro was all show. He had been elected on the back of the former district attorney taking a bribe from a politician who'd been caught with an underage girl. The ever-prescient Castro took that moment to run for the office on an anti-corruption ticket. To separate himself from the other candidates for DA, he wore a white or pale suit. It was supposedly an idea from one of his advisors: it wasn't good enough to say he was clean – people had to have a visual reminder of his untouchable character. Like everything else, it was a gimmick. The word around the halls of justice was that Castro's white-suit routine hid his true nature – the guy was as dirty as they come. It had been Castro who'd set up the politician into bribing Castro's predecessor, thereby paving the way for a district-attorney election in the first place.

This guy was a player.

'If I had wanted a comment from Jackson's lawyers, I would've called Al Parish,' said Castro, buttoning his pants. 'Maura!' he called out.

A woman in her thirties came hustling into Castro's office. She was dressed in a black skirt, blue blouse and she had a notepad and pen in her hand. Her hair was supposed to be tied up, but some strands had fallen loose and stuck to her cheek with sweat.

'Yes, Mr. Castro,' said the woman I presumed was his secretary, Maura.

'How did he get in here?' asked Castro.

'Well . . . well, I-I-I'm not quite sure. I . . .'

'Never mind,' he snapped. 'Clean up this place. Get the garbage off my desk and, by the way, the tuna salad was awful. Don't ever get my lunch from that place again. I'm not paying for your mistakes. I'm taking that ten bucks out of your paycheck.'

Maura said nothing. She just bowed her head and almost tiptoed round Castro to his desk where she bunched up the remains of his lunch in her arms and made for the door. At this point I was grateful Kate wasn't here. If he'd spoken to Maura like that in front of Kate Brooks, Castro would've needed a fresh pair of pants.

'And where the hell is my speech?' he cried. 'As you can see, Flynn. I'm a little busy. If you're not here to plead out your client, you can leave.'

'I actually came with advice before you open your big mouth to media. Drop the charges against Jackson – he's innocent. This case is not gonna go your way and I wouldn't want you embarrassing your-self in public.'

'Get out,' he said.

I leaned back, looked at Castro. He found his white jacket on a hanger attached to a coat rack in the corner. He put it on, bellowed, 'Speech, now!'

An assistant DA, his white shirt stained with sweat, came into Castro's office with two pages of typed script.

'Is this the revised version?' asked Castro, snatching the pages and scanning them.

'This is the latest version with your edits,' said the ADA.

'Better be . . .' he said, and folded the pages before placing them inside his jacket.

The ADA left, Castro turned to me and said, 'You still here?'

I said nothing. I watched him step into his slip-on leather shoes, waited for him to take a step toward the door. When he did, I moved too. He was a little smaller than me, and when I shouldered him in the chest he bounced back two feet.

'My apologies,' I said. 'After you,' and I held out a hand to lead the way.

'You're a goddamn juvenile, Flynn. You don't scare me,' he said, and I followed him out of his office. Just as he got to the end of the corridor he was swamped by a crowd of ADAs as he made his way through reception and to the elevator. I watched him go, and stopped by Maura's desk.

'Why is it so hot in here?' I asked.

'He won't let us put on the AC. Says it's a waste of public money.'

DAs who save money are popular with the mayor's office. This guy was something else. He would make every one of his personnel suffer in the Manhattan heat just to save a few grand so he could suck up to a higher power.

Maura stared at her computer screen, dabbed her forehead with a tissue. Only being this close to her did I notice the collar of her blouse was frayed from too many washes – the color had faded too. Her lunchbox was by her feet, which were clad in pumps with one of the soles peeling away from the shoe. With inflation, rent, food prices and gas going through the roof – times were tough for everyone. One thing Castro was not short on was money. He'd come from a wealthy middle-class family and married an heiress to a mining company. Now, he lived in a mansion two blocks from West 74th Street.

I peeled off a hundred-dollar bill from my fold, placed it on Maura's desk.

'Don't tell him I gave you this. He'll make you give it back and he'll still take his lunch money from your paycheck. Just between us, let's say his lunch is on me and you take the rest as a tip. And if you ever get tired of this job call my partner, Kate Brooks. She could help you find something else. Lot of law firms in this town crying out for great support staff.'

Maura stared at the bill, then crumpled it in her hand and stuffed it into her purse.

'Thank you,' she said.

'No problem. Are you going to watch his press conference?'

She rolled her eyes, said, 'I have to. Part of my job.'

I smiled, said, 'I think you might enjoy this one.'

II

Eddie

As a former con artist, I have an advantage over some of my fellow lawyers. A trial verdict is rendered by twelve members of the public who form a jury. For the skilled lawyer, or ex-conman, a group of people presents an opportunity. Success or failure as a lawyer is not determined by your knowledge of the law – it is, however, greatly determined by your knowledge of human behavior. When cross-examining a witness, you should know the answer to a question before you ask it – not because you can see the future – but because you know the witness, you've studied them, and you have, through the timing, phrasing and intonation of your question, pre-determined the response. And that answer, which has been manipulated from the witness, is designed solely to help influence those twelve jurors in your favor.

It's all about people. And it's much easier to influence a group of people than a single individual.

Plenty of philosophers, sociologists, psychologists and every two-bit hustler on the street make it their business to understand how individuals and groups think. It's not just academic, it's big business. That's why every soda ad has a bunch of happy, attractive people drinking ice-cold cans together. In the publishing world a book really takes off when it gets that magic quality of 'word-of-mouth'. Most

TV shows get popular when groups of people talk about them on social media. Videos with mass appeal go viral. And the lemmings who don't know what they're doing buy stocks in the market when everyone is buying that same stock. It's powerful stuff.

And you've got to know how to use it.

With my back to the wall of the courthouse building, I watched Castro, flanked by his assistants, take up a position in front of a group of eager journalists.

I checked the street. It was busy. Lots of folk leaving their offices for the day to go get food and drink, or make their journey home.

The stage was set.

It wasn't the best start for the DA. I watched him for what felt like ten minutes, but was probably only ten seconds. He made a brief introduction, then stood there in silence while he patted his jacket pockets, looking for his speech.

'Ahm . . . aahhhmm . . .' he said, mumbling, 'Where is the . . .'

An awkward silence wrapped around him like ice forming on a car windshield. It was excruciating. Another five seconds of cameras rolling, reporters coughing just to break the heavy, embarrassing atmosphere. Castro stopped searching for his speech, grabbed the podium like he was steadying himself on a ship sailing through stormy seas.

There was nothing else he could do but start talking.

'Ahmm . . . when . . . when murder came to my neighborhood, I mourned the loss of Margaret Blakemore. Now, I'm taking down her murderer . . .'

'You come out all guns blazing when there's a murder on *your own* doorstep,' said a voice, through a bullhorn behind me. A man in a black suit raised the bullhorn over his head, let everyone on the street see him standing thirty feet from Castro. His name was Morgan Montgomery, or Momo to his friends. He was Castro's opponent in the upcoming DA election.

'What about the young black man murdered in the Bronx last

week?' said Momo, 'Or the five hate-crime attacks on Asian men and women in Chinatown just this month? Or the eight murders last month in Harlem? Where's their press conference?'

The press had turned away from Castro – they were staring at Momo.

And that's when I saw Porsche Bloomingdale, in her sweatpants and hoody, crossing the street to stand in front of Momo, watching him speak. She was quickly joined by Eric Fong and Veronica Colville-North. Eric Rothschild stopped in his tracks beside them and, slowly, it happened. Other people, not in the employ of Al Parish, stopped in the street to listen to Momo, observing every available law of human crowd behavior – if people were stopping to listen to this guy – then they wanted to stop and hear what he had to say too. Crowds formed like gravity. All I did was help it along a little. Human behavior did the rest.

Within thirty seconds, a crowd of around twenty people had gathered around Momo, and he addressed them and the journalists directly. Soon as that crowd built up, the journalists stepped away from Castro, the cameras turned away from the DA too, the media ran the short distance to stand in front of Momo and cover his speech.

Momo said, 'This DA only cares about victims if they happen to be in *his* neighborhood. He's not a DA for the people – he's all about himself . . .'

Harrison Washington III, still looking a little sore about his ruined designer jeans, redeemed himself in my eyes by starting the chant.

Mo-mo.

Mo-mo.

Mo-mo.

The chant took over the crowd organically. The story that would be on the news that night was not about John Jackson. Now, it was about the DA's disastrous press conference, his record – and his bias – and the fact that he only cares about this murder because it happened in his neighborhood. The coverage would all be focused on Momo.

Castro's assistant ADAs hung their heads, or casually broke away from him and wandered back to the office.

Not Castro.

He was staring straight at me.

I took his speech from my jacket pocket. I'd swiped it from him in a bump-lift when I almost knocked him over in his office. He didn't feel my light fingers reaching into his jacket.

I folded his speech again, tore it half.

Castro pointed at me, then turned and walked away.

It was on. Total war. Just the way I like it.

After ten minutes, Momo finished his speech, did a few soundbites for the cameras and the crowd dispersed. Momo put his bullhorn in his backpack and came over to me.

'Thanks for that, Eddie. The donation too.'

'It's only twenty-five grand, but it should help. I hope you win. I don't like Castro.'

'Good luck to you, and your client. See you around, Eddie.'

He left, and I put my back to the wall of the courthouse and waited.

I scanned the street.

An SUV was parked across the street. The doors opened, Bloch and Lake got out and came over to meet me.

'Any eyes on me?' I asked.

'Nothing,' said Lake.

Bloch shook her head.

'Well, keep them peeled. Somebody is going to take up that contract. I'd like to live long enough to defend Jackson.'

'We'll take you back to the office,' said Lake. 'Bloch got the super to put some extra locks on the door. You'll need to stay there till we come back.'

'Where are you two going?'

'We're going to take a look at the crime scene,' said Lake.

Bloch's head swiveled to the left. She watched a man in a long raincoat come out of the courthouse. He watched us as he left, then crossed the street and headed away.

I hadn't noticed, but Bloch had reached for her piece. She took her hand from the inside of her jacket, said, 'I don't like this.'

'I ain't exactly happy about it either. Just don't tell Harry or Kate. Like we agreed.'

Bloch nodded, said, 'I wish I knew who was coming for you. I don't like waiting.'

'It's a waiting game. What's the alternative?' asked Lake.

'A hunting game,' said Bloch.

12

Ruby

Tonight was the night.

From her little pot of savings, Ruby had taken two hundred dollars and gone shopping. She wanted to look her best for the party. It would become a party, of course. No gathering in this street happens without a lot of money being spent on food and booze. The excuse that had been given was that this was an emergency neighborhood-watch meeting. To talk about the murder and John Jackson's arrest and what, if anything, the neighbors could do to protect themselves.

This translated as what the neighbors could do to get the Jacksons out of the street.

And Ruby had a front-row seat. In fact, she would be the star of the evening.

Gossip was rife on the street and everyone knew Ruby worked for the Jacksons, first as a cleaner and then solely as a nanny for Tomas. Ruby had the inside scoop on exactly what was going on in the Jacksons' home. Had she seen something suspicious in the lead-up to the murder? Had she ever seen a gun in the house? Were John Jackson and Maggs having an affair? Even though Ruby had also worked for Maggs, from time to time, they would not ask much about her, if anything. They had already made up their minds about poor Maggs. Like Ruby, she was not accepted. Unwelcome. A woman of loose morals, some said. But, to Ruby, Maggs was free. Because she never cared what the rest of the street thought of her. She was beyond them. The only question they might ask tonight about Maggs was whether she was having an affair with John Jackson.

This, and other questions, would be posed to Ruby before the end of the evening. She was sure of it. For once in her life, Ruby Johnson got to be the center of attention. And she couldn't wait for it. That afternoon, she got a manicure. Even spent two hours in the salon getting her hair done. She had thought about getting her make-up done, but decided against it. She put on the same foundation she always wore, but added just a little eyeliner and a brighter shade of pink lipstick.

She wanted to look her best. This was her moment with the neighbors in West 74th Street.

In the evening, Ruby stood on the sidewalk gazing up at the home of Peter and Petra Schwartzman and their four children. Lights were on inside. The soft lilt of a piano escaped from the bay window – Peter was a big jazz fan. Petra never did anything by halves. The frequency of her little community gatherings had increased of late. Now that Peter and Petra's children had all grown up and were either in college or working, they had more time to socialize. The downside was they no longer needed any childcare and all their cleaning needs were met by a company. Ruby knew the family, but hadn't been in the house in a long time.

Petra could be hard work. She was the real gossip on the street. Knew everyone's business – who was having an affair, who had shares in a company that was about to skyrocket in value, who hadn't chipped in for the street's annual charity gathering. It had been over a year since Ruby had had any contact from Petra. Then she got the invite to the WhatsApp group and Petra invited her to the gathering tonight.

She pulled her pink, cashmere sweater down. Smoothed out her new jeans. She couldn't remember the last time she had bought clothes that didn't come from a thrift store. Not in a very long time. She had thought about buying a party dress, or a cocktail dress. She wasn't exactly sure of the difference, but in the end she decided against it. She wanted to wear something nice, but not formal. This wasn't officially a party, after all.

And the last thing Ruby wanted tonight was to embarrass herself.

And here she was, in her new outfit, her heart beating twice as fast as normal and a strange fluttering sensation in her throat.

Ruby didn't get nervous. Not often. She was used to being around money – serious money. But she was normally there just to clean the toilet or change the diapers.

Now, Ruby was going to meet these people as equals. Okay, perhaps not exactly equals, but she was there as *a person*. Not *the help*.

She would be *seen* tonight. She had to build on the trust she had established. It would make everything easier in the end.

Clearing her throat, Ruby climbed the front steps and rang the doorbell. It was answered by Petra herself – a small lady wearing a green dress with diamonds in her ears and a big fake smile.

'Ruby, darling,' she said, and embraced her. 'Thank you so much for coming. Let's go to the kitchen.'

She led Ruby through the hallway and they passed the living room, already crowded with guests.

'Tell me, how is your mother these days? It's been so long since we've seen her.'

'She's okay. Not so mobile these days, you know, with the illness.'

'Of course. Please give her our best when you see her.'

The kitchen had a full staff tonight. A chef in whites was taking hot trays of food out of the oven while another prepped smoked salmon. A young female server, dressed in black, waited to take food out to the guests.

'Everyone, this is Ruby. Ruby, this is Chef Antonio. He'll get you up to speed,' said Petra.

Ruby gave Petra a confused look. The nerves in her stomach were suddenly replaced by a hollow, empty feeling.

'Chef, please give Ruby an apron. Ruby, I can't tell you how happy I am to see you and thank you so much for helping out tonight. The guests in the conservatory haven't had any food yet. Could you be a darling and go straight there?'

As Petra turned away, the smile on her face fell away. The server gave Ruby an apron and pointed at a tray of canapés.

She wasn't here as an equal.

No one wanted to talk to Ruby.

No one wanted her insight into life inside the Jacksons' house.

Tonight she was not *a person*. She would not be *seen*.

She was *the help*.

She was here to give out canapés and top up wineglasses.

'Are you okay?' asked the server.

Forcing a smile, Ruby nodded, put on the black apron over her new clothes, tied it at the back and picked up the silver tray.

'You've got smoked-salmon blinis and venison-sausage profiter-oles,' said Chef Antonio, a big man with thick hairy arms.

Ruby nodded.

'Speak,' said the chef. 'Say, "Yes, Chef,"' he said.

As Ruby's eyes filled with tears, she said, 'Yes, Chef.'

'Good, now get the fuck out of here and give these people some food and then come straight back for another tray. Go, go, go . . .'

She reversed out of the kitchen door, balancing the tray in one hand as she dabbed at her eyes with the other.

Once in the hallway, Ruby took deep breaths. She could feel her face flushing. The combination of heartbreak and embarrassment was burning her cheeks. She could not allow herself to cry. It would ruin her eyeliner. People would point at her. People would stare. They would see her and know that she wasn't like them. Taking two deep breaths, Ruby calmed herself. Then she willed her features into a smile and checked her reflection in the large, oval mirror in the hallway. It looked as if she'd been given electric shock treatment; her expression looked contorted, even painful. She relaxed her shoulders, closed her eyes and let out her breath. When she looked at her reflection again, she appeared more natural. The smile no longer appeared mechanical.

She stepped into the living room and was enveloped in sound. Music, voices, laughter too – the rich make jokes even when discussing a murder.

The first person Ruby approached was Todd Ellis. He stood with his back to the wall, champagne in hand, nodding as he pretended to take in the conversation of the little group that had formed around him. He had a striking appearance – his head shaven to the skin, eyebrows sculpted to thin rows of dark black hair. Dyed, obviously. Small, bald and thin. His head turned red whenever he got angry, making him look like a matchstick in a suit. Ellis made it big on Wall Street in the nineties. He now served on the board of a bank and was the most regimented person Ruby had ever met. She had sat for his kids a few times. Two horrible brats who broke their toys for fun.

Just like their father.

Ellis had his PA send him his schedule for the next day at ten p.m. the night before for review. If something upset his schedule, Ellis would fly into a rage. She'd seen it once before. The car was late to take him and his wife to the ballet. He'd punched a mirror in the hallway, smashing it and cutting his knuckles. Ruby remembered staring at him as he pulled a shard of glass from the webbing between his index finger and thumb, and then sucked on the blood.

He was an empty man. His billions couldn't fill him up. And only work, money and pleasure kept the anger in check. A year ago, Ruby had caught Mrs. Ellis in the kitchen, crying. It took some gentle coaxing, but Ruby found out that Todd was having an affair with Maggs. Maggs had ended it, but Todd wouldn't take no for an answer. So Maggs had called Mrs. Ellis to tell her to keep her husband on a leash and spilled all of the dirty truth of the affair. Somehow, Mrs. Ellis had stayed with her husband. They'd patched it up. It was around the same time that Todd bought her a mansion in Hawaii, which Ruby supposed would have helped ease the situation.

But there was no easing the resentment in Ellis. It lived within him.

And he had continued to pursue Maggs. Ruby had seen Maggs sneaking him into her house, about a week before the murder. If Ellis's wife had found out he was back with her, there would have been a divorce. The price of that, according to the gossip the last time his wife threatened to separate – was close to three billion dollars.

That's an expensive affair.

He didn't even look at Ruby as he snatched an hors d'oeuvre off the tray.

She moved on. Saw Petra in the corner, making the rounds. She moved toward her, gestured for her to come over.

'Is there a problem with the canapés?' asked Petra.

'No, nothing like that. I just overheard some conversation. People are scared,' said Ruby. 'It would be good if someone could reassure them.'

'The DA isn't going to make it tonight, I'm afraid. I don't blame him after that press conference today. Did you see it?'

Ruby nodded, said, 'I think the neighborhood is angry and frightened. Somebody needs to do something. People can't be expected to live in the same neighborhood as a killer.'

'And yet you continue to work for them,' said Petra, and quickly followed her jab at Ruby with a solid right hand, 'Oh, I'm not judging you, darling Ruby. I'm sure you need the money . . .'

Petra waved her fingers at Ruby to continue passing around the appetizers. Ruby smiled with the full breadth of her mouth, forcibly, and moved on. Her little suggestion had been enough. She had planted a seed.

Petra would grow that into an oak tree. She moved to the front of the room, stood on a chair and tapped her champagne flute with a spoon.

'Thank you all so much for coming . . .'

Ruby had been making her way around the room. She stopped

and looked around for somewhere to put down the platter. No dice. She held it in front of her.

Just as Petra began speaking, Brett Bale brushed past her, taking an appetizer from her tray as he moved. He was rake thin – tanned and athletic – with a flop of thick brown hair, which gave him a preppy appearance. He'd been a tennis prodigy in his teenage years, but an ACL tear that led to a total knee replacement two years later ended any high hopes he may have had of turning pro. Instead of switching careers, Brett, with the backing of his parents, opened a tennis camp upstate. It proved popular. Really popular. Another four camps followed – two in Florida, one in Miami and the last in Texas, of all places.

Having four wildly successful tennis camps had given Brett the excuse to travel, and he then embarked on a series of affairs. Now, Brett at forty-five had been unfaithful to all four of his previous wives. Out of the four of them, only three survived. The last one had died suspiciously. She'd drowned while swimming from Bale's boat. Accidents at sea happen all the time, even to two-time national swimming champs like the late Mrs. Bale. Her family didn't buy it and had used their wealth and influence to pressure the police to charge him, but nothing worked. Bale's wealth was greater, and his lawyers were better.

None of this had stopped Maggs from getting involved with Brett. At least he was single, and some of the wives in the neighborhood were glad she had taken up with Brett as it might stop her flirting with their husbands. Maggs once told Ruby that she would like to be her for a day. To be unseen. For all her beauty, Maggs was insecure around women and men. She never thought she was good enough, pretty enough or smart enough. If only the neighbors had known that, they might actually mourn her. They were more concerned about the crime and the perpetrator than the poor victim.

Gossip was always hot on West 74th Street.

'As some of you may know,' continued Petra, 'our brave district attorney was due to give an address to our little soirée, this evening. However, due to circumstances beyond his control, he is no longer able to join us tonight. But he sends this message.'

She unfolded a note, perched her Gucci reading glasses on the end of her nose and read.

'*I want all the residents of West 74th Street to know that we will get justice for Margaret. Jackson has betrayed our trust, and has brought murder to our community. I will personally see to it that he spends the rest of his life behind bars. For now, until we can rid our street of this devil, be watchful.*'

She finished reading the note, folded it and held it in her hand.

'Now, if our illustrious DA were here this evening, I would run this by him, but, as you know, I'm very attuned to the mood of this street. I've been here a long time, and I know everybody is scared and angry. Well, we're not your average neighborhood. We can do things other people cannot . . .'

They had gathered to drink champagne, and eat canapés, and gossip, and plot, but none of the people in this room had the slightest remorse for poor Maggs. None of them mentioned her. Not one word of sympathy. Ruby bore Maggs no ill will, and she'd liked her company and her kindness, but Ruby was not built to grieve, as her grandmother had guessed – something wasn't quite right. Yet, she was sorry she was dead. Of all the residents, Maggs's kindness to Ruby made her stand out. And made Ruby hate them all so much more.

Petra continued, 'I propose we do the following . . .'

Ruby didn't listen to the rest of the speech, delivered in Petra's Upper West Side drawl. She knew Petra could never resist the opportunity to increase her standing in the community. She had the chance now to give the residents exactly what they wanted. All Ruby had done was point her in the right direction. Ruby's goal for the evening was complete. Now, she had other things on her mind: the two men in this room whom she'd gotten close to tonight. None of them paid her any attention.

Todd Ellis, the psychopath banker and matchstick man.

And Brett Bale, the tennis coach who may have murdered his wife.

Ruby had seen one of these men recently.

She'd watched him shoot Margaret Blakemore in the head, then skip down the porch steps and hide the gun in a garbage bag before casually walking back into this very house. And he had not noticed her that night. Just as he had not noticed her this evening. That was her great strength. Ruby thought herself foolish to have expected to be welcomed and treated as an equal this evening, treated like a member of this community. She was not one of them any more. She was the help.

Silent. Invisible. But that was also her power. She was a poisonous spider, lurking in the dark corners of every home on the street.

Ruby intended to keep it that way. For now.

Later that night, as she helped the caterers tidy up, she made plans. Ruby needed serious money.

And now she was going to get it.

So many spider threads she had yet to lay out. Some she could now begin to gather.

One thing was for sure – Ruby's game was just beginning.

And she had flies to catch.

13

Bloch

'Must be a party,' said Lake.

They stood outside Margaret Blakemore's address on West 74th Street. It was coming up on midnight, and down the street a group of people were filing out of a house, waving their goodbyes and making the short trip to their neighboring homes.

'I don't like parties,' said Bloch.

'One of their neighbors has been murdered. What kind of people throw a party at a time like this?'

'Rich people,' said Bloch.

An unmarked NYPD pool car pulled up beside the two investigators. A small, rotund cop with a belly that hung over his pants, got out of the passenger seat of the Ford and flashed his badge.

He was Detective Marvin Neeson. A thirty-year veteran. His career had begun when the city was climbing out of the grip of drugs, gangs and prostitution. When the murder rate was higher than his blood pressure was now. His face had a ruddy hue to it. Not just his cheeks, it looked as if someone had spraypainted his head in a pinkish-red.

'Bloch?' he asked.

Bloch nodded, took out her ID, showed it to him.

'Why are we doing this now? I should've been home in bed two hours ago. Instead, I have to come down here and babysit you two,' said Neeson.

'We wanted to take a look at the scene around the same time the crime was committed. It helps,' said Lake.

'Helps what?'

'Helps us get a better sense of the crime,' said Lake.

'You don't need to be a friggin' crime-scene expert to know what happened here. We got the murder weapon. End of story. Say, I didn't see your ID.'

Lake nodded, said, 'That's right.'

'You ain't getting inside until I see ID.'

Bloch said, 'He's with me.'

She said it as both a statement of fact, and as an end to the conversation. Bloch was well known in New York law enforcement. A few years ago, she had trained some of their best officers in hand-to-hand combat, and advanced driving skills. At first, some of the cops were resistant to being taught self-defense by a woman. A couple were downright mad about it. Those two decided to take her on, on the mats, full contact. One of them was an NYPD golden gloves champion. The other had been an amateur wrestling champ and self-described ju-jitsu expert. Both of them had to eat a lot of shit from their lieutenants when they had to take a couple of months off, on paid sick leave, after their bouts with Bloch.

'I know you,' said Neeson.

Bloch nodded.

'If he's with you, fair enough. But you're responsible for him,' said Neeson, and handed Bloch the key to Margaret Blakemore's house and got back in his vehicle.

Before Bloch put the key in the door, she stood back, lit up the lock face with a flashlight.

'No toolmarks,' she said, then tried the key.

Bloch and Lake went inside and shut the door behind them. Found the light switch.

The hallway was large, dominated by a beautiful wooden staircase with a red carpet in the center of the stairs, held down by brass runners. The floor was pale tile. They spent five minutes with their flashlights tracing the floor, looking for anything out of place, any spot of blood, markings on the floor, anything out of the ordinary. There was nothing.

'No back door in these houses,' said Lake. Bloch nodded, and they continued into the room on their left.

What had once been two rooms had been converted into a single living space. Wide and long. Couches, an antique roll top and side tables in the bay window area, and the second area at the back was the kitchen. A large chrome stove and porcelain sink, with a long table in the center of the room. A bench on one side, chairs on the other. It looked like a space for socializing. The stove top looked as if it had never been used. Along the opposite wall was a wine rack.

They scanned the kitchen area quickly and then focused their attention on the living area. Even though cleaners had been employed, there was still a darker grain to the wooden floor just in front of the window. Everything else was neat and in its proper place.

'What do you think?' asked Lake.

'No forced entry. No signs of a struggle. She knew her killer,' said Bloch.

'That doesn't help us with defending the good doctor.'

'It is what it is.'

Down on her hands and knees, Bloch examined the stain, turned and then stared up at Lake.

'We know the killer fired three shots,' she said. 'One took her in the chest and lodged there. No exit wound. Then, when she was on the floor, two shots to the head. The rounds were .22 caliber. No exit wounds from the skull. There's not much blood here. Massive intercranial hemorrhaging would have led to bleeding from the nose, ears and the entry wounds,' said Bloch.

'With the head shots, both entry wounds were mid temple. Half an inch between them. That's decent grouping,' said Lake.

Bloch nodded.

'No scorch marks around the entry wounds. No pressure bruising from the barrel of the pistol. Same on the chest wound. He stood back, aimed and fired,' she said.

'Jackson doesn't know how to shoot,' said Lake. 'You can get lucky with one shot. Not three. Not when you're drawing down on a real-life, moving, breathing, defenseless human being.'

'It looks like an execution. Someone who knew what they were doing.'

'Not much of a defense,' said Lake.

'It's a start,' said Bloch.

Together, they scanned the downstairs rooms again, then made their way to the upper floor. There were four well-proportioned bedrooms spread over two floors. A bathroom, a main bedroom with its own bathroom and a small guest room on the second floor that had been converted into a dressing room. Two more bedrooms on the third, both with adjoining bathrooms.

Nothing out of place.

Everything looked neat and tidy. Even the bed.

'Has Alan Blakemore spent the night here since the murder?' asked Lake.

'No,' said Bloch. 'There was a story in the *Post*. He came back to the city to ID the body, checked into a hotel, flew back out to Madrid the next day.'

Lake nodded, and they set about checking the drawers and closets in the main bedroom.

Bloch peered out of the window. The light from the chandelier threw her reflection onto the glass. She unlocked the window, pulled it up and stuck her head out. The smells of the city came to her. The smell of rain in the air, sewage too. The street was mostly in darkness. The residents were now at home in their beds.

Lake joined her.

'Listen,' said Bloch.

Stilling his breathing, Lake remained motionless, his ear cocked. The only sounds were distant rolls of tires on the avenue at the end of the street and the low hum of the city.

'I don't hear anything.'

'Exactly,' said Bloch. Reaching into her pants pocket, she came out with a handful of change. She aimed it at the trash can resting against the lamp post next door. The quarters hit the can with a crash and rattled and danced into the gutter. A few stray coins bounced off the hood of the police car parked outside. Detective Neeson got out of the car, looked around.

Bloch watched the lights come on in the bedrooms of the houses opposite. She leaned out of the window further. Lake did the same.

Only when they leaned forward did they spot the young woman across the street staring up at the window. She had long dark hair, tied up in a ponytail. A pink sweater and blue jeans.

Bloch met her gaze.

The young woman didn't flinch. Didn't look away.

She just stared.

A key part of being a detective is developing a sense of people. Being able to read expressions, body language, changes in tone of voice. Bloch wasn't good at reading people. Never had been, and never would be. Her brain operated on a different level. Numbers. Facts. Science. Logic. People were unreliable, and therefore a slight mystery to her.

As she stared at the young woman across the street, Bloch felt something stir inside her. Whatever hormones and chemicals the central nervous system needed to deal with a threat – they were swirling around Bloch's body right now. This wasn't the emotional part of her mind – this was the old, dormant, lizard part of her brain. The survival instinct.

The young woman looked away, continued to walk up the street, away from the house. She didn't run. She walked slowly, like she was out for a stroll.

'Who was that?' asked Lake.

Bloch shook her head.

Front doors opened, windows opened and people gazed out into the street to see what the noise had been.

'The neighbors are on edge,' said Lake, 'but I guess this is the kind of street where folks pay attention to noises in the night. There's a lot of rich folks here who don't want to get robbed.'

They both came back inside, and Lake closed the window.

'Medical examiner put the time of death between midnight and one a.m. We know the victim wasn't found until the morning,' said Lake. 'There was a party down the street, which would have made noise, but not everyone was there. How come none of the other neighbors came to check on her when they heard the shots?'

'The rounds taken out of Margaret Blakemore were .38 grain hollow points. Subsonic. The shots don't break the sound barrier when fired, so no crack of gunfire. You combine a subsonic round with a suppressor and each shot will be no louder than forty, maybe fifty decibels,' said Bloch.

'What does fifty decibels sound like?' asked Lake.

'Normal conversation is about sixty decibels.'

'Shit, so the killer knew her, knew the area, knew how to shoot and knew his ammunition. This is looking more and more like a professional hit. I know the husband has a solid alibi and he's way out of state for the time of the murder, but could he have hired a hitman?'

'We can rule out the husband. No real motive. And this is not a professional hit,' said Bloch.

'Why not a professional?'

'Because she wouldn't let a stranger into the house and a hitman would've shot her when she opened the front door.'

Lake shook his head, stared at the ground. They both fell silent for a time, considering their thoughts.

'The cops have searched these rooms,' said Bloch. 'They haven't tossed the place, but they would have completed a cursory search, trying to build a picture of Margaret's life. They kept it tidy, though. This is all exactly as it was when the murder occurred.'

'Agreed. The rooms and contents would have been given a quick once-over. There's, what, half a million dollars of jewelry just sitting on the dressing table in the other room. If nothing there was taken, no need for the cops to tear the place apart. This wasn't a robbery.'

'They knew it wasn't a robbery when they saw the body,' said Bloch. 'She was still wearing her engagement ring. That's a big rock.'

'Fair enough,' said Lake. 'So what is our motive here? It's not robbery. Postmortem shows she wasn't assaulted in any way – so it's not sexual. It's like you said – it's an execution.'

They began to examine the bedroom – the nightstand, the closet, both working different sides of the room.

Bloch closed Blakemore's underwear drawer, opened the second drawer and began looking through her socks when she stopped.

'Lake,' she said, and from inside a pair of rolled-up socks Bloch pulled out a cell phone.

14

Eddie

I sat in my office chair, feet on the desk beside a cup of cold coffee.

Kate had gone home with her copy of the Jackson files, taking the night to go over pre-trial motions. Harry stood at my office window, a glass of Scotch in his hand, bathed in neon green from the sign for the bubble-tea shop across the street.

'What the hell is bubble tea, anyway?' asked Harry.

'I have no idea. Denise likes it. Says they do all kinds of flavors.'

'Do they have bourbon flavor?' asked Harry.

'I don't think it's that kind of deal. There are little gel balls in the bottom of the cup. It's huge in Japan and they charge eight bucks for a cup.'

'Eight dollars? It's almost one a.m. and there's still a line of people outside. Maybe we should quit the law, open up a tea shop.'

'What do you know about selling bubble tea?' I asked.

'About the same as you know about practicing law.'

'Thanks, Your Honor. Is that NYPD patrol car still across the street?'

'Been there for forty-five minutes now.'

'The red Buick pick-up?'

'Same spot. You want to tell me what's going on?'

'Nope.'

Swirling the liquor in his glass, Harry said, 'You know Lake already told me and Kate.'

I swept my feet off the desk, said, 'I didn't want to worry you. And I trusted him to be discreet.'

'Discreet? Lake?'

I nodded, said, 'You wearing your old Colt?'

'It's in my desk drawer. Going to wear it when we go home. When are we going home, by the way?'

I shook my head, finished the cold coffee in my mug.

'I don't know, Harry. We need to wait for Bloch.'

'She just pulled up outside.'

A few minutes later, Bloch and Lake came into the office.

'There's a red pick-up outside with two guys in leather biker gear in the front. They look twitchy and they're watching this building. Getting ready to make a move when that patrol car moves off,' said Bloch.

'It seems as though Harry and Kate know all about this,' I said.

'I told them,' said Lake. 'It kinda slipped out. What do you want to do?'

'I don't know yet. Tell me what happened tonight,' I said.

Lake and Bloch exchanged a look.

'Bloch found what looks like a secret cell phone in Margaret Blakemore's sock drawer. It's with our lab techs downtown. We should know more in a couple of days. They have to break into the phone. After we left the house there was a lady down the street, taking some interest in our visit. Nice lady, a real gossip. Her name is Petra Schwartzman. Been a resident for a long time,' said Lake.

He pulled out one of my office chairs, took off his messenger bag and dumped it on the table. Lake's suit looked as if someone else had worn it when they'd died in their sleep, and Lake had taken it from the corpse. His foot tapped on the floor and he scratched at his dark, curly hair. Bloch moved to the window, stood beside Harry so she could keep an eye on the street.

'Lake said Petra said Margaret had a string of affairs. Her marriage has been open for many years. Her husband Alan knew all about Margaret's steady stream of gentlemen callers. None of them Jackson.'

'Did she give you any names?' asked Harry.

'Lake said two. She says one of them was a long-time affair. Guy named Todd Ellis. Margaret broke up with him about a year ago, but the guy wouldn't take no for an answer. Apparently, he has anger issues. Eventually Margaret called Ellis's wife and told her about the affair. Still this asshole wouldn't give up. He patched things up with the wife, let things settle and then Margaret took him back. Second guy is Brett Bale, single, filthy rich like Ellis. String of divorces and guess what?'

'What?' I asked.

'He is suspected of drowning one of his wives. The last one,' said Bloch.

I sat forward, grabbed a pen and began to tumble it across my knuckles. An old cannon's trick. It keeps the fingers supple, dexterous, light enough not to notice when they dip into someone's pocket.

'If Jackson didn't kill Margaret, we need to be able to point to an alternative suspect,' I said. 'A jury will need that. I wonder if the cops interviewed any of these guys about their relationship with the victim. If they did, they'll want to bury those interviews. It doesn't suit their case right now. They've got their man – our client. We need to take a look at these two.'

Lake nodded, 'These men have serious money. Both are extremely wealthy and no doubt well protected. It won't be easy.'

I nodded, fell into silent thought.

'We've got bigger problems right now. Those bikers in the truck outside aren't waiting for a pizza. Do we stay here all night hoping they leave?' asked Lake.

I let the pen fall to the desk. Leaned back in my chair, and spoke slowly, 'I thought about that, but I'm not going to be a prisoner in my own office. The cop in the front passenger seat of the patrol car is Sergeant Ben Gray. He's part of New York's Finest. I recognized him when I first saw the car. When I set one foot outside the door his car is going to drive away. That's the signal for the bikers to come out shooting and I'll be dead in the street.'

'Jesus,' said Harry.

I paused, said, 'I never thought I'd say this, but I think the best thing to do is call the police.'

'Ready?' I asked.

'All set,' said Harry.

He was standing at my window, a pair of Bloch's tactical field binoculars in his hands. Raising them, Harry focused on the patrol car. Particularly, the small part of the interior visible through the windshield from our elevated position.

'Make the call,' I said. Lake dialed 911 on his cell, and together with Bloch moved out of my office, down the stairs to the front door.

'What do you see?' I asked Harry.

'Nothing yet. Wait, there it is. The driver just switched off the radio.'

Lake had called 911, said his girlfriend had just been assaulted and her bag snatched one block over from my office. The two cops in the patrol car outside the bubble-tea shop were easily the closest police unit. They didn't flash their lights. Didn't turn on the sirens. Didn't even start their car. They just turned off the radio so they could pretend there was a malfunction, and they didn't hear the call. I guessed they had already turned off their bodycams and their personal radios. The dispatcher would have their vehicle location on GPS, and no doubt they'd given the call sign to say they were dealing with a problem before going dark. But really they were waiting for me to come out of my office, then they would drive off and let the bikers in the red pick-up gun me down.

'Okay, Harry. Are you sure their radio is off?' I asked.

'I watched the driver turn it off. What do think – I'm blind?'

'Alright,' I said, getting up out of my chair. 'Let's go. You want to make the call or shall I?'

'Oh, leave this one to me,' he said, placing the binoculars on my desk and reaching for his phone.

Harry dialed 911 as I made my way downstairs.

I stood facing the closed front door. My heartbeat quickened. Harry finished the call, and I heard his footsteps descending the stairs behind me. I licked my lips. My mouth felt dry and I was suddenly aware that my hands were shaking.

'Call is in,' said Harry. 'Just answer me one thing. What happens if they turn their radio back on?'

'Then we walk out this door and I get shot. Maybe you get shot too?'

'Who would want to shoot me?'

'How many ex-wives do you have?'

Harry stood beside me, facing the door.

I felt his presence, solid, real. Since my old man died, Harry had been like a father to me. A cranky, eccentric, alcoholic father – but a good one.

I felt my friend at my side and my hands weren't shaking any more.

'Thank you,' I said.

'For what?'

'For putting your life on the line for me. I'm glad I'm walking out this door with you.'

Harry didn't say anything. He didn't need to.

I checked my watch.

Ninety seconds since Harry made the call. I'd estimated two, maybe two and a half minutes would be enough.

I checked my phone. No calls.

The little hallway that led directly to the street was just wide enough for Harry and I to stand shoulder to shoulder. Concrete painted walls and a faded charcoal carpet that we'd been meaning to replace for weeks.

I stared at the door. Looked at my phone. Breathed.

The most dangerous part of this was in the first few seconds of stepping out onto the street. One second after I opened that door, the patrol car would drive away, the doors on the Buick across the street would open and the two leather-clad, hairy-ass bikers would be on the street too, with weapons in their hands pointing straight at me.

I stared at the door.

Checked my phone.

Breathed.

Two minutes since the call.

We couldn't tell what weapons the bikers were carrying. Since they were in a truck, and not on their bikes, Bloch guessed it would be small semi-automatic rifles. The kind that spit two hundred rounds a minute and kill everything in their path.

I stared at the door.

Breathed.

My phone rang.

Caller display read – BLOCH.

'That's the call,' I said, and reached out to open the door.

Only Harry had pushed in front.

'Wait, Harry!'

But I was too late. He'd opened the door.

Stepped out on the street.

I bolted out after him and then a lot of things happened all at once. The hitmen bikers were in the Buick, two cars down from the cops in the patrol car across the street. Bloch and Lake were standing ten feet from me on our side of the street. They'd all stood still. Waiting. Like a spring that was coiling tighter and tighter with every passing second and now, suddenly, unleashed with tremendous speed and force.

Soon as I set foot on the sidewalk, I heard the sirens. They were close.

I heard the engine starting on the patrol car. The wheels beginning to turn. They were ready to get the hell out of there before the shooting started.

The bikers were half out of the pick-up. The one closest to me, the driver, had a short-barreled AR-15 in his hand. He had a long gray beard over a black leather jacket. His eyes were red and wild. It was obvious that he'd passed the time in the pick-up smoking an eight-ball, or something equally dangerous, to get his blood up enough to kill me in the middle of a Manhattan street.

I couldn't see his pal. He was on the other side of their pick-up. But the driver stopped dead before he could raise the rifle.

He'd heard the sirens. He got back into the pick-up fast.

An NYPD car screeched round the corner one block away to my left, tires smoking. I heard the engine gun over the siren as it accelerated toward me. The car hit the brakes right in front of the pick-up.

Sergeant Gray's patrol car had pulled out, but then braked hard as another patrol car came down the street the wrong way, sirens blazing, blocking the entire road.

Cops poured out of the vehicles. Except the one that had been waiting for me.

Bloch ran over to the first cop out of the car. She pointed at the pick-up, cried, 'Gun!'

The cops who were in front of me drew their sidearms, focused on the pick-up. I saw both bikers now, in the front. The passenger looked even more loaded than the driver. He still had the barrel of a riot gun sticking up in the air.

The cops who were blocking the road were out of their vehicles. They passed Gray's patrol car and ran to assist their colleagues who were zeroing in on the pick-up, guns drawn, barking instructions.

The driver's door of the pick-up opened an inch. The short barrel of an automatic machine gun stuck out.

The storm of gunfire from the police was deafening. Glass exploded from the windshield and driver's window. From the rapid fire, the glass looked like the surface of a still pond that was broken with a sudden, heavy downpour of rain, shards dancing in the air.

The firing stopped. The bikers were a bloody mess.

Sergeant Ben Gray stepped out of his patrol car and marched

toward me, a look of undiluted fury on his face. Bloch looked at me over her shoulder. She could step in and stop him.

I shook my head, walked out onto the road to meet him.

His lips curled into a snarl as he got right into my face. He was trembling. Panting. Eyes fierce and lips drawn over his teeth. His nose almost touched mine.

I smiled and he put two hands on my chest and pushed me.

I stumbled back a couple of yards.

'Look, I've been two steps ahead of you the whole time. Even in court I was four moves in front. Call this shit off, right now.'

He glanced to his left, the four cops who'd arrived were all focused on the pick-up. They wouldn't hear him.

'I'm not calling anything off,' he said. 'Now you've embarrassed me in front of my brothers. I'm gonna watch you die.'

'Careful,' I said. 'Everyone who has ever come after me made a bad decision.'

He laughed, said, 'What? You sued them, lawyer man? You're gonna tell me they regretted it?'

'Hard to tell. They're all dead.'

His expression changed, but just for a second. A flash of ice in his veins before the adrenalin and anger trampled it back down.

'Next time you won't see them coming for you.'

'I'm going to give you a choice. Call this off and walk away, and I'll forget about it. If you don't, I'm coming after you,' I said.

He turned his back on me, said over his shoulder, 'And what you gonna do? You don't know me.'

I took his wallet from my jacket pocket. I'd lifted it when he came close, just half a second before he pushed me.

He had two hundred bucks in the wallet, give or take, a bunch of credit cards and loyalty cards, and something else.

'212 North Baker,' I said.

He stopped, swiveled around on his heel. I put his driver's license back in his wallet and tossed it to him.

'Here,' I said. 'You dropped this.'

The wallet hit the street, and his partner grabbed a hold of him before he could take a run at me. He was still screaming at me when I got into the back of Bloch's car, beside Harry. Lake sat in front of Harry in the passenger seat, Bloch got in, turned on the engine and pulled away.

'I don't think that was smart,' said Lake. 'Goading him like that.'

'Probably not,' I said. 'But it felt good.'

'What if he's right?' asked Harry.

'Right about what?' asked Lake.

Harry said, 'What if next time we don't see them coming?'

Lake looked at Bloch. Bloch said nothing.

I felt the weight of Harry's words on my chest. There was nothing else I could do.

15

Mr. Christmas

The Desert Dragon ranch in Jackson, Wyoming, was not located in a desert, nor did it have anything to do with dragons. The smallholding of a hundred acres had cost Charlie Hutchings a pretty penny – five million dollars.

He had made that money back in less than a year.

In the last ten years, the valley of Jackson Hole had become home to a new kind of prospector – multi-millionaires. The cowboys, farmers and small-town folk were finding it hard to adjust to these immigrants from New York City, Los Angeles and San Francisco. Wyoming, with its mountains, lush green grass and empty spaces, had become home to a host of new tech companies.

The rush to Wyoming was fueled by its tax laws.

Corporations in Wyoming pay zero tax. The sales taxes are also some of the lowest in the United States. This was Switzerland to greedy tech companies and their CEOs.

Charlie Hutchings saved seven million dollars in income tax the first year.

The only problem was Charlie had to register his companies, and keep their profiles low, hiding his involvement through a string of shell companies, leaving a long and complicated trail. He was a wealth manager, from Chicago. A very successful one. Wyoming was nothing like Chicago – it was hard to find good pasta, and there wasn't much in the way of theatre in the mountains. Still, Jackson Hole was the perfect place for Charlie.

He had needed a deep hole to hide in.

But it wasn't deep enough.

The man in his kitchen had found him, about an hour ago.

The man was dressed in a black suit, white shirt and black tie. The fedora he'd worn when he arrived was hung on Charlie's coat rack, beside the man's trench coat. It had taken the man about two weeks to find Charlie. He had put in the time online, tracing all those companies right back to this bald, middle-aged Charlie, sweating through his pajamas in his dining chair.

The man in black poured hot water on ground coffee that sat in a filter over a glass dome. He had slow, deliberate movements. Graceful. Like a dancer. His voice had a mellifluous quality, as if he savored every syllable of every word. His language was formal, yet warm. Like a benevolent official in a position of enormous power.

'So, Charles, tell me, what do you think of Marlon Brando?' asked the man as he put down the kettle.

Charlie was finding it hard to breathe. The panic that had set in as his arms and legs were duct-taped to his Baccarat dining chair had not subsided. If anything, Charlie's fear had only increased.

Between gasps, he said, 'You mean the actor?'

'But of course,' said the man, sweeping his hand through his blond hair.

'I-I-I don't know. Do you like him?' asked Charlie.

The man stared at the water filtering through the coffee grounds and dripping into the flask below.

'Come, come, Charles. We're all friends here. This is not a trick question. But, to put you at your ease – yes, I like him very much.'

'Yeah, yeah, yeah, he's great,' said Charlie, and finished his sentence with a breathy wince.

'Relax,' said the man. 'You'll hyperventilate. Breathe with me. We're going to try the physiological sigh. Do you know what that is?'

Charlie shook his head.

'You're going to take a big breath in. Deep as you can, and then, you're going to inhale a second time. Your lungs will already be quite full, but, trust me, you can manage another brief inhalation. You're going to hold all of that air for three seconds and then exhale slowly. Are you ready?'

Charlie nodded, vigorously.

The man turned toward him, and to assist Charlie, he moved his hands over his chest as if conducting the air, puffing his chest at the second inhalation, then turning his hands over, delicately, and brushing them downwards to the floor as he exhaled. It was like watching a great maestro conduct an orchestra. The man's movements were almost hypnotic. You couldn't take your eyes off him. Charlie breathed in and out on his command.

'Feel better, Charles?' asked the man.

Charlie nodded. His chest no longer rose and fell like an old bellows. His eyes shot to the medical bag that sat on the dining table. It was old, black leather with a metal clasp at the top. Charlie knew enough about the man in his kitchen to be afraid of what might be in that bag.

'That's just a little tip for you. It's proven to lower anxiety levels. Now, where were we? Yes, Brando. I've been revisiting his oeuvre lately. Student of Stella Adler, you know.'

A confused look spread over Charlie's face. So far, the man had not harmed him. There had been no violence, apart from being secured to the chair with duct tape.

The man in black removed the filter from the flask and poured fresh, hot coffee into one of Charlie's mugs. He tasted it, nodded agreeably at Charlie and continued his speech.

'He was a fiercely intelligent actor. During one of Adler's acting classes, she instructed her students to imagine that they were chickens and the atomic bomb was about to fall on them from the heavens. Well, as you can imagine, the class got up and they were running around, clucking and flapping their imaginary wings in a cacophonous panic. Except one student, Brando. He didn't run around. He calmly spread his legs and hunkered down on the floor. Adler asked what the hell he was doing. Why wasn't he afraid of the oncoming atomic Armageddon? Do you know what he said?'

At first Charlie didn't react. Then he shook his head, said, 'No.'

'Brando said, "I'm a chicken. I'm laying an egg. What the fuck do I know about atomic bombs?"'

The man smiled. Charlie was too petrified to move.

Just then, the man's phone rang. He smoothly removed a black cell phone from his inside pocket, hit answer and placed the device at his ear.

'Good evening,' said the man. 'Mr. Christmas speaking.'

'You're always so polite,' said the voice on the line.

'Manners cost nothing, my friend. May I be of assistance?'

'I heard about a job in New York. A lawyer. New York's Finest are floating the paper in the open. Fifty grand, flat fee. No expenses. Thought I should let you know.'

'Not to be impolite, but it's a little below my paygrade.'

'I realize that, but, you know . . . It's a tough economy.'

'Someone in New York will pick it up. That's not my usual territory.'

'Well, that's the thing,' said the voice on the line. 'Jimmy the Hat knows this guy. Nobody in New York will touch it. I heard there's people flying in from all over.'

Mr. Christmas took another sip of coffee, then said, 'Whom?'

'The guys you might expect. Mid-level earners, but one in particular who is very much in your paygrade. I didn't think the job would be for you, but I didn't want you to hear about it afterwards and get pissed at me. Thought I should at least give you the option.'

'That is most considerate of you. I'm just engaged at the moment, but give me a little time to think about it, if you wouldn't mind, and I'll call you back.'

'Sure thing.'

Mr. Christmas ended the call and turned his attention to Charlie.

'This has been pleasant, Charles, but I'm afraid time is short, and I have to bring our meeting to a conclusion. You know Chicago sent me. They want the files you took with you when you left so abruptly.'

'Files? I haven't stolen any files. I haven't taken a dime from Mr. Moresco—'

'You are being indicted in Chicago for fraud. You are out on bail and yet you've managed to move states. Mr. Moresco correctly believes the FBI don't want to put you in prison – they want Mr. Moresco. You have access to a large amount of his personal financial information. Enough to cause him some considerable legal concerns. We can't have you making a deal for your freedom. I need you to give me Mr. Moresco's files.'

'I don't have anything . . .' said Charlie, sweat now running down his face.

Mr. Christmas held up a palm to silence Charlie and then approached him, slowly. He moved like a cat, each stride delicate and in perfect balance.

'Charles, normally at this point things would get unpleasant. But, as I said, I don't have a lot of time. Torture is a blunt tool. People will say anything for the pain to stop. We can begin that process and before the end you will have told me where I can find the files. I will know if you are lying. Unless you're Marlon Brando, you're not going to be able to fool me. If you want to play dumb, that's your choice. I will cut off your hands, then your feet, put out your eyes and then things will *really* get nasty. Or, you can tell me what I wish to know, and I can make things easier. I can give you a shot that will make you drowsy and then you will fall asleep, quite peacefully. I like you, Charles. I like your home. I like your coffee. And you have been co-operative and polite. Please choose quickly.'

He turned away from Charlie, moved to the medical bag on the dining table and twisted open the clasp. He spread the top of the bag open and removed a syringe, and a vial of clear liquid, which he set on the table. Next, he took out a hammer and a saw, and put them on the table as well. With each item that came out of the bag, Charlie's eyes widened, his heart rate went up and his chest began to pump air through his trembling lips.

'It's in the first drawer of my desk. There are no other copies,' said Charlie.

Moving to the hallway, and then the study, Mr. Christmas found a pen drive in the desk drawer, brought it back to the kitchen and inserted it into a small laptop he had in his bag.

Charlie watched him with dead eyes.

'Thank you, Charles,' said Mr. Christmas. He picked up the syringe and the vial in his left hand and stepped behind Charlie.

'I have money. I could give you twenty million, right now. You could disappear, pretend you never found me,' said Charlie.

'But *someone* would find you, Charles. And then Mr. Moresco and his associates would come looking for me. That would be . . . messy. I'm sorry. This is the way it has to be.'

'Will I feel anything?' asked Charlie, blinking away tears.

'Nothing. I'll make sure of that,' said Mr. Christmas as he drew a pistol from his jacket. He pointed the muzzle at the back of Charlie's head and pulled the trigger twice.

'See, you didn't feel a thing,' said Mr. Christmas.

He repacked his bag, took out his cell phone and dialed a number.

'That was quick,' said the voice on the line.

'My business concluded earlier than expected. Please inform our friend in Chicago. He will be pleased. I must confess, your proposition intrigues me. You mentioned some of my colleagues were interested in this job . . .'

'A few.'

'Angel?'

'I don't work with him, but I imagine he would be interested.'

Angel was a world-class sniper. Ex-military. Navy seals. He pre-ferred to take out his targets from a different ZIP code. He got the nickname Angel because he could make fire rain from heaven and disappear before the smoke cleared. Few people had ever met him. Mr. Christmas had caught sight of him once, in Guatemala City, from a skylight. He had taken prey that had belonged to Mr. Christ-mas. And that was rude, to say the least. Mr. Christmas did not care for rudeness.

'If you would be so kind, book me on a flight to New York, please.'

PART TWO

16

Ruby

In the two weeks that followed Petra's neighborhood gathering, a new kind of tension trod the sidewalks and twitched at the curtains of West 74th Street. Ruby had felt it. That night, Petra had taken Ruby's subtle suggestion about John Jackson for her own, as Ruby had expected, and even though there was a consensus for the plan agreed that night among the residents, it had taken some time for it all to be prepared.

A few days ago, Alison had asked for a quiet word with Ruby in the kitchen. She looked pained, and not with worry for her husband.

'Ruby, I don't really know how to say this, but I want you to know that I trust you and I'm in no way implying anything, but did you happen to see my old necklace anywhere around the house? I can't find it,' said Alison.

'Oh, which one?' asked Ruby.

'It's very fine silver. Looks like lace? There are a few small stones in it. It was my grandmother's necklace. You know the one?'

'I think I do. I remember seeing you wear it once. It's sooooo beautiful.'

'It's old and it means a lot of me. Yeah, sorry, I just can't seem to find it. Normally, I keep it in my drawer upstairs, but it's missing.'

'I'm so sorry. The last time I saw it was when you must've worn it.

My mother used to have something similar except it's nowhere near as beautiful. She loved to wear it with her black cocktail dress.'

'Does she still wear it?' asked Alison.

'No, they . . . they took it. The banks. After my father left us . . .'

'Oh God, Ruby, I'm so sorry. I didn't mean . . . I feel *terrible* now . . .'

'Don't be a *goofball* – it's not your fault,' said Ruby. 'That's all in the past now. It was . . . difficult at the time. My dad just ran out and left us with all his debt. Millions of dollars. They took everything. Mom and I were left to deal with all of it. But we got through it. The hardest part was the shame, you know? But I'm so grateful to you and all the neighbors for everything. I'm sorry about your necklace. I'll keep a look-out for it.'

'How is your mom doing?' asked Alison.

'Not good,' said Ruby. The truth. Along with everything else that had been taken from Ruby and her mom, health insurance went too. If they had at least held on to that, maybe her mom would have had a check-up sooner. Maybe they could've caught the cancer early. Maybe she could have been saved . . .

It was too late now.

'Mom has a year left. Maybe two,' said Ruby with a heavy sigh.

Alison gave Ruby a hug, said, 'I'm so sorry. I knew she was sick, but I didn't know it was that bad. Oh, God, I feel terrible. I'm so consumed with John and the case . . . and my stupid necklace. It's silly. I'm sorry.'

She had not brought up the necklace again. But on a few occasions she'd seen Alison pulling out the contents of drawers in her bedroom, lifting the cushions on the couch in the lounge and even emptying the bathroom cabinet. Ruby had said nothing.

Now, Ruby stood in the hallway of the Jackson home, waiting for Tomas to finish brushing his teeth before she took him to school.

She stood by the kitchen door.

Facing the front door.

Her back to the painting of the red priest.

She heard buzzing.

At first, she tried to ignore it. Like a fly dive-bombing around her head.

As the buzzing grew louder, she tuned in to its sound. It was no longer a buzzing sound.

It was a voice. A fast, hissing whisper.

Looking over her shoulder, she could see John was in his study, beside the lounge. Alison was in the kitchen preparing some fruit for Tomas's lunch box.

Neither of them were whispering.

John had kept himself busy. Working all hours. But then all of that had stopped.

Last week, John had opened a letter from the hospital, read it, let it fall from his fingers and then quietly walked out of the kitchen. Even before Ruby reached down to retrieve it, she knew what it said. The way John moved out of the room, unsteady on his feet, like he'd just been hit on the head with a shovel . . .

'The management, in consultation with trustees, have concluded that in the interests of the patients and the hospital, you should be placed on suspension . . .'

There was a tension in this house. The place was quiet. Yet a low pulse filled her ears whenever she set foot through the door. It wasn't real. More of a feeling that her mind manifested into noise. Or maybe it was just the sound of her own heart beating. It reminded her, in a way, of being young and listening to the *clink clink* of ice tumbling into her father's bourbon glass. A signal for the fear to begin. Josef managed a property portfolio inherited from his father. This empire provided their income, but his gambling was out of control. When he lost big, he sold a property and doubled his bets, trying to get even. But he always lost. And when he lost – he drank. Even now, all of these years later, whenever Ruby heard the tinkle of ice in a crystal glass, it set her teeth clamping together, a flash of heat at her neck and pressure in her head. She knew as a young girl, when she heard that noise, that within a few short hours, her mother would be cowering somewhere in the house – hiding from him. And then the banging and the breaking of glass.

And then the screaming.

And then quiet.

Like a hurricane passing over the house. And the next day, the hurricane would have no memory of the devastation it had caused. Her mother would sweep up the broken glass early, before he woke. Upturned tables righted. Pictures put back on the wall. The floor mopped clean. The swelling on her mother's face brought down with ibuprofen and more ice. The looming bruises hidden beneath layers of make-up.

Ruby had heard some of the neighbors, women, in hushed conversation, when they thought she wasn't listening, gossiping about her mother – calling her common, and not their kind of people because of the amount of make-up her mother wore. They didn't know she was hiding her husband's sin. They blamed her. Said that only whores wore their make-up that way.

Her mother's silence was so loud it roared inside Ruby's head. And when her father left them with his debt, the banks came and all their possessions were loaded onto trucks, and the neighbors had stood and watched. Ruby felt the heat of shame that day. An inferno in her mind that still burned with the very thought of it.

Now, standing in the hallway, watching John typing on his laptop, another sound began layering over the clicking of his keyboard.

The whispers . . .

The letterbox in the front door flapped open and mail landed on the welcome mat. Alison came quickly from the kitchen, and John met her in the hallway. These days, the mail brought all kinds of bad news into this house. John's suspension letter. Legal bills. Letters from the bank about extending their credit and demands for down payment from the construction firm Alison had hired to do a remodel on their brownstone interior. And of course there was worse.

Hate mail. Death threats.

Alison got to the mail first. Flicked through the pile of letters and stopped when she reached a white envelope. It was addressed to John. Handwritten.

He took it from her, tore open the envelope and read the letter. He said nothing, gave it to Alison to read.

'What is it?' she asked, a slight tremble in her voice.

Ruby moved into the kitchen to give them some privacy. She didn't wait to be asked. From the kitchen Ruby hollered upstairs, 'Tomas, come on, munchkin. We have to get going or you'll be late for school.'

John and Alison whispered in the hallway, but there was no masking the hurt in Alison's hushed voice.

Ruby couldn't hear them at first. She didn't need to. She already knew what was in the letter. After all, it had been Ruby's idea, stolen, of course, by Petra.

It was a letter to John from the residents' association of West 74th Street. It said that they didn't feel safe with him still living in the street.

They wanted John to move out.

It would only have taken Petra a half-hour to write the letter, but it took another two weeks for it to be signed by every single household.

'They want us out of our home,' said Alison, her breaking voice increasing in volume.

'I'm so sorry,' said John, over and over again.

Ruby stepped out of the kitchen.

'Maybe it's a blessing,' said Ruby quietly.

'What do you mean?' asked John.

'All this terrible stress you've both been under. It's a nightmare for you, and Tomas. Maybe getting away from it all might be for the best.'

'Mom? Dad?' said Tomas.

The young boy stood on the staircase, frozen, watching his parents. Ruby turned and glanced at Alison and John.

They stood at the end of their hallway, holding each other, their backs jerking as they cried. The stain of the murder accusation had bloomed into fire. A hot poker of stigma that seared their flesh, burning the family with shame. Just as Ruby had once felt.

Tomas ran down the last few steps, past Ruby, and grabbed hold of his parents. They knelt and embraced him.

'Do we have to move?' asked Tomas.

'Maybe Ruby's right. We should get out of the city for a while,' said Alison. 'Just get away from everything. Maybe even kill two birds with one stone. Get the construction firm to start the remodeling early. They could work while we're out of the house.'

John smoothed his son's hair, cupped his face, said, 'No, we're not going to leave our home. I didn't do anything wrong, son. This is all one big mess, but we're going to stay here. And we're going to fix it. Things will get better soon.'

Even though Ruby's teeth clenched tightly, she forced her lips into a smile.

Mother. Father. Son. All of them holding each other. An invisible tether between them. Even though neither Ruby nor anyone else could see this ethereal connection, she knew what it was.

The love of a family.

Something Ruby had never truly felt. There'd been nothing from her father but fear. And her mother was too damaged.

Love was alien to Ruby. As alien as the smile she now wore. Her expression was of compassion and admiration.

Inside, Ruby was screaming.

The family moved into the lounge, and Ruby backed away.

Down the hall.

As she moved, the whispering became louder.

And louder.

She looked at the floor. And watched her feet stop three feet from the first stair. They turned to face the wall.

Turned to face the painting of the red priest.

Ruby kept her eyes on her shoes.

She knew the painting like she knew her own face.

The whispering was louder now.

Ruubeeee.

Ruuuubbbbeeeeee.

Her head shot up and stared at the painting.

You could have killed them all by now. There isn't much time. You need to get the money, said the red priest.

Ruby didn't need to speak aloud for the priest to hear her. He could hear her thoughts, just as she could hear his. All the same, she couldn't help but move her lips, soundlessly, as her voice flowed through her mind.

Killing them won't help. It will make things worse, said Ruby.

They are coming for you, Ruby. Just kill them and . . .

No.

Then do something . . .

Ruby nodded.

'Who are you talking to?' said a voice.

Out loud.

A female voice.

Ruby swung round toward the front door.

There, in the hallway, Alison's mom, Esther, stood in her blue slacks, white blouse, Tommy Hilfiger bag and her heels, and her accusing eyes.

'I *said*, who are you talking to?' repeated Esther.

Ruby shook her head. The priest's voice shouted at her, but she couldn't listen. Not now.

She didn't like having that voice so loud in her head. It sometimes gave her a migraine. Once, she had talked with the priest for hours, while babysitting one evening – little Tomas asleep upstairs. It was only when the blood fell over her lips that she realized her nose was bleeding. The voice was too loud to listen to for very long.

'Sorry, I'm just talking to myself,' said Ruby innocently.

Esther held her ice-queen gaze upon Ruby for what felt like a long time.

'Just do your job. Look after my grandson, keep your mouth shut and your greedy eyes to yourself,' said Esther. Then she turned, closed the front door and greeted her daughter. Alison was in a state again. And her mother held her, but as she gripped her child she eyed Ruby warily.

John Jackson's last words replayed in Ruby's mind.

Things will get better soon, he'd said, just a moment ago in the hallway.

No they won't, thought Ruby.

She would make sure of it.

17
Eddie

I had started leaving my car in the garage.

Too easy for somebody to hide a device in or on the car some place where I wouldn't find it. Car bombs are a lot more sophisticated than they used to be. Getting down on your knees and glancing under the body, or even popping the hood and searching for suspicious bulges, wires or boxes, didn't work any more. There was an Armenian in Queens who took out a rival boss with six beads of C4 threaded on an insulated wire, hooked up to a waterproof miniature cell-phone receiver and then fed into the gas tank of a Lincoln Navigator. The resulting explosion put a six-foot-deep crater in the blacktop and launched the Lincoln through a semi hauling six hundred live chickens. The city spent two days cleaning burnt metal, blood and feathers off a quarter-mile of the street.

I took the subway and watched my back.

It had been two weeks since the NYPD wiped out two hitmen from one of the more violent motorcycle gangs out of New Jersey. No more tails. No eyes on me from parked cars outside the office, nor outside my apartment. I imagined Sergeant Gray had put the word out to cool things down, at least for a while. He would've had heat from the brass for sitting in a patrol car with his partner with their radios turned off, twelve feet from two heavily armed bikers in a pick-up truck.

If he was smart, he would call off the hit. Cancel the paper on me and forget about it.

Unfortunately, I didn't think he was too clever. Even if he had some brain cells to spare, it was personal now. I'd made him look like a fool in front of his brother officers and his crew. He'd probably convinced his boss, Buchanan, that I was a threat. Now, I was a severe pain in the ass.

It was only a matter of time before somebody else came calling at my door.

I walked the four blocks from the subway to my office. It was coming up on ten in the morning when I climbed the stairs and made for my desk. I stopped. Denise was on the phone, listening. She gestured toward Kate's office. Harry and Bloch were with Kate, standing around her desk. I pushed open her door and heard a voice coming from her cell phone. It was Al Parish.

'What's going on?' I asked.

'Hi, Eddie,' said Parish. 'Just to quickly bring you up to speed. John isn't doing so well. He got a letter this morning, signed by all of his neighbors. They asked him to move out. He's probably lost his career too. This is all becoming too much for him. We need to do something.'

'You want a meeting, Al? I could give him the talk again,' said Kate.

'I think you got him this far, Kate,' said Al. 'But I'm not sure he's got a lot left in the tank. His kid is getting harassed in school. Alison says the neighbors cross the street instead of passing her on the sidewalk. Is there anything we can do to move this case along? I think things would be better if we could give them a trial date.'

'We don't have a trial date,' said Kate. 'And we're not close to being ready yet.'

Al said, 'I know, I know. I was just wondering if we could somehow get a trial date. Then at least there's an end point for John and his family. That would help. I just . . . I just don't know how long he can hang in there.'

'Okay, Al. We hear you. Leave it with us and we'll see if there's some way to grease the wheels,' I said.

Al thanked us, hung up.

'Even if we could get an early trial date, we're not ready,' said Kate.

'I know, but we can be ready. Bloch, any updates on finding us a ballistics expert?' I asked.

Bloch said, 'I got the last refusal this morning. That list of experts you gave me, everyone turned us down.'

'Why?' asked Harry.

'They all said the same thing,' said Bloch.

'Conflict of interest?' I asked.

Bloch slowly nodded.

District Attorney Castro was dirty, narcissistic and power-hungry, but that didn't make him stupid.

'Castro carpet-bombed the field,' I said.

As well as briefing the top ballistic expert in the country and securing him as a prosecution witness, he'd also sent prosecution papers to another five of the most respected ballistics experts. The only people with enough experience and credibility to challenge the prosecution expert were also paid by Castro to read the case materials. That meant they had knowledge of the case, potentially confidential knowledge and therefore couldn't act for the defense. It would be a conflict of interest.

'The DA's case hangs on that ballistics report and the DNA report,' said Kate. 'If he proves the gun that fired the rounds which killed Margaret Blakemore was found in our client's closet with his DNA on it, then that's it. We need our own heavyweight ballistics expert to challenge that testimony. Without it, we're done. What are we going to do?'

'I don't know,' I said. 'I haven't had enough coffee yet.'

They all stood in silence, staring at me.

'What are you waiting for? Go get coffee,' said Harry.

I left them in Kate's office, ignored the ton of files and paperwork on my desk and made for the coffee machine. It came from my old office. The timer no longer worked, and the hot plate wasn't as hot as it used to be, but, on the plus side, I had never cleaned it. Didn't matter what kind of blend you put in, all the coffee that filtered into the bun flask tasted the same. I liked it that way.

No one else used this machine but me. I brewed a pot. Drank half of it quickly.

I put down my cup. Found that I was absently twirling a pen in my hand – tumbling it between my fingers and over my knuckles. It helped me think.

The pen stopped moving. I went back into Kate's office.

All three of them were still in there, waiting for me. Harry was going through the discovery documents we'd received from Castro. He picked up a page, and a curious look crept over his features.

'What's this latent-print expert's report from Mr. Bude?' asked Harry.

'It's a dud,' said Kate. 'There was a palm print on the gun. They couldn't match it to our client – said it was only a partial print and not enough for identification.'

Harry rubbed the top of his head. He often did this when he was thinking. Like he was Aladdin rubbing a lamp and hoping a genie, or an ingenious idea, might pop out at any moment.

'Let me see that DNA analysis,' said Harry. Kate moved files on the desk, handed the report to Harry.

'Look at this,' he said, and gave the report back to Kate.

'What am I looking at here, Harry? It's the DNA analyst's report. It confirms the DNA found on the gun belongs to John Jackson.'

'Yes, but look where they took the sample from.'

I moved beside Kate, read the preamble to the DNA report.

'He got the DNA from the partial palm print on the lifting tape, not from the gun itself,' said Kate.

Due to the advances in DNA analysis, forensic techs can now extract DNA samples from the tape that lifts palm prints or fingerprints, rather than swabbing the object upon which the print was found.

'So what?' I said. 'Does it matter if he took the DNA from the gun or the partial palm print? The print expert says the latent partial print is a palm, and it's too small an area for comparison.'

'Now you're thinking logically,' said Harry. 'That's the mistake. Think about it. Why do we have this palm print report in the first place? It doesn't help Castro.'

'He has to call the latent-print expert because the DNA came from the print on the lifting tape. He needs the print expert to testify that he took that print from the gun. If he wants to use the DNA evidence, he has to use the palm-print evidence.'

'Exactly,' said Harry. 'Otherwise, Castro would bury this latent-print report, like he's buried some of the statements we haven't seen yet. There's something here. Something important, but I can't see it yet.'

'I'm not sure I follow, Harry.'

'How is it possible that someone can leave their DNA behind in a palm print, but that same palm print doesn't match their palm. That's like me touching this desk,' and at this point Harry placed his hand on the desk. 'So I leave behind my DNA, which is extracted from the print tape, but I don't leave behind my actual palm print? That's not possible. Something doesn't make sense here.'

'It makes sense if there's not enough of the palm print to analyze for comparison purposes,' said Kate.

'You mean, it makes sense if we believe Castro,' I said.

'There's something in this,' said Bloch.

Kate said, 'Maybe, but right now Castro has a rational explan-ation, and we don't. That means we don't have shit to throw. Keep thinking, Harry. But try to find a way to get the statements that he hasn't yet given us. I bet the cops interviewed Todd Ellis and Brett Bale. It was the talk of the neighborhood that they were involved with the victim. I've filed a discovery motion, but Castro can kick that can down the road for months.'

Harry looked at me, said, 'Eddie, have you had enough coffee yet?'

I nodded, said, 'I have a plan to get those interviews of Ellis and Bale too. It's not perfect, but it should work. Harry, go talk to some of your brother judges.'

'They're not my brothers any longer. I'm retired, remember?'

'You still have some friends in there. Are any of them trustworthy? I mean, could they keep a secret?'

'Maybe one or two. The rest are just like other lawyers – gossips.'

'Great, go talk to the gossips. The looser their tongues are, the better. Tell them John Jackson is starting to crack. He can't handle the thought of a public trial and against all our advice he wants to plead the case down to manslaughter, or murder two. We know he's innocent, but he wants to plead anyway. Ask for their guidance. Tell them you're struggling with this – it's a moral and ethical weight on your mind. Plus, you want to make sure your ass is covered in case he changes his mind once he's spent a year in Sing Sing, and then decides to sue his lawyers.'

Harry looked at me quizzically.

'Kate, you go see Castro. Tell him we're not impressed by him scorching the earth for decent ballistic expert witnesses and we're going to need time to find one. Tell him we want to put this trial on the back burner for as long as possible. Tell him we're investigating possible romantic links between two alternative suspects and the victim. Don't ask him to put the trial off as a favor. I want you to basically *beg* him for as much time as he can give us.'

'Why me?' asked Kate.

'Because you're a straight shooter and he doesn't trust me.'

'Hang on a second,' said Kate. 'Al Parish thinks we need to get this case on as soon as possible. How does this help? Isn't that the opposite of what our client wants?'

'Exactly,' I said. 'Castro will hear the rumors from the judges that our client can't face a trial and is thinking of making a deal. If you convince him we want to delay, that matches up with the rumors

Harry has spread around. Castro will move heaven and earth to screw up our defense and get this case to trial quickly in order to put as much pressure as possible on Jackson, in the hope it forces him into taking a plea. I'd bet my life Ellis and Bale told the cops they were at the party all night, and at the time of the murder they had nothing to do with Margaret Blakemore. Those statements, on the face of it, blow our alternative-suspect theory out of the water. We'll get a trial date within six to eight weeks and those statements within twenty-four hours.'

'Six weeks? We're not going to be ready for trial in six *months*,' said Harry.

'We'll be prepared. We're not going to get a decent ballistics expert even if we waited two years. So it doesn't matter. Castro will cut corners too. That gives us a fighting chance. Let's do it. Bloch, you're with me.'

'Where are we going?' she asked.

'The DA has the murder weapon in our client's house. Our client's DNA on the gun. He has all the evidence in the world apart from one thing. He doesn't have a story to tell the jury. There's no motive for John Jackson to murder Margaret Blakemore. We're going to go find the real story behind this case.'

18

Eddie

Eating out with Gabriel Lake was not an easy endeavor. He shaved every four days, whether he needed to or not, and his hair was in a constant mess, but not enough to distract anyone from the state of his suits. There was so much going on in Lake's head that he didn't have room to think about ordinary everyday life. The only thing he was particular about was what went into his body. When I say particular, I mean it was bordering on some kind of condition.

Junior's restaurant, between 45th Street and 8th Avenue, is a hot-spot for tourists who have had their eyeballs blown out in Times Square. It's a little haven of Americana, dressed in orange, with seats at the counter, fifty tables and the best cheesecake within a hundred miles.

Bloch ordered the cheeseburger, medium, and an ice-cream soda. I said I'd have the same. The waiter, dressed in black jeans and a black polo shirt, thought this table was going to be easy. No problems. No fuss.

Lake stared at the menu.

Little did the waiter know he had inadvertently dressed for his own funeral.

'How are the eggs cooked? Is it on the hotplate or a pan?' asked Lake.

The waiter's eyebrows shot up into his forehead, and stayed there for the next ten minutes while Lake went through his repertoire of questions that would test the patience of Mother Theresa, if she'd happened to wait tables in Manhattan. Lake wasn't being rude, just thorough.

'Where do your eggs come from?' asked Lake.

'Chickens,' said the waiter, who was beginning to lose the will to live.

'I meant where . . .'

'He'll have the omelet,' said Bloch, rescuing the waiter.

'She's right. I'll just have the omelet, five whites and two yolks, still water and a coffee, please.'

The waiter snatched the menu out of Lake's hands.

Bloch gave Lake and I copies of the report she'd picked up from Raymond, Bloch's tech expert.

Lake's right heel bounced on the floor as he read.

The report discussed the burner phone Bloch found in Blakemore's home. It had only ever called two numbers. Both of them were burners and both seem to have been disabled the day after the murder. Both of the unknown burners made calls to Margaret's phone the day before the murder. The single SMS message on the phone was sent six or seven hours before the murder, sent to one of the burner numbers.

TRANSCRIPT OF TEXT MESSAGE EXTRACTED FROM NOKIA 3310.

SMS message sent to CONTACT: SMS sent at 17:05.

After all we've been through, you're still treating me like a piece of shit. I'm always second best, aren't I?

I'm done being your fucking piece on the side.

I can end you with one phone call.

Maybe I should tell everyone what you've done.

How would you like that?

Then you'll know what pain feels like.

'Has Jackson seen this?' asked Lake.

I shook my head.

'Is this a defense?' he asked.

'Not yet. I'm guessing one of the numbers on the phone was for Brett Bale and the other Todd Ellis. We have two alternative suspects. We were on our way to check out these guys when Bloch got the call from Raymond. I need you two to look into them. Deep dive,' I said.

'From the looks of that message, Margaret Blakemore was playing a dangerous game with at least one of these men. That message is a threat. It sure looks like motive.'

The waiter came with our drinks. Lake tried to ask him a question, but he pretended to hear something on his mic and practically ran from the table.

'We need to get to know Ellis and Bale. I think we should wait until we have their statements, or interview transcripts from Castro. Then we'll go shake their trees.'

'What if nothing falls out?' asked Lake.

'Then we shake harder,' said Bloch.

19
Ruby

Holding the page up to the light from her desk lamp, Ruby surveyed her work.

The lettering appeared uniform, all capital letters. She had used a Sharpie, the thick line less likely to show any personalization in her handwriting. She had practiced for a few hours on cheap copy paper, making sure to work out any kinks in her lettering. After fifty or so pages, she had the paragraph locked down, and could reproduce it as if it had come out of a Xerox machine.

She lifted a pad of paper from her desk drawer, spying the clock on the desk in her bedroom. It was almost eight in the evening and her hand was beginning to cramp. Mom would be growing impatient around now. It might be a good time to take a break, but she was in the zone. Now was the time to finalize her letters.

'*Ruby! Ruby! Is there any soup?*'

The voice came from the living room of her small apartment.

'I'll be there shortly, Mom!' called Ruby.

'*Thank you, sweetheart.*'

She looked around her bedroom. A single bed, tight against the left-hand corner of the room. The bed didn't fit on this side, and the door could only open a couple of feet before it hit the mattress and base. But Ruby needed her desk on the right side, where the sockets were and the light from the window. No family pictures. The walls painted white to maximize the light. A bookcase beside the desk. There were only a handful of books on those shelves. Mostly non-fiction. Cookery. Home maintenance. Mindfulness. And a selection of self-help books that proved to be no help at all. A single poster above her bed.

She had seen the poster in a second-hand record store. They also sold old pieces of memorabilia – classic Americana to go with the rockabilly records – their specialty. The poster was faded on one side, as if it had long been exposed to a bright sun. Ruby didn't mind; it meant someone else had loved it enough to display it. And Ruby loved this poster. She gazed at it for hours at a time. She wasn't sure, but she guessed it was from the eighties advertising a convertible Cadillac Eldorado. The car looked nice, but that wasn't what made the poster special. Behind the wheel was a woman, her blond hair blowing in the wind as the car sped along an arrow-straight road through the desert.

That lady looked like she had the perfect life. No one around her. No whispering from the red priest, no family, no responsibilities. And no problems.

Total freedom.

Ruby desperately wanted to be that lady. And she knew one day she would be. Everything she was working for was to get onto that road, with nowhere to go, forever.

She finished the first letter for Todd Ellis. She would need another for Brett Bale.

Knowledge is power.

Maggs was a talker. Ruby had spent many afternoons with Maggs, talking while she cleaned, and sitting for a coffee afterwards. It wasn't just out of politeness, or loneliness, it was kinship. Two outsiders. Ruby told her about her father, and mother, and that she envied Maggs, in a way.

'Trust me – you wouldn't want my life,' said Maggs.

'But you have money. And freedom. You can go anywhere and do anything,' said Ruby.

'Money can take care of a lot of things in life, but it can't fill your heart. And it sure as hell can't mend it when it breaks.'

Ruby thought that if the other residents knew Maggs like she did, they would accept her. They would see her kindness, and the emptiness in her life, and they would want to make her feel better. That's what Maggs did – she wanted everyone to feel good. Out of all the wealthy clients in the street, Maggs was the only one who gave Ruby a bonus at Christmas, as well as the only person to give her something even more precious – her time and her care and attention.

People in the street were still talking about Maggs, thought Ruby.

She had two men, desperate to hide their relationship with Margaret Blakemore, for very good reasons. Bale already had suspicion on him from the death of his last wife. And if Ellis's wife found out he'd been seeing Maggs it would cost him at least half his fortune. Ruby had seen one of them kill her friend, Maggs. And the other man was perhaps just as dangerous. Provoking a killer was something not to be taken lightly. But Ruby had no choice.

Ruby needed money. Her mom was getting sicker and needed care.

And Ruby wanted freedom.

'*Ruby*,' came the voice again.

'I'm coming, Mom,' said Ruby as she made her way to the small kitchenette. She opened a can of soup, poured it into a pot and heated it on the stove.

As the soup bubbled, Ruby thought about the Jacksons.

Today was a bad day for them. Tomorrow would be much worse.

As she moved away from the stove to fetch two bowls, she heard a crunch. Lifting her right sneaker, she saw the remains of a huge cockroach crushed beneath it. The damn roaches were getting so bad she didn't even have to go looking for them any more. She could just walk around the kitchen, killing them casually.

She poured the soup into two bowls, giving most of it to her mother. She set the bowls on the little table and sat down to eat.

'Soup is ready,' she hollered.

'*I'll be right there,*' said her mom.

Ruby picked up her spoon and began to eat. The soup was hot and salty, but the beef was still tough. For a moment, she wondered if Mom could eat it. She hadn't been swallowing very well lately.

She heard the *thock* of the cane first, the noise resounding within the small apartment, followed by the soft shuffling of slippers across the wooden laminate floor.

Ava Johnson sat down at the little table across from Ruby. She thought her mother's eyes had aged even since this morning. It was as if they were swimming in milk. They were pale, and unmoving. Her limbs were so thin now. Ruby could close her hand completely over her mom's wrist. It was as if she was shrinking. Like her flesh was being sucked out of her while Ruby was away at work.

She didn't speak to Ruby, just stared into her soup with her creamy eyes.

Things would be different soon. Her mom needed more care than Ruby could manage on her own. Making sure Mom was somewhere safe was a top priority.

Even if things went according to plan, Ruby knew she would have to leave New York. Moving from city to city. Town to town. She would enter each new place bearing a new name, and a new story. And she could spend her days driving in the desert. Far away from West 74th Street. Far away from her old life.

Far away from the red priest.

But that also meant leaving Mom.

It was all coming together now. This was not just for Ruby.

It was for Mom, too.

'Mom, did you manage to take a look at any of the brochures I left with you?' asked Ruby.

Her mom shook her head, then brought a trembling spoonful of soup to her mouth.

'You know, some of them are really nice places. It's not a nursing home, you know. It's like a retirement complex, with nurses. For people like you. Nice folks.'

'We don't have the money,' said her mom. 'We can't afford any of those places.'

'I've been saving,' said Ruby.

Her mother eyed her warily.

'Where did you get the money?'

'Working. For families on our street.'

'That's not *our* street any more. They kicked us out. Remember? When your father took all our money. Now you're going to leave me too. Everybody leaves me,' said her mother as her shoulders shook and tears fell into her canned soup.

'I'm not leaving you, Mom. This is for the best,' said Ruby. 'It's better for you. There will be someone to take care of you twenty-four hours a day.'

But her mom didn't hear her. Or didn't want to. Her spoon fell from her thin, bent fingers and landed in her soup, splashing on her blouse, neck and face.

Getting up from her chair, Ruby grabbed a napkin and moved round the table. She knelt before her mother, turning her around to face her. She dipped the napkin in a glass of water and wiped the soup stains on her mother's clothes.

When they were clean, she carefully raised her mother's head, wet the napkin again and gently dabbed at her mom's face as a mother would wash a baby's face – slowly, so very gently and with great tenderness. Her skin was so thin it was almost translucent. She was afraid that if she was rough she might tear it.

Ruby wondered if she loved her mom. She thought that she did. That, whatever love was, this was the closest she could come to it.

'It's going to be okay, Mom,' said Ruby.

'You're a good girl, Ruby.'

*

Later, when her mother was asleep, Ruby slipped quietly out of the apartment. The elevator hadn't worked in weeks, so she made the descent down the four flights of stairs, past the rotting garbage bags outside the apartments. A short bus ride brought her to an old hardware store in East Harlem. They were just closing up for the night as Ruby entered the store. She promised the store owner she would be quick.

She paid cash for a bag of masonry nails, spray paint and a four-pound crack hammer with a forged-steel head and shock-resistant grip. She put all the items in her backpack and took the bus home.

In her bedroom, in their little apartment, Ruby held the hammer. It seemed very heavy at first, but after some practice swings she soon got used to the weight. The key was to swing it. Not to use force. Let the momentum, gravity and the weight of the head do the work.

The little pebbles that Ruby had been throwing down the hill were slowly eroding the slope, knocking into bigger stones, which rolled into even larger ones. The landslide was beginning.

All Ruby had to do was make sure that it buried the right people.

The letters she would deliver tomorrow morning, before sunrise, would be the first boulders rolling down that hill.

20

Ruby

At seven the next morning, Ruby stood in front of the Jacksons' front door.

She had never been given a key to their house. Some residents didn't mind Ruby having a key. She could clean, shop for groceries, keep the place secure and in shape for their return from vacations or long weekends in the Hamptons.

Not the Jacksons.

Ruby's finger hovered in front of the doorbell.

When she pressed it, things would be set in motion.

She had to be quick.

Accurate.

Silent.

She dropped her hand away from the bell. Stared at the door. Yawned.

Took a moment to think.

Alison would answer the door. She always answered the door. These last few weeks, it had seemed as though every morning that Alison opened the door, a month had passed instead of twenty-four hours. The weight of her troubles was squashing her spine and drying her skin. The woman was aging at incredible speed. Crows' feet clawed deeper into the skin around her eyes with every passing day. And that skin grew more pallid. Gray now, instead of her usual pink glow. It had occurred to Ruby that Alison now looked almost the same age as her mother – Esther.

She suddenly remembered that Alison rarely left the house.

She might not see it.

Ruby had to make her notice. And, for that to happen, Alison had to see something in Ruby. Some reaction. Ruby could not risk Alison failing to notice.

She pulled up the sleeve of her shirt, exposing her right wrist. Before Ruby did anything else, she took a second to scan the street. No one around. A quiet moment.

She had to be quick. Accurate. Silent.

Ruby bit into her right arm. Just above her wrist. Her teeth took hold of the flesh, pulled. She whimpered. The pain was intense. Ruby didn't want to break the skin. That wouldn't do. She just wanted the pain.

She bit down, harder.

Her eyes squeezed shut. Her fingers began to tremble. She pulled her wrist away, stretching the skin, and just when she thought she couldn't hold on any longer, she jerked her head up.

That did it.

Tears squirmed from her tightly shut eyes.

Ruby opened her mouth, wiped the saliva from her wrist and folded her shirt over the teeth marks, deep and already turning purple. There would be bruising for a few days at least. She had to remember to keep that arm covered.

Her cheeks were flushed and she felt her breath ragged.

Ruby hit the doorbell. Within thirty seconds, Alison opened the door. Her head bowed, eyes on the floor. Another day in hell for the woman married to the man accused of murder. Another day to suck the life right out of her.

Ruby didn't move.

She stood on the top step. Her left arm cradling her wrist.

When Ruby didn't step into the house right away, Alison glanced up.

'Oh, Ruby, what's wrong? You're crying,' said Alison with genuine concern in her voice.

Ruby said nothing.

She just stared at the front door.

Alison opened the door another few feet, and followed Ruby's eyeline.

The door was painted a pale lilac. A brass knocker in the center of the door.

And scrawled across the door, in bright red spray paint – a single word.

MURDERER

Alison's fingers flew to her lips as she staggered back a step. As if the word had wounded her. She let out her breath all at once, and sank to her knees. The strength had left her shaking legs.

Ruby had to act swiftly.

She wiped the tears from her face, and gently lifted Alison back to her feet.

'Is Tomas out of bed yet?' asked Ruby.

Alison shook her head.

'Okay, let me go get some cleaning products. There's some strong bleach in the bathroom cabinet upstairs. You'd better take a picture of this for your attorney. They should know you're being targeted.'

'Ruby, thank you,' said Alison through the tears, her phone in her trembling hands.

Moving past her, Ruby heard soft, sibilant laughter from the red priest as she took the stairs to the upper floor. She moved quickly past the bathroom into the main bedroom. John was downstairs in his study, the door closed, already hard at work. She opened the jewelry drawer, grabbed a diamond bracelet and stuffed it into the front pocket of her jeans. She took the bleach from the bathroom on the way back down to the kitchen.

At the sink, she filled a dish tub with hot water and found some scouring cloths. Taking the tub, cloths and bleach to the front door, Ruby set them down on the top step.

'Did you get a picture?' asked Ruby.

'I took a couple. Oh my God, I can't believe this. Why are they doing this to us? Don't they *know* us? Don't they know we're not bad people?'

Alison was in a mix of panic, deep frustration and sadness. The message scrawled across their door was an attack.

John must've heard the commotion. He came out of his study, his noise-canceling headphones round his neck.

'What's happ—'

His question became redundant before he spat it out. His eyes locked on the graffiti sprayed across the front door.

Doctors have strength. Ruby had always thought so. To deal with life and death on a daily basis builds an internal fortitude. Of course, it's different when something terrible is happening to them. That professional distance that allows a cool head cannot be reached. The hurt hits the heart before the head.

His face flushed red. Eyes glistened. He opened his mouth to speak, but no words came, only a groan, his throat strangling his voice.

'I'll take care of it,' said Ruby. 'It'll be okay. Go back inside.'

John's lips trembled as he held Ruby in his gaze. In that moment, Ruby was hope. Someone helping them in another dark moment in what was becoming a perpetual night.

Somehow, Alison found strength – for John. She took his shoulders, turned him away from the door and spoke softly as she guided him to the lounge. Ruby closed the door, poured a small amount of bleach into the tub of water and soaked the cloth. She set to work, gently probing at the edges of the *M*. She didn't want to remove the paint too quickly.

She checked her watch.

Althea would be arriving any moment.

Glancing behind her, Ruby made sure no one was on the street, no faces at the windows of the houses opposite. She reached over the stone porch and discreetly emptied the bottle of bleach into the storm drain.

While she worked, Ruby kept one eye on the east side of the street, waiting for Althea. Just a few minutes later, she saw her marching toward the house, her old, worn-out Converse sneakers flapping on the sidewalk. As Althea ascended the stoop to the front door, Ruby squeezed the last drops of bleach into her tub of water.

'Hi, Althea. Isn't it terrible?' she asked, gesturing to the door.

Althea didn't react to the graffiti, nor to Ruby. She had an uncanny ability to keep her expressions neutral.

Ruby did notice Althea shifting her eyes to Ruby's right wrist. Following her line of sight, Ruby noticed small dots of red on her wrist. The exact type of mist that would blow back onto someone who is using a can of spray paint.

Rubbing at the paint on her wrist, Ruby said, 'It's starting to come off. Mostly onto me. But I'm out of bleach. Could you be a dear and get me a second bottle from the bathroom cupboard?'

Althea looked at Ruby's hands again. There was some red tinging to the cloth, and Ruby's fingers. It was clear she was making the calculation that the flecks of paint on Ruby's wrist could have come from cleaning. Althea nodded, and Ruby stepped aside to let her get through the door.

Once Althea stepped into the hall, Ruby used the cloth to remove the last of the paint from her wrist. She thought she had washed her hands thoroughly last night. She must've missed these spots.

One mistake would be catastrophic. Ruby could not afford any more mishaps. Now, she was relying on Althea doing what she normally does. Every day she comes to the Jacksons' she dumps her backpack in the hall. Same spot.

Listening, Ruby heard Althea's footsteps on the stairs.

This was her opportunity.

Ruby quietly stepped into the hallway, making sure not to go too far, so that Alison or John wouldn't be able to see her from the lounge. She bent low, unzipped Althea's backpack, took the diamond bracelet from her jeans pocket and placed it inside the pack. She didn't zip it back up, just left it where she had found it.

Returning to the door, Ruby worked harder now on the letters. In a few strokes the *M* and *U* were almost gone.

Footsteps coming down the stairs. Althea's rubber soles flapping on the tiles.

The door opened further and she gave Ruby the bottle of bleach. Pausing, taking a breath, Ruby wiped at her brow before taking the bleach. Althea returned to the house and moved to the kitchen. She was heading for the utility cupboard to fetch her sweat-stained apron.

Any plan requires elements of luck. People not paying too much attention to what is going on around them.

Althea hadn't noticed her bag was open. Everything was set.

Ruby picked up the tub of water, pushed open the front door and dropped the tub onto the tiles. She let out a cry, nothing too dramatic, but enough to summon Alison to the hallway. Two seconds later, Alison and John came bounding out of the living room, wondering what fresh hell was waiting for them. They saw the spillage. Ruby's hands on her head, swearing at her incompetence.

'Jesus, I'm so clumsy. I'm sorry. Alison! The water – grab Althea's bag before it's soaked.'

As the puddle of water spread across the tiles, Alison stepped forward and took hold of Althea's backpack, not wanting it to be ruined. She didn't realize the bag was open. As she snatched it upright, the bag tilted. A purse fell onto the floor. A granary roll wrapped in a plastic baggie, a set of keys . . . they all clattered onto the mosaic tiles.

And then a bracelet hit the floor.

Alison swore, at her own clumsiness this time. But then she paused as soon as she saw the diamond bracelet. Slowly, she bent low, picked it up and examined it.

'I'll get a mop,' said Ruby.

'No!' said Alison forcefully.

Ruby stood still. Waiting. Watching.

Althea came out of the kitchen to see what had happened. She hadn't even gotten to the cupboard yet to put on her apron. She stared in confusion at Alison, at both the expression on her employer's face, and puzzlement as to why she was holding her backpack.

'This was in your bag,' said Alison, holding up the bracelet. 'This is *mine*. John gave it to me for our tenth wedding anniversary.'

'I don't know what you're talking about,' said Althea.

'It fell out of *your* bag,' said Alison.

Fear crept into Althea's voice, 'I swear to God I didn't put it there. I've never seen it before.'

'John, call the police . . .' Even as Alison said it, her face crumbled. The police had put her husband on trial for a murder he didn't commit. Their happy, elitist beliefs had been shattered. Now, they didn't trust the police.

'You took my grandmother's necklace too,' said Alison. The shock of Althea's betrayal was subsiding, replaced by anger.

'Get out!' said John. 'Just get out of our house.'

Althea began to speak, but John shouted her down. He took hold of Alison, steadying her. And Althea gathered her own belongings, wet from the water on the floor, and stormed out of the house, muttering in Spanish.

Ruby found the mop and the bucket and soaked up the water, then quickly removed the spray paint from the door.

As she washed her hands in the kitchen, she heard Alison behind her.

'Thank you so much, Ruby. I honestly don't know what we would do without you.'

The rest of the day passed without incident. Esther called in, as she did more regularly, to check on Alison. She heard Alison telling Esther about what had happened that morning. The graffiti on the door, and Althea's betrayal.

Ruby listened from the hallway and Alison and her mother spoke in the kitchen over herbal tea.

'I just can't believe it,' said Esther. 'Not Althea. The other one, Ruby, I could believe.'

'No,' said Alison. 'Ruby has been amazing. She's so kind. And she's stood by us.'

Even though the conversation fell quiet, and Ruby could not see the two women from the hallway, she knew Esther was giving her daughter one of her looks. One of her skeptical, motherly looks.

Esther was beginning to become a major problem for Ruby.

21

Kate

When Kate arrived in the office, Denise was already there, working the Xerox machine.

Eddie's plan had worked.

Yesterday she had met with Castro, and told him she needed time. Her client was on the ragged edge, ready to crack and plead to a crime he didn't commit. The odds of getting an acquittal with the DNA evidence against him were just too great. She told Castro they needed time to find a DNA expert, a latent palm print expert and a ballistics expert who was probably going to have to come from overseas, seeing as how Castro had poisoned the pool of experts in the US.

Castro said he would think about it.

Harry's talk with the judges corroborated what Kate had told him. Lawyers talk.

Trial date was set for four weeks from today. And the interviews of Brett Bale and Todd Ellis had come through to the office that morning.

It was clear the investigating officer, Detective Chase, had thought Bale and Ellis were suspects. They were interviewed days apart. But both men had stuck to their stories. Yes, they'd had a relationship with Maggs, but that was all in the past. They'd been at the party, with forty witnesses, and they'd stayed until after three in the morning.

A separate statement from Petra Schwartzman confirmed both men left after three a.m. The medical examiner put the time of Margaret's death at between midnight and one a.m., but absolutely no later.

Castro would have held these interviews back, buried them. And then unleashed them in court if Eddie and Kate had decided to use Bale and Ellis as alternative suspects. He was sharing them now, to try to add to the pressure on John Jackson to throw in the towel.

No way was that going to happen. And they now had a trial date, which helped John focus on getting through this ordeal.

Kate left a note for Eddie and a copy of the statements, then left the office and saw Bloch pulling up in her Jeep. Kate got into the passenger seat.

'Let's go shake some trees,' said Kate.

They drove to Brett Bale's tennis camp in Yonkers, where he had offices and managed the rest of his empire – a base close to his home in Manhattan. Bloch parked in the lot beside Bale's Ferrari, and walked with Kate into the reception area.

There was a tennis shop on the left, and an office on the right with a reception window. Kate could see a formidable lady sitting in that office, focused on her screen. A bell sat at the reception window. A corridor facing the entrance doors led to changing areas and tennis courts beyond. A set of stairs led up to the next floor.

'His office must be upstairs,' said Bloch.

If no one was stopping Kate going to find Bale, she wasn't about to ask permission. Better not give people a reason to say no.

Kate followed Bloch up the single flight of stairs. At the top was a storeroom on the left, and a short corridor leading to an office.

The plaque on the door read *Brett Bale #1*.

'How do you want to handle this?' asked Bloch.

'Diplomatically,' said Kate.

Bloch raised an eyebrow.

'That means we don't threaten to remove any limbs,' said Kate.

'I'll play it by ear, for now,' said Bloch, considering the advice.

Kate knocked and opened the office door in one smooth motion. Again, she didn't want to give anyone an opportunity to stop them.

Bale stood behind a large desk. A wide window behind him overlooking the tennis courts. He wore an expensive white silk shirt and navy chinos with, as Kate expected, tennis shoes. He held his phone to his ear.

The office was neat, with a few filing cabinets on one side and two chairs facing the desk.

'Hold on a second,' said Bale into the phone, then lowered it and addressed Kate and Bloch, who were both now standing in his office.

'Wait a second, who are you?'

'Hi, Mr. Bale, we're here to talk to you on behalf of a resident of West 74th Street,' said Kate. Not lying, but not exactly telling the truth either.

'How did you . . .? Wait one second,' he said, then returned the phone to his ear and said, 'Look, I pay Rudy Carp a small goddamn fortune every month. When I call him, I want him to pick up the phone. I'll call him right back and he'd better answer or I'll get myself another lawyer.'

Kate knew the name Rudy Carp. He was a celebrity lawyer, one of the richest in New York. Eddie had worked with him once, briefly. A real barracuda.

Bale looked at his phone, began typing a message, said, 'Just one second . . .'

Kate glanced at his desk, saw a piece of paper sitting there. Letter-sized. Nothing unusual about a letter on a desk, but this was unusual. It was handwritten. Block capitals. In red pen.

Angling her head, Kate read the first line . . . *I SAW YOU AT* . . .

Bale must've seen Kate looking at it, because his hand snaked out at great speed and snatched it off the desk, crumpling it into his fist.

'Sorry, I hate mess,' said Bale.

'No problem,' said Kate, taking out her phone. 'Oh dear, I'm sorry.

Now, just a second . . . God these cell phones are torture, aren't they?' said Kate as she typed something quick on her phone. A text message to Bloch.

CALL ME NOW. DON'T HANG UP.

Bale forced a smile, said, 'Sorry, I'm confused. Did you speak to my secretary or the office manager before you came up? It's just I'm really busy. I have to make an urgent call . . .'

'No, sorry. There was no one at reception. We won't take up too much of your time . . .' said Kate, taking her handbag from her shoulder. She placed it in her lap as she sat down on one of the chairs facing Bale's desk.

Bale's lips peeled over his teeth, just for a second, and his eyes darkened with a flash of irritation.

Kate felt her phone vibrate. Keeping the screen pointed toward her, she accepted Bloch's call, put her handbag on the floor and, most importantly, her phone beside the bag.

'Who did you say you represent?' asked Bale.

'A resident of West 74th Street.'

'Which one?'

'John Jackson, he is falsely accused of the murder of Margaret Blakemore. I believe you knew Mrs. Blakemore.'

Bale's tone, which up to now had been polite, changed.

'This conversation is over. If you want to talk to me, you need to speak to my lawyers. Now, please leave.'

'Oh, I'm sorry, we're just looking for some background—'

'Get out or I'll call the police,' said Bale.

Kate picked up her handbag, left her phone and exited the room with Bloch. They walked down the corridor and stood at the top of the stairs. Bale's door was closed. Bloch raised her phone so they could both listen.

'Rudy, it's Brett Bale. I think someone is trying to blackmail me over Margaret Blakemore . . .'

They couldn't hear Rudy Carp's side of the conversation.

'I got a letter. Handwritten. Red ink. Demanding a lot of money or this person is going to tell the police they saw me murder Margaret . . .'

'I know . . . I know . . . but with the accusations still flying around about Jane . . . Okay, just keep the letter . . . Can I— Look, I just want this to go away . . . No, okay, I won't pay a dime . . . Well, what do I pay you for? . . . Okay, okay, Rudy, bye . . .'

He hung up, swore and said some unsavory things about Rudy Carp. Jane was Bale's late wife – the swim champ who'd drowned while on vacation in Florida with Bale.

Kate opened his office door, said, 'Oh, God, I'm sorry. I think I left my phone . . . Yes, here it is . . .' She bent down, picked it up. Bale gave her a look like he wanted to strangle her.

As they made their way downstairs, Bloch said, 'That was a cute move with the phone.'

'I'm spending far too much time with Eddie Flynn,' said Kate.

In the parking lot, Kate called Eddie, gave him an update.

'What do you think?' asked Kate.

'I don't know. Could be a scam artist. But maybe not. John didn't get a blackmail letter. Some anonymous caller started this entire case against him. There are definitely people somewhere in the background of this case that are playing dangerous games. Could be multiple people.'

'But it might just be one person,' said Kate.

'I don't understand any of this. Harry and I have tracked down Ellis. He goes for lunch in the Cardozo Hotel every Tuesday. We're going to go see him tomorrow. I made arrangements with the concierge.'

'What are you going to do?'

'Harry's going to offer him some legal advice.'

22

Ruby

Alison and John left early to go meet their lawyers.

Tomas sat in front of the TV in the living room watching *Rugrats* reruns and Ruby busied herself cleaning the kitchen. Since Althea's departure, Ruby had taken over the housekeeping. There were baskets full of laundry upstairs and trash that needed to be emptied from the bathrooms.

She sprayed disinfectant on the counter and wiped it down. A large blowfly swooped by, then flew into the hallway and landed on the painting of the red priest. Ruby closed her eyes and tried to drown out the noise.

Thankfully, the house phone rang. Tomas ignored it. He was lying on the couch, mesmerized by the TV. Ruby saw the number displayed on the phone's screen.

Mom.

When the phone stopped ringing, the light came on the base to say a voicemail message was being left. Ruby quietly closed the living-room door and hit the speaker on the phone base.

Esther's Manhattan drawl came over the speaker.

'. . . *I know you have enough going on. I'm not interfering. I'm just worried about my grandson. I never liked Ruby. There's something not right about that girl. Anyway, before you blow your top, I wanted to tell you I met Althea. Lovely girl. She was terrified when I called and it took a lot of persuasion before she agreed to let me into her apartment. Look, she lives with her family and half of them are undocumented. The last person who would risk getting arrested is Althea. She didn't take the bracelet. She says Ruby hates her and it was Ruby who planted the brace-let in her bag. I think she's right . . .'*

Leaning over, Ruby placed both hands on the hall table and closed her eyes as she listened.

'. . . Did I tell you I saw Ruby talking to our painting in your hallway? She was talking to it. Or herself. I mentioned this to Althea and she said she saw the same thing once. Ruby was whispering to it. I never told you, but I had that painting valued a long time ago. It's Renaissance period and worth more than Ruby will make in her entire life. Don't you get it? Ruby took my mother's necklace. The one I gave you. It's our family heir-loom. I saw how Althea is living. Trust me, if she stole an expensive necklace and sold it, she wouldn't be living like that . . .'

Ruby's jaw tightened.

'. . . I know you're both going through hell. And I'm sorry for digging this up, but someone had to. It's not fair what's happened to Althea. I think Ruby took the necklace and that painting is next. You have to fire Ruby. When you get a chance, call me. I love you.'

The phone base chimed as Esther hung up the call.

Another beep came from the base as a symbol of an envelope appeared on the display.

Ruby accessed the message menu on the phone.

She hit delete and the envelope icon disappeared.

'Alexa,' said Ruby, 'send flowers to Mom.'

'Okay, which flowers would you like to send?'

'A bouquet of lilies.'

'Okay. Which address would you like to use for delivery? Would you like to use 1819 West 74th Street, or 14 Henderson Place?'

Ruby picked up a pen, wrote down Esther's address on Henderson Place and said, 'Cancel.'

'*Order cancelled*,' said Alexa.

The noise from the fly filled Ruby's ears. Then the hissing and whispering began.

The red priest wanted to talk.

23
Ruby

The diner's coffee was hot and cheaper than Starbucks, but, more importantly, it was next door to Althea's apartment building. Ruby had long ago followed Althea home. She had been a target for Ruby, and, like her grandmother always said, knowledge is power.

Ruby took a refill from the waitress, and sat in the window booth.

She'd left the Jacksons' a few hours ago, after they got back from their appointment. Then she'd taken a bus to the Bronx.

On the way, she'd made the call to Immigration and Customs Enforcement.

There were no set response times as far as she was aware. But Ruby figured they would respond as soon as they could get a couple of officers free.

'May I have your name, please?' asked the ICE officer.

'It's Esther Hanson,' said Ruby.

It had taken ICE an hour and a half to respond. Not bad, considering. Ruby watched the ICE van pull up at Althea's building. Saw the officers climb out of the car and make their way inside.

Ruby finished her coffee and waited. She guessed maybe twenty minutes. Five to get to Althea's apartment. Another five to get inside. It brought back memories of Ruby staring out of her childhood bedroom window on West 74th Street as the cops pulled up at her house.

Neighbors, or perhaps even a couple passing their house on the street, had heard noises. Screaming, probably, coming from her mother. The cops came to the house. One in the living room with her mom. One outside on the street with her dad.

And her mom lied every time. It was a fall down the stairs. A slip on the icy sidewalk. A misjudgment in her squash game and she got a ball in the eye.

The cops knew she was lying. And sometimes they would press her. Ultimately, they knew unless she co-operated there was nothing they could do. They couldn't arrest her husband if she didn't make a complaint about him.

So, after a while, around twenty minutes usually, they just left.

Twenty minutes after the ICE officers went into Althea's building, they were back on the street with Althea's uncle, her aunt, her mother and her two little cousins. The van filled up with Althea's people – ready to go to some processing center. Ruby didn't really know what happened when undocumented immigrants were taken away. Nothing good, she guessed. And she was unlikely to ever see any of them again.

Althea stood on the sidewalk, shaking with fear and shock. Ruby understood fear all too well. She could not say that she understood what Althea was feeling, but Althea was smart and Ruby could well imagine what she was thinking. For almost two years, Althea's family had lived in fear of the ICE agents. The fear dissipates. Althea was careful and there was no reason for anyone to report them.

What had changed in Althea's life?

She had been fired and accused of theft, but no cops had been called. A few days later, Esther visits Althea. She sits in the apartment, meets Althea's family – and the very next day ICE agents are at their door.

Fear leads to mistrust. But, even without the mildest paranoia, it would be a logical conclusion to associate Esther's visit with someone suddenly calling immigration. At the very least, Althea would not be able to rule that out. She would strongly suspect Esther was the one who had taken her family away from her.

America could be cruel.

The Statue of Liberty stood tall, with its back to New York City.

Ruby left five dollars on the table for her coffee and the tip, and made her way to the subway.

It took forty-five minutes to get to Henderson Street.

Ruby didn't do anything at first. It was still light. She wanted to wait until it got darker. But not late. Knocking on a door when it was fully dark made it more likely she wouldn't get inside, and it might attract more attention from the neighbors. While she waited for the sun to dip behind the buildings, Ruby made circles of the block. Watching the windows of the houses opposite Esther's. Making sure no one was watching her.

Her backpack felt heavy. The weight was reassuring. Her back was covered in sweat, but the long black overcoat she wore concealed it. The coat was breathable, but in this heat it was like having a furnace draped over her shoulders.

While she walked, she went over her speech. In her mind.

She would do exactly what the red priest had told her.

Esther Hanson lived in a redbrick, three-story townhouse. A basement apartment below, one set of steps up to her house. Thankfully, no lights were showing in the basement apartment. This was a really nice area to live. And, like most of these places, few people actually lived here. Probably half of this street was vacant properties, bought as investments, occasionally rented out on Airbnb, or short-term leases with stringent terms on cleaning and occupation.

These were no longer homes. They were money. Just big piles of money and, usually, if you left them well enough alone – those piles just grew bigger all by themselves, so when the property was back on the market after seven or ten years, prices had gone up and the investors could make their return.

Esther's house was occupied. And a lamp lit the living room that overlooked the darkening street.

Taking a deep breath, Ruby climbed the eight steps to Esther's front door and, covering her little finger with the sleeve of her coat, she rang the doorbell.

She waited only a few moments before Esther opened the door. No security chain. No checking through the peephole before she opened up. She was quicker than Ruby had expected, almost as if she was waiting for a caller.

The welcoming smile fell from Esther's lips as soon as she saw who was on her doorstep. Replacing it with a look of confusion, and then something else. Something approaching disgust.

'What are you doing here?' asked Esther.

'It's about Althea,' said Ruby. 'I need to talk to you.'

'You can talk to my daughter, your employer, about Althea. I have nothing to do with it,' said Esther, coolly, and she stood back, started to close the door.

'Wait, it's because of Alison that I'm here. There are things you don't know. Alison cried for two days after she lost that necklace. The silver lace one that you had given to her. She was inconsolable. I didn't want to tell you because she was so worried about how you would react. When she found out it was Althea who stole it, I knew Alison would do anything to get that necklace back from the person who took it. But she didn't do anything . . .'

She paused then, for dramatic effect, and in an effort to let what she had said sink in. Esther was not stupid, but perhaps she wasn't the quickest. She just shook her head and started to close the door again.

'Wait, please, do I have to say it out loud? Alison should have called the cops. I think Althea made sure that Alison couldn't call anyone. I'm pretty sure Althea is blackmailing your daughter. I think it's something to do with John and the gun the police found in the house.'

The door's path had already concealed Esther's face. It was an inch from shutting when it stopped, and gradually Esther pulled it open again. She had finally put together what Ruby was saying. Even if Ruby had to spell it out. Of course, Alison had to call the police. She would do that a hundred percent. Esther knew her daughter. A family heirloom with so much pain and history and love attached to it – it didn't make any sense for Alison to just let that go.

'How do you know Althea is blackmailing her?'

'Can I come in? I don't want to talk about this out here?'

Esther thought about it. Cast her eyes from side to side to see who else was on the street. It was quiet. No one around. But, still, she didn't want the neighbors gossiping.

'You'd better come in,' said Esther.

She turned away, and Ruby stepped into the house and closed the door behind her. Ahead of her, in the hallway, Esther's shoulders slumped as she exhaled. Perhaps she was thinking that she had been a foolish person, being taken in by Althea. Not only had this woman stolen from her family, but Esther had been stupid enough to get fooled again.

Turning right into the living space, Esther disappeared from Ruby's view.

Slowing her pace, Ruby had a few seconds to put on her gloves before she went through. She managed to get them on, then put her hands in her pockets to conceal them.

Esther moved through the living room, and approached a table in the dining area where she pulled out a chair. As the legs dragged across the solid wooden floor, Esther paused again. Second thoughts, maybe. Perhaps Althea had been right all along, and it was Ruby who was playing her now.

Ruby saw the look of doubt creep in. The expressions on Esther's face were easy to read, even for someone who didn't have the greatest understanding of emotions.

'You need to explain yourself right now. Because, if my daughter is in danger from anyone, I need to know,' said Esther, gazing into Ruby's eyes for the first time.

'Why don't you sit down. I think John and Althea are having an affair and that has something to do with that gun. I think Althea is trying to get money from Alison. This is really complicated. Do you mind if I get a glass of water?'

Waving a hand at the kitchen behind her, Esther sat down, a confused expression on her face.

Ruby wanted Esther confused. She had deliberately told her something so complex and strange, but with it an implied threat to her daughter, that Esther would have no choice but to hear Ruby out. Even if it was to confirm in her own mind that Ruby was full of shit.

Ruby moved behind her into the kitchen.

She ran the faucet, fast.

Loud.

She slipped off her backpack.

Took an apron from it and slipped it over her head.

'I don't understand what you're saying, Ruby. This is really confusing,' said Esther, shaking her head.

Ruby took the five-pound hammer from the backpack and then set the bag on the floor.

She stepped closer to Esther, who had her elbows on the table. Her back to Ruby.

Raising her arms, Ruby swung the hammer high above her head.

'I don't know if I should trust you . . .' said Esther.

Ruby took another step toward her.

'I saw you, one day, talking to the picture in Alison's house. The one with the cardinal. You were . . . whispering . . . to it. You want it, don't you? I see you. You want the life my daughter enjoys – the money. But you're not like us, Ruby. You can never be one of us. If you say my daughter or son-in-law are being manipulated – I don't believe you. I want proof.'

Esther angled her body, to look behind.

Ruby took another step. She was close now. Just two feet away. Esther must've sensed her approach.

She froze as she saw Ruby with the hammer.

'I wasn't whispering to it. I was listening. He tells me things, the red priest. He's very bad, you see. Mostly, I just do what I'm told . . .'

Esther tried to get up, but her legs caught beneath the table and it lifted an inch off the ground before she lost her balance. She fell back on the seat, then tried to stand and twist out of the chair, desperate to move, to get away.

As the hammer hit the back of Esther's skull, Ruby continued to talk.

'He told me I had to kill you. This isn't my fault. This is your fault. You could've really messed things up for me.'

She raised the hammer. Let it swing down again.

The left rear chair leg buckled with the force of Esther's body being pummeled. The chair collapsed, sending Esther to the floor.

She was already dead.

24

Mr. Christmas

At eight thirty, on a hot Tuesday morning, Mr. Christmas sat behind the wheel of his black Lincoln Continental and watched Eddie Flynn and Harry Ford enter the lobby of the Cardozo Hotel. This was his first time seeing Flynn in the flesh. Up until now he had studied photographs only – pictures taken by newspaper photographers. He had seen pictures of Flynn, his partner Kate Brooks, mentor Harry Ford and their detective, Bloch. Today, he hoped to get a flavor of the real people.

He had researched his target. It didn't matter that Mr. Christmas was paid for his craft – ending a life was never merely business, particularly for his victims.

Murder was always personal.

The more he delved into Flynn and his history, the more intriguing the man had become. There were even odd parallels to Mr. Christmas's own life. Flynn was a man with a foot in two worlds. He was, by all accounts, a gifted trial lawyer. His past, however, was much more interesting. The son of a small-time grifter, Flynn had followed that same path, but excelled as a con artist. His quick wit and cunning allowed him to build his own reputation in the criminal underworld with the moniker Eddie Fly. Like so many brought up underprivileged with a criminal parent, he practically inherited a life of crime. His childhood friend Jimmy Fellini, whom he'd met in Mickey Hooley's Boxing Club, was now head of the Italian crime families in New York. Everything pointed to Flynn making a mistake and ending up serving a nickel in one of the state's less salubrious prisons. But something had happened before his luck ran out.

Flynn had turned away from being a con artist and went back to school. Passed the bar exam and clerked for the man who was now his best friend – former Judge Harry Ford. This was a turning point in Flynn's life, and the reasons behind it were not clear for Mr. Christmas. Most of the men in his line of work just focused on finding a target. That was not enough for him. Their location was important, but knowing who they were, how they behave and how they react to certain situations was essential. It was, to him, the difference between knowing where one can find a piano, and being able to sit down at the instrument and play Chopin.

He wondered what Flynn was doing. Judging by the news articles he could find, Flynn was in the middle of a major case, defending brain surgeon John Jackson in a murder trial. The victim was a minor celebrity and aging Manhattan socialite. That bought the case some column inches, as did the location of the murder – West 74th Street – a notably high-end neighborhood in a city full of high-end neighborhoods. Interestingly, Jackson's mother-in-law had been found murdered just a few days ago, and a young woman arrested. There was much more going on than appeared on its surface.

Perhaps Flynn was meeting a witness. The Cardozo Hotel has an exclusive club for dining and drinks, frequented by bankers, business types, lawyers and general high rollers. The cost of membership ensured only the very rich and elite were allowed to join. Flynn wasn't in that class, but he had been to see the concierge and booked a room for the night.

Mr. Christmas checked the rearview mirror. Then side mirrors.

The sidewalks of Manhattan were rivers that flowed with people. And he was looking for a particular kind of fish. One that stood out among the crowds. It wasn't particularly difficult to spot them. Their eyes gave them away. And their dress.

A large man wearing blue jeans, tan boots and a tan work jacket, carrying a large tool bag over his shoulder. A single AirPod in his left ear. He had watched Flynn, Ford and Bloch enter the building. Walked slowly along the same side of the street. Once they were inside the hotel, the man in work clothes hid his gaze with a baseball cap and put his back to the building, leaning against the wall. He'd stood out not because of where his gaze had been fixed, but because he walked slowly, and his clothes, while portraying him as one of the thousands of construction workers who flooded the city every day, also gave him away.

They were new. Spotless.

He was a mobile spotter. Tracking Flynn along the pavements. He would have a mobile base. And there would be at least one other person behind the wheel of a vehicle. A two-man team. Minimum.

Mr. Christmas cast his eyes around the street. At first, nothing leapt out at him. Then a black panel van turned the corner. It parked on the other side of the street, twenty feet from the hotel entrance and facing Mr. Christmas. A driver and a passenger in blue overalls. Both men alert. Eyes scanning the street.

They clocked his Lincoln. The passenger's gaze quickly moved on. But not the driver's.

Mr. Christmas checked his watch, took his cell phone from his pocket and pretended to look at it, keeping the driver in his peripheral vision. After a few seconds, the driver shifted his attention to the rest of the street.

The hotel entrance was busy and Mr. Christmas watched people go in and out, mostly tourists, their luggage unloaded from town cars onto trolleys by the bellhops. The concierge and greeters were out front ferrying guests.

A half-hour went by. Tourists checked in and checked out. The man in pristine work clothes lit a cigarette and studied his phone.

Adjusting his side mirror, Mr. Christmas was able to get a better look at the man in workwear – the eyeball on the street. Mr. Christmas sat forward, squinting, trying for a closer look. The left pocket of his jacket bulged. A small handgun. Or maybe a taser. He also noticed there was a tattoo on the back of the man's wrist, a snake that curled over his hand and onto his knuckles. He believed he knew that tattoo, but he had to get a closer look to be sure.

The crew made up by the occupants of the panel van and the construction worker were good. They kept each other in sight, while covering all bases and means of exit from the hotel.

Mr. Christmas waited, and forty-five minutes later he got his opportunity. A truck pulled up in front of the row of parked vehicles and the driver got out, threw open the rear door of his trailer and retrieved a handcart. He was about to make a delivery to the hotel and, for however long that took him, he would obscure the view between the panel van and the man on the street.

Just as Mr. Christmas opened the driver's door of his Lincoln, his messenger bag in hand, he thought over what would happen when Flynn left the hotel. His contacts had told him Flynn wasn't planning on occupying the room he had booked; it merely allowed his contacts at the hotel to get him into the club. Flynn could leave the hotel any time.

When he did, things would move quickly.

The van would pull out into the middle of the street and the man in workwear would move swiftly to intercept his target. The mobile vehicle was a van, which meant there was probably someone in the back to open the rear doors for the workman to make his escape after he had executed Flynn and Ford. If he slipped, there would be at least one shooter in the van – back-up. Either way, both Flynn and Ford would certainly be killed. No point in leaving a living witness.

Mr. Christmas stepped to the sidewalk, placed his black felt fedora smoothly onto his head and buttoned his light black overcoat. His movement was lithe and elegant – like Fred Astaire in top hat and tails.

The contract on Flynn's life had attracted attention. Mid-level

hitmen, mostly. When Mr. Christmas drew nearer to the man in
work gear, he got a closer look at the tattoo on his left hand. As the
man smoked his cigarette, the sleeve of his jacket slid down.

The snake coiled into a figure eight over the back of his hand.

Even though he couldn't see it, he knew there would be a corres-
ponding eight on his right hand.

These men, known as the 88s, were part of a small professional crew
who were normally based out of Fort Worth, but they had operated in
Miami, Chicago, Upstate New York and Houston. Ex-specialists. Two
were former Marines. One Green Beret. Two Rangers. They had built
a reputation for a number of terror attacks, although none of the incidents had been classified as such by the FBI. They were mostly
bombing African American and Jewish-owned businesses and retail
stores. All five members had been dishonorably discharged from military service for a variety of offences – mostly race-related violence.
Their planned terror campaign needed financing, and of course none
of them were psychologically capable of holding down regular
employment – and they didn't have a service pension to get by on
either.

They began taking jobs from whoever paid. Small-time stuff at
first, working security for a people trafficker named Grady Banks. A
particularly nasty fellow who sold stolen children to the highest
bidder, mostly foreign nationals, or sometimes to Mr. Christmas's
current employers – New York's Finest, who then sold them to broth-
els dotted around the city. Grady Banks and the 88s were friends.
They were also neo-Nazis.

The eights on their hands represented the eighth letter of the
alphabet – H. Double H was some kind of bullshit code for *Heil Hitler*.

Mr. Christmas didn't care for Nazis.

However, on this occasion, their skewed bigotry was not the reason
he felt the need to intervene. When he had heard a number of his
fellow professional killers were interested in the contract on Eddie
Flynn, it became a matter of economic propriety. Not only would

Mr. Christmas be the one to put a bullet in Eddie Flynn, but it also gave him an opportunity to pick off his market competitors before he killed the lawyer. With fewer professional hitmen in operation – the market would adjust. Prices would go way up.

Murder is often an economic force, especially in the world of assassins.

As Mr. Christmas approached the man in work gear, he noticed him angling his phone screen to get a look at Mr. Christmas as he approached. He could almost sense the man tensing. The workman had good survival instincts. His other hand dived into his coat pocket, his fingers no doubt wrapping around the compact pistol hidden in there.

He stopped just a few feet from the man, retrieved a soft pack of Lucky Strikes from his pocket, a lighter, and tapped a smoke to his lips as he turned his back. Cupping his hand round the lighter, Mr. Christmas struck the wheel a few times but to no avail. He always carried an empty lighter for just such an occasion. The man was watching him, and Mr. Christmas swung round.

'Excuse me, sorry to bother you, but could I borrow a light?' asked Mr. Christmas.

The man threw the butt of his cigarette into the street. The muscles in Mr. Christmas's jaw twitched. He didn't like litter. Throwing trash onto the ground was a symptom of an unevolved mind.

The man appeared irked, but he let go of the pistol in his jacket and placed his right hand into his pants pocket and came up with a Zippo, which he snapped open on his thigh and then lit, in a practiced back-and-forth whipping movement.

'Thank you,' said Mr. Christmas as he held the cigarette to the flame.

The man flicked his wrist to close the lighter.

'Pardon me for asking,' began Mr. Christmas, 'and I don't at all mean this question to sound flippant, or compendious – I'm genuinely interested to hear your answer. Tell me, sir, what do you think of Marlon Brando?'

25
Harry

Before the young conman had come into Harry's life, he'd felt as if his path was settled. He had grown up poor, in the back of his father's Buick while he drove all over the South preaching the gospel. Harry didn't have much in the way of an education, apart from the paperbacks his mother loved to read. She liked racy novels, with titles like *Texas Two-Step* and *Anything Goes*, much to the annoyance of Harry's father, who made sure those books were safely locked in the trunk when they stayed in a town for a week or so. At first he objected to her choice of reading material, but he knew better than to argue with Harry's momma. That was a road no man ever wanted to walk down. But it was James Baldwin's books that caught Harry's attention. It was as if someone was writing just for him – a young, poor African American in the South.

Harry got out and into the US Army, just in time for the tail end of the Vietnam War. He saved a lot of men and progressed through the ranks. He left the military after the war and got his high-school diploma and a college education. Then the bar exam and he was off, flying high in his own law firm and fighting the injustices that had haunted him for most of his life. He built a reputation for an implacable knowledge of the law, a great empathy for his clients and a respect for the constitution. He rose to be a judge, but during this time in his life there was something missing. He was no longer in the fight.

He began drinking more, and his marriages tumbled into the abyss, one after another, until one day a young man spoke in his courtroom, pretending to be a lawyer. He destroyed a witness on the stand. Harry remembered feeling the blood pop in his veins as Eddie took apart that guy's testimony. Here was the best natural talent he had ever seen in a courtroom.

Harry had no children and his relationship with Eddie wasn't really a father-and-son type of deal. They were best friends. Eddie's recklessness, his vibrancy and his disregard for the law were appealing to Harry. It kept him young. Or at least feeling that way.

He liked the electric juice – the thrill of working with the young man. And, in truth, he loved Eddie. And he believed in him.

And that was all that mattered.

Harry reminded himself of this as he walked through the lobby of the Cardozo Hotel.

Eddie knew people all over the city. A booking was required at the hotel, to make it easier for Harry, Bloch and Eddie to get through the front door in the first place, and then into the members' club. Residents were not permitted, and Harry suspected Eddie was paying off the concierge to get them in, and even this small thrill made Harry feel more alive.

Bloch peeled off, took a seat in the hotel lounge opposite Gabriel Lake, who had been there for some time, making sure there was no one in the lobby who might pull out a gun on Flynn. There was still a price on his friend's head, and Harry was glad that all precautions were being taken.

Eddie walked slightly ahead of Harry as they made it to the end of the lobby, then turned left down a long ornate hallway to a set of double doors marked PRIVATE MEMBERS ONLY. The man in a suit on the door checked Eddie's room card, nodded and let them both through.

The private members' dining room had low lighting, large circular tables with four chairs at each one, the full silver service, low jazz playing in the background and the smell of cedarwood and good food.

Todd Ellis sat at a table by himself, three empty chairs around it. Business suit, red silk tie over a white shirt. Head shaven and catching the light from the candles on the table. His head was down, looking at his phone. A single glass of water had been placed in front of him.

There was no way to get to him apart from either accosting him on the street or breaking into his office. He wouldn't take an appointment with Eddie, so there was no point in trying. This was his safe space, and the only place to offer an opportunity to talk.

'Mr. Ellis?' said Eddie.

He raised his head, looked at Eddie and Harry, said, 'Yes, what is it?'

Harry didn't like this guy. Money didn't buy manners.

'My colleague and I would like a minute of your time, if you don't mind,' said Eddie.

Ellis's gaze returned to his phone as he said, 'Make an appointment with my office.'

Before Eddie could say anything else, the waiter appeared beside Ellis, and put down a large plate of salad, scrambled eggs and caviar. The waiter didn't even have time to take a step away before Ellis started complaining.

'These eggs are overdone,' said Ellis. 'Take them away and do it again.'

Harry could see the eggs weren't overdone. They were cooked just right, moist and glistening in the atmospheric light.

'Sir, the eggs are—'

'I don't give a fuck what you say. Take these fucking eggs, throw them away and do the entire dish again from scratch. You just blew your tip, by the way.'

Without another word, the waiter took the plate away.

Eddie and Harry had rehearsed an introduction – subtle ways to get Ellis to open up, and get something useful out of him. Harry noticed Eddie's fingers tightening into a fist on his right hand. The time for subtlety had passed. Before Eddie said something he regretted, or grabbed Ellis by his tiny head and put him up against a wall, Harry decided he had better cut to the chase.

'We represent John Jackson. We want to ask you about your relationship with the late Margaret Blakemore,' said Harry.

Ellis stood up. Harry thought it didn't make much of a difference – he still looked like a kid at a grown-ups' table.

'I don't care who you are. Get the hell out of here,' said Ellis.

'Should we go talk to your wife instead?' asked Eddie.

Ellis called for security.

'Are you nervous about your wife knowing you were having an affair with Margaret Blakemore when she was murdered?'

'There's not a single piece of evidence for that. Now get the hell out of here. And . . .' Ellis stopped speaking. The look on his face darkened further, as if he'd made some kind of connection in his mind that Harry couldn't fathom.

'You're Eddie Flynn, right?' he asked.

Eddie said yes, and Ellis nodded then put his hands on his hips. He had acted at first as if he was confused about who was asking him about Margaret Blakemore.

Harry made the connection.

'Has someone mentioned that name to you recently?' asked Harry. 'Has someone threatened you?'

The look on Ellis's face confirmed it.

'Get. The. Fuck. Out.'

'It's been nice talking to you,' said Eddie.

Harry followed Eddie out of the dining room just as a large man in a suit came toward Ellis.

'It's okay. We're leaving,' said Eddie.

Once in the lobby, he said, 'Well, that didn't go as planned.'

'We did get something important,' said Harry. 'Now we know Ellis is being blackmailed too. Did you see his face?'

Eddie nodded, said, 'I saw it. What the hell is going on in this case? John's housekeeper, Althea, murders Alison's mother, and now Ellis and Brett Bale are being blackmailed about their possible involvement in Margaret Blakemore's murder? And that anonymous call accusing John? I have a really bad feeling about this one.'

Harry thought for a moment. Bloch and Lake saw them in the lobby, got up, stepped into line ahead of Eddie.

'This all started with Margaret's murder and that anonymous call. We need to know why John Jackson is being framed. That's the real question here.'

26

Mr. Christmas

The man in work gear moved through a range of emotions. All of them writ large in his expressive face.

At first, confusion.

'What do you think of Marlon Brando?'

Random strangers who ask for a light and then randomly seek your opinion on old movie stars are rare. It's not an interaction that happens even occasionally. The man in work gear was surprised by the question. He didn't even get as far as thinking about an answer – he was so bowled over at being asked that his brain couldn't function.

He was momentarily stunned.

That confusion deepened as Mr. Christmas stepped forward smartly, almost nose to nose, gripping the workman's right arm and pinning it so that he couldn't get to the gun in his jacket. Before fight-or-flight response kicked in, the workman's expression changed again. This time from surprise to shock.

And then pain.

'Don't move. Don't struggle. There's a blade in your thigh,' said Mr. Christmas, his voice calm and almost soothing. 'Do what I ask, and I'll take the knife straight out. You'll bleed, you'll limp for a week, but you will live. If you don't co-operate, I pull the knife a half-inch to the left, at forty-five degrees, and I sever a major artery. You will die in seconds. *Do not* struggle.'

The man's eyes widened in fear.

'Now, on your coms, I want you to tell your friends to drive away. Say Eddie Flynn made it out of an exit into an alley and he's gone.'

Mr. Christmas, confident he had full control of the man in front of him, sensed movement to his left. He pushed in closer to the man, angled his body slightly to give himself some cover.

Bloch moved slowly out of the Cardozo lobby. Checking right and left. She saw the workman's back, and Mr. Christmas standing close to him, glancing over his shoulder. Unusual, but not suspicious. Just two men in conversation. She was looking for a more immediate threat. From the angle of her gaze, Mr. Christmas guessed she had spotted the van.

It was unlike Flynn to move around the city without protection. He had obviously guessed, correctly, that it was more likely he would get hit coming out of the hotel, or inside the building. Which is why Bloch had been inside.

Mr. Christmas knew he could draw his gun, aim over the workman's shoulder and take out Flynn as he stepped outside the hotel. It was a difficult shot. Forty yards. A moving target. Possible other bodies in the way. The Nazi might make a move while Mr. Christmas was distracted.

Too risky.

'Tell your colleagues in the van to move,' said Mr. Christmas. 'I won't ask again.'

The workman pressed a stud on his inner-ear device, said, 'Abort, abort, NYPD.'

Instantly, Mr. Christmas heard the van's engine starting up and then the change in tone as it found a gear and began to move.

If he let go of the workman's arm to take out his own gun, the workman might try to get free – maybe even reach for his weapon. He glanced to his right. An alleyway. He gently pulled the man toward the alley, knowing, with a blade in his leg, he would have to follow.

Sweat broke out on the workman's face as Mr. Christmas forced the man's back against the alley wall. The entire alley was in the shade. Dark and cold against the morning sun. Narrow, maybe only ten feet wide.

'You know, if you weren't a Nazi, I'd probably let you live.'

Mr. Christmas skipped to his left, toward the mouth of the alley. He didn't look back. He heard the wet crash of arterial blood hitting the opposite wall like a fire hose. Then he drew his pistol, leaned out from the alleyway and pointed it at the front door of the hotel.

Eddie Flynn and Harry Ford stepped outside.

It was too soon.

Too public.

But Mr. Christmas had learned never to pass up on an opportunity.

He shut his right eye. Used his left to find and align the iron sights on his Sig Sauer with Flynn's torso.

He inhaled.

Began to apply pressure on the trigger. It's always a squeeze on that trigger, never a pull.

The pressure increased.

He exhaled, stabilizing his body, making sure there were no movements to throw off his aim.

More pressure on the trigger.

The gun steady in his hand. Ready to adjust for the recoil.

More pressure.

A man in a wrinkled suit came out of the hotel behind Flynn.

Mr. Christmas gasped.

BANG!

27

Eddie

The lobby of the Cardozo was always busy, day or night.

More business was conducted on the grounds of this hotel than in the US congress. I had hoped to get more of a reaction from Ellis. Feel him out. But he was too damn abrasive. Still, Harry was right – we'd gotten some important information. Somebody was blackmailing him too.

Bloch stood as she saw us, walked ahead to make sure the street was clear.

Lake stepped in behind us, making sure there was no one in the lobby who had managed to go unnoticed and would now make their move.

Harry made it through the revolving doors first and into the bright sun. I followed him. He stopped. Bloch was straight ahead. Stationary. A van drove past, from left to right. Her gaze followed the van. I noticed the driver wasn't looking at the road.

He was looking at Bloch. His eyes were hidden behind wraparound tactical shades. His beard was long and thick and brown and hung over his chest.

Harry and I stood on the sidewalk. Waiting for Bloch to give us the all clear. She followed the path of the van as it got to the end of the block and made a turn.

I had the sudden feeling that something was wrong. Bloch turned her head side to side – scanning the rest of the street. Lake came out of the hotel and stood behind me.

'Are we good?' he asked.

Bloch said nothing.

'You see something?' he asked.

Bloch said, 'No.'

'Then why are we standing here?' asked Lake.

'Because I *feel* something,' said Bloch.

I felt it too. An electricity in the air. The sun was already over the building directly opposite us. Coming from the muted lighting of the hotel into a neon furnace of sunlight momentarily blinded me.

Then things happened all at once.

Someone stood in front of me, blocking the sun. My eyes couldn't adjust immediately.

I blinked and something wet hit my face.

I flinched and at the same time I heard a sound. Unmistakable.

A gunshot.

At the same time as something wet slapped me, I realized I was falling. A force, hitting my chest, throwing me to the ground with tremendous velocity.

The back of my head hit the sidewalk. I don't know if I blacked out, but I couldn't see anything for a few seconds. My eyes couldn't focus.

There was a weight on my chest. I wiped my face. Something red on my fingers.

Blood.

I tried to move, but I couldn't.

Something was pinning me to the ground.

The back of my head was wet, blood running down my neck and into my shirt collar, my heart thumping in my temples.

Then, inexplicably, the weight lifted off me.

I sat up.

Harry was on the ground. He'd fallen into me, knocking me over. His shoulder must've hit my chest.

I looked down at the blood gushing from his stomach. He gazed up at me. Lake flung himself on the ground, planted both hands on Harry's belly and cried out for somebody to call a paramedic. Blood, glistening in the sunlight, pooled over Lake's fingers.

Everything was quiet.

Harry tried to talk. I took his hand. He coughed and more blood spat from his lips.

Suddenly, it wasn't quiet any more. Bloch, still on her feet in front of me, was firing that hand cannon. Pointed up. At first, I thought she was shooting at the sun, then I heard glass breaking and chunks of masonry falling into the street.

She was shooting at a window, high on the building opposite.

I told Harry I loved him.

He squeezed my hand.

I told him to hold on.

He gripped tighter.

Lake was screaming at him to stay awake.

Harry's eyes began to close.

Bloch reloaded, let out a howl of anger and grief and shock and then emptied another load at the building.

As the echoes of gunfire faded in the steel, concrete and glass canyons of Manhattan, I heard a siren in the distance.

Harry's fingers went limp.

28

Mr. Christmas

The gunshot made him flinch.

At first, he didn't know what had happened. He had not fired.

The man who followed Eddie Flynn out of the hotel, and stood behind him, was known to Mr. Christmas.

Gabriel Lake.

He had not realized Lake was working with Flynn.

His senses, his mind, bombarded with shocks, soon came back online.

The shot had come from his left. Up high. He shaded his eyes, looked up. A half-open window, twentieth floor of the building opposite.

Angel. The sniper.

He always dealt death from above. A perfect position. Elevated. A choice of exits. And firing from a position in line with the sun, to make it harder to spot him. Anyone looking at his point of fire would have to gaze into its fierce glare.

Mr. Christmas looked back at the street and the hotel entrance.

His mind put together everything that had happened.

Right before the shot, Harry Ford had stood in front of Flynn. The force of the bullet hitting Ford had thrown him back, and he'd tumbled into Flynn, the kinetic force knocking them both to the ground like bowling pins. Flynn was on his knees, beside Ford.

Lake was trying to staunch the bleeding.

Bloch must've made the same calculations as Mr. Christmas. She'd spotted the open window – made the connection. The angle, the origin of the gunshot, the firing position from beneath the sun.

She drew a Magnum and began unloading. The half pane of glass above the opening in the window disintegrated. Dust and brick exploded around the frame as Bloch fired, reloaded and fired again.

Mr. Christmas ducked back into the alley.

Stepped over the creek of blood on the floor from the dead workman, and began to run down the dark alley.

Angel had interrupted his plans. The ex-sniper would need to be dealt with before he could go after Flynn.

He could not kill the lawyer without knowing more. The former FBI agent Gabriel Lake was now working with Flynn and that changed everything.

How did he know Flynn?

And, more importantly, what did Flynn know about Lake?

Did he know the truth?

PART THREE

29

Eddie

Clarence lay down on the grass, rested his head on his front legs, sighed and stared at the tombstone in front of him.

He stayed like that for a while. Unmoving.

Leaving me to my quiet thoughts.

I put my hand on the cold marble stone.

I made my silent promise and then stood for a while.

The graveyard was quiet this time of the morning. The only sound was the distant thrum of ride-on mowers cutting the grass.

'Come on, Clarence,' I said.

He got up and we walked back to my car. I opened the passenger seat of the Mustang and Clarence leapt in without a word from me. I closed the door, got into the driver's seat and buzzed the windows down about a foot. Normally, Clarence would stick his head out, let his tongue flap in the wind as we drove.

Not this time. Not for a while now.

Clarence curled up in the passenger seat and whimpered. I put my hand on him, stroked him a few times, said, 'I know, pal. I miss him too.'

The ride into the city took forty-five minutes. Clarence didn't move for the entire journey. I kept a hand on him when I could. I wanted him to know that I was there for him.

I left the Mustang in a lot on 99th Street, between Park and Madison, and walked Clarence across the street to Mount Sinai. We took the elevator to a special ward of the ICU. Dogs are not allowed into hospitals, but I dropped a couple of hundred bucks on the right desks in city hall, in front of the right people, and got a special license. Clarence was now officially a therapy animal and could get into more buildings in the city than I could.

Kickbacks and greenbacks.

I opened the door to the private room, unhooked Clarence's leash and he hopped up onto the bed and sat at Harry's feet.

It was the only time Clarence was at peace.

I took a seat beside the bed and put my head in my hands. Listened to Clarence breathing. Listened to the machine that breathed for Harry, and the steady metronomic ticks of his heartbeat monitor.

The paramedics had kept him alive. His blood loss had caused hypovolemic shock, and before the paramedic got blood plasma into Harry's body his organs had begun to falter. Between the blood loss, the shock and the bullet that ripped through his lower ribs and nicked his liver, Harry had a lot of problems. Emergency surgery saved his life.

But everything had taken a toll. Harry had not woken from the operation. EEG showed normal brain function, or as normal as it could be, given he was unconscious and unresponsive.

Harry had not opened his eyes since they'd closed on the sidewalk outside the Cardozo Hotel. Not in weeks.

The surgeon told me Harry could hear me. He could hear Clarence too. Maybe even feel him. Every day I came by with Clarence. Kate and Lake came most days too. Bloch had not come by since he was admitted. I didn't push her to go. Neither did Kate. Bloch didn't do emotions. She kept that all inside. Seeing Harry in a hospital bed was more than she could deal with.

I sat up, looked at Harry. Touched his hand.

'I went to see Harper's grave this morning,' I said.

Harper had been my investigator. Our friend. And maybe could've been someone I might have spent the rest of my life with. I loved her. And I believed she might have loved me too. Until the night she was taken from both of us. It broke my heart. Harry's too. He had just found Clarence not long before Harper was killed. She saw Harry making friends with a stray on the street. And the stray followed him home. And he'd kept him, named him Clarence, after Darrow – the famous civil rights lawyer.

Harper had looked at me when she said Harry liked picking up strays.

I had been a stray too, a conman working the streets, when Harry found me.

'I miss her,' I said out loud. 'I miss you too, Harry. I need you to come back to me.'

I sat for a while and didn't know what I should say. So I just started talking.

'Denise is looking after Clarence most nights. He likes her place. Tony Two Fucks is over at her apartment a lot, and that guy is like a big teddy bear whenever he sees a dog. They're feeding him too many snacks.'

Clarence's head shot up, he looked at me as if in mild indignation, then settled his snout on Harry's ankle.

'The Jackson trial starts in the morning. I'm amazed John has lasted this long. The family has been through hell. Alison is on meds now. Her mother's murder has all but destroyed her. In part, she blames herself, I think. She's barely hanging on. Bloch and Lake have been busy liaising with the police about Alison's mother's murder. Of course, the police don't want to let us talk to Althea. Lake thinks it's too much of a coincidence. He thinks there's a connection with Margaret Blakemore's murder, but we can't find it yet. Althea steals jewelry from the Jacksons – has a piece of bad luck and gets caught. Then Esther, Alison's mother, calls ICE on Althea's family. Althea takes her revenge on Esther. Cops found a bloodied apron in the trash at Esther's home. Once they made the connection that Esther called ICE on Althea, that provided Althea a motive – the cops pick her up, run her DNA and find a match for the DNA left behind on the bloody apron . . .'

The machines hum and beep and wheeze.

And Harry is still and quiet.

'I don't know. There's no connection between Althea and Marga-ret Blakemore. That doesn't stop Alison from tearing herself apart with guilt. What if she hadn't fired Althea? What if she'd called the cops on her as soon as she found out she was a thief? Poor woman. Kate wants to explore the possibility Althea planted the gun in the Jacksons' home. Doesn't make sense to me. She didn't work for Mar-garet Blakemore. And there was nothing missing from the Blakemore home. I don't buy it. Kate says the jury doesn't have to buy it either – but if they consider it a possibility then maybe we have reasonable doubt. It's a stretch. Right now, we don't have anything solid on Todd Ellis and Brett Bale other than rumors and that phone message – but no way to prove the message went to Bale or Ellis.'

I squeezed his hand, let it go. Wiped my face and ran my fingers through my hair.

'I wish you were awake. I need you, Harry.'

His chest rose and fell in time with the rhythm of the machine. His eyes were closed. Sometimes, if I looked at him long enough, I would kid myself into thinking he was waking up. I would see a flut-ter of eye movement. A ripple in the small muscles of his liver-spotted forehead. A twitch of his fingers.

But it was all in my head.

The tubes in his throat kept his mouth open. A trickle of saliva had dried over the corner of his mouth, and crusted the stubble on his chin, which was now almost a beard. I'd asked if I could shave him. The hospital said no. Said one of their staff would do it, but they were busy with other patients. I grabbed some paper towels from the shelf beside the bed, dabbed at his mouth and chin.

Whispered to him that I loved him.

I didn't have to say it. Harry knew it.

I replayed that day, over and over in my mind. The sun had blinded me. And it had all happened so fast – the sudden shadow as Harry stepped in front of me – my eyes hadn't had time to adjust before Harry thumped into my chest, knocking me to the ground.

He was protecting me. Just like he'd done weeks ago when we'd left the office together and faced those bikers parked across the street. Only this time Harry had caught a bullet meant for me. And I hated him and loved him for it. I didn't want the people in my life to suffer because of me – because of what I do. But they always did.

That's why I pushed away my wife. That's why I rarely saw my kid, however much I wanted to be there for her.

Because if something happened to them because of me I just wouldn't want to go on living.

I felt that pain again, in my chest. A tightness and a burning sensation that felt like I was being strangled from the inside. My breath grew ragged and I sat down, hung my head. Forced my lungs to open, my rib cage to expand, sucking the air into my body as best I could. Holding it. Letting it out slow.

It was frightening. The doc said it wasn't my heart. I was way too young and all the tests came back okay.

It was psychological. A panic attack.

Usually followed by neck pain, then headache.

Not for the first time, I wished that I didn't know Harry – that I'd never met Kate, or Bloch, or Lake – that I didn't have a firm with a single employee.

I wished that I was completely alone. Then no one could get hurt because of me.

When my breathing returned to normal, I stood and stretched my neck. The headache was on its way and I popped three Advil dry. Before Clarence got off the bed, he turned and looked at Harry.

Carefully, he picked his paws up, put them down around Harry's body so as not to step on him, and made his way up the bed.

He licked Harry's hand, whimpered.

'Come on, pal,' I said.

Reluctantly, Clarence leapt to the floor.

We stood there for a while, the two of us. Looking at our friend in his hospital bed. Thankful he was alive, but deathly worried that he would never wake up. And it seemed that both of us knew that with the passing of each day the likelihood of Harry opening his eyes was diminishing.

'Mr. Flynn?' said a voice.

I turned, saw one of the nurses who was looking after Harry.

I greeted her and she asked if I had a moment to talk.

'I see you here all the time,' she said, 'and there has been a meeting of the clinical staff in Harry's case and we decided to talk to his relatives and friends. Since you're the main contact, we thought we should tell you first . . .'

My throat tightened, but I managed to find the words.

'Tell me what?'

'Harry is stable, we want to make that clear, but in these types of cases where coma has lasted this long, we often tell the family that it might be time to start thinking about letting go . . .'

'Letting go?'

'Most people who have been under this long don't wake up. I think you and your friends should start preparing for that.'

She smiled, and gently touched my arm. Then turned and walked away.

Clarence whimpered.

We left the hospital, shared two hot dogs in the park, and then I dropped Clarence off at Denise's place.

'Any news? Any change in his condition?' she asked.

I shook my head.

'He'll come around, Eddie,' she said.

I didn't tell her about the conversation I'd had with the nurse. I didn't want to take away her hope.

I fumbled for a response, then asked, 'How can you be so sure?'

'Because Harry Ford is too damn stubborn to lie in bed for long.'

I made my way to the office, watching my back, taking long circuitous routes through the city, and waited by the phone for Bloch to call while I read over the Jackson files for what felt like the fiftieth time. I sat there for hours. Thinking. Reading. Sometime in the evening my eyes must've closed, because when I opened them the office was in darkness and my neck was in agony.

And I was no further forward in finding a defense for John Jackson. I needed to sleep. I had been staying in a different place every night. On my toes all the time.

I wished that this case was already over.

Tomorrow was the beginning.

I wondered if I would live to see the end.

30

Kate

The defense table was annoying Kate.

It must be the floor, she thought. She bent below the desk, saw that one of the rubber feet at the bottom of the table leg closest to her had come away. That made the table rock back and forth, half an inch, whenever she leaned her elbows on it. This caused the row of four pens in front of her to roll out of alignment.

She tore off half a dozen pages from her legal pad, folded them together until they formed a wedge, which she slid underneath the table leg. At first the corners ripped, but, using the toe of her shoe, she managed to force the wad of notepaper between the tiles and the foot of the table.

With both hands on the desk, she tested it for stability. Solid.

She rearranged her pens. Checked her phone, made sure it was on silent. Checked her iPad, made sure it too was on quiet mode. Adjusted the items on the desk, ensuring they were equidistant from one another, square and to hand.

Nodded to herself. Satisfied.

Kate thrived on order – or so some would say. In truth, what Kate truly enjoyed was *restoring* order. Fixing things: organizing files into neat piles with multicolored tabs stuck among the pages, tidying her pens into a neat row in front of her a half-inch apart with the pen clips on the caps all facing to the right, and leveling wobbly defense tables. The habit, or compulsion, applied to people too: taking out corrupt bosses who harassed their staff, adjusting Eddie's tie to make it straight and even, flicking the more unruly parts of Harry's hair until it came into line, making sure Eddie didn't have more than one drink on the rare occasion he joined Harry with a glass of bourbon . . . She drew the line at Gabriel Lake, though – that man's appearance was so disheveled he sometimes made her feel dizzy.

Order needed to be restored in this courtroom. The jury needed to know that John Jackson was an innocent man.

She turned around and glanced at John and Alison.

John's eyes were closed. When the jury came in, he would take his seat at the defense table. For now, he sat in the front row, holding hands with his poor wife. He'd lost twenty pounds since Kate had first met him. And he didn't have twenty to lose. Now, instead of athletic, he looked gaunt. A gray hue permanently shadowed his eyes and bloodless cheeks. A nervous tremor had begun in his left hand. She'd first noticed it after Esther's murder. On Kate's insistence, he went to a doctor. Someone who didn't know him, way out of Manhattan. He got tested, and it wasn't neurological. Which made it psychological. The strain was beginning to tear him apart.

Beside him, Alison stared into nothing, her mind a thousand miles away. Maybe years away. Maybe thinking about the before times. The good times with her family. Before her husband had been accused of murder. Before her mother had been so brutally killed. Before her perfect life had imploded. It was one thing to lose a parent. It was quite another when that parent was the victim of a brutal murder. And the killer was someone Alison had fired. Even now, weeks later, Kate remembered the sight of Alison at the funeral. She hadn't cried at the graveside, she had howled. Kate knew that cry. She had echoed it herself when her own mother died. It was a cry of pain and loss and regret made only by those who are savagely broken. Sometimes, grief can be a machine that grinds your very bones. And Alison was still in that grinder.

Alison hadn't been eating either. She covered up the worry lines that crept around her eyes, but no amount of make-up could disguise the hollow look on her face.

She'd almost lost everything. If John was convicted, Kate dreaded to think what might happen to Alison. Some people can take whatever life throws at them. Alison had taken some heavy hits in the last few months and one more might knock her down so hard that she would never get up.

Kate smiled, reassuringly, but it seemed that neither John nor Alison could see her. Their minds were overcome with pain and terrible fear.

Al Parish sat beside Alison. He was checking his phone. Probably work emails. To Al, the Jacksons were just another couple of clients. They meant nothing more to him than how a stockbroker would think of a portfolio of products, or a carpenter would think of a piece of pinewood or ash. They were commodities. A file. A name on top of an Excel spreadsheet of billable hours.

To Kate, they were people. Broken people who needed her help to get fixed.

Kate looked to her right. There were two chairs there. The one on the end would soon be taken by John. The chair beside Kate, the chair for lead counsel in the case, was empty.

Eddie said he would be late.

Kate would take a note of Castro's opening statement, then give her own.

Jury selection had been uneventful. Twelve ordinary New Yorkers, none more biased or more even-handed than the next. Thanks to Eddie, this case had not received anything like the media attention Castro had craved. Kate also suspected that he had a hand in keeping Esther's murder out of the papers so as not to risk the jury feeling in any way sorry for the Jacksons. Still, the main thing was the jury pool had not been infected with fifty news articles speculating on why her client might have killed the one-time starlet Margaret Blakemore. Most of the jurors had not heard of the case before. Some had remembered a mention of the killing around the time of the murder, but nothing else. And certainly nothing that would sway their opinion when it came time to deliver a verdict.

Crime journalists, mostly for the web, huddled in rows at the back of the courtroom. There were few other people in attendance. Even the victim's widower had not shown up. Maybe it was too much for him. Or he had moved on already. Kate got the impression Margaret Blakemore had lived in a loveless marriage.

Noise from the prosecution table to her left drew Kate's attention. Castro was standing over his assistant district attorneys, pointing at a laptop screen and whispering. Even though he was trying to keep the volume low, Kate could see he was having trouble keeping his emotions in check. His cheeks were flushed, but he didn't look pissed off. Still, his pale, ivory-colored suit set off the redness in his complexion. The man in white. The hero. Or so he would have everyone believe. One of the assistants hit some keys on the laptop, then Castro noticed Kate staring at him. He reached over and quickly slammed the laptop closed.

He was up to something. Even though he wore a white suit, he was no innocent.

She glanced over her shoulder at the doors of the court.

No sign of Eddie. Not yet.

She could handle the case, and was confident in her skills, but she felt better having Eddie beside her. Whatever Castro could throw at them – Eddie could throw back a lot worse. Kate was a straight shooter. But to win, with the entire weight of the State of New York thrown against you, sometimes you had to play a little dirty to even the odds. That was Eddie's department.

Right now, he wasn't even in the building.

She thought about Harry, lying in his hospital bed. She missed his strength and his wisdom. Most of all, she missed his friendship.

'All rise,' said the clerk.

Everyone in the courtroom stood. The excited chatter from the prosecution table ceased. John kissed Alison, and left the public benches to take his place at the defense table beside Kate.

The Honorable Arthur Zell took his seat in the judge's chair. He wasn't a bad judge. Not a lot of experience and very little of it in criminal law. Fair minded in that he often had to check the law in the privacy of his chambers. He didn't just rely on what the prosecutor told him. He was still getting used to wearing the robes of his office. There were stitches visible all along one side of his robe where he had repeatedly caught it on doorknobs and stair railings. With any luck, he wouldn't interfere too much in the case, which was all you could hope for in a judge.

Judge Zell reminded the jury of their obligations to keep an open mind, not to discuss the case among themselves until all the evidence had been heard, and then asked Castro to give his opening statement.

Kate felt the defense table rocking. She bent down to check if the paper wedge had come loose. It was still in place. It was then that she noticed John was shaking. His hands were clamped together, resting on the table.

Gently, Kate put her hand over his, and separated his fingers from each hand, told him to put his palms on his thighs. He couldn't help his hands from shaking, so there was no point in him trying. But Kate told him the best thing he could do was not to let the jury see his nerves. People interpret others' anxiety in different ways. Some would see John sweating, shaking in fear, and believe him to be guilty – right then – right there. No need for any testimony or evidence. The guy looks guilty, so he must be guilty.

Kate didn't need any more hurdles to leap over. Not with this jury.

She leaned over, whispered to John, 'Take it easy. I know this is hard, but the jury are watching now. Don't react to anything Castro says. He wants you to get pissed off and show anger in this room, in front of this jury. Just keep your expression neutral. No nervous smiling, no angry looks.'

John nodded.

'Remember, Castro has some forensic evidence, but he doesn't have a story to tell the jury. There's no motive. That's our first strong point in this case. We need the jury to have unanswered questions in their minds. No story, no conviction. Okay?'

He nodded again, took a deep breath.

Kate turned her attention to Castro, who stood in front of the jury.

'Members of the jury, I want to thank you for your service during this trial. By the end of this case, you will have performed your sworn civic duty. You will have returned the only true verdict in this case – guilty. And you will have put a murderer behind bars for life. That is what this city requires of you. And I have no doubt you will not shy away from this duty. When it all comes down to it, this case is very simple. The defense . . .'

Castro pointed at Kate, and then continued. 'The defense will try to make this more complicated than it really is. It's up to you if you want to listen to them. Me, I keep things simple and true. Facts, ladies and gentlemen of the jury. We deal in facts. The who, what, where and when.

'Who killed Margaret Blakemore? What happened during that crime? Where and when did it happen? The prosecution case will prove the following, beyond all reasonable doubt. Margaret Blakemore died from multiple gunshot wounds. She was shot in her home on June second, sometime around midnight. The gun that fired those fatal shots was found during a lawful police search of the defendant's property. The murder weapon was in his closet. And it has his DNA on it.'

None of this was news to Kate, or to John – it was as she expected. A simple, clean and powerful statement to the jury. An attempt by Castro to frame the case within his parameters. She had made a note while he talked. Castro had talked about the facts – Who? What? Where? And when?

But he had left out the most important question. The one the jury would be asking themselves constantly.

Why?

'That is more than enough for any jury to convict this defendant . . .'

Kate knew Castro was winding down. She felt that tingle of nerves in her stomach. It would very soon be time for her to make the defense opening statement.

'. . . and, members of the jury, once you have heard the testimony from the prosecution witnesses, those facts will become concrete in your mind. And, with that, there is only one verdict – guilty.'

Castro sat down. The judge offered Kate her chance to frame the case for the jury. Like all good lawyers, she knew the best thing to do was to ball up the prosecution's speech and throw it right back at them.

'Members of the jury, my name is Kate Brooks. I represent the notable pediatric neurosurgeon, John Jackson. He is an outstanding member of our community.'

She glanced at John. He had threaded his fingers again, held them on the table, shaking the whole damn desk. One thing Harry had taught her was that a disadvantage, or a weakness in a case, was just a matter of perspective. If you looked at it from a different angle, maybe it could be a strength.

She continued, 'Hundreds of children have had full and meaningful lives because of the skilled hands of my client, John Jackson. Take a moment, please, members of the jury, and just take a look at my client's hands now.'

The jury turned to look at John. They saw the fear and hurt in his eyes, and ripples of that pain fanned out into his shaking fingers.

'My client is afraid. He is an innocent man on trial for his life. And all he has done is serve our community and save the lives of our children.'

Kate knew to pause, let the jury take a good look at John. She wanted them to adjust their thinking – to take a different angle on what was in front of them. This wasn't a guilty man who had been caught by the system – this was someone who has been wronged and has paid for it dearly.

'Now, John Jackson needs you, members of the jury. His life, his career, has been destroyed by these false allegations and at the end of this trial we will ask you to give him his life back. The evidence that Mr. Castro outlined is all disputed, and you will understand by the end of this case how forensic evidence doesn't always tell the full story. Speaking of stories, that is something very important to bear in mind. The prosecution want you to answer the who, where, when and how questions. But they don't want you to think about the most important question of all. Why? Why would John Jackson kill his neighbor? There is no answer to that question for two reasons. First, the prosecution have no connection between John Jackson and the victim in this case. They can't tell you *why* because they don't know. They don't know because John Jackson didn't kill Margaret Blakemore. He had no reason to harm her. But someone else did. Someone with motive who is not sitting in front of you today . . .'

'Objection, Your Honor,' said Castro.

Kate turned round, genuinely surprised. It was relatively unheard of for a prosecutor to object to a defense opening statement. The judge called for both parties to approach the bench.

'What is the meaning of this?' asked the judge.

'My apologies, Your Honor. I had to object. Defense counsel was misleading the jury.'

'What?' was all Kate could manage.

'I will give Miss Brooks the benefit of the doubt. I don't think she did it deliberately. Maybe she hasn't had time to read our latest filing,' said Castro.

Kate felt a chill on her neck.

'What filing?' asked Judge Zell.

'We have filed a motion for witness anonymity . . .'

Kate's mind flashed on Castro's hushed conversation before the judge entered the room. His ADA must've hit send on the electronic filing right before the judge came into court. Kate left the judge's bench, retrieved her iPad from her desk and came back. Sure enough, she'd received a copy of the prosecution motion. They'd held it back on purpose, making sure she wouldn't see it until after her opening statement, so they could interrupt her, ruin the opening of her case.

'What is this?' asked the judge.

'Your Honor, the prosecution have obtained new evidence from a witness who will only testify anonymously. They are fearful of retribution from the defendant, and we believe this witness qualifies for anonymity. This witness will tell the jury exactly why John Jackson murdered Margaret Blakemore.'

31

Eddie

'Could I have two organic eggs – poached – lightly toasted sourdough toast and a cup of hot water with a slice of organic lemon, please?'

The server squinted at Lake, pursed her lips together and gathered her thoughts before replying.

'We don't do poached,' she said.

'What about boiled?' asked Lake.

'We got a grill and a hotplate. You can have scrambled, fried or raw, *honey*.'

The word *honey* came out of the waitress's mouth, for sure, but it sounded an awful lot like *asshole*.

'For the sake of my sanity, he'll have fried eggs. I'll have the pancakes and lots of coffee, please, ma'am,' I said.

'Same,' said Bloch.

The waitress gave me a nice smile, gathered our menus and disappeared with the order. We'd been up most of the night. I'd crashed at Bloch's place, found Lake there. They'd been spitballing and working all the angles. It was coming up on seven in the morning. I needed food, coffee, a shower and then it would be time to meet Kate after the mid-morning recess. She said she could handle the opening statement on her own. I wanted to be there, for support if for nothing else, but it was more important right now to try to figure out what the hell was really going on behind this case.

'I can't get my head around all of this,' I said. 'I get the feeling there's a whole other story going on that I can't see. We have two murders on or connected to this street. We have Margaret Blakemore, but there's no link to John beyond the murder weapon turning up in his home. Then Alison's mother, supposedly killed by their maid who got caught stealing and Esther reported her family to ICE. I know Kate thinks Althea planted the gun, but Althea has no connection to Blakemore.'

Lake said, 'There's no connection between Althea and Bale, nor Ellis either.'

Bloch said, 'I get that Althea had a motive to kill Esther Hanson, but why dump her apron, with her DNA and the victim's blood on it in the trash at the victim's home? That seems dumb to me. And yet there were no other forensics found in the house so far to link Althea to that address. Could be the same person who killed Blakemore? All I know is the killer wanted Althea arrested for murder,' said Bloch.

I leaned back in the booth, let that roll around in my head. The waitress brought coffee and Lake's hot water with lemon. I thanked her and she smiled at me then shot a dirty look at Lake as she left.

'How would the killer know to pin the murder on Althea? How would they know Esther reported Althea's family to ICE?' I asked.

We sat there in silence for a moment.

'What if Esther didn't report Althea's family to ICE? Those tip lines aren't like 911. The calls are not recorded. Tips can be anonymous. Why give a name at all?' I asked.

'Okay,' said Lake, 'so this perp kills Esther, for some reason we don't know, and frames Althea. That kind of MO fits with the Blakemore killing. Margaret was shot – okay, different method – but then our client was framed. There are some similarities.'

'I'm with Bloch. I'm not sure it's the same person who killed both victims,' I said. 'There's someone who is very smart, pulling a lot of levers here. Maybe we're wrong about everything. Maybe Kate is right. Maybe Althea is behind some of this and she's working with someone else. I just can't piece it all together . . .'

The waitress came over with our breakfast. We ate in silence. Bloch and I worked through the food. I ate without really tasting anything. I just needed the calories. Flipping over his eggs, Lake examined them, weighed his options and finally just ate his toast.

When I finished my plate, I asked for more coffee and looked out of the window. It was a Manhattan summer morning and the sun was never lazy in this town. It burned the sidewalks it could reach and boiled the sewers beneath. The people who flowed past the diner wore shades, caps and tees. But there was no escaping the heat in this city. Traffic rolled slow, hot tires greased the faded asphalt and the wind was taking the day off.

'I wish Harry was here,' I said.

Bloch said nothing.

Lake said, 'I'll check on him tonight.'

Bloch still said nothing, but I saw her shoulders fall when she heard Lake say he'd visit Harry.

'It's not your fault, Bloch,' I said.

'I never should've let you two leave the hotel,' she said. 'It is my fault.'

'How could it be? The whole reason this happened is because I threatened to expose a corrupt cop. I brought this pain down on all of us.'

'But you did the right thing. I felt something that day outside the hotel. I didn't act on my instinct. Harry's gone because of me.'

'He's not gone. He's still alive. He'll pull through . . .' My throat tightened, and I couldn't finish the sentence.

Taking in a huge breath, Bloch expanded her chest, held that air, then blew it out.

'You know he stepped in front me,' I said. 'Like he did when those bikers were outside the office. He took the bullet for me. Don't beat yourself up. This is all on me.'

The waitress brought over the check and I counted out some bills, waved away Lake's attempt to pay. Bloch couldn't speak. Didn't say much at the best of times, but she held her thoughts close. She had said too much already. Whatever pain she felt over Harry, she wanted to keep the rest inside.

Both of them left the diner. I sat there with my thoughts and a hot refill of coffee. My mind ablaze with guilt, theories and a terrible worry that the only man who would end up paying for these crimes would be the wrong one – our client John.

The sun moved behind a cloud and a man walked into the diner.

He wore a black suit, crisp white button-down shirt and black silk tie. In his right hand he carried a black fedora. I noticed him because of the sharp suit, and the fact that he didn't wait at the sign for a table. Instead, he made his way toward me as soon as he came in. When he reached my booth, he stopped. Looked at me.

No one was going to shoot me in a public diner. Even so, I had my right hand in my jacket pocket and my fingers threaded through my ceramic knuckles.

The man had pale skin, and pale eyes. They were a strange color, as if they'd once been a bright, saturated blue and they'd faded with time and light into pastel.

'Mr. Flynn, I am extremely pleased to meet you,' said the man, but didn't offer a hand in greeting. 'I would shake your hand, but I can see it's wrapped around a weapon in your pocket. Please don't be alarmed – you will have no need of it. Not at the moment, anyway.'

Without a word from me, he sat down across from me where Bloch and Lake had been just a few minutes before. His movements were smooth and controlled. He slid into the booth with all the grace of an old movie star.

'I know you are busy, but you and I should talk. My name is Mr. Christmas. I don't want this to appear rude, but I have been planning to kill you . . .'

32
Ruby

Ruby had been busy this past twenty-four hours. She didn't like talking to police. And the district attorney, Mr. Castro, gave her the creeps with his white suit and big smile.

They were pleased with her. Told her she was doing the right thing. That there was no longer any reason to be afraid.

They would protect her.

They would make sure John Jackson paid for the murder of Maggs.

The red priest's voice was in her mind now. She could hear him even when she wasn't in the Jacksons' home. It had first happened last night, as she put her mother to bed. At first, she thought it was a fly, buzzing around her. Then the buzz intensified, the tone altered, the pitch changing, morphing, becoming the whispers . . .

Rubeeeeeeeeeeee . . .

It was unsettling, at first, to have the red priest in her head. The pressure felt enormous, and it had caused her to stagger, lose her balance. Almost falling on top of her mother. She'd held on to the bedrail. Closed her eyes, breathed in and out.

'Are you okay?' asked her mother.

'Fine, it's just a headache.'

'Take some Advil and drink some water.'

Even at her age, in her condition, she was still her mother. Soon she would have a new home. People to look after her. Wash her. Dress her. Feed her. Ruby had to get away. She had to silence the red priest and go somewhere where no one could ever find her.

There was a strange comfort now in the whispers. Somehow, she didn't feel so alone. The red priest was with her. He was wicked and cruel, but he loved Ruby. And, if she did as he told her, he wouldn't shout.

Ruby hated it when he shouted. The pressure in her head would build like a boiling pot, her ears felt like they wanted to explode, and the pain . . . and then the blood. Her nose would bleed, but only a little. She told him she would do as he asked. And he would calm down. His voice no longer like a booming mic in her head, just a soothing breeze of whispers.

Ruby's letters to Ellis and Bale gave them time. They had the money, of course, but they would need time to ensure that it could be paid without anyone else noticing that money had slipped from their accounts.

The letter gave detailed bank account instructions. The money had to be paid today. Noon was the deadline. Ruby had needed time, too, to make arrangements to hide the money from anyone who might try to trace it.

Ruby would need to move the money straight away. She now had accounts set up in more than a dozen banks under different company names. She had watched a tutorial video on how to move money, and in what amounts, so as not to arouse suspicion or trigger any money-laundering inquiries. She just had to wait for the transfer to hit that first account, then she could work.

She would have time. The Jackson trial started this morning, and Ruby was supposed to be looking after Tomas, but only until the end of the trial. The Jacksons were planning to leave town for at least a month, no matter what the verdict. If it went well, John would be coming too. If he was convicted, Alison would take Tomas and get away from the nightmare of media and abuse that would inevitably follow.

Ruby couldn't wait for them to leave. In truth, she couldn't believe that they had stuck around for this long, despite the hellscape that their lives had now become. God knows, Ruby had tried to make it as bad as possible.

Once they were gone, Ruby could act.

After that, Ruby was leaving too.

Her mother would be in her new care facility, and Ruby, well, Ruby would be free. She had begun dreaming about open-top cars and long desert roads.

Far away from all of her problems.

33
Eddie

'What kind of a name is Mr. Christmas? Where's your red suit?'

The man across from me in the booth smiled. With his ivory skin, milk-blue eyes and sharp suit, he didn't look like the kind of guy who laughed easily, but his amusement seemed genuine.

'I'm just beginning to like you, Mr. Flynn. You are endowed with many admirable qualities. Of course, that doesn't mean I won't kill you, but not now, at least. So you can relax, take your hand off that weapon in your pocket. I can also assure you that I am not the person who injured your mentor, Mr. Ford. I am much more discerning in my professional approach. I am not carrying a firearm presently. There's a blade in my sleeve, but I don't foresee the need to use it. Not unless you force my hand . . .'

His voice was deep and strong. It came from his chest. And on the way out of his mouth his lips and tongue moved eloquently to make sure he hit every syllable for perfect pronunciation. While his tone seemed friendly, even though he'd just told me he was planning to kill me, his language was formal. I guessed he was an educated man. His fingers laced together and he placed his palms on the table, extending his elbows. Chin up. Good posture. There was a confidence that oozed out of him. There was an odor from the man, something citrusy, with wood and tobacco. It smelled expensive. Like the suit.

I took my fingers from the ceramic knuckles in my jacket pocket and put my hands on the table. He watched me, his expression neutral. I got the impression that he could move fast if he wanted to. And I had no doubt he could use the blade he had in his sleeve. Who keeps a knife in their sleeve? Someone who had a special sheath made for it, no doubt. A custom job. This wasn't Mr. Christmas's first rodeo.

I'd been around killers from the time I was a kid. I remember sitting on a bar stool in a Brooklyn dive, sipping a Pepsi and eating peanuts when I was eight years old while my father shot craps in the back, or played cards. The big guys with moustaches and suits who read the paper in that bar knew my father was working, and they were taking a cut from whatever he could con out of the regular clientele. Those big men kept the Pepsis coming, and I sat and listened to them talk and tell jokes. There's something about men who have killed other human beings for a living. It's in their eyes. It's in their voice. They seem both regular people and completely alien. They understand that there are social conventions, relationships with peers and loved ones, but they also know there's an off switch. That if they have a problem they can solve it by putting three .22 rounds in the other person's head.

Mr. Christmas was a killer. And it showed.

But only to those who knew what they were looking at.

'Who shot Harry?' I asked.

'We can talk about that later. There are other, more interesting matters to discuss.'

'If you came to buy me breakfast, you're too late. I already paid and I ain't hungry,' I said.

'This isn't a social call, Mr. Flynn. While I am not technically here on business, hence your current good health, I am not here to make small talk either. Now that I have introduced myself, I think we can get to the point.'

He paused, caught the waitress's eye and politely asked for coffee. The waitress brought over a cup for him, and gave me another refill. I was glad I'd tipped well.

He first stared into the cup, warily, then brought it to his lips. There was a mild look of distaste as he smacked his lips and set the coffee cup down.

'I spent eight years in Sicily. It spoiled me. The coffee was so good there I can still smell it. And this . . .' He pointed to the mug. 'Forgive me – I digress. I wanted to enquire as to the nature of your relationship with Mr. Lake.'

When he'd sat down, I had no idea what this guy wanted to talk about. I had never met anyone more polite who appeared intent on killing me at some point down the line. It was a little like meeting the guy who was going to make your coffin. Whatever guesses I could've made about what Mr. Christmas wanted, I would not have thought Gabriel Lake would have been his point of interest.

'He's my friend. And my investigator. Freelance. Do you know him?'

'We've met,' said Mr. Christmas. 'It was a brief interlude, but pleasing nonetheless. My interest in Mr. Lake is professional, mostly. He used to work for the Federal Bureau of Investigation . . .'

He gave the feds their full and correct title. It was the Bureau of Investigation, not Investigation*s*. If a guy ever flashes a badge and says he's from the Federal Bureau of Investigation*s*, you can be pretty sure the badge and the guy that goes with it are fake.

'I know his résumé,' I said. 'He worked in the Behavioral Analysis Unit. Lake hunted serial killers. He's taken that business into the private sector now.'

Again with the smile, Mr. Christmas said, 'I am aware he is no longer with the Bureau. Has he ever told you why that is the case?'

I nodded.

'Did he tell you the whole story, I wonder?'

'He said he got a tip-off from a federal informer about the whereabouts of a serial killer. Lake went to the property, kicked the door down, but by then it was too late. It wasn't a killer's home – it was a heroin bank. Lake was almost killed, but he took out every armed man in the building before he passed out from blood loss. That much was in the newspapers. Or most of it. By the time Lake woke up in the hospital, the informer was dead. Lake thinks someone in the Bureau set him up and sent him into a death trap. That last part didn't make the news cycle.'

Mr. Christmas cocked his head, his expression curious. 'There are certain aspects of the events of that evening that have lain hidden. Either by necessity or design. He didn't tell you the identity of the killer he was searching for that evening?'

His tone had changed. The timber more somber. He didn't need to spell it out.

'He was looking for you?' I asked.

Mr. Christmas softly closed and then opened his eyes as he gave a slight nod by way of agreement.

'Mr. Lake drew the ire of agents in the Bureau because of his some-what radical approach to the identification, pursuit and detection of those who regularly commit murder, either by desire or as a legitimate business enterprise. Some in the Bureau thought he was right. If he had been allowed to remain in the service and progress, he would have altered that organization. He could have embarrassed some agents. Ended the careers and the life's work of others. Mr. Lake had been warned – or perhaps *threatened* is a better description – that he may become a target. I may say that his courage and determination drove him onward, but I could equally offer the comment that he is both stubborn and perhaps over-confident in his beliefs. Needless to say, the outcome was predictable.'

'What's your interest in Gabriel?' I asked.

'He intrigues me. I have been in my current line of work for a very long time. It is not often that I meet an opponent of that skill. And, I feel, in another life, it could well have been *me* chasing *him*. He may be your friend. He may be a brilliant investigator. But he is also a killer. I think you knew that already.'

'Are you targeting Lake?'

'No. I have no interest in killing Mr. Lake. It so happens that he has stumbled into my business here, with you . . .'

I'd had enough. My best friend was in a coma. I had a case starting for a client I knew was innocent and there was a real killer out there, somewhere, walking free.

I leaned forward, said, 'I don't really have time for a walk down memory lane with a hitman. Even one as polite and well-mannered as you. I got shit to do, so if you want to kill me, I suggest you make your move. Plenty have tried and failed. You know who shot Harry?'

He nodded.

'Who is he?'

'His name is Angel. Or at least that is his moniker in the trade. He is a former Special Forces operative. Seal team sniper. Quite skilled. His identity should not be difficult to discover. As I understand it, his experiences in Afghanistan and Iraq were unpleasant, to say the least. His team was tasked with tracking and executing an ISIS operative who targeted US military patrols. This operative's method was to strap explosives to children and make them get close to the American soldiers before . . . well . . . you can imagine. Angel provided cover for the patrols. In the military, soldiers are conditioned to kill on the basis that if they fail to execute the enemy, they are essentially sacrificing one of their comrades. Kill to protect the man next to you. That works quite well. In Angel's case, he had to shoot more than a dozen children in order to protect his team. Not all of those children were carrying explosives. It's difficult to know if it happened after he shot the first child, or the twelfth, but it appears that something inside Angel broke. Something that could not be put back together. I have respect for him as a fellow professional, but if you don't kill him I think I might.'

'Why would you kill him?'

'There are a number of reasons. First, he took out one of my targets before I could pay them a visit. He is a competitor, but in my line of work competition is, shall we say, cutthroat? Let's call it a Darwinian

approach to the economics of murder. With fewer professionals operating, prices will go up. There is also the challenge to consider. Most
of my targets don't know I exist until they feel my blade at their
throat. Angel knows my work. I'll enjoy the test.'

I got up, slowly, confidently, so Mr. Christmas would not see it as
a challenge.

'Give New York's Finest a message from me, will you?'

'Certainly,' he said.

'Tell them to back off. Before it's too late.'

'I'm afraid they won't respond well to that message. Angel and I
are not the only ones chasing the contract on your head. The 88s are
looking for you too.'

'The neo-Nazis?'

'The very same.'

'Any other good news for me?'

'Yes, I think matters are coming to a head. All of this will be over
quite soon. One way or another.'

34
Ruby

Since Althea's betrayal, Alison had relied on Ruby more and more. She'd even given her a key to the house. When Ruby arrived at the Jacksons' on the first morning of the trial, and let herself in, Alison was in the kitchen wearing her dark business suit. She was getting used to seeing her without make-up. Not that she usually wore much, just foundation and some light touches here and there. Since her mother's death, there was no point. Alison cried every day. It wasn't just loss – it was a dark wound deep inside her that would never fully heal. And today was the start of the process that would see her husband sent to prison for the rest of his life. It was, in a manner, another form of grief.

'Let Tomas lie in bed for as long as he wants,' said Alison. 'None of us are getting much sleep. There's leftovers in the . . .'

A great burst of emotion erupted from Alison's chest. She almost convulsed with worry, her stomach and chest heaving out great sobs. Ruby pressed her lips together, moved closer and gently rubbed Alison's back, like one would a child.

'It's going to be okay. I know it. John is a good man. He didn't do this terrible thing. People will see that,' said Ruby.

'I just . . .' Alison tried to voice her thought, as if doing so would bring her some ease. 'I made a family lasagna last night. John loves my lasagna. I keep cooking him his favorite meals. I can't help it. It's so stupid. He's too sick with worry to eat, but I keep thinking he better enjoy this food now because if it all goes wrong he'll never get to eat with us again . . .'

It's the simple things that sometimes hurt people in times of great trouble. Smells, food, souvenirs on the fridge, keepsakes, an old coffee mug, the sound of a key in the front door, even a chair with its cushion worn thin and still bearing the impression of that person – little everyday landmines that the mind latches on to – bringing all the pent-up existential emotion crashing into the real world. For Ruby, it was the sound of ice cubes tumbling into a glass, the smell of bourbon. The worst of all was the buzzing.

The interminable hum of the blowfly's wings.

'I'll look after Tomas, my little sweetie munchkin. Maybe play a game with him. Try to take his mind off things,' said Ruby. 'He's a tough cookie.'

John came into the kitchen, pale, drawn, as if he'd not seen the sun or a decent meal in weeks. Which was probably true. The half-inch gap between his shirt collar and his neck told the same story. It was as if his life had stopped. Ruby knew he was hanging on to a thin rope – blind hope and faith in his lawyers.

Ruby would be there, in the courtroom, one day very soon, to watch the last thread of hope snap in John's eyes.

'Good luck today,' said Ruby. The couple gathered themselves and left. No sooner had the door closed than the buzzing sounded. Louder and louder.

Ruuubeeeeeee.

Look at me.

She moved to the hallway and stared at the red priest. His face had changed. His eyes had turned black and fearsome, his lips drawn back to reveal sharp, pointed teeth and a long black tongue that slithered from his mouth.

Kill the boy.

'No, I can do it another way.'

Your way is not working.

'They are leaving after the trial.'

Kill the boy, kill the boy, kill the boy . . .

Raising her eyes to the ceiling, she imagined Tomas upstairs, sleeping peacefully, and the priest's murderous mantra faded back into so much buzzing.

Ruby opened her laptop and logged into her deposit account. The money should be in by noon. Ruby needed that money. She had worked hard for it. Killed for it.

She checked the balance.

One dollar.

She kept refreshing the screen. At first every ten minutes. Then every eight minutes, then every five minutes and so on, as the clock ticked down and it got closer to noon.

11.55 a.m.

Refresh.

Balance one dollar.

'Ruby, can I have a sandwich, please?' asked Tomas.

The boy stood at the kitchen counter, still in his pajamas, rubbing sleep out of his eyes. She had let him have a lazy morning. His parents were in court, facing the end of a nightmare and, Ruby hoped, the beginning of a new one when John was convicted. Courtrooms were frightening places where trauma, pain and death collided in a war of words. Ruby was not looking forward to being in court either. But she had no choice. She had to go, and make sure John was convicted. She needed the family gone from her life.

'You haven't even had breakfast yet,' said Ruby.

11.56 a.m.

Refresh.

One dollar.

'I don't want breakfast. I just want a peanut butter and jelly sandwich. And some juice,' said Tomas, the crackle from a night's sleep still in this throat.

'Just go wait in the living room, honey bunny. I'll bring it to you.'

'Can't I just have it right now?'

11.57 a.m.

Refresh.

One dollar.

Ruby ignored him, all her focus on the laptop screen. Her mind rolling through possibility after possibility. They had both paid, but there was a delay in the transfer. Neither of them had paid and it was going to be a fight – one she couldn't win because Ruby's time was almost up. She needed to run. And she needed that money.

Goddamn it, why hadn't they paid? Did they want to get their lives ruined? Or get themselves killed?

'Ruby . . .'

11.58 a.m.

Refresh.

Screen loading.

One dollar.

'Ruby! I'm hungry!' Shouting. Whining.

She smiled at him. A big, beaming smile. Inside, her plans were crumbling. Her teeth squeaked as she ground her molars against one another.

What the hell? This can't be happening.

This. Can't. Be. Happeninggggggggggg . . .

'Ruby!'

'Shut the fuck up, Tomas!'

The child stumbled backwards, his somnolent eyes suddenly and shockingly wide open. His mouth agape. Body frozen. Tears welled in those big eyes and as Ruby caught hold of herself, and reached for him, fear took hold and he backed away.

'Tomas, I'm *so* sorry. Please, I just got distracted. I'm sorry.'

He ran out of the kitchen and his little feet pounded up the stairs.

Ruby swore. She couldn't go after him now. He would need to calm down first.

Then she heard him calling from the landing. Anger and sincerity in his little boy's voice.

'I'm going to tell my mom what you did. You used a bad word and you yelled at me!'

Oh no, no, you're not, thought Ruby. She was so close now. Just another few days. Just another few jobs. Tomas could not wreck things now.

No matter what, he could *not* tell his mother.

Tomas would see that soon. Either he would calm down and forget what had just happened, or Tomas would not be here when his mother returned.

12.01 p.m.

Refresh.

All the air left Ruby's body.

Balance $500,001.

'Tomas, little buddy, I'm sorry . . .' said Ruby.

35
Mr. Christmas

The little revival movie theatre was empty, apart from one man.

He sat in the eighth row. In the dead center. Row H. Seat fifteen of thirty. The one seat that gave him the closest view of the entire screen which his field of vision could comfortably accommodate.

The house lights were down, but the up-lighting was on, illuminating the red velvet curtains lining both sides of the screening room. The thirty-five millimeter projector wasn't even switched on. A sixty-foot-wide screen sat dead and gray in front of him. The smell of popcorn rose from the floor, along with other more unpleasant odors.

Mr. Christmas rarely ate as he watched movies. Occasionally, when he craved the darkness and solitude of the movie theatre, he sometimes bought a soda and a hot dog. He had no taste for popcorn. Yet, he did enjoy that smell. It was wrapped up in his childhood, and his teens, and, for that matter, it was an odor that had accompanied him for his whole life. Rarely did a week go by without a visit to a cinema, no matter where he found himself.

He had enjoyed drive-in theatres in hot, filthy parking lots in Arizona, mouse-infested 1920s movie palaces in Detroit, modern multiplex theatres in LA and single-screen revival houses that attracted hipsters and cinephiles alike.

He tipped his head back and let his gaze rest on the ceiling. He used to do this as a kid, letting the vast blackness of the paneled ceiling wash over him. And the same sensation came, just as he had experienced as a child – the overwhelming belief and fear that the ceiling was going to collapse and fall on top of him. The sensation was so strong that an electric tickle travelled from the back of his legs down through his calves and into his ankles.

He shivered with the pleasure of fear.

Mr. Christmas raised a hand to the projectionist. While he sometimes enjoyed the company of a few strangers in the movies, he much preferred having the screen all to himself. Which, just as on this occasion, necessitated Mr. Christmas purchasing every seat in the house. It was not a small amount of money, but while his finances were not infinite they were very large indeed. He enjoyed some of the finer things in life, but his lifestyle was not in any way extravagant. He owned several properties, drove a Lincoln,, but didn't have a boat, nor a plane, nor any other item that proved an effective way to burn through a fortune.

He spent his money on fine clothes. Good coffee.

And going to the movies.

The up-lighting dimmed, sending the vast room into darkness. This screen was now a spaceship. A magical thing that could transport him to anywhere in this world, or out of it.

The screen came to life and the Paramount logo filled his heart.

His phone began to vibrate.

He raised his hand. Nothing happened at first. Then he waved it and the screen froze and died.

Mr. Christmas retrieved his phone from his jacket and took the call.

'I'm just enjoying some thinking time,' said Mr. Christmas. 'I don't wish to appear rude, but I thought I would just explain why I would like to keep this call short.'

'Don't you ever just say hi?'

'Hi,' said Mr. Christmas.

'Forget it. Look, I'm just giving you a courtesy call. While you're on the Flynn job. Seeing as how you're in town, another job just came in and I thought you might want to double up.'

'Is it an open contract?'

'Closed. It's a private party. And it pays a little better than the Flynn contract. Seventy-five, plus expenses.'

'Interesting. It might be worthwhile to take an intellectual detour and cover my expenses for the whole trip. What's the job?'

'Recovery and closure.'

'Tell me more.'

'Our client wants his two hundred and fifty thousand dollars back. He paid it so he could trace his blackmailer, following the money trail. It's a young woman called Ruby Johnson. Get the money back. Kill the girl.'

36
Eddie

I rode the subway to the courthouse, watching my back the whole time. You don't survive as a con artist on these streets without eyes in the back of your head. I knew the basics. Altering my route. Criss-crossing streets. Stopping and doubling back. Watching my angles so I could catch glimpses of what was behind me reflected in the store windows, train windows and polished granite tiles as I made my way through the city.

I also couldn't help but glance up, keeping watch for any windows that were ajar, and making sure I was never out in the open on the sidewalk. I kept pedestrians close by, matching their pace – keeping their bodies between me and those open windows.

Moving through Manhattan on the subways and sidewalks, you can see a thousand faces. Burning them into my memory, I had to make sure I didn't see any of them again on a corner, or a platform, or on the stairs. Somewhere where they shouldn't be. It was like bathing in people and paranoia. By the time I reached my destination, my brain was fried.

I called Lake. 'Where are you?'

'On West 74th Street. Nobody has moved this morning. Bale and Ellis are still home.'

'I just had an interesting conversation with a guy who says he knows you. His name is Mr. Christmas,' I said.

Lake said nothing for a moment, then, 'Has he taken the contract from Buchanan's crew?'

'He's planning on taking out a few of his colleagues first. But, yeah, I think he will.'

'Then he's a dead man.'

'He said you were chasing him when you got lured into that stash house.'

'That's right. And I came out alive. He's on my list.'

'Anything else you need to tell me about him?'

'He loves old movies, Marlon Brando, and he's a total psychopath.'

'Good to know,' I said, and ended the call. There was a time and a place for asking Lake more questions about this man. Now was not that time.

I felt safer as I stepped inside the courthouse. I breezed through security and got into the elevator alone. As the doors closed, I let my eyes shut too.

My head felt like it was in a blender.

Harry was unconscious in the hospital and it was likely I was going to lose him. A crew of corrupt cops had hired an array of killers to take me out. An innocent man had placed his life in my hands. I had a case I couldn't solve. And someone was playing around on the edges of it all, killing on the periphery of this trial.

I listened to the elevator mechanism. The whirr of cables and rollers. Allowed my mind to cool.

The elevator car stopped on my floor. As the doors rolled back, my eyes opened.

Kate was waiting for me in the hallway, her arms filled with files and her legal pad. A pen slotted into the bun of hair at the back of her head and a look on her face that spoke to the weight she was carrying too. All my problems were Kate's problems. And I hated that.

'Did you get my message?' she asked.

I joined her in the hallway and we headed for the courtroom. 'I did. We've been ambushed.'

'Castro has dug up an eyewitness. Someone who says they're afraid of reprisals and they'll only testify if the court grants them anonymity. Looks like we'll be cross-examining them blind.'

'How are John and Alison?' I asked.

'They're wrecks. I don't think we can put John on the witness stand. He looks like he's been living in a cell for months and he's ready to crack. Who knows what he's going to say on cross-examination.'

'Ordinarily I don't like putting clients on the stand. Castro can accuse him of lying. His DNA is on the murder weapon, but he told the police he'd never seen it before. If he can handle that, it's worthwhile. I think people will believe him when he says he didn't kill Margaret Blakemore.'

Kate tore off a page from her legal pad, handed it to me.

'This is the list of the first set of witnesses. Castro is calling the investigating officer to open the case. Setting the scene for the jury. Oh, and Bloch wants to see you,' she said, pointing up the hall.

Up ahead, Bloch leaned against the cool walls of the hallway. Head down. Lost in thought. Her gaze fell on me as I approached.

'I pulled a favor, got Esther Hanson's phone records. There's no record of a call made to ICE.'

'So maybe this was a set-up to frame Althea?'

Bloch said, 'Maybe not. Maybe she made the call from a payphone. But it makes a set-up more possible, maybe not probable.'

'Go join Lake in case one of our suspects makes a move. We need to keep tabs on Bale and Ellis. And remind Lake to get his own damn car. He's been promising that for weeks. So, you two, any ideas who our mystery witness might be?'

Bloch shook her head. Kate took the pen from her hair and started to chew on the end of it. I waited, let her mind rattle through the possibilities.

'Whoever it is, they are speaking to motive,' said Kate. 'I have a feeling there's more to it. I've never dealt with a case where the witness is anonymous. Think the judge will grant his motion?'

'I'm sure of it,' said Eddie. 'It happens more and more now. You see it a lot in mob trials and trafficking cases.'

'So we have to cross-examine a witness totally blind, in a major murder trial? How is that fair?'

'This is the justice system,' I replied. 'Nobody said it had to be fair.'

'So what the hell are we going to do?'

'You stick to the plan. We still have a strategy. Let me worry about the anonymous witness. The thing about an unfair legal system is that all bets are off. If the prosecution isn't playing fair, I'm not going to run a straight game either. They're forgetting something . . .'

'What's that?'

'You can't cheat a conman.'

37

Eddie

Detective Arthur Chase took the bible in his right hand and swore to tell the truth, the whole truth and nothing but the truth, so help him God.

He was a career NYPD man. Dark suit. Dark shirt. Set off with a dark navy neck tie and flashy silver cufflinks. A chunky chain on his right wrist and a thick Rolex Submariner on his left. Both silver. To match the cufflinks, and the tie pin. He was a man with a mission. Places to be. Bad guys to catch. A year-round tan. A little gray at the temples, but age hadn't slowed him down or dulled his wits. Sharp green eyes flashed like the cufflinks and seemed to take in the whole room. Artie Chase had a good rep. How could you not, with a name like that. He looked after the officers on his team. Filed his reports on time. Pushed up his precinct's clearance rate. Always bought the first round at the bar. He was a straight operator. No ties to New York's Finest. He'd never beaten a suspect. Never broken the rules. He just looked after his team and closed his cases.

Which, in a way, made him the worst kind of cop.

Bad cops see out their twenty years in the job because of guys like Chase. Cops look after cops. All cops. The bad ones too. If you rat on a fellow officer, your life is turned into a living hell and your career takes a nose dive off a ten-story building. And that's the best-case scenario. Chase learned this early. And, like all cops, he learned to keep his mouth shut. That's hard at first, but it becomes easier when you're doing good police work. The price you pay for doing good in New York is ignoring all the bad that goes on under your own roof. The more good you do, the easier it becomes to look the other way.

Chase did a lot of good.

He never got a hard time on the stand from defense attorneys. They knew, instinctively, any jury would admire a guy like Chase. And, if they didn't know it beforehand, the looks jurors would give him during his testimony put all doubt out of their minds. Any criticism of Chase risked alienating the jury. And he told the truth on the stand. The trouble with cops who told the truth in court was that you couldn't catch them out in a lie. There was no weakness in their battle lines. No way to put a hole in their testimony or even shake it.

A defense attorney's worst nightmare.

Castro played up to Chase's charm and natural magnetism, taking him through his résumé – his years of service and seniority – before he got to the juicy parts of his testimony.

'I got a call to attend a possible homicide on West 74th Street. A neighbor had noticed a front door lying open. Unusual for that time of the morning. He called out, then went inside and found Margaret Blakemore dead on the floor. He called the police right away . . .'

The neighbor had been Norman Tuttle. He was a tech investor who had moved into the street just a month before the murder. When he left for his five a.m. run, he'd seen the door open. Didn't touch anything, didn't disturb the body by attempting CPR: it was clear Margaret was dead and beyond help. Bloch and Lake had looked into Norman extensively – he was as straight as they come. Much like our client. We had agreed Norman's deposition could just be read to the jury and admitted into evidence. He didn't know Margaret, didn't really know anyone yet, and the less bodies on the stand the quicker this case would be over.

'I arrived at the scene and spoke to the two response officers who had secured the property. I ran through my standard questions about what they had touched, what areas of the house they had been to, what they had found and recorded all of it. I opened a crime log and called for forensics and the medical examiner.'

'What did you find when you went inside the property?' asked Castro.

'I saw a woman lying in the living-room area on her back. Her head was pointed toward the bay window. There was what appeared to be two bullet wounds in her temple and one wound in her chest. Her eyes were open. She was clearly deceased.'

'Were there any signs of a struggle?' asked Castro.

Right then, I knew the anonymous witness was going to testify to some kind of relationship between our client and the deceased. Castro was setting it up.

'No obvious signs, no.'

'Was there any sign of forced entry to the property?'

'None.'

'Given your expertise in investigating homicide cases for more than twenty years, were you able to draw any insight from the fact that there was no sign of a struggle and no sign of forced entry?'

There was no point in objecting. Some lawyers would in the hope the judge would intervene and ask the cop to stick to the facts. The jury liked Artie Chase. Best thing to do was to turn that to our advantage.

'It raises the distinct probability that the victim knew her attacker.'

Some members of the jury nodded, agreeing with Chase.

'After you had examined the crime scene, and a forensic examination was conducted of the living room and the victim, what happened next?'

'Our officers canvassed the neighborhood, but no one saw anything suspicious or heard anything on the night of the murder.'

'What course did your investigation take?'

'We spoke to the deceased's spouse, Alan Blakemore, who was not in the state at the time of the murder . . .'

He was a good witness. Closing off avenues of potential attack from the defense. Most married women whose lives end in violence are murdered by their spouses. Chase was long enough in the job to know that's an area that defense might go to and he was shutting those doors before we could open them.

'. . . and we built up a picture of the deceased and her social circle and her life. We continued our investigations and two weeks later we got a breakthrough. An anonymous tip from a caller. The call came in from a public payphone.'

'Your Honor, we would like to play the recording of that call for the jury, People's exhibit nineteen.'

The DA and his team fussed with a laptop that was connected to the sound system in court. And then the call started to play. I'd heard it already. The caller was disguising their voice. It was low, gravelly, but there didn't appear to be a great deal of depth to their tone. I got the impression the caller was young and more than likely female, but it wasn't possible to tell for sure.

I know who killed Margaret Blakemore. I was across the street that night, hiding behind a line of parked cars. I watched John Jackson shoot her, then leave and go back to his house. He still had the gun on him when he left . . .

The line went dead. The caller never acknowledged the call handler, never answered any questions, just made this statement and hung up.

'What did you do when you received that tip?' asked Castro.

'I applied for a warrant to search the home of John Jackson and arrest him for questioning. There was specific corroborating evidence in that anonymous call. We had not released the information to the press that Margaret Blakemore had died from gunshot wounds. The only people who knew that were the killer and the potential witness. The warrant was granted and we made our search and arrest.'

'What did you find at the home?'

'Officer Pettifer found a .22 caliber pistol in the defendant's bedroom closet, high up on a shelf between some spare bedding.'

'What is the significance of the caliber of the weapon?'

'It's the same caliber ammunition found in Margaret Blakemore's body. She was shot three times. This weapon holds a nine-round magazine. Three rounds had been fired from the magazine in this weapon.'

'Was a forensic examination made of this weapon?'

'Yes, an urgent one. A partial latent palm print was found on the gun, but this print wasn't enough to provide a match for the defendant. However, our forensics lab was able to extract DNA from that same print.'

'Experts will testify about his forensic examination and DNA testing, however, from your perspective and understanding, is DNA evidence *more accurate* than palm or fingerprint identification?'

'Yes, sir,' said Chase.

Castro paused for a moment, flicked through the papers on his desk. He was creating tension – building up the finale.

'Did you ask the defendant about the gun that was found in his closet?'

'Yes, and I should say, at that time, we didn't have ballistic evidence to confirm that it was the murder weapon, but we strongly believed it to be so. In any event, I asked Mr. Jackson about the gun in his closet and if he could explain how it got there.'

'What did he say?'

'He said he'd never seen it before.'

'And it was subsequent to this denial that the DNA found on the murder weapon matched the defendant's DNA?'

'Correct.'

'Do you believe the defendant when he said he'd never seen the gun before?'

'The gun that we found in the defendant's home, we believe, is the same gun that fired the rounds which killed Margaret Blakemore. It has the defendant's DNA on it. There's a simple explanation for this. The defendant shot and killed the victim. And then he denied it. Like he's denying it today. He's lying.'

'Nothing further,' said Castro.

I got up, walked round the defense table and stood in the well of the court. The no-man's land between the judge, the witness, the lawyers and the jury. Center stage. Hands in my pockets. I glanced over my shoulder at John.

He sat at the defense table looking utterly lost. Defeated. His eyes were glazed with fear. A man whose life was about to end too soon. He'd lost weight since I'd first met him, and he didn't look the better for it. That suit hung off him. Like a death shroud.

This happens every day in America. Innocent people get caught in a machine that destroys them and their families. I didn't have a magic button to stop the machine. No failsafe device. No cut-off switch. Amid the roar of the grinding steel wheels of justice, I only had words. They were my sole weapon.

The temptation was to scream and rant. And make myself heard over the thunder of the machine.

Yet, I knew, the best thing now was to speak softly. So that those twelve people who could stop the machine might lean in and listen. Really listen. Because, if they didn't, then the machine would roll right over John and Alison. And Tomas.

I nodded at John. I wanted him to know that I was going to fight for him. That there was hope.

He couldn't see it. Not yet. I had to make him hear it.

That meant throwing Chase off balance.

'Detective Chase, is there anything about your investigation that you would do differently?'

This is an open question. Anything can happen. This is the exact opposite of what lawyers are trained to do in cross-examination. They want to keep their questions tight. Yes or no answers. Control the witness. Control their testimony. But I knew the answer Chase would give.

His eyes blazed wide when he heard the question. Not one he was expecting. He thought for a second, and then gave the only answer he could and put a little sugar on top.

'No, not at all. I believe our investigation led us to the truth. That your client murdered Margaret Blakemore.'

Castro winced and then smiled at his assistant DAs, like he was watching me get pummeled by a pro fighter. I was expecting the hit. Chase was an experienced witness. And cops who are used to testifying know that when they are given the ball, and they have an opening to make a three-point shot – they'll throw it through the basket every damn time.

The hit was worth taking. Chase had gotten his three points. But the game was just beginning.

I cleared my throat, audibly, looked at the jury and said, 'Let's talk about this investigation, and the evidence your officers missed, and the evidence you're keeping from this jury . . .'

38
Ruby

The house was quiet. It had been like this for the last twenty minutes as Ruby worked on her laptop, moving money from account to account.

No pings, whizzes or pops from Tomas's iPad games. No music. No sound of his feet on the floor above. It wasn't a calm silence. The air was filled with a heavy stillness. A tension that Ruby had to break.

Tomas could not tell his parents that Ruby had been mad at him. They trusted her. And nothing, absolutely *nothing* could be allowed to damage that faith. Not when she was so close to being free, and resolving the problem that had threatened her world and consumed her thoughts for months.

She breathed out, poured some orange juice into a glass. Then, using two spoons, Ruby crushed a Xanax into a fine powder and tipped it into the glass. A spoonful of NyQuil and another of Benadryl. And then Ruby stirred up the mixture. The color of the orange juice dulled into a muddy yellow. She washed the spoon, picked up the glass of OJ, took a chocolate-chip cookie from the jar in the cupboard and went upstairs.

Tomas's door was closed. She put her ear to the door and listened.

At first, she heard nothing, and then sniffing.

Ruby cradled the cookie in her wrist, opened the door and stepped inside. White walls, white shelves, a pop of bright blue on one wall behind Tomas's bed, and toys neatly arranged everywhere. Tomas was curled up on his pillow. A small, dark, damp stain next to his head where he had been crying. His back was to Ruby, and he tensed as she walked in.

'Tomas, I'm so sorry. My mom is sick. I just got word she is going to have to go into a special home to be looked after by nurses and doctors. That's what I was doing on my laptop when you came into the kitchen. I'm sorry I yelled,' she said, softly.

'You said a bad word. A real bad one.'

'I know, sweetie. I was upset. I won't ever use that word again.'

As Ruby slowly walked round the bed to face Tomas, he screwed his chin into the pillow. He didn't want to look at her. Sometimes, with children, if they can't see something bad in their mind, it isn't there. It just goes away.

Rubeeeeeeee.

The buzzing began in her head.

Her foot stood on something. She looked down. Saw it was Tomas's skipping rope. It was a thick, white woven fiber rope with wooden handles painted red. Some of the paint had chipped off.

Rubeeeeeeeeeeeee.

She shook her head.

'I brought you a drink, and a cookie. To say sorry.'

His little fists grabbed the pillow, twisted it, trying to move the whole thing over his head.

'Come on, little buddy. I know you're hungry. You must be thirsty too. Drink this juice all up and you can have this cookie.'

For a second, his head came out from under the pillow and he saw the glass in Ruby's hand, then dug his face back into the pillow again. Deeper, this time.

His voice was muffled as he spoke. 'Don't want it. I remember that drink from last time. Dirty juice. It tasted funny.'

'It's just orange juice. Come on. We can watch *Star Wars* this afternoon if you like?'

He must've been struggling to breathe, because he shifted his body and turned his face away from Ruby toward the door.

'Come on, it'll be fun, munchkin man. I can show you how to make popcorn?'

No response. The boy lay there in the bed.

Ruuuubeeee . . . take the rope. Do it now. He'll ruin everything . . .

Ruby sometimes caught a look in Tomas's eyes that tugged at something inside her. It was the same look Ruby had once worn, when she was about Tomas's age or perhaps older. A fear that a child carries inside them, all the time. Only at certain moments does it rise to their face and express itself fully.

Ruby remembered seeing herself in a mirror, maybe four years ago. Mother had sat her down in the living room and told her that she had to be strong. That men were coming to look for her father and he had to go away.

'What men?'

'Bad men. Men he owes money to.'

'I know we're not rich any more. But we have money, don't we? Can't Daddy give them the money?'

Her mother fell silent, but her face let Ruby know that she was composing her response and carefully choosing which words were least likely to wound her child.

'Your father works hard, Ruby. But he also gambles and drinks too much booze. This is a bad combination. Because he's no good at either of those things. We might have to move away from here.'

'What? Move away?'

She nodded, said, 'With your father. He's upstairs now, packing. He says he will go and get a place for all of us somewhere far away. And, once he's got it, he will come back for us.'

As young Ruby had tried to take in that information, she'd stood and walked around the living room. It was then that she caught sight of her face. A layer of grime and dust covered the surface of the mirror. Although her home was clean, her mother never polished the mirrors.

Perhaps because her eyes had dulled, and her lip now hung down a little on the right side. Maybe her mom didn't want to look at her reflection. Her face was becoming an indictment of her husband. But, that day, Ruby saw through the dirt on the mirror, and saw real fear in her own face.

'He told me he has a plan. Everything will be alright, Ruby . . .'

Ruby.

Ruuubeeeeeee . . . the rope!

Ruby shut her eyes tightly.

We are so close. Alison will throw you out of the house . . .

'Please . . .' said Ruby, and as she spoke, she wasn't sure if she was talking to the red priest or to Tomas.

She put the glass of juice on Tomas's nightstand and placed the cookie beside it. Slowly, she sat on the bed.

Tomas didn't move when he felt her weight on the mattress.

Take the rope now . . .

With trembling fingers, Ruby reached down and touched the skipping rope. The white, woven fibers were strong. One of the wooden handles made a hollow tinkling sound as it rolled on the wooden floor when Ruby began to gather up the rope in her hands.

'Please . . .' she said.

Choke the boy . . .

Wrapping the rope around her fists, a length about a foot long in between her hands, Ruby knew there was no arguing with the red priest this time. His voice was getting louder, angrier. Soon her head would begin to ache and her nose would bleed, and he was right. She couldn't risk this.

Do it NOW!

She leaned forward, the rope taut, and for some reason she could not understand tears formed in her eyes.

She would make it quick. It would not be painless, but it could be quick. She could get the rope round his neck now, then kneel on his back and pull. With any luck, his neck would break before he suffocated.

Ruby got onto her knees, her heart hammering.

Lips dry.

Cheeks wet.

Rope taut.

And she hesitated.

For Tomas's little hand reached out for the cookie. He lifted it from his nightstand, and took a bite.

Ruby let the rope fall from her hands and tucked it into the bottom of the bed between the mattress and the foot stand.

'I'm sorry too, Ruby,' said Tomas.

'That's okay, sweetie. That's just fine. Have some juice.'

Tomas did as he was told, the fury of the very young who had felt their first taste of injustice, subsiding. He took a sip, made a face.

'Drink it all down,' said Ruby.

He did. The whole glass. Even the thicker juice, which was mostly medication, that had congealed at the bottom of the glass. His mouth twisted and his tongue poked out from between his lips, seemingly trying to absorb the air, or anything for that matter, to get rid of the taste.

'Eat your cookie,' said Ruby, and stroked his hair.

'Is your mom going to be alright?' asked Tomas.

'Yeah, I think she is. She needs people to be around her all the time. To give her the care that she needs. She deserves it.'

'Good,' said Tomas, and took a big bite out of the cookie and crunched it around his mouth.

They sat together, quietly, on the bed. Sometimes talking. Sometimes not. But within half an hour Tomas's eyelids began to look heavy.

'Why don't you have a nap? I'll be downstairs if you need me.'

Without another word, Tomas rolled over and let his eyes close. He would sleep, heavily, for five or more hours. Ruby would tell Alison that Tomas was in a foul mood, maybe running a fever, and that at one point she had to raise her voice, because he was screaming, but she hated doing that. Tomas had a lot of sedatives in his system. He would be groggy for many hours after he woke. His brain just as clouded. That's the way he was last time Ruby had given him some special juice when she'd wanted him to fall into a deep sleep.

Ruby felt things would be alright now.

It was nearly over.

She had one more shopping trip tonight. To a hardware store in the Bronx. One she had not been to before. She needed heavy-duty plastic garbage bags. Thick. Black. The kind used for industrial waste.

The kind you could put a body in.

39
Eddie

Artie Chase butted in before I could ask a formal question.

'This was a good investigation. My team and I were thorough, meticulous and professional.'

Ordinarily, I would object. Have the judge direct the jury to disregard the witness's last statement.

I didn't. Instead, I reminded the jury exactly what Chase had said, counting off his points on my fingers as I spoke.

'Thorough. Meticulous. Professional. Is that right?'

'Dam— Sorry, *absolutely* right.'

Chase was getting a little tetchy. He didn't like any criticism. Real or inferred. He was going to have to get used to it.

'When you inspected the crime scene at Margaret Blakemore's home, you found no evidence of a struggle. Did you find any evidence that anything in the home had been disturbed?'

'No. The house was clean and orderly, with the exception of the victim lying on the floor and the fact that the front door was left open.'

'This home had a lot of expensive furniture, fittings, lighting. There was jewelry sitting on dressing tables upstairs, and the deceased wore a number of expensive rings. Is it safe to say you did not consider this to be a robbery?'

'At first, I didn't rule anything out, but you are right. After looking around the property, there was no evidence of items being stolen. As you say, there were a number of pieces of personal property that could have been taken, but were not. Mr. Blakemore also confirmed, later that day, that nothing in the property had been taken. I then formed the theory this was not a robbery homicide.'

'Detective, most women in the United States are murdered by someone close to them. A partner, a boyfriend, a spouse. Correct?'

'Correct. However, Mr. Blakemore was not in the state at the time of the murder. That alibi has been verified.'

I didn't ask him if he suspected Alan Blakemore. He had anticipated my line of questioning, and tried to head me off at the pass. This was Chase's first mistake. One that I was going to jump on.

'I didn't ask you if Alan Blakemore was a suspect. I asked you about homicide perpetrator statistics. So you're telling me that Alan Blakemore was your first suspect until you ruled him out of the investigation?'

'Ah, I— Well, he was never an *official* suspect, but, like I said, my team was thorough, meticulous and professional.'

I could've argued with Chase, made him confirm that he had investigated Alan Blakemore and had him as suspect number one. But I decided it was better to use Chase's reluctance to admit this.

'You have already confirmed there was no sign of forced entry, so, with your thorough, meticulous and professional approach, you were looking for people who knew Margaret Blakemore who might have a motive to kill her?'

'We were looking for other suspects, yes.'

'Suspects who perhaps were romantically involved with Margaret Blakemore?'

'Perhaps. We did ask Mr. Blakemore if he knew of anyone who might want to harm his wife and he confirmed that he didn't know of anyone.'

It was time to bring this thing to a head.

'So, if Mr. Blakemore wasn't an official suspect, are you telling me you had identified no suspects prior to the anonymous caller?'

I liked this question. It gave no room for a good answer. If he said there were no suspects prior to the anonymous call, he looked incompetent. If he said there were, then it looked as though he was keeping something from the jury.

He paused to think.

'Is that a difficult question?' I asked. 'It's just that we know there were no less than two suspects identified by police who were suspected of killing Margaret Blakemore – isn't that right?'

Chase nodded, said, 'Yes, there were.'

'So was your reluctance to admit that because you want to hide the existence of those alternative suspects from the jury?'

'No, not at all . . .'

'Detective Chase, you're not telling this jury the whole story, are you?'

'The two suspects identified were quickly ruled out. They had alibis.'

'They were at a party on West 74th Street on the night of the murder?'

'Correct.'

'Together?'

'With other individuals, yes.'

'Would it be possible, at a busy and noisy party, to slip out of the front door unnoticed?'

'No,' said Chase, and now he was in trouble.

'It's *not* possible to do that? So your officers spoke to every person at the party, right?'

'Correct.'

'And every minute that those individuals were at the party was accounted for by witnesses?'

Chase said nothing. He just bit down on his lips. Smoothed his pants.

After a few seconds more, he said, 'No, they did not account for every minute.'

'I see,' I said. 'So when you told this jury it was not possible for either of these two individuals to slip out the front door unnoticed, that was a lie?'

'Not a lie – I was just momentarily inaccurate.'

'*Momentarily inaccurate* sounds a lot like *alternative facts* to me. You understand you are under oath today, Officer?'

He nodded.

'Having made assumptions in your investigation as to possible motives, neither you nor your officers conducted a thorough search of the upstairs bedrooms, did you?'

'We carried out a once-over search. It was not a search and seizure situation.'

'You were looking for possible motives, suspects, yet you didn't find this . . .'

I walked back to the defense table and Kate handed me our first exhibit.

'This is a cellular phone, registered to Margaret Blakemore, and hidden in her sock drawer in the bedroom upstairs. This phone contains only two contact phone numbers, and one text message remains on the phone. From the text message, it's clear the deceased was involved in a sexual relationship with at least one of these contacts. You were not aware of this, were you?'

'No, this is the first time I've seen that phone.'

'Your Honor, this should have been disclosed . . .' Castro was on his feet, objecting, blood filling his angry cheeks as we both approached the bench.

'Your Honor, I didn't know if the police had seen this phone, and ignored it, or had never seen it before until I asked this officer. For all I know, they'd examined it and deemed it irrelevant. Obviously, we want to submit this as a defense exhibit,' I said, stretching the truth as far as I was comfortable with in front of a judge.

'This is blatant ambush tactics, Your Honor,' said Castro.

'Maybe he's right? He knows all about ambushing his opponents . . .'

'Alright, alright,' said Judge Zell, and stared at me.

He knew I was getting blindsided with an anonymous witness by Castro. This gave me a little leeway of my own.

'Is there anything else relevant that you have not disclosed to the prosecution?' he asked me. 'What's on this phone?'

'One text message, sent by the victim maybe six or seven hours before the murder. We haven't been able to trace the other phone numbers to registered devices. But it's clear from the SMS message the deceased was involved with at least one of these contacts. There are phone calls from both numbers to the victim's phone the day before the murder.'

Zell was a decent man, and had the makings of a good judge.

'I'll admit the exhibit. But you have to promise me there are no more surprises.'

We returned to our tables, Castro shaking his head as he walked away.

'Detective Chase, read this message, sent by the victim just hours before the murder. My partner, Miss Brooks, will put this up onscreen so the jury can read it too.'

SMS message sent to CONTACT: SMS sent at 17:05.

After all we've been through, you're still treating me like a piece of shit. I'm always second best, aren't I?

I'm done being your fucking piece on the side.

I can end you with one phone call.

Maybe I should tell everyone what you've done.

How would you like that?

Then you'll know what pain feels like.

The courtroom fell silent.

'Detective Chase, Margaret Blakemore is threatening to reveal information. If you'd read that message before the anonymous call came in, you would have had a high priority suspect, correct?'

Chase said nothing for a moment. His jaw worked back and forth as he ground his teeth. He knew what he had to say. The answer was clear in his mind, and to everyone else in the courtroom, but it was as if his body refused to let those words out of his mouth. After another few seconds, the silence was becoming uncomfortable. He realized he was making things worse.

'That's possible, but—'

'Wait, you have a threatening conversation taking place with an unknown person hours before the victim was murdered, and it's only *possible* that person would be a suspect?'

'They would have become a suspect, but they would have been the wrong suspect, Mr. Flynn. Your client had the murder weapon in his home with his DNA present on that gun.'

I had been waiting for this.

'Detective, you don't know how long that gun was in my client's closet, do you?'

'No.'

'So it's possible that this unknown suspect could have shot Margaret Blakemore, and planted that weapon in his home.'

'Not possible,' he said.

I had been expecting this. Waiting for it.

'Are you sure? Could you be *momentarily inaccurate* about your answer? Take a moment before we have that conversation again. Just think carefully now. It's possible an unknown suspect could have shot Margaret Blakemore and planted that weapon in my client's home, correct?'

'Possible,' spat out Chase, but he added, 'but not likely.'

I had three more questions. I wanted to increase the tempo of question and answer. Chase was already pissed off. I stepped closer to him, fired out the next question fast, with a little spice in my tone.

'You said at the beginning of this cross-examination you and your team were thorough, meticulous and professional. It was unprofessional to miss that cell phone, laziness not to search her property fully – isn't that right?'

'No, I—' said Chase, firing back his answer immediately.

'You wanted to make an arrest alright, but it didn't matter who you arrested, did it?'

'We got the right man,' he said, leaning forward, spitting his answer into the courtroom.

I had done my best with Chase, introduced the possibility of doubt. I didn't want to name Bale and Ellis yet, not until we had more evidence. Getting specific on these two would only give Castro a chance to knock them down and eliminate them one by one. Now, the jury was left with questions. Who were these suspects? Were they having an affair with the victim? Juries asking themselves questions is where the defense wants to be. Doubt is the defense attorney's nirvana.

The last question I tossed out just as fast. And I waited to see his reaction.

'You know the identity of the anonymous caller, don't you?'

His mouth opened, and he inhaled, and then shut it again. Castro was on his feet.

'Objection, Your Honor,' he said.

'What? Why? Either he knows who the anonymous caller is, or he doesn't. That information has not been disclosed,' I said.

But I knew, in my gut, why Castro was objecting.

We approached the bench, so the jury and the rest of the courtroom wouldn't hear our whispered conversation.

'He can't answer that question, Your Honor,' said Castro.

'I don't see why not?' said the judge.

Castro swallowed, looked at me sideways then back at the judge.

'Your Honor, the anonymous caller is now our anonymous witness.'

40

Bloch

'What the hell is up with these guys?' asked Lake.

He sat in the passenger seat of Bloch's Jeep, and sipped at his filtered water. They had been there since the morning. Parked at a position in the street that gave them a view of both Todd Ellis's and Bret Bale's homes. Bale's home was furthest away, but there were no cars parked in front of Bloch, and the elevated driving position of the Jeep made sure they could see if anyone went into or out of those properties.

So far, neither man had left home. And no one had come calling.

'Something is going on, for sure,' said Lake, and this time he turned to look at Bloch. She hadn't acknowledged his first statement, and was so far ignoring his second.

'I've never asked you this, but how come you don't talk much?' he asked, his fingers drumming the arm rest.

Turning her head slowly, Bloch looked at Lake. Raised an eyebrow, asked, 'When are you getting your own car?'

Lake nodded.

That seemed to be enough.

She brought her gaze to the front and sighed. Lake talked too much. His fingers were either tapping on the dash, or his foot thumping on the floor, or he was messing with his hair, humming, or just talking for the sake of it. Lake had the kind of energetic mind that just had too damn much going on.

Bloch was still.

Composed.

Her mind worked in a different way. Logic. Numbers. Facts. Then conclusions. Lake more than made up for what she didn't understand about human behavior, which was a lot. He could think like the men he hunted. Bloch didn't like to consider that too much. Lake had a capacity to put himself in other people's shoes. He had great empathy, but not for ordinary people. Not so much. He studied the worst of humanity, and could understand their twisted motives and desires. Bloch sometimes wondered if Lake saw parts of himself in those monsters.

'What do you think their play is?' asked Lake.

Bloch was silently praying one of the men would leave home. She would then kick Lake out of the car to keep an eye on the other target, and she would follow the first man in the Jeep. She was trying to think. The case and the events surrounding it were like broken pieces of a mosaic in her mind. She was tossing them around, seeing which ones fitted together and what kind of picture that made. So far, few of them fitted. And, even when they did, there was no clear picture. There were too many missing pieces.

Right then, the contemplative part of her mind shut down and another piece of her brain fired up. Because up ahead, Brett Bale stepped out of his front door and made his way down the porch steps to the sidewalk. He wore a navy Puffa jacket and blue jeans with sneakers. Ball cap and shades. Dressing down. That's what she thought at first, then she glanced at the temperature reading on the dash – 93 degrees. Far too warm for a jacket like that. And it wasn't as if he wore it loosely – he had it zipped up to his neck.

He walked past his sports car, and his Land Rover opened as he approached. His gait had changed. Normally, Brett Bale walked like a man with four billion dollars in cash in his bank account. A certain swagger. Shoulders back. Hands loose. Chin in the air.

Not this time. His right arm swung in time with his footsteps, but his left arm was close by his side and stiff.

Bloch noticed these things. It was her gift. Something that had given her a career. A calling. It was perhaps sometimes a curse too. While she could read a crime scene and observe and see what others could not, she couldn't get a sense of when someone was upset, or vulnerable, sad or happy.

It took the one and a half seconds for Brett Bale to get into the Land Rover for Bloch to interpret what she had seen and come to a logical, theoretical conclusion.

She didn't have to say it either. Lake was just as fast, and he liked to talk.

'He's wearing a piece,' Lake said.

Bloch nodded. People who don't normally wear a concealed weapon don't know how to carry it. An average-sized loaded handgun weighs between one and a half and two pounds. Plus the holster, if it's a good-quality leather shoulder piece, that's another half a pound at least. It feels alien to those who don't wear it every day. It subtly affects your balance, but more than that – you are conscious of it at all times. It's like carrying around a hammer strapped to your side.

That's why Bale's left arm was stiff. He was holding it against the side of his jacket where he wore his piece. Making sure it was there. That it wasn't somehow going to fall out. And the heat. It wasn't weather to melt the blacktop, but it was hot. No other reason to be wearing a warm jacket on a day like this other than for concealment.

Bloch fired the engine.

'Should I get out?'

She nodded.

Lake exited the Jeep, Bloch pulled out into the street five seconds after the Land Rover. She followed Bale, keeping her distance. He made a left at the end of the block. Stopped at a set of lights. No other choice but to roll up behind him. She kept her distance, but was now close enough to see into his vehicle. The back window had a dark tint, but not so dark that she couldn't make out the figure of Bale in the driver's seat.

The lights changed.

Bale moved.

She followed.

He didn't touch his indicators, but turned left. Bloch swore under her breath, made the turn with him.

Was he using counter-surveillance techniques? This one was pretty standard. You begin with a few loops of the block, then random turns. Tight and quick. That creates a crazy trail of movement that no other normal driver behind you will make, so you know, right away, if there's still the same car in your rearview after that – then you've got yourself a tail.

The Land Rover indicated left.

Shit.

He was making a loop, now driving back into West 74th Street.

Bloch contemplated driving on. Not following him. He must've been on counter surveillance.

She should drive on. She knew it.

That's what her brain was screaming at her to do.

But something else happened. She didn't know if it was gut instinct, or that elemental lizard-brain again, but whatever it was, she hit the indicators too, made the left four seconds after Bale.

Then he did something else Bloch wasn't expecting.

The Land Rover pulled into a parking space on the right side of the street.

Bloch drove past the vehicle and, as she did so, she checked her mirrors, got a good look at Bale in the driver's seat and realized then what he was doing. That was a moment which shifted some more tiles in the broken mosaic of this case and caused Bloch to suck in the air.

She drove on up the street another two hundred yards, past Lake who was walking along the sidewalk. She turned the corner. Waited.

She saw him in her rearview, flashed the lights. Lake got into the passenger seat beside her.

'What the hell? He was running a loop! Did he make us?'

'No,' said Bloch. 'I'm pretty sure he didn't notice me. Did you see
where he parked?'

'No, why?'

'He's armed and he's watching a house on this street.'

Lake's eyes widened. 'He's parked outside the Jacksons' house?'

41

Eddie

'How do you think it went?' asked Alison.

We were on our way out of the building. Staff exit. I tried, when possible, never to leave a building the same way I came in. There was still a sniper and God knows how many other people who wanted me dead.

No reporters waiting for us. I knew most of the security personnel. I couldn't always get out this way, but if a few friendly faces were working those back corridors, we could skip out onto the sidewalk unnoticed. I held the door open, letting Alison and John through first, then Kate, who met my gaze as she walked past.

I didn't know how to answer Alison's question. Soon as I took one step out of the courtroom, the first thing that banged into my brain was the image of my friend lying unconscious in a hospital bed. Even though I knew there were no new messages on my phone, I would check it anyway. In some ways I feared hearing from the nurses. A message from them could only mean one of two things – either Harry was awake or, more likely, something far worse.

My mind was still on my friend, and it was taking too long to get my head back into the game to give our client a fair assessment. Kate saw me struggling, and didn't want to leave Alison hanging.

'We were never going to win this case on the first day,' said Kate.

'All that we could have hoped for is to make the jury curious. We want them to be asking questions. Who else might have been involved in this murder and why didn't the police investigate? I think some of the jurors are at least beginning to wonder. We have to build on that tomorrow.'

'Thank you both, so much. I mean it . . .' said John, his throat thick with fear.

'This was the first battle. Stay strong,' said Kate. 'The war is just getting started.'

My phone buzzed. It felt like the thing was wired into my heart, the vibration like an electric shock. Instantly, I was panicking, scrambling to get my phone out of my jacket, already silently pleading that this wasn't bad news from the hospital.

It was Lake, and my eyes closed for a second. The tension left my shoulders and I hit the answer button.

'Are you with the Jacksons?' he asked.

'Yes.'

'Step away for a second. I don't want them to see your reaction.'

'Give me a minute,' I said, and moved underneath the scaffolding that currently enveloped this side of the building.

'What's wrong? Is it Harry?'

'No, he's still the same. I saw him this morning. It's Brett Bale. We think he's carrying a gun and he's in his Land Rover parked outside the Jacksons' address. He's watching the house.'

'What the hell is going on?'

'We don't know.'

'Is the babysitter still in the house with Tomas?'

'Yep.'

'Has he made any attempt to get inside?'

'Not yet. He's just sitting there, but he's watching the place. I think he must be waiting for John. I don't want to have to kill one of our suspects to save our client. Not when we don't know if he's really the one who killed Margaret Blakemore.'

I felt a stabbing pain at the back of my neck. The beginnings of a bad stress headache. I used to get them a lot. Five years ago, I would've gone to a bar. Two shots of something hard and then a beer. That took the edge off the pain. Nowadays I was on coffee and soda, which didn't do the same trick. I rolled my shoulders, stretched my neck and breathed slow. Checked my pockets. No Advil.

'How long has he been outside?'

'Coming up on an hour now.'

I looked over at my client and his wife. They were standing with Kate. She was trying to keep them from crashing. John had to hang tough for a few more days, on the off chance we could pull off a miracle and get him an acquittal. Right now, that seemed very far away. It felt like I had to win a crap shoot in Vegas, but I wasn't even *in* Nevada – I was in Brownsville trying to start a rusted Buick with four flat tires.

'Okay, hang tight. Let me know if there's any movement.'

I ended the call and politely pulled Kate away from our client.

'There's a problem at the Jacksons'. Brett Bale is watching the house. He's armed. I need you to stall John and Alison for a while. Tell him you want them to go back to the office for just a half-hour. Go over his testimony and brainstorm this anonymous witness some more.'

'What are you going to do?' she asked.

'You know me – I'm going to do something stupid.'

I had hidden my car in a parking lot three blocks from the courthouse. Before I'd stowed it away, I'd had Bloch check it for GPS trackers and other less savory devices. Even checked the fuel tank. It was clean. I'd made sure no one had followed me into the lot or out of it. I picked up the old Mustang and for a second enjoyed the purr of the V8 when I fired it up, then drove to West 74th Street.

A light rain was falling. Just a shower. The sun was still high and casting blues and purples through the fine mist. I parked behind Bloch, got out, approached the driver's window. Bloch buzzed it down.

'Any change?' I asked.

Bloch shook her head.

'Alright, I'm going to go talk to him. When he looks in the rear-view mirror, show him Maggie. Then put it away. One more thing. If he shoots me, kill him.'

Bloch began to protest as I walked away from the car and headed straight for the Land Rover. I stood in front of the passenger door. His attention was in the other direction, looking directly at the Jacksons' home. I knocked on the glass.

Startled, he turned and looked at me. Held my gaze for a second. I gestured that he should open the window. He waved me away.

I didn't move.

He took another few seconds and looked me over. I was in a suit. My hair was a mess and my tie was undone but I clearly wasn't a homeless person looking for change.

He pressed a button on the door panel and the window cracked an inch.

'You going to let me in. It's raining. I think we need to talk.'

'Who are you?'

'My name's Eddie Flynn. I represent John Jackson.'

The information rolled around in his head for a few seconds. His hand reached for the zipper on his jacket.

I tensed. Stood my ground.

He moved the zipper down below his chest, then put his hand on his stomach. The gun in his jacket could be in his hand and pointed at me in under a second if he moved fast.

'What do you want?'

'I already told you. I want to talk.'

His gaze shifted and he stared out of the windshield. There was a lot to process. He was sitting outside an alleged murderer's home, someone who he might have framed. He was weighing up the options. If I got aggressive, he had a gun.

His left hand was still on the door console. I heard the mechanical clunk of the doors unlocking. I opened the passenger door and got in beside him, shut it behind me.

That right hand moved a little closer to the opening in his jacket.

'Let's be clear about this. I just want to talk. Nothing else. So relax.'

His right hand stayed where it was. He kept his eyes on me.

'I'd appreciate it if you put your hands on the wheel. There's no need to reach for that piece you've got in your jacket.'

His eyes flared, and his finger moved an inch, just inside the zipper.

'Take a look in the rearview mirror. See that woman in the driver's seat of the Jeep behind you? She's showing you a .500 Smith and Wesson Magnum. She calls it Maggie. It's loaded with seven hundred grain rounds. Armor-piercing. That thing will go through this car like paper. The exit wound would leave a hole in your chest the size of a basketball. So relax. Take your hand away from the gun in your jacket and tell me what the hell you're doing here.'

'I'm just sitting in my car. On my own street. Minding my own goddamn business,' said Bale.

'So why did you drive around the block and park outside my client's house?'

'It's a free country.'

'No, it isn't. I don't know if it has ever been that. But it sure as shit isn't free for you. Not today. So tell me what you're doing here. Or would you rather talk about Margaret Blakemore?'

His face registered the name. He tried hard to keep his expression neutral, confident. But his pupils dilated and his lips parted when that name came out of my mouth.

'I don't want anything to do with your client or his family. I don't want to talk to them. I have no intention of harming them,' he said.

My father was an Irish conman. My mother was Italian, from a long line of strong women that hailed from Palermo. There was nobody on this planet that my father couldn't fool – except one. My mom. She could spot a lie on a fly's ass at five hundred yards, or, more accurately, she could read the lie in my father's face before he even opened his mouth. You can't grow up in a household like that without picking up some of those skills.

When Brett Bale said he wasn't there for my client, he was telling the truth.

'So what the hell are you doing here, then?'

He said nothing.

'It's just . . . someone parked outside my client's house with a gun makes me nervous. Especially someone like you. It's not a good idea to make me nervous, Mr. Bale.'

'Someone like me? What have I ever done to you?'

'Nothing yet. Wasn't your last wife a swim champion? And yet she drowned swimming off your boat, in a calm sea with perfect weather. It seems accidents happen around you, Mr. Bale. Did Margaret Blakemore have one of your accidents?'

His teeth began gnawing at his lip, then grinding together, his jaw muscle working back and forth. He had a strange, detached look in his blue eyes.

'You've got enormous financial resources,' I said. 'You're ruthless, determined, possibly sociopathic. For many people, you are the worst enemy they could possibly have. But I've had worse. And I'm still here. So don't get any bright ideas. Here's what's going to happen now – I'm going to get out of this car and you're going to drive away. My people will be here all night, keeping watch. You won't see them. But they will see you.'

He checked the rearview mirror again. The sight of Bloch with a Magnum that could punch a hole in an armored Humvee is not a pleasant one. Bale was a psychopath, but he wasn't stupid.

'Get out.'

'Keep that gun in its holster. Until next time, Mr. Bale.'

I opened the passenger door, but gave Bale a parting gift before I left.

'Actually, there won't be a next time. I don't think we'll meet again. If I come for you, you won't even know about it until it's all over.'

I stepped onto the sidewalk and slammed the door shut. The engine came to life, and Bale pulled out of the space and hit the gas. Bloch drove the Jeep forward, level with me, and then stopped and opened her window.

'What do you think?'

'He's not after the Jacksons. He said as much, and I believe him.'

'Then what is he doing here?' asked Lake.

'I don't know, but he's dangerous. I'll need you two to take it in shifts tonight. Keep an eye on our people. Bale is the immediate threat, but I need to know if Ellis makes any moves.'

'You think he killed Margaret Blakemore?' asked Bloch.

'I'm not sure yet. And for God's sake, Gabriel – go buy a car.'

42
Ruby

The red priest was screaming at Ruby when the front door opened and Alison and John walked into the house. He shut up as soon as the Jacksons came inside, but Ruby's head still hurt. At times it felt like his pale hands were in her skull, pushing down on her brain, squeezing it.

Court was finished for the day.

John looked finished too. He looked even more tired and beaten than he had this morning. It had been interesting to Ruby to watch his decline over these last weeks. A vibrant, fit young father had become a wan, ghostlike figure. As if his life had been sucked right out through his eyes. Alison could see it too. Ruby noticed. She saw the concern in the looks she gave her husband. In her small touches. Brushing his shoulder, taking his hand. At times, Ruby wondered if Alison was concerned her husband might take his own life.

Ruby was concerned about this too. She didn't want that. John had to live, for a little while longer at least.

She explained it had been a rough day for Tomas. He might have been running a fever and she had given him some infant paracetamol. He'd had a tantrum, but Ruby had dealt with it and there was no point in going over it again. He was upstairs asleep. Had been most of the day.

Alison thanked her, and they both went upstairs to see him. Ruby followed, at a distance. She watched John and Alison wordlessly climb into Tomas's bed. One on either side. And together they held their son. Tomas stirred, but only a little.

'Dad,' he said, and put his little hand on his father's chest and snuggled into him. His father's tears fell into Tomas's hair, but that didn't seem to disturb him from his slumber. Alison's body shook as she cried. John was still. And very quickly his tortured eyes closed.

Ruby walked silently downstairs, took her bag and her jacket and opened the front door. As she stood on the stone steps, she felt the small hairs on the back of her neck rise. A feeling started in her legs, then the small of her back and zoomed up her spine, through her shoulders and down into her arms, finally making her fingertips itch.

It was the same feeling as being in a dark wood and hearing a twig snap behind you; the same sensation experienced when leaning over the railing at the top of a tall building; the same central nervous system warning that's triggered when you're in the wild and you see a bear coming over the top of a ridge ahead; it's the body's alarm system flashing a red alert – flooding your muscles with adrenalin.

Someone was watching Ruby. She knew it. Instantly.

She patted her pockets, as if making sure she had her keys with her. It allowed her to take a moment, to be still, and to allow her peripheral vision to locate the watcher.

There, on the other side of the street.

One of the people who worked for John Jackson's lawyer. The woman, Bloch. Sitting in her Jeep. Staring at her.

Ruby wasn't used to being watched. As a cleaner, maid, babysitter, no one paid her any attention. She came into many homes in this street and spent hours there every week, and yet nobody seemed to even notice she was there. They didn't speak to her if she didn't engage with them. They certainly didn't look at her.

She was the help.

She was the server.

She was invisible.

But now she could feel the blood warming her cheeks as Bloch's eyes burned into her. Nothing to do but ignore it. She hoisted her backpack onto both shoulders, trotted down the steps and turned sharply along the sidewalk in the direction of home, and her mom, who would be waiting for her. Hungry.

She was smart, this investigator. The red priest would want her to kill this one. It wouldn't be easy. Best to avoid her, for now at least. Ruby knew she was a threat.

She kept her head down, pounded the wet pavement as she headed up the street. With every step, she felt the heat of those eyes upon her. And with every step, she heard the red priest's voice purring in her mind. She tried to think of something else. A way to get rid of this priest for good.

As she turned the corner, she couldn't resist glancing over her shoulder, back down the street. The investigator, Bloch, was out of her vehicle. Standing beside it.

Watching her.

Ruby turned the key in the door to her apartment and immediately heard an unfamiliar sound.

Voices.

'Mom?' she called out.

No answer. Just the murmur of conversation. Two men.

'. . . you found paradise in America . . . you made a good living . . . the police protected you . . . there were courts of law . . .'

The voice was familiar. Someone she knew?

No. It's the TV. Mother hardly ever watched television. She listened to her records. She read her paperback romance novels, but her mom never put on the TV. Ruby rarely watched it. Sometimes for the news, but that was it.

She stepped into the small living space, which was lit only by the glare from the screen. Somehow, Mom had rearranged the only two chairs in the room. They were both facing the TV. Mom sat in her chair. And a man wearing dark clothing sat in the other.

'*. . . someday . . . I may call upon you for service . . . Until that day, accept this justice as a gift on my daughter's wedding day.*'

Ruby liked movies. She knew those lines. The movie was *The Godfather*.

Written by Francis Ford Coppola and Mario Puzo. The actor who played the title role . . .

Marlon Brando.

'Good evening,' said the man in the chair.

43
Ruby

'Hi,' said her mom, cheerfully. 'You never told me about this nice gentleman. A friend of yours, I believe?'

Ruby stood very still in the dark. There was a filleting knife in the kitchen drawer, eight feet behind her. A crack hammer and a crowbar under her bed. She had no weapons on her. Not even a penknife. The man's face was calm. His lips curved into a welcoming smile. His eyes blazed, illuminated by the TV screen. Like the beams of a headlight hitting a big jungle cat's eyes through the darkness.

The man said nothing. He didn't move. His long legs were folded over one another. Sleek black pants, polished expensive leather shoes. Black again, like the rest of the suit. Only a pressed white button-down shirt and dark tie gave any contrast. It was hard to tell in this light, but his hair seemed to be a lighter color, and his skin the same hue as rice paper. So white it was almost translucent. Ruby could see, even in the glow from the TV, thin snakes of blue and red veins in his cheeks.

She had never seen him before. But he knew Ruby.

That is to say, he could see the true Ruby. The real Ruby. She could tell. He was one of those few who gaze right into you. This man, with his pale eyes, could see a black soul beneath a pretty pink sweater. The same feeling she had when Bloch was watching her – it returned now. Only this time it was dialed up to eleven.

'Aren't you going to say hello?' asked her mom.

She was cheerful, delighted to have had a guest in their apartment. When they first moved here, there were a handful of her mother's friends who wanted to come over and visit. But her mother refused them all. She didn't want them to see how far they had fallen. From West 74th Street to a two-bedroom, roach-infested apartment in Hell's Kitchen was a long way down. And so, eventually, her mother's friends stopped calling. And Ruby and her mother were alone.

'Hello,' said Ruby.

The man stood smoothly, with a pleasing and seemingly effortless agility, like a gymnast who is in absolute control of even the smallest muscles. The movement was unnerving and yet marvelous to behold. Ruby felt fear gnawing at her guts. She didn't need to look down to know that her hands were trembling.

'Your mother and I were just watching one of my favorite movies,' said the man.

'Mine too,' said Ruby, and he smiled unexpectedly. 'Yeah,' said Ruby, 'I love Brando. He deserved the Oscar. Pacino should've won too, for best supporting actor. Joel Gray won for *Cabaret*. I liked how Pacino gave up his life . . . to protect his family . . .'

As she said that last sentence, she glanced at her mother.

Mr. Christmas acknowledged the subtext with a slow blink of his eyes.

'Aren't you the cinephile. Your mother and I were just killing time, as it were, until you returned. I made her soup. We ate together. I didn't know what time to expect you, so I didn't fix you a bowl. There is some left over on the stove. For later . . .'

'I'm not hungry,' said Ruby.

Who the hell was this man? He wasn't a cop. That much was clear.

'Well, I don't wish to disturb either of you ladies a moment longer. Ms. Johnson, if you and I could just have a word in private? I've told your mom how influential you have been in the neighborhood watch. How we, in West 74th Street, just couldn't do without you . . .'

Ruby nodded and backed out of the room.

She turned as she heard the man say his goodbyes to her mother.

'Thank you so much for your hospitality, madam. You have a lovely home. It's been an absolute pleasure to enjoy your company this evening, Mrs. Johnson . . .'

Ruby was ahead of the man now. Maybe five feet. She could make it to the knife drawer in the kitchen. But not without him seeing her. If she was going to get a weapon, now was the time. She could dart into her bedroom and close the door. There was time to do that. The only question was what would happen to her mother if Ruby was safely behind a locked door.

Then she stopped panicking. Started thinking. He wasn't going to kill her tonight. He had spent time with her mother. Cooked her dinner. And they had talked. He seemed to know Ruby had a connection with West 74th Street, but she wondered how much this man really knew about her.

As Ruby moved through to the kitchen, she noticed two bowls and two spoons on the kitchen draining board by the sink. He'd not only heated the soup, but he'd washed up. Even draped a kitchen towel over the pot to keep flies and whatever else crawled along the kitchen tops out of her soup.

His DNA was all over this apartment. He had not come here to kill her. At least not tonight.

She opened the front door and stepped out into the dim hallway. The motion sensor in the corner wasn't working, and the only light came from the apartment or the open elevator door, but of course the elevator was out of order. Ruby had to feel her way to this floor using the flashlight function on her phone.

She flipped on the flashlight as the man followed her into the hallway and closed the door.

Now that they were alone, and out of earshot of her mother, the man spoke softly.

'Thank you for playing along with me. I wouldn't want to frighten your mother unduly. She is a remarkable woman, having been through so much.'

'How do you know what my mom has been through?'

He cocked his head, half smiled at Ruby's question.

'Before we turned off the lamps, I saw her face. I know the face of a woman who has been beaten for half of her life. I know that you care about her very much and she doesn't have a lot of time left on this earth. That apartment is clean and your mother is well attended to, considering your financial means. Which brings me to the purpose of my visit. My client would like his two hundred and fifty thousand dollars back, if you would be so kind.'

So that's who this man was. A fixer for either Ellis or Bale.

'I don't know what you're talking about?' said Ruby.

'Shall I ask your mother?' he said, and this time there was no warmth on his tongue as he spoke.

Ruby stood very still, even though the fear was trying to shake her body. She had to be very careful with this man. Choose her words well.

'I don't have it,' she said.

'The money trail went cold after you moved it through Panama. That was clever. But you should have used that bank first. My client has a lot of resources and he was able to trace you very quickly. It's only a matter of time before someone picks up that trail again. People are working on it right now. You haven't cashed it, I'm guessing. I had a look while I made the soup. There's a bag of clothes, tools and burner phones in your wardrobe, so I guess you're getting ready to run, Ms. Johnson. You should perhaps have moved faster.'

'I couldn't,' she said, and her gaze moved from the ice man in front of her, to the door of her apartment.

'Your mother?'

'I spent it,' said Ruby. 'I've paid for her care at a facility in the city. A nursing home. Retirement community, call it whatever you want. I don't have the money. She's moving . . .'

'Tomorrow morning,' said the man, cutting her off. 'Some nice men are arriving to take some of her things and move them to her new home, so she said. I noticed her bag was packed too. While I admire the sentiment, that does put you in a rather difficult position with my client . . .'

His pale eyes seemed to fire red in the torch light.

'I can get it . . .' said Ruby, sputtering.

'You are a resourceful young lady, no doubt . . .'

'Twenty-four hours. I'll have all of it. In cash,' said Ruby, because of course she had another two hundred and fifty thousand in a different account. Ruby had got a quarter of a million in blackmail money from both men. But that was her running money. That was her ticket to freedom, after she'd solved her huge problems.

The man said nothing for a time. He just stared at Ruby. Like a great white shark. Dead eyes. Either he would swim away, or he would take Ruby's head clean off in one bite. He was deciding, right then and there.

Ruby held still. Her body was screaming at her to run. To get back into the apartment. *Get a knife. Get a hammer. Defend yourself.*

The red priest was beginning to stir. He had lain still, watching all of this in silence. Ruby could hear his voice. A rumble in her brain, his red mouth open, ready to scream . . .

'I don't normally do this, but I have of late, experienced some degree of alternative working practices. Ms. Johnson, we have an agreement. Twenty-four hours. You will have the money for me, but if you fail then I will make you regret it with every nerve fiber in your body.'

Something inside Ruby that had been holding her up straight seemed to falter and bend at that moment. The relief came quickly and left just as fast.

'What's your name?' she asked.

The man seemed surprised by the question.

'You can call me Mr. Christmas. I'll be keeping an eye on you, Ms. Johnson.'

He nodded, and his heels clicked together. Then he moved past her and his heels bounced down the staircase. He didn't look back.

Ruby listened to his shoes on the stairs. Only when the sound had completely disappeared did she let out her breath.

44
Eddie

'Good fuckin' morning, Fly Man. You want some fuckin' eggs or what?'

I lifted my head off Denise's couch and immediately felt pain soaking into the back of my neck. Tony Two Fucks was in the small kitchen of her studio apartment fixing breakfast.

'I'll just have coffee and Advil,' I said.

'You ain't fuckin' drinkin' again, ya fuck?'

'No, it's the couch. Not the bottle.'

I stretched my legs to the floor, sat up and rubbed my left shoulder. Stretched my neck and back. It wasn't the couch. It was stress, but I didn't want Tony nor anyone else to know about it.

'That suit looks like Lake wore it,' said Denise as she came into the kitchen wearing a dressing gown, her wet hair caught up in a towel. She kissed Tony, and they whispered something together. I couldn't hear it. Whatever it was made them both smile. I was happy for Denise.

I'd slept in my shirt and suit pants. The blankets Denise had given me last night were still folded neatly on the chair opposite. I heard the sound of nails on a hardwood floor and then felt a long, wet tongue licking my face. I said good morning to Clarence and gave him a belly rub. Tony cut open a whole packet of bacon and dumped it in the pan. Denise was vegetarian. Half the pack was for Tony. Half for Clarence, who, once he'd said good morning to me, scampered over to the kitchen and sat at Tony's feet. The smell of bacon hitting a hot pan was too tempting for him.

'Don't go into the office today,' I said.

Denise poured me a coffee, brought it over to the couch with a bottle of painkillers.

'Breakfast is served. So what's going on? Are we closing?'

'For the next few days I want you safe at home. I'm sleeping on people's couches, never staying in the same place two nights in a row, and this case . . . I just need to end this. All of it. The price on my head, the crazy person who's working behind the scenes on the Jackson case, and I need to find whoever really killed Margaret Blakemore.'

'How are you going to do that?'

'I don't know exactly, but I have a rough idea how to start.'

I rubbed my neck, then dry-swallowed three pills.

'Easy on those,' said Denise.

'Tony, I need you to do a couple things for me today, if that's alright?'

'Sure, whatever the fuck,' he said.

For a second, I didn't register it. Then, I noticed he'd only dropped one f-bomb in that sentence. Denise saw the realization on my face.

She whispered, 'We've been working on our language. I don't want my mother, who's eighty-seven, to throw him out of the house two seconds after he walks in.'

'He's meeting your mother? Must be getting serious.'

I took a gulp of hot coffee, stood, stretched and then talked to Tony.

'I'll talk to Lake this morning. He'll call you and help out with this. I need an apartment in Leonard Street, in the old Clock Tower Building.'

'What do I look like – a fuckin' realtor to you?'

'*I* don't want to rent it. I want somebody to rent out their place. I couldn't afford that building. I just need it to go up on Airbnb or some place like that. Just for a couple of days. I'm sure there's regulations that state you can't rent out your apartment like that, but I'm sure you can convince a suitable candidate. I'll compensate them accordingly.'

'You gonna pay their fuckin' hospital bills?'

'Don't hurt anyone in that building. Be subtle. And don't kidnap anybody either. Just, you know, use your powers of persuasion.'

Tony nodded, tipped the bacon onto a plate and started breaking eggs into the pan.

'Oh, and I need one more thing. Ask Jimmy if he can set up a meeting with Buchanan. It's time I met New York's Finest.'

'A meeting? Jimmy don't fuckin' meet no cops.'

Denise had been listening, and gave Tony the eye – he was swearing.

'Not for him. For me.'

'You're going to have a fuckin' sit down with a bunch of crooked cops who are trying to kill you?'

'Do you have any better ideas on how to end this?'

'Sure, fuckin' kill 'em all.'

'Tony, watch your mouth,' said Denise.

Tony held up a hand by way of apology.

'I can't take on a whole crew. Not without more people getting killed. I'm not going to ask Jimmy to start a war for me. Just ask him to set it up. I'll go on my own. I want to be in a room with Buchanan. Tell Jimmy I want to make them an offer.'

Tony started laughing, said, 'You got some fuckin' balls on you, kid.'

Denise tossed her head in frustration.

'I need time to think. I'm going for a long walk to West 74th Street,' I said.

'Eddie, just be careful,' said Denise.

'I have to finish this. I'm sick of being careful. It's time I started being smart.'

45
Eddie

Manhattan is life.

Walking these streets is like plugging your brain directly into humanity itself. Some people think that this city is defined by its great buildings that reach for the sky, the sheer volcanic opulence of Times Square at night, the grandiose romance of Central Park or the enormous scale and wonder of the Brooklyn Bridge.

It is none of those things.

Manhattan is made by the people who pound its sidewalks, by the cab drivers who battle through its traffic, by the sounds and spirit of those who pour beer, sell newspapers, flip burgers, buy and sell the world, count the money and the people who protect them all.

In Manhattan, it's hard to see starlight. The people make this city burn too brightly.

Clarence and I made our way through the park, headed west. The summer sun was beginning to warm the sidewalks and the cars and the people. And all the while my brain boiled with questions. Especially after I'd taken the call from Bloch. She'd gone home for an hour to shower. There had been no movement from Ellis or Bale last night.

'You said last night that Brett Bale told you he wasn't targeting the Jacksons,' said Bloch.

'That's right,' I said.

'And you believed him?'

'Yeah. Do you think I got it wrong?'

'No, I think you got it right. I think he's interested in the nanny – Ruby Johnson. I didn't know who she was until last night. She was the girl who watched Lake and me in the Blakemore house. She saw me outside the Jacksons' last night. There's something about her . . .'

'What do you mean?'

Bloch sighed, said, 'I'm no good with people. But I know how to think. And I know how to fight. When I see Ruby, I make fists. My jaw clamps down. And I can't take my eyes off her. Same thing happens when I see a spider. Or a snake. I don't know why it happens. It just happens. That's the best way I can explain it.'

'Are you telling me you're afraid of the babysitter?'

'I *think* I am,' said Bloch.

We talked some more, and I let her know the plan so far. It was risky.

'The meeting with Buchanan, where are you going to get the money? How am I supposed to watch your back?'

'You can't watch my back when I meet Buchanan. I'm on my own. I don't know where I'm going to get the money yet. Trust me, I'll find a way.'

'A lot can go wrong. I don't want you in a bed beside Harry,' she said.

'If something goes wrong, I won't be in a hospital bed. I'll be on a slab in the morgue, but I can't think of any other way to do it.'

'What do I tell Kate?'

'Don't tell her about the meeting. Tell Kate I'll need her to play along with Castro. The key to this case is in that latent palm print and the DNA. Harry focused on it. We'll deal with the anonymous witness as best we can.'

I hung up. Clarence glanced up at me as we walked. He didn't look convinced by my plan.

I wasn't convinced either. I grabbed his leash and we headed out.

We got to the Jacksons' place on West 74th around eight that morning. Alison answered the door and let us inside. I had never been inside their house. At first it looked like a perfect family home. Clean, tastefully decorated. Lush couches and thick carpet in the living room. Patterned black-and-white tile in the hallway, which led into the kitchen on the left.

A little boy sat at the counter eating a bowl of cereal. He looked like he'd just got out of hospital – that tired, weary, sick look.

Being accused of a major crime that you didn't commit does something to you, and to your family. It's a cancer. It eats people from the inside out. I could see it in John. Alison too, that haunted aspect. Even when she smiled at Clarence, who got a bigger welcome than I did.

'How are you holding up this morning?' I asked.

'I miss my mom, Eddie. She could be tough sometimes, and cruel, but she loved me and I loved her. She was always there for me and now . . . I just . . . I can't lose John as well. I just can't . . .'

'I'll make sure you don't,' I said.

'That's a nice doggy,' said the kid, rubbing his eyes. He put down his spoon and carefully climbed off his breakfast stool to stand beside Clarence.

'Tomas is still a little groggy,' said Alison, wiping her raw cheeks. She'd been crying through the night, I guessed. 'Tomas was given some medication last night for a fever and it kind of knocks him out for a day or so,' said Alison.

'Can I pet him?' asked Tomas.

Even the kid's voice sounded strained and fatigued. His eyes had brightened, though.

'Sure,' I said. 'This is Clarence.'

'Hi, Clarence. I'm Tomas,' said the boy.

I heard footsteps on the stairs, and John came into the kitchen. He looked worse than yesterday, but, for a moment, the fear subsided as he watched Tomas stroking Clarence, who was loving the attention.

'Nice dog,' said John.

'He's not mine,' I said. 'He's . . .'

'Harry's?' said Alison, and I nodded, welcoming her finishing my thought. My friend was still on my mind, every second. I wanted him beside me. So we could talk, and I could hear his laughter. The nurse had basically told me to expect the worst. I hadn't processed that information yet. I didn't want to.

'How is he?' asked John.

'Still the same,' I said.

'Coffee?' asked Alison.

I sat at another stool at the kitchen counter and watched Tomas and Clarence get to know one another. Tomas giggled as Clarence licked his face.

'Thank you,' said John. 'I can't remember the last time I heard him laugh.'

We fell silent. Alison poured coffee for me and I sipped it, then put it down to let it cool and looked around the kitchen.

Like the living room, everything was nicely put together. Tasteful. Alison, I guessed. She had a great eye. It looked like a home you might see in a commercial, or a catalogue, but lived in. Not cold and clinical. There was a toy firetruck on the floor by the window; pencil markings on the door frame, which I guessed was John taking note of Tomas's height as he grew; and the large refrigerator door was covered in souvenir magnets, which pinned up bills, letters, drawings, Tomas's paintings and technical drawings of the hallway and living room – plans for renovation. Alison liked a project, I guessed.

Alison and John watched Tomas and Clarence play, and then I heard something.

It was faint at first, but grew louder.

A buzzing sound.

A bee, or a wasp?

Then I saw it. A big fat blowfly whizzed by. Clarence saw it too. He tracked its movements through the air.

The fly swooped through the kitchen, and Clarence was locked onto its flight path. He followed it into the hallway.

'Clarence,' I said, and went out after him.

In the hallway, Clarence stood very still, looking at something on the wall.

The fly, I presumed. He let out a low growl, and a whimper.

'What is it, boy?'

As I got closer, the buzzing got louder. Clarence seemed to be staring at the painting on the wall. It was strange. At first, it seemed out of place with the rest of Alison's decorative scheme. A gilded frame and, within, an old man in black and red robes, a crucifix in one hand, sat in a chair, staring out of the painting. It wasn't like those pictures I saw as a kid, where the eyes of the people in the picture follow you around the room. But it was well done. And old. Very old.

The fly crawled over the small ridges of paint, buzzing around it. Clarence barked.

'Hey, it's just a fly. Calm down, pal,' I said.

The blowfly launched itself off the painting, and flew back into the kitchen. For a second, Clarence watched it go. But he didn't follow. He was on all fours, staring at the dark, unnerving picture of the old man. He barked. He didn't like it. I didn't like it either.

'It was my mother's,' said Alison, joining us in the hallway. 'It was her mother's before that, and she passed it on to me. Like many things. Most of them I still have. Apart from my necklace. I would give this thing away in a heartbeat if I could have my necklace back.'

'You caught Althea trying to steal a bracelet. The police never found the necklace?' I asked.

She shook her head, then said, 'My grandmother spent a fortune finding this picture after the war. It had been hidden in a basement in Warsaw, by a friend of hers. She had it shipped over here in the fifties. I never liked it as a child. It scared me. I sometimes thought the priest in the picture was looking at me. Silly. I had to put it up when my mother gave it to us as a wedding gift. No choice. I didn't want to at first, but whenever she visited she would ask where I'd put the painting of the priest. She could be difficult. I miss that. Eventually, John hung it here to shut her up. Kinda out of the way. You see it every time you go up the stairs, but it's hidden away enough that most people don't have to look at it. I've been meaning to take it down since Mom . . . but I haven't had the heart to. Not yet.'

She wiped away a tear, and John joined us in the hallway, put an arm around Alison's shoulders and lightly kissed her hair. It was a gentle gesture, just a reminder that he was there for her in her grief.

'Ruby is afraid of the red man too,' said Tomas.

Their cleaner and nanny, Ruby. I hadn't met her yet. But it was time to rectify that.

'What's that, sweetie?' asked Alison.

'Ruby's scared of the man in the painting. I see her looking at him sometimes and she looks scared.'

A strange look came upon Alison's face.

Now I really needed to meet Ruby.

'Look, this wasn't an entirely social visit,' I said. 'Court is in an hour or so. Alison, I know how much support you give to your husband. And we need you beside him, but could I ask you to come to court later today? This morning, I need you to pack up whatever you need for a few days and check into a hotel. We are making the arrangements. This is for your safety, plus it frees up some more of my team. We're going to need to move fast, because this case is going to move fast. Do you think you could do that for me?'

'I can't,' said John. 'This is what the neighbors want. They want me out of this street. I haven't done anything wrong. I won't leave my home.'

'John,' I said, 'I know how proud you are. And you have every reason to be. However, this is not about you. This is about the safety of the family. I know you're a good protector and provider. Right now, I need you to be smart.'

'But they'll see that we've left. They'll think I'm guilty.'

'They already think you're guilty. You want to win? Let my team do their job. Go to the hotel. Get room service. You'll be much safer there. Trust me.'

John put his hands on his hips. This felt like the final straw for him. He had tried to hold on to his reputation, his job, his marriage, his family, his sanity. And this was one last thing that was being taken from him – his home.

He swallowed. Nodded.

Good enough.

'Tell me more about Ruby,' I said.

Alison explained that Ruby and her mom used to live on this street, but her father was an alcoholic and a gambler and lost everything. He ran out leaving them to deal with all of it, including the repossession of their home. Alison couldn't be sure, but she'd heard Ruby's father was a violent man. There were rumors that he regularly beat Ruby's mom.

'The thing is, with a background like that, you just wonder how she survived. Her future was ripped away. But she didn't get angry or sullen, she just looks after her mom,' said Alison.

'Is her mom sick?' I asked.

Alison nodded, said, 'I don't think she has long left. Look, I believe in Ruby. She has been such a rock for us these past months . . .'

I was about to say that Alison had also trusted Althea at one point, but I bit my tongue.

The sound of a key sliding into the lock drew our attention. The front door opened and a young woman in her early twenties stepped into the hallway. She wore a T-shirt, blue jeans and a light green jacket. Her hair was tied up in a ponytail and she carried a backpack. Soon as she got inside, she realized that everyone in the house had stopped to stare at her.

'Hi, Ruby,' said Tomas, breaking the awkward, stagnated quiet.

'Hi, my little angel,' she said.

She seemed perfectly nice. There was a cotton-candy sweetness to her voice and her easy smile. I wondered what the hell Bloch saw in this young woman that I did not.

And then I saw something. She looked at me.

For a second, maybe even just half a second, the smile dropped. It was like someone holding up a shelf, and just letting it fall moment-arily before pushing it back up there again – level.

'Ruby,' said Alison, 'John and I are going away for a few days. We're taking Tomas. Could you help me pack?'

Ruby's smile grew wider. Her eyes lit up.

'I think that's for the best. I can help you pack,' said Ruby.

And before I said my goodbyes and took Clarence, I wondered what the hell was going on with Ruby Johnson.

She was hiding something.

46

Kate

Kate remembered Eddie telling her that a cross-examination was best treated like an armed robbery. Get in fast, get what you want and get out.

Given that her father used to be a cop, Kate disliked the analogy. But it was accurate.

With the jury settled, and all the players in court, Castro called the medical examiner to the witness stand.

The medical examiner, Dr. Joanne Kilter, testified that the victim, Margaret Blakemore, died from three gunshot wounds. One in the chest. Two in the temple. She was able to retrieve those rounds from the body and they were preserved in evidence for the ballistics expert – Mr. Harris.

The ME was not a contentious witness. She told the facts as she found them. Kate knew there were things the ME didn't find, and they could help John Jackson's case.

'Dr. Kilter, you examined all three entry wounds caused by the gunshots. You didn't find any evidence of bruising to the skin around those wounds?'

'I did not.'

'You didn't see any scorch marks?'

'I did not.'

'What is a star-shaped entry wound?' asked Kate. This was a loose question, but there was only one factual answer. Worth the risk.

'It is a tearing and ballooning of the skin around a bullet entry wound consistent with the barrel of the weapon being in contact with the skin when the round is fired. This causes the gases from the firing of the weapon to be trapped under the skin, which will erupt and tear because a minor explosion has happened beneath the skin.'

'And there was no sign that this happened in this case?'

'None.'

'So whomever fired the fatal rounds did so from a distance, correct?'

'Correct.'

Kate thanked the witness, and sat down.

Castro now turned to the rounds that had been retrieved from Margaret Blakemore's body.

Harold Hugh Harris had signed his ballistics report with his initials.

He always used his middle name and pronounced it with a flourish as he stated it for the record after accepting his oath. Castro took some time to run through his credentials. He didn't hold a doctorate. Didn't have a college degree. He was, by trade, a gun seller. At least he used to be, until he discovered that he could make a shit-ton more money as a private consulting ballistics expert. The money was on display – it had paid for a tailored navy pinstripe suit, perfectly cut at the ankle to show off his brown leather cowboy boots.

He hailed from Texas, as if anyone couldn't guess.

His qualifications entailed a one-month training course with a recognized professional body of ballistic experts. He had paid the course fees, completed the assignments and training, then collected a certificate with gold foil on the edges. The remainder of his qualifications as an expert witness came from what he described as 'extensive casework experience over a period of fifteen years'.

'Mr. Harris, did you receive any weapons for examination in this case?'

Harris was another graduate of the school of expert witness testimony. He faced the jury, giving the lawyers a profile view only. He knew the only people who mattered in the courtroom were the jury, and it was easier to stay out of an argument with a lawyer if you didn't look them in the eye.

'Yes, sir, a Sig Sauer pistol . . .'

'Wait just a second, Mr. Harris. When you received the weapon, did you also take into custody any other evidence seized from the scene?'

'I did indeed, sir. Yes, I also took custody of three shell casings from the crime scene, and three rounds which I believe were retrieved from the victim. However, I only examined one of those rounds.'

'Why did you only examine one bullet?'

'To my understanding, sir, this was the only bullet that had not suffered significant impact damage. It was slightly deformed at the tip, but otherwise intact. The other rounds were heavily damaged.'

'Just tell the jury what examinations you undertook?'

'I carried out tests to determine whether the bullets fired came from the pistol found by police in the defendant's closet.'

'And how did you go about this?'

'I was able to test-fire five rounds from the pistol into a water tank, and then undertake a microscopic examination of those control rounds, comparing it with the bullet recovered from the victim. You see, when a bullet is fired, there are tool marks impressed upon the bullet as it passes through the barrel of the weapon. Each barrel has been machined with a spiral-type pattern, or rifling, as we call it, which spins the bullet as it leaves the barrel in order to keep the projectile flying straight. There are characteristic markings left on the bullet, but each weapon will leave individual marks. These are fairly unique. I was able to determine that the markings on the control shots matched those marks found on the bullet used in the shooting.'

Castro took a second to make sure the jury was following. Most of them were. Some were not. He decided to make it a little easier for the rest of the jury to follow.

'The markings on the bullets, are they like a fingerprint for the weapon?'

'Yes, very similar to a fingerprint. Each bullet carries the markings of the weapon that fired it. And, in this case, there was a sufficient match for me to be sure that the weapon found in the defendant's closet was used in this shooting.'

47
Kate

Taking on an expert in his own field is daunting.

It's even more daunting when a man's life is in the balance. Kate put those thoughts aside. It was almost an unconscious act. She had been taught to leave the outcome of the case to the jury. Not to think about the consequences of every mistake – while it was happening. Nothing could be allowed to cloud her mind.

It was then that Kate ignored her training. She took a breath, inhaled deeply and felt the weight of her responsibility flood her mind and her body.

An innocent man's life lay in her hands right at that moment.

She had to carry John with her if she was to win this fight.

First thing to do was break Harris out of his witness training. She couldn't have his attention locked on the jury. Harris needed to look at her. Otherwise, he'd never be drawn into the trap Kate was going to set.

'Mr. Harris,' said Kate, 'you didn't do all of these tests, and invest your time and effort into this case for free, did you?'

He smiled, but kept his head pointed at the jury and said, 'No, ma'am. I am an independent ballistics expert, but I do charge for the work I do. I charge the DA exactly the same amount as I would charge a defense lawyer like you, little missy.'

Little missy.

Harris wore a condescending smile.

Not for much longer, Kate thought.

'Tell me, how much is the DA paying you for all of your work in this case?'

'Objection, relevance?' said Castro.

'Your Honor,' said Kate, 'the people who elected the district attorney are paying for this expert. There are perfectly qualified NYPD forensic experts who are trained in ballistics. Instead, the DA has chosen an alternative expert. The people are entitled to know how much that costs and if there is a motive behind this expert's selection.'

The judge nodded. Kate continued before he could change his mind.

People don't like to talk about how much they earn. In this case, Harris was getting paid because a murder had happened. The members of the jury were on forty-five dollars a day, plus lunch. And Harris would know this. The jury sure as hell knew it.

Harris looked away from the jury, straight at Kate, and said, 'I have been paid one hundred and thirty-five thousand dollars.'

Now he had broken eye contact with the jury, it was Kate's job to keep him talking to her. Sever that eye-to-eye dialogue with the jurors permanently. The best way to do that was to start a fight.

'Is that how much you charge for lying in court?' asked Kate.

'Little missy, I don't tell lies. I have conducted thorough forensic examinations of a weapon and ammunition and provided my expert opinion to the court. It don't matter who pays me – I tell it like it is.'

'You've done the opposite, really, Mr. Harris. You've been telling the jury like it isn't. You are a member of the Association of Firearms and Tool Mark Examiners?'

'I am a fully paid-up member.'

'What is the criteria set for examining projectiles and determining their common origin?'

'The marks have to be *in agreement*. I believe that is the phrase,' he said with some authority.

'That is not correct, is it? The actual wording of the guidelines are that for projectiles to be determined to have a common origin, there has to be *sufficient agreement* in their markings.'

'That's what I said. Agreement.'

'The markings left behind on a projectile can vary over time and use. So that the same weapon can produce certain markings one day, and different markings the next week?'

'That is true.'

'Your comparison of the markings left behind is completely subjective, though. Isn't that right?'

'I undertake a microscopic comparison of the projectiles. When I am satisfied that they have the same markings, then I have to say that they have a common origin. In this case, there were ridges and furrows on the projectiles which I felt were common to a single weapon.'

'But another ballistics expert may find that same evidence inconclusive? Do you accept that?'

'That's their *opinion*,' said Harris.

Kate tried not to smile. Her line of questions had narrowed to this point, and to this precise word that she had coaxed from Harris. She moved his testimony from a bullet being a fingerprint for the weapon to mere *opinion*.

'There is no objective scientific proof that these projectiles were fired by the same weapon – it's just your *opinion*, having carried out a comparison?'

'My *expert* opinion.'

'Other than the tests you carried out, what else influences your opinion?'

Harris thought about this, said, 'Not a single thing. Sometimes I am given details of the crime scene, but it doesn't matter. I go by my comparison studies.'

'I see, well, what if we did a small comparison study right now? Of the cases in which you were retained by the district attorney's office – how many times have you found that the disputed projectiles in those cases matched the defendant's weapon?'

'I don't recall. I've worked a lot of cases.'

Kate marched to the defense table, picked up a small file and opened it. She had done her homework on Harris.

'Let me remind you, Mr. Harris. You appeared as a prosecution witness in forty-three cases. In all of those cases you said the bullets matched the weapons linked to the defendants.'

'If you say so. I don't recall.'

'You have appeared as a witness for the defense in twenty-six cases in thirteen states. In all of those instances, you disputed the prosecution's case that the bullets matched the weapons belonging to the defendants.'

Harris tilted his head, said, 'In each of those cases I conducted my examinations faithfully.'

'But you have already admitted your expert opinion is just that – it's *opinion*, not fact. Correct?'

'I carried out a microscopic comparison of those bullets . . .'

'You base your opinion on whoever is paying you, Mr. Harris. The jury doesn't need a microscope to see that,' said Kate.

48
Ruby

Sunset Senior Living facility sat on 46th Street and 10th Avenue between a dog day-care center and a liquor store.

The sign in the reception area read: 'Making Your Sunset Years Beautiful' and beneath it was a picture of an old lady sipping a margarita on a rooftop, watching the sun set behind the buildings of Manhattan.

The facility manager, Lula, did point out that they'd had to close the rooftop refreshment area, as two residents had managed to throw themselves off the top of the building. She also explained Saturday night was movie night, meatloaf was Wednesdays, Tuesdays was aerobics and Thursdays was karaoke night. Both suicides happened on a Thursday. Lula helpfully added that she didn't believe there to be any correlation.

For a place that cost eighty-nine thousand dollars a year, and was cheap in this part of New York, it struck Ruby that taking a fall off the roof might make economic sense to some folks.

'I'm sure your mother will be very happy here,' said Lula as she walked with them toward her mother's room, passing some elderly gentlemen with walking frames and cheeky grins.

The room could've been better. The floral wallpaper had peeled away at the corners, and there was an orderly kneeling down at the locker beside the bed, putting stuff into a blue garbage bag. There were fresh sheets, a TV, a chair and a comfortable bed and bathroom. Stains on the wallpaper where pictures had been freshly removed.

'We encourage residents to place their own art on the walls. Our porters will bring your personal items of furniture right up,' said Lula.

Her mom looked around the room and smiled, then patted Ruby's arm.

'I'll be well cared for here,' said her mom. 'You go and live your life. I can't believe you spent all your savings on this . . . you . . . you've worked so hard for me . . .'

Ruby choked up when she heard the emotion breaking her mother's voice.

'He left us with nothing. You've saved me, Ruby. I love you so much.'

She felt the last of her mother's strength in that embrace. She inhaled her. The Oil of Olay on her skin, the smell of strawberries from her hair. Ruby's tears fell onto her mom's gingham dress.

'I'll be back in a day or so –' she almost said out loud she would come to say goodbye, but checked herself at the last moment – 'to check in. Just call my cell if you need anything.'

Ruby didn't mind handing over a quarter of a million dollars for her mom's care. She deserved somewhere decent to live. And this was way better than their ratty apartment. She would be looked after for the remainder of the short time she had left in this world.

It was more than her father, Josef, had ever done. All he knew how to do was spend and lose money, and hurt people.

By the time Ruby left the facility, she was already planning.

She thought about going home and packing up her possessions, but apart from some clothes there was nothing she wanted to take. She had no heirlooms like the Jacksons. Anything of value had already been taken and sold by her father's debtors, who failed to track him down. Ruby wondered if they had looked very hard at all, because her father had signed liens on all their property and possessions. The banks and businesses he owed could just take the house and everything in it, and sell it. And that is exactly what they had done.

She would go to the Jacksons and look after Tomas and think things over.

When Ruby arrived at the Jacksons', she met their lawyer, Flynn. She didn't like him, didn't like the way he looked at her.

Ruby found it hard to contain herself when Alison said they were going to a hotel. She helped them pack. John would go to court, and Alison and Tomas would be at the hotel today.

Ruby quickly formed a plan.

She would get her money. Go home and pack her stuff. Rent a vehicle. Go to the Jacksons' tonight.

And find a way to deal with Mr. Christmas.

She was sweating by the time she reached the bank, a brand-new duffel bag in her hands, which she'd just bought from a Target. When it was her turn at the teller, she explained she had called ahead and wanted to make a withdrawal. One of the bank's supervisors was called, and he tried and failed to get Ruby to keep her account with them.

Twenty minutes later she was on the street, her account closed.

Two hundred and fifty grand in her new bag.

And a plan forming in her mind.

The man who called himself Mr. Christmas was formidable. Frightening, even. And smart. But not entirely honest. Ruby knew if she gave him the money, his next move would be to put a bullet in her head.

49
Lake

As Gabriel Lake sat behind the wheel of his new car, he thought about the morning's events. Tony Two Fucks had met him at the old New York Life Insurance Building. Lake got out the driver's seat, closed the door and hit the fob to lock it.

'What the fuck is that?' asked Tony.

'It's my new car.'

'You paid money for that fuckin' thing?'

'It's a car. It's got four wheels and it drives.'

Tony shook his head, and Lake followed him into the grand entrance of 108 Leonard, which had originally been home to the New York Life Insurance Company, before it was extended, and then subsequently had its clock tower erected. Now, a hundred years later, it was home to more than one hundred and fifty luxury apartments. Tony whispered something to the building's doorman, who took them straight to see the building manager in a side office off the marbled-floor reception area.

Lake waited on the leather couches, admiring the ornate gold filigree on the ironwork that decorated the walls. Tony came out of the office with the manager, carrying a floor plan. Lake selected an apartment on the south side. Top floor. Beneath the clock tower.

'We can accommodate our resident in one of our hotels while the maintenance work takes place. The apartment will be on all major rental sites within the hour,' said the manager.

Tony swore at him in a way that Lake took to be greatly affectionate, then bear-hugged the man until his face turned Coca-Cola red and then let go of him enough to allow his feet to touch the floor. Lake wondered what it must be like to be on the wrong side of Tony Two Fucks if this was how he treated friends.

Lake sent a text message to Eddie to confirm the apartment was ready, then headed back to his car.

Tony didn't like his car. Still, it was a car. Lake didn't care much for aesthetics.

After a phone call with Eddie, he drove to the Jacksons' to meet Eddie and Clarence.

'What the hell is this?' asked Eddie as he got into the backseat with Clarence.

'It's my car,' said Lake.

'It's a Pontiac Aztek,' said Eddie.

'Is it? I don't know. It's white, which is a surprise. I thought it was brown when I bought it. But it drives okay.'

Clarence took a look around the interior and let out a moan.

'I'm going to walk Clarence home then get to court. Bloch will watch Ellis and Bale. You follow Ruby Johnson, the Jacksons' nanny. If I'm right, she is going to make some plays. Get pictures.'

And so, for the rest of the morning, Lake had followed Ruby Johnson. He'd watched her wave off Alison and Tomas to a hotel. John left for court, then Ruby left. He watched her go buy a sports bag, and then head to a bank.

The bag was empty when she went in.

The bag was full when she came out.

Lake took pictures on a digital camera with a zoom lens. Slowly, he pulled out into traffic and drove for a hundred yards. Then pulled in. Ruby didn't use the subway, and for that he was glad. Lake didn't like underground spaces. She seemed to prefer the bus, and that was easier to follow, as most New Yorkers who drove the city got stuck behind a bus for at least part of their day.

He kept back a couple of cars, not wanting to alert Ruby that she was being followed. After ten blocks, he noticed that the car up ahead stopped when the bus stopped, and had a couple of opportunities to get around it, but never did. A sleek, black Lincoln.

Lake felt something cold walk over his skin. The Lincoln was following Ruby.

He once knew a man who drove Lincolns just the same as this one. Didn't matter what city he was in, the man always hired or bought black Lincolns to drive.

A man he never wanted to see again. The man that Eddie had met.

Ruby hopped off the bus a block from her apartment building. Lake pulled ahead of the bus and the Lincoln. He looked at the driver as he passed, but the man had his arm on the window rest, hiding his face. Unable to get a good look, he sped up, overtook the car and checked his rearview mirror. The driver had his head down.

An uneasy feeling began in his stomach, and he felt a dull pain in his right shoulder. That joint was held together with wires and screws, limiting his full range of mobility. A .45 caliber round had torn through his shoulder, some years ago. It was one of a number of bullet wounds he'd suffered. Trauma surgeons had saved his life, and stopped the bleeding from the stomach wounds and the shot that cut through an inch of his thigh. Those injuries had healed well.

The shoulder was a problem some days.

Usually, it ached in the cold.

Or when he had nightmares about the shooting in the heroin stash house where he'd almost died from those wounds. He would wake up covered in sweat, his shoulder screaming.

Lake shook his head. Tapped a beat on the steering wheel as he came around the block and parked across the street from Ruby's building. He just got stopped in time to watch her go inside.

There was a Starbucks on his side of the street. He connected to their Wi-Fi, emailed the photographs of Ruby to Eddie.

His phone rang one minute later.

'Is that blackmail money?' asked Eddie.

'Got to be. I'm sure she didn't save enough cash to fill a gym bag from changing diapers and washing floors.'

'How much is in there?'

'No idea.'

'Send the name and address of the bank to Bloch. She'll find out.'

'What about Bale and Ellis?' asked Lake.

'We don't have enough bodies to watch everyone. Right now, the game is all about Ruby Johnson. Stay on Ruby and keep me updated.'

As Lake ended the call, his passenger door opened. There were internal locks on the Pontiac, but either they didn't work or Lake didn't know how to switch them on.

A man dressed in an expensive black suit got into the passenger seat beside Lake and shut the door. As he got in, Lake's nervous system went into overdrive. Adrenalin flooded his veins, the fight-or-flight instinct kicked in and Lake, instead of moving, was frozen in place for half a second from the shock of seeing this man. The incongruity.

It was like watching a five-hundred-pound alligator get into your car. Disbelief comes first. Then reaction.

Lake reached for his gun, but the man gave him a look. Wagged his forefinger in the air, like he was remonstrating with a child, and then tutted.

'You're not as fast as you used to be, Gabriel. Do you mind if I call you Gabriel? Mr. Lake seems too formal. Especially after all that we've been through together.'

'Are you going to tell me your first name?' asked Lake.

'I think Mr. Christmas is just fine, for me. Oh, what the hell – let's go crazy . . . You can call me Christmas. What do you think of that?' he asked with a genuine smile.

'I think I'm going to kill you the first chance I get,' said Lake.

'Now, Gabriel, that *is* rude. Here we are, sharing a case together, getting to know one another, reconnecting after all this time . . . It's disappointing. Almost as disappointing as this car. Did you steal it from a junk yard?'

'What are you doing here?'

'We're talking,' he said, completely focused on Lake. Such intensity. Eyes like a traction beam locked on Lake as he asked, 'Why are you following Ruby Johnson?'

Lake didn't miss a beat and fired back, 'Why are *you* following Ruby Johnson?'

The questions were like two sharp blades clashing.

Neither of them spoke. Lake met the man's iron gaze. Silence filled the car's appalling interior. He could hear his own heartbeat like a timer ticking down to some horrific end.

Two killers. Inches from one another. In a car filled with boiling quiet.

Somehow, Mr. Christmas appeared to piece together Lake's motives.

'Your client's babysitter is really quite something, isn't she?'

'I don't know yet. She's a player in a game that has cost a lot of lives. How much money is in that bag she's carrying?'

It was an innocent question, and for a moment Mr. Christmas weighed whether he should answer. The exact amount didn't make a difference. It was clear to both men she was carrying a lot of cash.

'Quarter of a million,' said Mr. Christmas.

The tension that had built between them seemed to evaporate. Although Lake couldn't see it, he felt the man beside him take his state of readiness down a few notches. As if every muscle fiber that had been tensed now let go into easy company.

'We're two old hands at this game. You and I. Between the two of us, we have killed a lot of people . . .' said Mr. Christmas, but Lake didn't let him finish.

'Don't put me in the same coffin you crawled out of. We're not the same. I don't kill for money. I do what's right.'

'What's right? Is that what happened in that stash house? Was it right that you went through that building killing everyone in it, whether they were armed or not?'

'You seemed to think it was okay.'

'You were bleeding out, Gabriel. It was a valiant effort, but that last man . . . You were on the floor, barely conscious . . .'

'And you shot him in the face. I wouldn't have gone near that house if I wasn't chasing you down. It was your fault. All of it.'

'Was it my fault one of your colleagues wanted you dead and led you to walk into that trap? No. You were lucky I was following you. It was me that pulled your near lifeless body out of there and called a paramedic. You're alive because of me.'

'You mean I nearly died because of you.'

'Don't you see? We are the same. We're linked. Now, we have a common goal. Young Ruby's machinations are causing all kinds of repercussions.'

'You were given a contract to kill her. Who hired you?'

'Oh, come now, Gabriel. You know my methods. It's all done through the office. I'm not great at customer care, nor administration. I take the call; I pull the trigger. Someone else handles the paperwork.'

'Call your office, or your guy, or whoever deals with your shit. I want the name behind the contract. And Ruby Johnson has to keep breathing until I can prove my client is innocent.'

'I'm not entirely sure that is ethical,' said Mr. Christmas.

'You're a professional hitman. I'm not sure you can claim the moral high ground here.'

'What if I said no.'

'You'll say *yes*,' said Lake.

Mr. Christmas tilted his head to one side, said 'Why?'

'Same reason you pulled me out of that building.'

He considered this for a moment, said, 'The identity of my principal shall remain confidential. However, in the spirit of this conversation, I shall allow Ms. Johnson some additional time. Just as I am permitting your employer.'

Lake gritted his teeth, said, 'Thank you. Eddie isn't my boss. He's a friend.'

'And yet you didn't tell him about me.'

'We all have secrets.'

'Indeed. Now, if you don't mind, I do have to relieve Ms. Johnson of the funds she has so readily and fruitfully acquired. Give my regards to Mr. Flynn. I'm sure I will meet him again soon.'

As Mr. Christmas opened the passenger door and turned to get out, Lake thought about making a move for his weapon. The man's back was turned. He was vulnerable for one, maybe two seconds. Enough time for Lake to draw his pistol and put three rounds in the hitman's back. Two in the lungs. One shot in the spine.

Mr. Christmas gently closed the passenger door of the Aztek.

Lake's fingers crushed the steering wheel. Then he relaxed his shoulders, cleared his mind for a second, inhaled deeply and tried to get his heart rate below one thirty. The cold pain in his shoulder eased. After a few seconds, he took out his cell, called Eddie. Told him everything that had happened. The bag. The money. The hit. He didn't relay the entirety of the conversation. The part about Mr. Christmas saving him from the last shooter in the stash house, he kept that to himself for now. Eddie had already seen the photos Lake had sent of Ruby and asked him to send them to Bloch too.

'Where is Christmas now?' asked Eddie.

'He's just crossing the street to go into Ruby's building.'

'I'm on my way.'

50

Eddie

I ended my call with Lake in the hallway outside the courtroom. I went inside, sat beside Kate.

'The People call Ansen Bude . . .' said Castro.

'Bude is the latent-print expert,' whispered Kate.

'I was hoping we wouldn't have to deal with this today,' I said.

'What are we going to do?' asked Kate.

'Exploit the fact that the latent palm print isn't a match for John. That's our only point, but Bude has an easy out for that line of questioning.'

Kate swore under her breath. I closed my eyes, tried to focus. There had to be a better way. The print was important. Castro would prefer not to call Bude to the stand, but the DNA that matched John came from the print tape itself. He had no choice. The fact that the palm print didn't match John was important. It was a mystery. Juries don't like mysteries.

Something worked at the back of my brain. Something about this print.

Harry knew it was important.

But I couldn't grasp hold of it. Not yet. I had a theory, but it was crazy. And, yet, it just might be the truth.

'How are we going to beat Castro? What would Harry do?' asked Kate.

I bowed my head. Hearing his name, feeling his absence in the courtroom – it was a gut punch.

Gut punch . . .

'Harry often thought of cross-examination like boxing. Same tactics . . .' I said.

I thought for a moment.

There was a way.

'We can't beat him. Not today. Make sure you get permission for the judge to recall the experts. It's going to run like Foreman and Ali in '74. Today, we're going to lose.'

'Lose?'

'Lose. And lose badly. We're going to take a lot of punishment from Castro. And we're going to lean on the ropes and rest while we absorb those punches.'

'And then what?'

'We lose today. Tomorrow, we're going to take Castro's head off. Look, I've got to go. There's a hitman following Ruby Johnson,' I said. 'The answers we need for tomorrow are not in this courtroom. You okay to hold the fort?'

'I can handle it. What the hell is going on in this case?'

'I think either Ellis or Bale has hired someone to go after Ruby. They know she's the blackmailer. She's got a quarter of a million dollars in a gym bag. She's turned Margaret Blakemore's murder into a nightmare.'

Kate thought for a second, said, 'Remember what Harry used to say about Einstein? That if someone gave Einstein a problem with only an hour to solve it, he would spend fifty-five minutes defining the real question and then five minutes answering it.'

I didn't follow. Kate saw my confusion and elaborated.

'What if Ruby isn't just exploiting this situation? What if she created it? She could've planted that gun in the Jacksons' home, then she made the anonymous call. She's the witness. This is all about money for Ruby. It makes sense.'

'Maybe, but why testify anonymously if she has the money already? Why not just take off? And how did a palm print that isn't John's, but contains John's DNA, get on the murder weapon?'

'That's the problem,' said Kate. 'We've spent too long thinking about the answer. We need to go back to the beginning and think about the right question.'

The theory that had been working in the back of my head started to come together. I still didn't have all the pieces for it to make sense. They would come.

I had a lot on my mind. The contract on my life, the meeting with New York's Finest, Angel, Mr. Christmas, Castro, the Jacksons, Margaret Blakemore and – at the center of it all – Ruby Johnson. And my best friend lying in a coma.

'What are you going to do?' asked Kate.

'I have to meet Lake. Then Christmas. But, first, I need to make some calls and do some shopping. When you're done for today, and we've had our asses kicked, I want you to reach out to Castro. Tell him we can see which way this case is going and we want to make a deal. Drop a hint that we will talk to our client about second-degree murder, but I need to talk to Castro first and make sure it's on the table if we can convince our man to plead guilty. Tell him to meet me, alone, in the All American Diner opposite the precinct, at seven tonight.'

'You're going to have dinner with this guy?'

'I'm not going anywhere near the place. Just tell him to meet me there. Trust me.'

51
Eddie

Before I left the courtroom, I took a second to reassure John Jackson that things were going to be okay. That the rest of the day would be rough, but not to worry. We were going to come back strong in the morning. Al Parish sat in the row behind John. I tapped Al on the elbow as I left court.

'Walk with me,' I said.

On my way to the elevator, I opened my phone and hit dial for Denise.

'We're in trouble,' said Al.

'Don't I know it. Things are going to work out okay. I promise. I need your team of associates tonight. Same deal as last time. Street clothes. Dressed down.'

'What are you going to have them do this time? Assault the district attorney's office?'

'Not exactly. I want to buy them dinner . . .'

I explained what I needed. Parish didn't understand why I wanted it, but promised to make it happen. He was getting used to my method of legal practice.

Denise answered my call.

'You know I said you could work from home today?'

'Yeah . . .' said Denise in a tone that said she had never really believed it.

'I need you to call into the office and copy some documents for me as fast as possible.'

'You want me to go into the office and Xerox documents?'

'You and Kate are the only people on this planet who know how to operate that copy machine. Not even the man who built it can get it to work.'

'How much do you need copied?' she asked with a sigh.

'Around eleven pounds . . .'

I made a stop at the store where Ruby bought her gym bag. Checked the photos Lake sent me. Zoomed in. I walked around the aisles until I found the exact same bag hanging on a rail. There were only two left in the store.

I smiled.

When I exited Target, I then hailed a cab and got dropped off at Lake's Aztek, still parked across the street from Ruby's building. I got into the passenger seat.

'You been shopping?' he asked.

'Yeah, I was going to get you some snacks, but they only had human food. Has he come out yet?'

'Not yet.'

'How long has he been in there?'

'An hour.'

My phone buzzed. Message from Tony Two Fucks.

The Angel has checked in at the Clock Tower Building.

I had too many plates spinning in the air. It was time to start catching some of them.

'What's Christmas doing in there? Should we go check on her?' I asked.

'He's talking. He likes to talk. I don't think he's going to harm Ruby. Not yet. He gave me his word.'

'And you trust him?'

Lake shrugged, rubbed the steering wheel rhythmically as his heel bounced on the floor. As a naturally anxious man, it was hard to tell when he was genuinely worried or just conscious.

'I want you waiting outside for when he comes out. Tell him to meet me at seven thirty tonight. I'll be at 102 Norfolk Street – the Lower East Side Toy Company.'

'What the hell are you doing? You're going to meet a man that wants to kill you?'

'I've met a lot of people that want to kill me. My ex-wife, for one. Look, it'll be okay. I don't walk into any place that I don't know how to walk out of. Just set it up. After you talk to him, stay on Ruby. Kate thinks Ruby is at the heart of all of this. She saw the real killer that night. Somehow took the gun, planted it in John Jackson's home. She has access to that house. And she did it all to blackmail the real killer into paying her a quarter of a million dollars. I don't know how she got John's DNA, and there's no way to prove any of this. If Kate is right, and I think she is, then Ruby should be halfway to Rio by now. Why is she still here? I have a feeling she's going to make some moves and we need to be there.'

I left the vehicle, was about to close the door behind me when I stopped, leaned down and said, 'You know, the best place to look at this car is from the inside. And even that makes me feel ill.'

Lake gave me the finger.

As I stood on the street looking for a cab, I called Bugs. My guy who moonlighted as a tow-truck driver with his buddies, playing the part for me during the Jayden case against Sergeant Ben Gray.

'How would you feel about coming out of retirement?' I asked.

'I don't know, Eddie. I can't do any more time. I'm too old for breaking and entering.'

'I wouldn't ask if it wasn't important. I need you and a couple of your buddies tonight – Karl and Little Sacks. I'm paying fifty grand. What do you say?'

'For fifty grand I'll break into Fort Knox.'

'Relax, it's not that big a deal. Just some light B'n'E. There's two jobs. First one is real easy,' I said.

'What's the first job?'

I waved down a yellow cab, said, 'I need you to break into my car.'

52
Kate

Ansen Bude was one of the most handsome men Kate had ever laid eyes on.

He had those classic Scandinavian looks. Tall. Blond. An Olympian gymnast's build under a tasteful suit, violet-blue eyes that made her legs feel funny and cheekbones as sharp as the tail fins on a '57 Plymouth Fury. She wasn't the only one who was checking out Mr. Bude. Several of the female jurors were practically beaming at the man as he finished his oath and sat in the witness chair.

'Mr. Bude . . .' began Castro, pronouncing the name to rhyme with 'dude'.

'Actually, it's pronounced *boo-day*,' said the witness in perfect English, with only a slight Scandinavian accent. The ladies on the jury clearly liked his voice too.

'My apologies, perhaps you could outline your position and professional credentials for this jury,' replied Castro coldly. As well as a dirty player, Castro was also a vain man. Kate could see it in the way he checked his hair, adjusted the line of his suit every time he got to his feet. And, like most imperious men, he disliked Bude. Kate could tell by Castro's tone.

In that lovely accent, Bude said he had studied various biological sciences in Stockholm before moving to New York to study latent fingerprint extraction and analysis, and he was employed by the NYPD in their forensics laboratory.

'What is a latent print?' asked Castro.

'Well, first I have to explain what a palm print or fingerprint is,' said Bude.

Castro nodded, as if he was expecting it, and told him to go right ahead. Secretly, Castro was pissed – here was a pedantic witness picking apart his questions. Kate formed the view that Bude cared about his responsibility as a witness and as a scientist.

'Fingerprints, like palm prints, are formed before we are born. These are the friction ridges on our hands and fingers, which form whorls, loops and patterns.'

He finished his answer and looked to Castro. Bude was clearly an experienced witness. And one who followed the rules. Instead of going ahead and finishing the full answer, he stopped. Waited for the question. Witnesses who keep talking all have the same problem – inevitably they say something that comes back to bite them on the ass.

'And what are latent prints?' asked Castro.

'Natural oils and biomaterial like dead skin cells are constantly coating every surface of our skin. When we touch something, often we leave some of that material behind. And this is in the unique form and pattern of our fingerprints or palm prints.'

The forensic lesson was over – Castro got Bude talking about this case and asked him about the print he'd found on the weapon that killed Margaret Blakemore.

'I had dusted this weapon with metallic powder and brushed it carefully over the entire surface. This allows oils, material and moisture to become visible. We know it's there when we see the pattern formed by the ridges on our skin. I saw a pattern on the grip of the weapon. Using transparent lifting tape, I was able to take that print, and the biomaterial forming the print, and then marked it as evidence.'

'What did you do then?'

'I photographed the print, scanned the picture and fed it into our database of prints. This was a palm print, or part of one. Unfortunately, this print did not return a match.'

'Are there any particular reasons why someone could leave behind their DNA on a fingerprint, or handprint, but the print itself does not match?'

'There are many reasons. It can be the amount of pressure applied to the surface, the direction of travel, or the contact surface itself. In this instance, there just wasn't enough of the print, and that was why it did not match the defendant.'

Castro thanked Bude and sat down.

Kate rose and smiled at Bude. He smiled back. Kate got that funny feeling at the back of her legs again.

'Mr. Bude, just to be clear, your testimony is that the palm print you found on this weapon does not match the defendant's prints, correct?'

He smiled again, and for a moment Kate thought she was getting somewhere.

'I'm afraid it's not as simple as that. The print I examined did not have the characteristic markers in sufficient quantities to match the defendant's prints.'

If anything, that sounded worse for the defense. Kate got permission from the judge for Bude to be recalled as a witness and then sat down before she inadvertently caused any further damage. It wasn't her fault – it was the right question to ask, and she knew it. Bude knew it too, and so he'd been waiting for it.

Castro called what could be his star witness. Dr. Hopkins looked like a quiet man. He was carrying an extra thirty pounds, which filled his gray sweater neatly. He wore a smile, a suit and wide, comfortable shoes that you were only allowed to buy if you were over sixty-five years old or you're from Cleveland. He was sworn in, gave his qualifications as an expert DNA profiler and Castro led him through ten minutes of lowball questions on what DNA is, how it's extracted and tested.

'Were you able to obtain a DNA profile from the biomaterial in the palm print lifted from the pistol?'

'Yes, the biomaterial left behind, like skin cells, which form a latent print, had sufficient DNA markers for us to provide an analysis.'

'Just to be clear, the DNA came from the palm print itself?'

'Correct. The sample was taken directly from the lifting tape, used by Mr. Bude, which collected the biomaterial on the print itself.'

'And what was the result of your analysis of that DNA?'

'As I explained earlier, every set of DNA has specific markers. We have the technology now to check for twenty-four separate sets of markers from, say, someone's blood sample. In this case, we were able to obtain sufficient DNA for a profile. That profile was in all probability a match with the sample of DNA obtained from the defendant for comparison purposes.'

'Why do you say *in all probability?*'

'No, in DNA science there is no such thing as matching DNA, scientifically speaking. However, our probability figures were sufficiently high. That is to say, the DNA profile has a mathematical likelihood of matching the defendant. There is a one in three-point-four billion chance that the DNA belonged to someone else.'

'So the odds of the DNA on the weapon belonging to someone other than the defendant is one in three-point-four *billion?*'

'Correct.'

'Is that longer odds than winning the state lottery?'

'Much longer. That's like winning every lottery in the United States, with the same numbers, on the same day.'

'Thank you, Dr. Hopkins.'

Kate hated leaving the jury with those odds. It was a killer blow. She could see that they were clearly impressed by Dr. Hopkins. He didn't exaggerate his scientific findings; he was clear and precise. Some of the jurors looked at the defendant. Nodding.

They'd made up their mind.

Kate asked for the witness to be recalled at a later date. The judge adjourned the case for the day.

John Jackson closed his eyes, hung his head and tears fell on the defense table.

Kate's phone had been buzzing in her pocket.

There was a group chat now, for Lake and Bloch to keep Kate and Eddie updated on the whereabouts of the players in this game.

Bloch was parked on West 74th Street, focused on Bale.

Todd Ellis was on the move.

Bloch wanted to keep an eye on Bale, so she let Ellis go.

53

Mr. Christmas

The sleek, black Lincoln circled Norfolk Street for the second time. It was almost seven thirty.

As Mr. Christmas rolled around the block, he thought about his day and, in particular, his visit with Ruby Johnson. There was a young woman who was full of surprises.

He had expected she would not open the door to her apartment. She would not call the police, given the large bag of cash she had in the place, but he had thought she would resist. If she was anything, she was a fighter.

Except she didn't resist. She opened the door and invited him inside.

'I've got the money,' she said.

'I'm aware. Perhaps I could see it, please.'

She disappeared into her bedroom as Mr. Christmas waited in the kitchen, his right hand inside his jacket, ready to draw his pistol. Ruby came out of the bedroom with the blue gym bag, set it on the counter and opened it. Then stood back. Mr. Christmas brought the bag toward him, so he could look inside and keep Ruby in his eyeline. He didn't want to turn his back on this one.

He fanned the bound stacks of cash, making sure they were all hundreds and fifties, and no one-dollar bills had been slipped in. It came to two hundred and fifty. Neat.

'Do you want coffee?' asked Ruby.

'If you are attempting to delay the inevitable conclusion of our business, there is no need. I will not harm you today, Ruby.'

She nodded, said, 'There's still coffee, if you want some.'

'Why not?' said Mr. Christmas.

She poured two cups. Mr. Christmas asked for half and half and sugar, and they took their coffee to the small living room, Ruby in her chair, while Mr. Christmas occupied her mother's old seat.

'How does it feel having your mom in a retirement home?' asked Mr. Christmas.

'It's part nursing care too. For her illness. It's a relief,' said Ruby. 'She deserved to have people take care of her properly. She's been through so much. She had a terrible time with my father. He beat her, for years. Then, when he ran out on us and took whatever money we had left – that was hard too. She still loves him. And she hates him. But she got us through it. And I wanted to be able to give her something back.'

'Have you ever tried looking for him?'

'No. She tried, about a year after he took off. Last trace of him – he was working in a bar in Topeka, Kansas. He'd stolen the weekend's takings and run off with a waitress. The trail went cold after that. I pity the waitress. I bet she was afraid of him too. What about you? Are your parents still around?'

Mr. Christmas felt something in his gut, a warmth. He'd not had a conversation like this in a very long time.

'My father left us when I was five years old. He went out for a gallon of milk, never saw him again,' said Mr. Christmas. 'I have no idea where he is now. Probably dead. My mother couldn't cope. She called the police, reported him missing. She didn't tell them he was the type of man who would disappear for days on end, and come home with no shoes and a torn shirt. For the rest of her life, she spent her evenings staring at the front door. Waiting for him. She died when I was fifteen. Car wreck on the way to pick me up from school. She'd been drinking.'

'That must've been very difficult for you,' said Ruby.

'Not really, my dear. I knew from a young age that I was quite different from my peers. I knew right from wrong, of course. But I refused to see the appliance of that general societal norm to me. I didn't *feel* like other people do. I have a short temper, especially if people are rude. That is the extent of my emotive range. Other emotions rarely surface. When they do, I am invariably in the dark of a movie theatre. That's where my feelings lie, and I don't take them with me when I leave. They remain on the floor, like nuggets of spilt popcorn.'

'Is that why you are . . .' She couldn't finish the sentence.

'Yes, in this profession my ability to kill people without a second thought is a positive boon. I do have principles, and my own morals, after a fashion. Strange as they may seem, to some. Everyone needs guidelines. You are polite and wise enough not to try to kill me. That is, in part, why you are still alive. What are your guidelines, Ruby?'

'I do what I need to do to protect my mom.'

'And that is admirable,' said Mr. Christmas, and he sipped at his coffee and thought for a moment, then said, 'You are not afraid of me.'

'No, I am afraid. But I don't show it. Do I need to be afraid of you?'

He smiled.

'What are your plans now?' he asked.

'I have things I have to do. Then I am going to do what my father did. I'm going to disappear.'

'These things you need to do, are they to protect your mother?'

She nodded.

'And after that you are going where?'

'There's a poster on my bedroom wall. It's from the eighties, I think. An ad campaign for Cadillac. A blue one. Convertible. There's a woman behind the wheel and she's on one of those long straight roads in the desert somewhere that just goes on and on and on, and she's just driving. Her blond hair is blowing in the wind and the sun is shining. That's where I'm going.'

'I like you, Ruby Johnson. Someday, we should go to the movies together. Just as friends. You like movies?'

'I like movies. I like the ones where people drive. When they go on a road trip.'

'Then it's a date. Tell me more of your plans.'

'Maybe I shouldn't,' she said.

Mr. Christmas drew the pistol from his jacket, laid it on his lap, said, 'Would you rather discuss Marlon Brando?'

She looked at the gun. Mr. Christmas took another drink from his coffee cup.

'Alright, I'll tell you the truth,' said Ruby.

Mr. Christmas, upon exiting Ruby's building, met Lake on the street. Lake passed on the message about a meeting with Flynn.

Mr. Christmas never passed up a meeting with a target.

And now, here he was on Norfolk Street. He drove by a parked Mustang, Flynn's car, and pulled in, the memory of his afternoon with Ruby still playing in his mind. He got out of the car, stepped to the sidewalk and looked up and down the street.

Two men, he guessed they were homeless by their dress, halfway up on his side of the street. One of the men pulled a thin strip of dark metal from his pants and began to slide it in between the glass and the doorframe of Flynn's Mustang. More than half of the streetlights were in darkness. No security cameras anywhere. This was an ideal spot to steal a car, or just break in and grab whatever was inside, including radios, cash, bags. Mr. Christmas looked at his car, and his gaze travelled to the trunk.

He looked at the men. Then back to the trunk of his Lincoln.

He could not take any chances.

Using the fob, he clicked the button to release the trunk lid, retrieved Ruby's blue gym bag, closed the trunk and locked the car. The beep and the flash of lights briefly drew the attention of the two men breaking into Flynn's car. Mr. Christmas stared at them. They slowly moved away.

With the bag in his hand, he turned to try to find the entrance to his meeting place with Flynn. A small metal gate, about waist height, barred a set of stairs that led to a tunnel under the building. A hand-made sign on the gate said, *Lower East Side Toy Company.*

He pushed open the gate, took a firm grip on the handles of the gym bag and slowly descended the steps into the tunnel. When in dark, possibly hostile places, Mr. Christmas never used a flashlight. Instead, he stood there for a minute, letting his eyesight adjust to the darkness. No point in advertising your arrival. Plus, if he held a flash-light in his free hand, it would hamper him reaching for his pistol.

At the end of the tunnel was a small courtyard, and a large oak door. A large man, possibly made out of oak himself, stood beside the door. As Mr. Christmas approached, he stepped to one side, and opened the door for him.

Warm light spilled onto the cobbled courtyard.

Inside, it was a time warp. An antique parquet floor. A rosewood bar, wallpaper that was as old as the building, and a split-level staircase that led to leather seats and an open fire on the floor above. There were only a few patrons at the bar. The hostess, in a green flowing dress, approached him and said, 'Welcome to the Back Room. I'll take you to see Eddie.' Linking his arm in hers, she guided him up the stairs and across the room. There was no one in the armchairs in front of the fire, and for a moment Mr. Christmas wondered if he had misheard her, but then she walked right up to a bookcase and gently pushed on one side. A secret door was revealed to another room, in the same style.

Again, empty.

She approached the wood panel that covered the right side of the wall, again pushed, and this time led him to another room. It was small and had a row of booths, like a diner, on one side and a bar on the other. In the last booth, against the wall, was Eddie Flynn.

Mr. Christmas took a seat opposite him, the seat was narrow and slim so he slid his bag under the table.

A coffee cup sat in front of Flynn.

'They serve most of their drinks in coffee cups,' said Eddie. 'Or if you order beer it comes covered in a brown paper bag. Just like it did when this place first opened. It was a speakeasy. One of the finest in the city. It used to be the back room of Ratner's deli. Meyer Lansky and Bugsy Seigel were regulars. Jimmy Walker, one of the most corrupt mayors in the city's history, would sit right here, in this booth, and meet with cops, mobsters, union men, you name it. And they all paid Jimmy. Would you like a drink?'

'No, thank you. I thought you didn't drink any more.'

'I don't. This is just coffee.'

'The place does have some period charm.'

'It's private, which is the main thing. Most people don't know about this secret room. I wanted somewhere we could talk, openly. I want to make you an offer.'

'You and I already have business together, Mr. Flynn.'

'That's what I'm talking about. I need more time before you try to fulfil the contract. I'm meeting New York's Finest tomorrow night.'

'Are you going to try to pay them off?' asked Mr. Christmas.

'I've got no choice. Like they say in that movie, I'm going to make them an offer they can't refuse. I heard you're a Brando fan.'

'The word fan comes from fanatic. You could say that, yes.'

'So I'm asking you for a truce. Let me have the meeting. If there's still money on my head afterwards, well, you can try to collect it then.'

'Mr. Flynn, even if the meeting does not result in a resolution, there will be no contract to fulfil. They'll kill you right then and there. You know that, don't you?'

'The thought had crossed my mind.'

'I am rather busy, but what is to stop me from collecting the prize right now? There's no one here.'

'I thought you were going to take the time to narrow your field of competitors.'

'Oh, I'm just *kidding*, Mr. Flynn. I'm in the middle of some other business. That will occupy me for this evening. Good luck with the meeting.'

And, with that, Mr. Christmas leaned down, lifted his bag and left the bar.

He walked to his car, put the bag in the trunk and got in. Fired up the engine and rolled out. He had another place to be.

The plumbing-supplies warehouse in Sheepshead Bay was in darkness. The gate was open and a Bentley was the sole vehicle parked in the lot. A side door lay open.

Mr. Christmas parked, retrieved the gym bag from the trunk and went inside. The place was massive, but the towering steel racks filled the space, creating a central corridor.

Todd Ellis stood in the center of the warehouse. He wore a leather jacket, jeans and boots. Ordinarily, Mr. Christmas never met the principal. Safer that way.

Ellis had insisted on a personal handover.

'Is she dead yet?' said Ellis, as Mr. Christmas approached him.

'Good evening,' said Mr. Christmas.

'Is. She. Dead. Yet?' spat Ellis.

Mr. Christmas cocked his head. This was a man with too much power. He was sure that Ellis's parents would have brought him up right. Taught him some manners. The value of relationships. Basic etiquette. Mr. Christmas did not like rudeness. Even now, after this short exchange, he could feel the rage building inside him.

'No, she's not dead,' said Mr. Christmas. 'Not yet. For now, I have your—'

'Why? Why isn't she dead? Didn't you kill her when you took the money? What the fuck are you doing?'

Mr. Christmas felt his jaw tighten as he strode forward. When he was within five feet of Ellis he dropped the bag. Stepped back a pace. He was afraid that if he opened his mouth again it would only make things worse and, for the moment, he was struggling to contain his anger.

Snatching the bag, Ellis dropped to the balls of his feet and unzipped it.

'What the fuck is this?' he said.

Mr. Christmas gazed at the bag, and the bundles of copy paper inside. They were not blank, those pages – on each one was a picture. A familiar one.

An image of Marlon Brando.

'I *said*, what the fuck is this? Are you trying to screw me over?'

Ellis stood, his neck burning red, spit flying from his mouth as he swore.

Mr. Christmas planted his feet. Tensed. Said, 'You need to calm down, sir. I don't know what has happened here—'

'You're trying to screw me. You've made a deal with that bitch. You have no idea who you're fucking with. I'm going to *destroy* you. Do you understand? I'm going to—'

Ellis didn't even have time to change his expression. He was still ranting, his lips curled in a snarl of rage, as the first nine-millimeter round tore through his chest.

The second one went through his mouth.

Mr. Christmas lowered his weapon, picked up the gym bag and dragged Ellis's body out of the building. He burned the Lincoln, the body and the bag some miles away in an empty parking lot.

As he watched the car go up in flames, he thought about one man.

The man who had conned him.

Eddie Flynn.

54
Eddie

I watched the hitman take the gym bag from under the table, get up and leave the Back Room speakeasy. I waited for a full minute, making sure he'd gone. The hostess, Anne, stuck her head through the door, said, 'He left.'

I got up out of the booth, turned and knelt down. Knocked on the wood panel beneath the seat that I had occupied. The panel slid open and a gym bag appeared. I slid it out, then I reached in and pulled Little Sacks out of the hidden panel behind the seat. While Mr. Christmas and I had talked, Little Sacks had slid the panel back, taken the gym bag with the cash and replaced it with the identical bag I'd bought that afternoon, which Denise had filled with exactly eleven pounds of copy paper, with a little message for Mr. Christmas printed on the pages.

God bless corrupt mayors. Jimmy Walker had sat in this booth for many hours when he ran the city. And everyone sat down opposite him with a bag at their feet. When they got up, the bag wasn't there. Jimmy may have been crooked, but he wasn't dumb. Even in a hidden area inside an illegal speakeasy in the 1920s, there could be a cop at the next table. This way, even if a cop was standing right next to Jimmy, no one would be able to see money changing hands.

I put the gym bag on the table just as Bugs came into the room.

I opened it, stared inside at the cash and then counted it.

A quarter of a million dollars.

'That going to be enough for New York's finest?' asked Bugs.

I nodded, took fifty grand from the bag and gave it to Bugs.

'I'm putting my life in your hands – you understand that?' I asked.

'You gave me my life back when you stopped me going to jail. I owe you,' he said. We talked for almost an hour, going over everything in detail.

'You know what to do?'

He nodded.

'Good enough. You can split the fifty Gs with your guys. Thanks, Little Sacks.'

He patted me on the back, said, 'We got you, Eddie. Don't worry.'

I watched them leave, prayed that I had made the right decision.

I took out my phone, called Al Parish.

He picked up, said, 'Well, my associates dressed as you suggested and they got what you wanted. You owe them three hundred and fifty dollars for dinner.'

'Put it on my expenses.'

'I still don't know what all of that was in aid of? How does it help us win this case? Castro is mightily pissed off that you stood him up.'

'Good. I want him pissed off. But that wasn't the whole reason.'

'Then what? Why did my associates spend two hours in a diner just to get a few pictures of the DA?' he asked.

'You know, best advice I ever heard was from Harry. He told me when I was in court never ask the witness a question if you don't know the answer. Nine times out of ten, he's right.'

'But I don't know what all of that was about? How does it help our case?'

'Al, for your sake, I think it's best if you don't know.'

I had another call coming in. I said I would see Al tomorrow in court.

Incoming call was from Lake.

'I've lost Ruby. She was on the street, caught a bus, then went into a commercial-vehicle hire yard. A half dozen vehicles have left and I couldn't see inside the cab of half of them. I think she's hired a van or a pick-up. Either way, she's in the wind . . .'

We'd lost Ellis earlier.

Text message from Bloch.

I'VE LOST BRETT BALE. CAME OUT OF HIS HOUSE AND JUMPED ONTO THE BACK OF A COURIER BIKE. I FOLLOWED HIM TOWARD LONG ISLAND, AND HE LOST ME.

'Did you see that text message from Bloch?' I asked.

'Jesus, everyone is making moves tonight,' said Lake. 'What'll we do?'

'Get to the Jacksons' house. It's a hunch. Nothing else. Just get there asap. I'm on my way . . .'

I called Bloch.

'Get back to West 74th Street. Bale was leading you away from the street. It's all going down tonight.'

55
Ruby

It was dark when Ruby pulled up outside the Jacksons' house.

The family were safely gone. They weren't slumming it either. Earlier that day, Ruby had helped Alison check in to a mini-suite at the Four Seasons, Downtown. Even though John was still on a salary, it wasn't what he usually brought in every month. They had savings, which they had relied on to a degree, but Alison was expecting an inheritance now, so the Four Seasons was the natural choice.

With her last quarter of a million gone, Ruby had about eighteen grand in her account. That wouldn't last long when she was on the run. No Four Seasons for Ruby. It would be most nights in her second-hand car, which she still had to buy, and the occasional stay in a Motel-6 when she wanted to shower and feel a bed under her bones.

But none of that could put Ruby off the thought of escaping the city. The road. A new name. A new life. Anywhere she wanted.

The thought of it gave her peace.

She closed the rear door of the panel van and hauled her backpack and some of her supplies up the steps and into the Jacksons' hallway. Two more trips unloaded most of what she needed. The street was quiet, even though it wasn't late. She was thankful for the peace.

Ruby grabbed a plastic ground sheet and unrolled it in the hallway.

Straightening the corners. She placed a bag of plaster on one corner. The leg of the hall table on another. For the last two corners she just used some Scotch tape. Two blowflies buzzed overhead. She could hear their wings beating against the painting. On her hands and knees, Ruby flattened out the sheet.

Then stood.

And stared at the painting of the red priest.

He stared right back at her. His face had contorted into something altogether demonic. Rage and anger pouring out of the picture. The house was silent.

Ruby's mind was a hurricane of noise.

The red priest was screaming. Crying. Howling.

The first she knew of the blood vessel that burst in her nose was when something warm trickled down her top lip, over her bottom lip and onto her chin.

She couldn't stop now.

This was her chance.

Ruby took hold of the painting, gripping the sides, and pushed up, levering it off the wall. She stepped back and placed it, face up on the sheeting.

The noise was deafening. She stumbled, held the side of her head. A ringing noise now.

And then . . .

Suddenly . . .

Silence.

Something had driven the priest away.

Instinctively, Ruby's head snapped to the side and she stared at the closed front door.

She heard the doorbell again. That was the sound she'd heard just a moment ago.

Someone was at the front door.

No!

She'd waited so long for this time alone in the house. Time to get rid of the red priest. Time to solve the problem that had haunted her day and night. Time to get away.

There was no door knocker, but whoever was on the other side of the door wanted in. She heard a fist thumping the wood.

Bang!

Three times.

Hard. Fast.

Insistent.

Ruby couldn't draw attention to herself or her presence in the house. Not now.

Please, Jesus, not now!

The neighbors would hear the knocking. There had been a murder on this street. They were on edge. Watchful.

BANG! BANG! BANG!

Louder now. She couldn't ignore it. This person wasn't going away. The lights were on in the kitchen and hallway. They knew someone was home.

Ruby had no choice but to open that door and fast.

She moved toward the door, glanced over her shoulder at the sheeting on the floor and the painting in the center.

She could always make up a story. She was just cleaning the frame. Yes, she could say that.

BANG! BANG! BANG!

Ruby took hold of the door lock and began to turn it . . .

56
Eddie

The Mustang's wheels locked as I stood on the brakes in West 74ᵗʰ Street.

A white panel van was parked outside the Jacksons' house.

The lights were on in the hallway. I got out of the car, sprinted across the street, up the steps and stopped in front of the closed front door. It was solid oak. Thick. Expensive. My shoulder and probably my hip would break before I could force the damn thing open. No element of surprise.

Ruby was in there. She'd hired that van. And whatever her end-game might be I knew in my guts it was happening right then in that house.

I rang the doorbell.

Waited.

Nothing.

I rang it again. Checked the street. No sign of Bloch or Lake, yet I knew they were on their way.

Maybe the doorbell was busted or disconnected.

I pounded on the door with my fist.

Waited. The neighbors would hear this soon and they would be poking their heads out their front doors to see what was going on.

Two cars arrived on the street. Bloch's Jeep and, behind it, Lake's

Aztek, already billowing black smoke from the exhaust. I smelled it before I saw it.

They pulled in, killed their engines and were out of their vehicles and running up the steps behind me.

I pounded on the door again.

And listened . . .

I thought I heard someone inside. Someone turning the doorknob. I bent my right knee, put my weight on my left foot. Ready to push my way in as soon as the door was opened . . .

57
Ruby

The doorknob turned slowly.

The springs inside the mechanism taking the tension.

Click.

The door was unlocked, and instantly it was pushed open, knocking Ruby on her back.

She landed heavily, her right arm twisting behind her.

When she looked back at the door, a man stood there. For a moment, she couldn't see his face.

His right arm was extended, and his features obscured by the gun pointed at Ruby's head.

'Get up, right now,' said Brett Bale.

Ruby's arm howled, the pain snaking up her forearm, into her triceps and the back of her shoulder. She didn't know if it was the pain or the sudden shockwave of fear, but Ruby found that she could not move.

'Up, now,' said Bale. He reached over with his free hand and grabbed Ruby's hair, hauling her to her feet as she let out a yelp of pain. Her scalp was on fire.

'Not here,' said Bale, and roughly turned her around, pointed her at the front door and still with a handful of her hair, shoved her forward. Ruby lost her footing, tripped and fell down the front steps to land on her back in the street.

She heard a door slamming, and managed to get her feet beneath her, ready to get up and run, when he grabbed her by her injured arm, at the wrist, and pushed her toward a Land Rover. The vehicle unlocked as he approached.

'Get in,' he said, and pushed the barrel of the pistol into her side, making her wince.

Ruby opened the passenger door, got in. Bale slammed her door shut, ran around to the driver's seat, closed the door and hit the ignition button.

With the seatbelt warning signal pinging, he pulled away, steering with one hand. His other in his lap, the pistol pointed at Ruby's belly.

'You got a quarter of a million dollars from me. I paid it so I could find you. There's no way you could know about me and Maggs unless she told you. Tell me exactly what she said . . .'

58

Mr. Christmas

Mr. Christmas had learned that if you have to burn your current mode of transport to hide evidence, it's best to do it close to an airport.

He'd walked for ten minutes through a dark neighborhood, putting some distance between him and the burning vehicle, and then called a different rental company, but they had no Lincolns available. He decided on a Cadillac, black, of course, and handed over one of many credit cards that he had in his wallet, under one of many names that he carried around like extra lives.

Soon he was back in Manhattan.

He'd driven around for a while, in likely places, looking for Flynn's Mustang, but couldn't find it.

Instead, he parked and waited.

While he waited, he thought about the seventy-five thousand dollars Flynn had cost him. And all the trouble of killing his client. Considering that development, he thought it best to tell his man now.

He always picked up quickly for Mr. Christmas.

'Good evening, it's Mr. Christmas calling . . .'

'How'd it go?'

'I'm afraid I have to report there has been something of a dip in my standards of customer care.'

'A dip?'

'More of a failure, or a collapse, in those standards, really.'

'How big of a failure?'

'Catastrophic.'

'So he's dead? I told him this wasn't a good idea. It's not how we operate, but he insisted.'

'In my defense, he was rather disagreeable.'

'What happened?'

'Well, at first he was discourteous. Then he was rude. There was a small problem with delivery of his money, which I would have rectified, but impatience and intemperance got the better of him. He threatened me.'

'Sounds like you did what you thought was right.'

'I have my standards.'

'Was the contract fully fulfilled?'

'No.'

'What about our other business. Is Flynn still alive?'

'He is, for now.'

'If you don't mind me saying, and don't take this as a criticism, but maybe you should think about closing out our contracts in New York?'

Mr. Christmas sighed, said, 'I didn't get to where I am by simply fulfilling contracts. As I've always said, there are wider considerations.'

'I'll leave it to you.'

Mr. Christmas hung up just as a woman fell down a set of steps a hundred yards ahead of him. He looked closer. A man followed her down those steps, picked her up roughly and threw her against a car. Focusing, Mr. Christmas recognized Ruby. He did not recognize the man who was mishandling her, but he saw the gun in his hand clearly enough.

Mr. Christmas turned on the Cadillac's engine and followed the Range Rover with Ruby Johnson in the passenger seat.

Before he turned left at the end of West 74th Street he heard the sound of an engine revving high. A distinctive sound for anyone familiar with cars. A V8 singing its irregular roar of a song. He checked his mirror, and watched Eddie Flynn's Mustang screech to a halt outside the Jackson house. Exactly the place Mr. Christmas thought Flynn might visit this evening. That was why he had parked there.

He knew then, exactly, what he should do. It was a matter of prudence, purely.

He was a professional, and professionals, before all else, perform their tasks with ruthless efficiency and reliability. Mr. Christmas should circle the block, come up behind Flynn and shoot him in the back of the head.

Hitmen fulfill contracts. They kill people and get paid.

This was logical. This was business.

This was what Mr. Christmas was supposed to do.

59
Ruby

Bale swore, made a right off Riverside Drive, caught the on-ramp for the Henry Hudson Parkway headed north. Traffic was heavy and as soon as they joined, he had to slow and stop. His left hand was still holding the gun in his lap, still pointed at Ruby.

The car in front moved off, and he let his foot off the brake to trundle forward ten feet before stopping again.

'What did she tell you about me?'

'She said she loved you.' Ruby lied.

'Did she say anything else?'

'Just that you were seeing other women. You had betrayed her. And she felt bad because she had stood by you . . . after . . .'

'After I drowned my wife?' asked Bale.

Ruby felt suddenly very cold.

The pain in Ruby's arm had not eased. If anything, it was getting worse. What occupied her mind more was that she was feeling something rare and electrifying. Fear. Total fear. She had no play here. No plan. She had to stop these strange feelings and think. The car was locked. She had watched Bale hit the button on his driver's door to lock all doors as soon as they'd moved off.

She couldn't get out. And if she tried, he would shoot her.

Somehow, she had to get that gun. There was no other way.

But her arm. Bale was strong and ruthless. She looked around the car. No weapons. Nothing other than a packet of gum in the console. The phone wasn't a weapon. And she had nothing on her that would work. Maybe the leather belt on her jeans, but he would see her taking it off before she could get it round his neck.

No, that wouldn't work.

The red priest hissed and buzzed.

Bite his throat. Stab his eyes. Get the gun . . .

For the first time in many years, Ruby felt helpless. She felt utterly alone. She knew she would die.

She shook her head, closed her eyes. What was this man going to do?

He didn't shoot her in the Jacksons' house. That was the same MO he'd used to kill Margaret Blakemore. Plus, Ruby's body would be found. The cops would look for a motive. They would find out she had paid a quarter of a million dollars to a care home for her mother, or they would at least search her financials and find the money coming into her account. They would trace it, working backwards, and that might lead them to Brett Bale.

Bale couldn't kill Ruby in the house and leave her body. He needed to make her disappear. That's why they were driving somewhere, and when they arrived at their destination, wherever that might be, Ruby knew that was when Bale would pull that trigger. It would be the end of the road for Ruby. No long days on desert highways with the wind in her hair – everything she had worked for, killed for, would be for nothing.

When she rubbed her face, her fingers came away wet. Only then did Ruby realize she was crying.

The car in front moved forward. A fat spot of rain hit the windshield of the Range Rover. Then another. And another. It was going to be one of those massive summer rain showers.

The windshield wipers activated on their own. Their car was in the left-hand lane, close to the barrier, with two more lanes on their right.

Bale moved the car forward, and then it lurched another five feet, violently, as it was hit from behind.

Bale swore and hit the brakes before he collided with the vehicle in front.

Ruby looked at the gun, but dared not make a move. In the rear-view mirror, a man in a black hat got out of the car behind and made his way toward Bale's driver's window.

'Shit, that's all I need. Don't say a word. I've still got this gun on you,' said Bale, and folded his arm over it, making sure the man who was coming to the window wouldn't be able to see it. 'You hear me, bitch? Don't say a goddamn—'

Ruby flinched, gasped, as glass and the front of Bale's skull blew out through the windshield.

Ruby hesitated. She didn't know what had happened, but the red priest was telling her what to do.

Get out! Get out! Get out!

Ruby leaned over and hit the unlock button on the driver's door. She then opened her passenger door and swiveled and turned, both feet hitting the blacktop at the same time. The jarring motion of landing on the asphalt sent a shockwave of pain through her arm. Saliva filled her mouth and her stomach heaved. Ruby couldn't remember the last time she had eaten, and she only wretched water and spit at her feet. She hadn't noticed the downpour until she wiped her mouth, felt the cold rain seeping through her clothes and soaking her hair.

Mr. Christmas stood in front of her.

'Good evening, my dear. Please switch on the vehicle's hazard lights.'

Her door was still open. Ruby leaned back in, hit the hazard lights.

'Thank you. Now, may I offer you a lift?'

Ruby didn't move.

'It's alright, our business has concluded. You have nothing to fear. Mr. Ellis is dead.'

Mr. Christmas watched Ruby as she gingerly got into his car. He tilted his head, then raised his chin, as he examined her arm.

'Roll up your sleeve, please,' he said.

Ruby pulled up her sleeve, but found that she couldn't straighten her arm. She winced, and bit down on her lip.

A car behind them blared its horn. Mr. Christmas tutted. Then took hold of her upper arm with one hand, her lower arm with the other.

'Your elbow is dislocated. This will hurt.'

He pulled and shoved her arm and Ruby heard a loud click and screamed into her fist.

Then he gently leaned over her, took her seatbelt, drew it across her chest and locked it in place. He turned his attention to the road, indicated and changed lanes, leaving the sound of horns behind them as they moved off.

'There is a medical bag on the back seat. There are some painkillers in there. But be careful – they are quite strong.'

Ruby turned around, managed to grab the bag with her injured arm. It was heavy, and she let out a moan as she brought it up front.

'Thank you,' she said.

Mr. Christmas smiled and nodded. As if he was expecting it, but at the same time quite grateful to receive the courtesy.

'What happened to Ellis?'

'He was the one who employed me to retrieve his money. I won't go into details, but let's just say his manners let him down.'

'Could you take me back to West 74th Street? I need to finish this.'

'Mr. Flynn is there. Or at least he was when I left.'

Ruby closed her eyes, shook her head. The red priest screamed at her, and she opened the medical bag and put a hand inside, searching for a bottle of pills.

'Be careful. There are some sharp implements in there. They should all be wrapped up in a leather carry case, but, nonetheless, watch your fingers.'

Ruby found the pills. Swallowed one of them.

'I didn't really get started. Bale came to the door. Flynn won't know what I was doing there. Take me back. I'll slip inside when they leave.'

'If there is anything that I have learned this evening, it is not to underestimate Mr. Flynn. You have a little money. Why don't you leave this all behind? There's nothing else you can do now.'

'I can't. Then they'll come after me. Maybe come after Mom. I can't risk it. Weren't you supposed to kill Eddie Flynn?'

He nodded, smiled. 'And, if anything, I have more reason to do so now than when I first started out. However, I have come to the reluctant conclusion that it would not be in my long-term best interests.'

'What do you mean?'

'I had my sights on Mr. Flynn. Ready to pull the trigger. I stopped when I saw a man with him. He was a former FBI agent. And, for a while, I'd been his target. Any damn fool can pull a trigger, but there are very few people in this world like us – true hunters of men. He is certainly one of them. I knew, when he was hunting me back then, that this man would find me. Then something unusual happened. He was set up. Someone in the FBI walked him into a house full of armed drug traffickers. He should not have survived, but he did. I followed him in, curious at first. I found him on the top floor of that house – out of ammunition, severely wounded. I killed the last man standing in front of him.'

'You saved him? Even though he was hunting you?'

'I did. And he saw me save him. That began something of an unspoken, but uneasy truce.'

'Why did you save him? Surely you should have let him die?'

'Do you play chess?'

'I never learned.'

'What is the point of being a grandmaster if everyone else is an amateur? Life would soon lose its pleasure. I know you don't play, but I trust you appreciate the analogy.'

Ruby nodded.

'When I saw Mr. Flynn and this man together I had to learn more.

Now, I understand that if I kill Mr. Flynn his compatriot will come after me. The thing about being a grandmaster chess player is that there will come a time when another grandmaster will defeat you. It is inevitable. If I kill Mr. Flynn, I know, in my bones, this man will hunt me down and I will die. In any event, Eddie Flynn's fate is likely out of my hands. He'll be killed tomorrow night at a meeting.'

'It would be better if he died tonight,' said Ruby.

'We can't always get what we want, young lady. What will you do now?'

'I have to see this through. I have to go to court tomorrow. There's a chance I can get into the house again. I have to believe that.'

They drove in relative silence for a time, and Mr. Christmas took them back into the towering streets of the city. They drove down West 74th Street, and Ruby checked the cars parked along the curb. None of them were from Flynn's team. She could get back into the house tonight.

'Why have you been so kind to me?' she asked as Mr. Christmas pulled in.

'Us grandmasters have to look out for one another from time to time,' he said, and then pulled a card from his jacket and gave it to her.

'If you ever need me, call this number. My long-suffering colleague will ask for the nature of your enquiry. Tell him you're a movie fan and you'd like to speak to someone about Marlon Brando. He'll do the rest. Farewell, Ms. Johnson.'

60

Eddie

The sound I'd heard was not from inside the Jacksons' home.

The sound of a mechanism moving came from another lock. The next-door neighbor opened her front door, a woman in her sixties perhaps, wearing an expensive-looking dressing gown.

'What the hell is going on? I thought when the Jacksons left, this place would quieten down. You're the second person banging on that door tonight. Can you keep the noise down?' she said.

'Someone else was here?' I asked.

'Sure, couldn't really see who it was. He looked familiar. Saw him parked outside on the street the other night in a Range Rover.'

Bale.

'What happened? Is he inside?' I asked.

'No, he left with the nanny. She got into his car and they drove off not five minutes ago, down the street there,' she said, and pointed.

'Lake, can you open this door?' I asked, but he was already working the lock with something small and black that looked like a key fob. It whirred and clicked and then the door opened. He pocketed the device and said, 'I'm going after them,' and then ran for his car.

The neighbor looked at us suspiciously, then said, 'You're the lawyer.'

'Yes, thank you, ma'am. Sorry for the disturbance.'

She went back inside, slamming her door shut, and I followed Bloch into the Jacksons' hallway.

Everything in the living room looked normal. The hallway and the kitchen didn't. In the kitchen, I saw a bag of tools.

'Don't touch anything without these,' said Bloch, handing me a pair of latex gloves. We both put them on. I closed the front door and Bloch said she was going to check upstairs, make sure there was no one else in the house. We had both seen the sheeting on the hallway floor and Bloch stepped over it to get upstairs.

I examined the tool bag first. It looked new, along with the tools inside it. A flathead screwdriver with a long neck; a trowel; a claw hammer; a crowbar and a hammer with a heavy flat-faced double head – a crack hammer. I took a moment to examine this closely. It still had a store sticker on the rubber covering the shaft. It looked new. No dents or scrapes around the steel head, but there was some staining. Dark spots. Could be blood. Could be Esther Hanson's blood.

Bloch came downstairs, holding an empty glass.

I pointed to the hammer, and the spots on it.

'Could be the murder weapon used to kill Alison's mother,' said Bloch. 'Looks like the type.'

'What's with the glass?' I asked.

'It was in the boy's bedroom, on the nightstand. There's some residue inside. Looks and smells strange – almost medicinal.'

'Alison mentioned Tomas had a fever and Ruby gave him some medicine. Maybe she put it in a glass of juice.'

A thick plastic sheet was spread out on the floor in front of the stairs. It was secured under furniture and a small, heavy hessian bag of what looked like sand, or plaster. There was no manufacturer's label or store sticker on the bag. The other corners were taped to the tile.

In the center of the plastic sheet was the creepy old painting.

This thing was important to Ruby. I knew that much. Alison had mentioned Ruby stared at it sometimes.

She'd got a lot of money out of Ellis and Bale before they'd worked out Ruby was the blackmailer. And she'd more than likely killed Alison's mother, Esther. And it had all started, I guessed, with planting another murder weapon in John Jackson's bedroom closet. A gun used by either Ellis or Bale to murder Margaret Blakemore. My working theory was that either Ruby had been in on the murder or, more likely, she was a witness. I couldn't discount the possibility she was part of the plot to kill Blakemore, but that part didn't entirely make sense. No, I was pretty sure Ruby had been lucky, or unlucky, one night, and secretly watched the murder.

Instead of calling the police right away, she had taken the gun from somewhere. Maybe she'd watched the killer dump it, then she'd quickly retrieved it, wiped any trace of the real killer and somehow planted John's DNA on the weapon – but, impossibly, not his palm print.

She'd got the money she'd wanted. Yet she was still coming to trial, I guessed, to testify against Jackson tomorrow. What was her endgame?

My mind, stalled, switched back on to the real world and my eyes seemed to flash open on the refrigerator door. That, or my subconscious was drawn to it.

I looked at the family collection of souvenirs and reminders on the door. Postcards. Artwork. Plans. Then joined Bloch in the hallway as she stood on the plastic sheet and stared down at the painting.

'Was she going to wrap this painting in plastic and steal it?' Bloch asked. 'This has all been about money.'

'She wanted the Jacksons out of the house,' I said. 'She probably stole the necklace too. Framed Althea for the theft and Esther's murder. But this painting . . . Maybe it is valuable, but . . .'

My breath caught in my throat as the priest in the picture moved.

Then I saw it wasn't moving. A fly had darted across the priest's face. It took flight, and landed beside another fly in the discolored space on the wall where the picture had hung.

Bloch looked at the wall, looked at me.

I went back to the kitchen, said, 'Take some pictures of the refrigerator door. We need to move,' I said.

I went outside, got into my car, started it up and called Alison.

'Hi, Alison, it's Eddie. I need you to make a call for me tonight . . .'

After I'd hung up on Alison, I called Detective Artie Chase.

The precinct patched me through to Chase on his cell phone.

'I need you to come meet me tonight,' I said.

'I'm a little busy right now, but you are on my list of people to talk to. I've got two dead bodies to deal with. You mind telling me your client's movements this evening?'

'He's in a hotel with his wife and son. Hotel staff and security cameras should be able to confirm that. What bodies are you talking about?'

'Two more of his neighbors are dead. Todd Ellis was found burned to a crisp in a rental car near the airport. Local cops ID'ed him from his wallet contents, some of which had managed to survive the fire. I'm standing on Henry Hudson Parkway right now, looking at Brett Bale. He was shot in his car. Doesn't look like a robbery to me.'

Somehow Ruby had escaped Bale. It wasn't Lake who shot Bale. He would've called.

'I can't help you with those murders, but I need you to come meet me tonight. I want to make a deal.'

61

Ruby

She watched Mr. Christmas pull away and felt her phone vibrate in her pocket.

Alison.

Ruby hit answer.

'Hi, Ruby, I'm just wondering if you could do me a favor tomorrow. The construction workers are coming in the morning, and I was wondering if you could be there to let them in?'

Ruby felt a sickness in her stomach.

'Sure, what time?'

'They should be there around nine. Please be there for me at that exact time. They charge by the hour even when they're waiting.'

'Sure thing,' said Ruby.

Alison thanked her and hung up. Ruby checked the street again. Quiet. None of Flynn's team's cars. They'd gone.

Her arm was still hurting. She was exhausted.

But she had no choice. She had to do this tonight. She went back into the Jacksons' house.

Everything was as she had left it.

Ruby walked into the kitchen, picked up the hammer and moved into the hallway.

She stood by the painting of the red priest.

She heard the buzzing.

He called her name.

Ruby raised the hammer. Her arm burned in pain. The hammer went up, over her head.

She let it fly.

And the red priest became silent.

'Hi, Ruby,' said a voice.

A real voice.

She turned, shocked, toward the staircase and the voice.

'We need to talk,' said Eddie Flynn as he walked down the stairs.

'I want to help you . . .' he said.

62

Angel

The man called Angel closed and zipped the carry case for his Sako TRG M10 and laid it on the vast emperor-sized bed.

The apartment he'd rented at extortionate cost was worth the money. 108 Leonard was an iconic building. With iconic apartments. The bathroom had more marble than most hotel lobbies. The price would eat into his bottom line when he collected his fee, but it was nice to enjoy the finer things once in a while. Angel didn't kill people for money. Sure, he got paid for his work, but he killed people because that was what Angel was put on this world to do.

Killing was purpose.

Protect the team.

Take out the target.

There was no team any more. Hadn't been for a while. Now, there was just the missions. Jobs he chose himself. The joy was in the execution of his work, not in the remuneration. Downtime was good. He owned a lot of nice cars. Some decent houses. And a place in the mountains of Ohio that allowed him enough space to practice his craft.

He put on a fresh T-shirt and black jeans.

Then tied his boots. Loosened them and then re-tied them. It was part of his ritual. Make sure your boots are tight – that's what his drill sergeant told him. He'd carried that with him through basic training, then BUD/S: Basic Underwater Demolition/Seal Team Training. This training is designed to be some of the most grueling mental and physical challenges ever devised. Only one in five trainees make it to week four – hell week. Few make it out of that part of the course. Most quit.

Some die.

Angel made it through and carried two friends with him.

Protect the team.

Four years later, he'd carried their flag-covered coffins onto the same C-130 transport plane in Bagram Airfield. And he'd vowed never to load another.

That's when the incidents began.

Children, mostly. Curious by nature, and they liked talking to soldiers. Children who may have had explosives hidden under their clothes, or may not. It stopped mattering to Angel after a while.

Protect the team.

He left the Seals a different man. A man with two hundred thousand dollars' worth of lethal training, who only knew how to do one thing.

How to pull a trigger and hit a target.

Any target.

He hoisted his tactical bag onto his back and his rifle case onto his shoulder, and left the apartment. In the hallway, there was one door to his right. Locked, but not alarmed.

He picked the lock in under a minute, closed the door behind him and ascended the winding staircase to the clock tower. There were two levels. First was the mechanism house, with four windows on each wall. Above were the clock faces. A north and a south face and the bell.

Angel stayed on the first floor, cut out the window overlooking Leonard Street and unpacked his rifle. The Finnish Sato TRG had a cold-hammer forged barrel and was likely the most accurate factory-built sniper rifle in the world. He loaded the weapon, adjusted the sight. The clock tower was two blocks from the front entrance to the Manhattan Criminal Court building on Center Street. The surrounding buildings with a view of the entrance were all public buildings. 108 Leonard was the closest private building, and the clock tower, with its elevated position, gave clear line of sight over the corner of the Family Court Building and Collect Pond Park.

About a quarter of a mile away. Four hundred meters. Maybe five hundred with elevation. The rifle had a factory-recorded accurate range of 1,500 meters.

Angel could put a bullet through a buttonhole with this weapon at 1,700 meters.

He checked his watch. It was coming up on nine a.m. Angel put on his ear defenders. The bell that chimed on the hour, every hour, would be deafening without them. The window was just below head height. He would have to bend his knees slightly but he could get comfortable. He was used to waiting for a shot, if he had to.

Eye on the stock. Sight lined up.

Eddie Flynn got out of the passenger seat of a Pontiac Aztek and stepped onto the sidewalk. The driver of the Aztek had unruly curly hair, and even from this distance Angel could see creases in the guy's shirt.

Angel began his breathing exercises and gently laid his finger on the trigger. Flynn was the target.

And he was on the street.

63

Eddie

The junior associates of Al Parish's offices were waiting for me on the sidewalk.

Soon as I shut the door on the Aztek, I was surrounded by expensive suits, all the way to the front door of the Criminal building.

Today was going to be a reckoning . . .

For New York's Finest. For Angel. For Castro.

And for Ruby Johnson.

As I waited for the elevator, I looked around the lobby, but Ruby wasn't in sight. When the elevator doors opened on my floor, Castro was waiting in the hallway, pacing the floor, a scowl painted across his face.

'I waited for you for almost an hour last night in that diner,' he said.

'Sorry, I got tied up,' I said.

'You ruined my night. And I'm not having a good day either. My secretary, Maura, she quit this morning. She said I should ask you about it.'

'Good staff are hard to find. If I have anything to do with it, your morning is going to get a hell of a lot worse. Say, do you have any gum? I meant to pick some up at the store this morning.'

'No, I don't have any gum. Are you telling me your client isn't interested in a plea deal?'

'Why should he? I'm going to get him an acquittal before lunch.'

Castro stormed off, his handmade Italian heels pounding the tiles.

I followed him into court.

John sat beside Kate at the defense table. Alison behind. The hotel had provided a babysitter for Tomas with impeccable credentials.

Kate knew what had happened last night. I'd called her around one in the morning, told her about my visit to the Jackson house and she had worked all night in preparation for today. She looked a little tired, but buzzed.

'Do you have any gum?' I asked her.

'No, I don't chew gum. You nervous or something? I didn't think you chewed gum?'

'I don't,' I said.

Neither John nor Alison had any gum. I'd get some before lunch, I was sure of it. I checked with Kate, and she had said she'd delivered our new discovery to one of Castro's assistant district attorneys.

I looked over at the prosecution table and watched Castro looking through the documents with an exasperated expression. He was pissed off and confused, the ideal state that any defense attorney wants for a prosecutor.

The judge came into court and we welcomed the jury back to their seats.

Kate stood up, flattened her suit jacket at the hem, took a pen in her hand, and re-called Ansen Bude, the latent print expert. As Bude took his seat in the witness chair, and was reminded that he was still under oath, I watched the man smile at Kate. She was right. He was handsome.

'Mr. Bude, just to remind the jury of your earlier testimony,' said Kate. 'You testified that the latent palm print on the gun was not a match for the defendant, correct?'

'It could not be matched, no.'

'Please take a moment to look at this . . .' said Kate as she leaned over and began tracing her finger on the mousepad of her laptop.

The large screen facing the witness came to life and displayed a palm print pattern. It was green and four foot wide. So the jury and the expert could see it.

'Mr. Bude, this is a latent print found last night. The original has been served on the prosecution this morning. You have not seen this print before, correct?'

'Correct.'

Kate clicked on the mousepad, moved her finger again.

The screen changed. The green print shifted to the left of the screen, and another print, in black, appeared on the right.

'This print you can see on the right of the screen is the print that you examined and confirmed could not be matched with the defendant, is that right?'

'Yes.'

Kate tapped the return key on the laptop, then placed two fingers on the pad.

'Watch what happens when these images are overlaid,' said Kate.

As her fingers moved across the pad, the print on the right moved and overlaid the green image on the left. It was like watching the last piece fall into place on a jigsaw. The whirls, lines and curves on the prints overlaid exactly.

'I'm not asking you to conduct a forensic examination right now on the stand, but do you agree that the patterns are very similar?'

'Do you mind if I take a closer look?' he asked.

The judge gave him permission. He came out of the witness stand and stood in front of the screen. His fingers traced the lines of the prints, sometimes placing his thumb on one point and stretching his hand to touch another point on the screen. He muttered to himself as his hands and eyes moved across it.

I held my breath.

He nodded, seemingly in agreement, and returned to the witness stand.

'Thank you, Your Honor,' said Bude. 'Latent print comparison, although sometimes done electronically, is better conducted by sight and measurement. There are at least eleven points of similarity between these two prints.'

'And what does that mean?'

'It means that these prints, from an expert point of view, would seem to be a good match at first glance. I would need more time to confirm, of course.'

I leaned over to Kate. She leaned down, worried. She thought I was going to tell her that she had missed out on asking a key question. Her concern faded when I said, 'Bude seems friendly. When he comes off the stand, ask him if he has any gum?'

'I'm not going to ask him for gum. I'll get you gum.'

'Thank you, Mr. Bude,' said Kate.

The judge looked to Castro. He was rubbing his temples and staring at the two images. He didn't want this evidence to settle in front of the jury's mind, but asking Bude anything else might only give him a chance to confirm the prints were a match. He told the judge he had no questions.

Bude then left the witness stand.

I re-called Dr. Hopkins, Castro's DNA expert.

A large man with a comfortable suit and comfortable shoes.

'Dr. Hopkins, you testified yesterday that the DNA you examined in this case was extracted from the latent print examined by Mr. Bude, correct?'

'That is correct.'

'And the DNA you extracted from that print did not yield a full set of markers for profile comparison?'

'Correct, but there were sufficient markers present to conduct a DNA profile analysis. That analysis confirmed, in my mind, the DNA had a high probability of origin from your client.'

Dr. Hopkins wasn't going down without a fight.

'Just to be clear, so the jury fully understands. Let's say there are one hundred markers you could use for comparison purposes. A cent for each one. A dollar would be a full DNA profile. How much did you have to work with the DNA extracted from the lifting tape?'

Some members of the jury nodded, this analogy was easier to follow.

Dr. Hopkins thought for a moment, then said, 'Around forty-five cents. Close to half.'

'Thank you, Doctor. You also testified that there was a 3.93 in a billion chance that the DNA you extracted from the latent print came from someone *other* than the defendant, John Jackson.'

'Correct.'

Kate was way ahead of me. She already had a piece of paper in her hand. She gave it to me, and I approached Dr. Hopkins.

'Doctor, the prosecution has been given a copy of this document. Please examine it.'

Hopkins took the page with some mild trepidation, which quickly turned to confusion when he examined it.

'This is a piece of handprint art. In green paint. It was taken from my client's refrigerator door last night. Mr. Bude just confirmed to this court that the print pattern on this page matches the latent print taken from the gun. Dr. Hopkins, how much DNA does a child inherit from their father?'

'Around fifty percent, sometimes more.'

'So that's around fifty cents?'

'Yes.'

'Doctor, the DNA you extracted from that latent print could have come from someone who shared fifty percent of my client's DNA, correct?'

The doctor looked at the page. Looked at the prosecutor. Looked at me.

'Yes, that's possible.'

'This piece of art is signed at the bottom of the page. Would you read out the name for the jury?'

'Tomas Jackson. Aged seven and a half.'

64

Eddie

Castro didn't want to take the chance of any further damage with his witnesses.

He still looked confident. He had an ace up his sleeve.

His anonymous witness.

'Your Honor, the People would like to call Witness Eight.'

I stood up, said, 'Your Honor, there is no property in a witness. Any party to this case can speak to any witness at any time. There is no longer a requirement for this witness to have anonymity. The witness is willing to waive that right.'

Castro was about to object, but the doors of the court opened, and Ruby Johnson walked in, flanked by Detective Artie Chase.

'Is this correct, Mr. Castro?' asked the judge.

Before he could answer, Ruby said, 'I want to tell the truth. I want to go on the record.'

Confused, Castro conferred with his ADAs. They were just as surprised as he was.

'In that case,' he said, with some trepidation, 'the People call Ruby Johnson.'

I watched her take the oath, sit down. She had her arm in a sling, and the bags under her eyes spoke of a restless night.

'Ms. Johnson, would you state your occupation for the record?'

'I am a nanny, maid and housekeeper to families in West 74th Street.'

'And where were you on the night Margaret Blakemore was murdered?'

Ruby looked at Detective Chase. He nodded.

'I was passing Margaret's house on my way home when I saw Margaret through the window of her living room, and I watched Brett Bale shoot her three times . . .'

Castro began to interrupt, but the judge stopped him.

'You asked the question, Mr. Castro. You deal with the answer,' said the judge.

'Permission to treat this witness as hostile?'

'Proceed,' said the judge.

'Ms. Johnson, you told me, and the police, you saw John Jackson murder Margaret Blakemore.'

'I did. I was lying.'

'So you're a liar. You admit that in front of this jury,' said Castro, desperately trying to prevent his case from imploding.

'I haven't lied to this jury,' said Ruby. 'I'm here to tell the truth. I lied to *you*, Mr. Castro.'

He stood silently for a moment. Thinking about what to do next. His best point had been made, that Ruby had lied to him. Any other questions could just make things worse. He sat down, and I stood to cross-examine.

'You used to live on this street, some years ago, is that right?'

'Yes, with my mother and father.'

'So you knew it well, and you knew the neighbors?'

'Yes.'

'After you saw Brett Bale shoot and kill the victim, what happened?'

'I followed Bale, saw him dump the murder weapon in a garbage bag and go back to the party at Petra's house. I took the gun.'

'This gun has been tested for DNA, which we have been discussing in this case. How did you get my client's son's DNA on that weapon?'

'I work for the Jacksons as their nanny,' said Ruby, and as she spoke she looked straight ahead, avoiding John Jackson's gaze. 'I drugged Tomas – I gave him a glass of orange juice full of liquid painkillers and sleeping aids, and when he was asleep I pressed the butt of the gun into his hand. Parents share their DNA with their children. I knew it would be enough to implicate John Jackson, as long as the police came looking for him.'

'So you made the anonymous call, implicating the defendant?'

'Yes, I made that call.'

'Why?'

'My mother was ill and I needed money. That was part of it. I knew I could blackmail Brett Bale and Todd Ellis. They were both suspects initially. Everyone knew they were involved with Maggs, sorry, the victim. If Ellis's wife found out he was back with Maggs, she would divorce him and take half of his fortune. Brett Bale knew that I had seen him kill Margaret. I got money from them both, and I spent it. But that's only part of the reason I did this. It's not the main reason . . .'

'Before we get to that, do you know why Brett Bale killed Margaret Blakemore?'

'Because she knew.'

'She knew what?'

'She knew Bale had killed his wife so he could be with Margaret. He'd told her as much. Then she found out he was still seeing other girls and she threatened to reveal his secrets.'

65
Ruby

Flynn was throwing questions at her, but Ruby didn't mind.

It was time to tell the truth.

Not all of it.

But enough.

'Why did you frame John Jackson for the victim's murder?' asked Eddie.

There was a simple answer.

'Because I needed them to leave the house,' said Ruby. 'I had spent many nights lying awake, trying to think of ways to get them out. I thought about a fire, but that wouldn't work. It might come back to bite me. I had to get them to leave somehow. Shame is a powerful weapon, Mr. Flynn. I needed them out of the street, and I knew if John was accused of murder then the residents would do everything they could to get him out. It's hard to walk down a street knowing everyone there hates you and wants you out. I did everything I could to pressure them to leave. I got the neighbors to write to them and tell them they were no longer welcome. I wrote MURDERER on their front door. I turned everyone against them . . .'

'Why? Why did you need them out of the house?'

'Because I was running out of time. Alison Jackson had arranged for construction work to be done on the house. And I couldn't allow that to happen.'

'Ms. Johnson, last night Detective Chase and I saw you in the Jackson's house after they left and checked into a hotel. You had a hammer in your hand. Do you remember?'

'I do.'

'What did you do with that hammer?'

'I swung it.'

This was hard. This was so, so hard for Ruby. Her eyes filled with tears, and her voice scratched and broke.

'You swung the hammer at something, didn't you?'

'I swung it into the stud wall. Breaking it.'

'Ms. Johnson, you confirmed earlier you used to live on this street with your mother and father. Just to be clear, you used to live in the house the Jacksons live in right now?'

'It was our house.'

'Why did you swing that hammer into the stud wall?'

'I had to break the wall down before the construction work began on the house.'

'Why is that, Ms. Johnson?'

'Because I had to move my father's body out from behind the wall before the construction workers found it.'

The gasp from the jury, and the rest of the courtroom, sounded like someone switching on a vacuum cleaner.

'Last night you confessed to your father's murder, to Detective Chase?'

And, as soon as Ruby had told him what she had done, the red priest stopped whispering. The voice inside her head, the red priest, *with the voice of her father*, stopped talking.

Ruby, at last, had silence. She was free from the red priest. Free from her father.

And that was the best kind of freedom.

'It was me. I killed him and buried him in the wall. My mother had nothing to do with it. *Nothing.* It was all me. She didn't know. She thought he'd run away. Alison's mother, Esther, she saw right through me. She knew I was up to something with the painting. I couldn't risk her getting me fired from working for the Jacksons. I needed Alison to trust me, and I needed everyone out of that house. I needed Althea gone too. Esther turned against me. So I had to kill her,' said Ruby.

Alison howled in pain, and John got up from the defense table, went to his wife sitting behind in the gallery and put his arms around her.

Ruby's own mother was dying, and Ruby had been given a choice last night by Flynn and Detective Chase. She could tell the truth, and her dying mother would have immunity.

Ruby always did what she had to do to protect her mother.

Even lie for her.

Josef had attacked her mom that night, before he left. She fought him off – finally she had fought back. And Ruby had taken a knife from the kitchen drawer, and put it in her father's neck. Together with her mom, they had pulled down part of the stud wall, put him inside it, and repaired it, plastered it.

Covered it up.

Flynn sat down, and the judge began speaking to the jury.

66

Eddie

Kate and I took a moment.

We stood in the hallway outside the courtroom, watching our client holding his wife. They cried hard. It was a mix of so much pain being released and so much joy at a life returned. Alison would need counseling, and Kate had already told her she would help arrange it. None of this was their fault. A monster had found its way into their home. It was no one's fault but Ruby's. The agony of what they had been through together would only deepen their love for each other. Detective Chase had agreed to visit John's hospital and speak to the director – get our guy his job back, any salary for the time he had missed work and an apology. In exchange, I agreed that John wouldn't sue the NYPD.

I hadn't told this to Al Parish yet. He was standing beside his army of associates as they patted him on the back and applauded him for a job well done. There would be no applause when I told him John wasn't going to sue the police. Al had made enough money out of John. I made a mental note to send Harold Washington III a new pair of jeans. I still felt a little bad about ripping a hole in his expensive pair.

I beckoned Al over.

'Thank you so much, Eddie. Kate, you were wonderful,' said Al.

'I need one more favor, Al,' I said.

'Anything.'

'There's a lady called Maura who is going to send you her résumé. She's a secretary, a damn good one. Hire her.'

'Do you know her?'

'Not really. She used to work for Castro, but she quit. Couldn't stand him.'

'If you don't know her, then why are you going out on a limb for her?'

'Because that's what people do, Al. Everyone needs a little help from a stranger.'

The elevators chimed and two people came out of it. Bloch and Castro. They weren't talking. I think Castro was still a little sore about everything and Bloch didn't talk.

Al and his associates left with John and Alison.

I still had business to attend to.

It was Castro who came up to us first.

'Ruby is in custody,' he said.

'Good. Detective Chase is better than I thought. I got one more favor to ask. Get Althea out of jail today, and get her family documented. It's the least you can do. And it's good for PR. And it might help prevent Althea from suing the city.'

'I hate you, Flynn. You know that, right?'

'You're joining an already sizeable group of like-minded people.'

He turned his back on me, walked away.

I asked Bloch, 'You get my text message?'

She nodded, put her hand in her jeans and came out with a pack of Juicy Fruit.

'I checked your car too. Like you asked. No devices anywhere. Even checked the fuel tank,' she said, and then gave me the keys.

'You top up the windshield wash and polish it too?'

Bloch raised an eyebrow.

I checked my watch. It was coming up on midday.

'I've got to go. Kate, can I borrow a page from your legal pad?'

She looked at me strangely.

'You mean you actually want to write something down? This is new.'

She tore off a page, handed me one of her pens.

'Stay here,' I said, and ran for the elevator.

On the way down I scrawled five words on the page. Big letters.

I chewed gum.

Checked my watch.

11.58 a.m.

The elevator doors opened in the lobby and I ran for the exit. It was a wall of reinforced glass. Two large panes on either side of the double exit doors.

A few people were filing out of the building ahead of me.

The sun was coming through the glass, bathing the faded tile lobby in golden light. I stood in that light for a moment. Breathing hard, but not from the run. From the adrenalin.

My fist clenched. Jaw tight.

I walked up to the solid pane of glass and stood in front of it. Then took the gum out of my mouth, set it in the middle of the page and slammed it onto the glass.

The page stuck.

I turned on my heel and walked away, toward the coffee shop on the ground floor.

I needed coffee. It would be another long day.

Tonight, I had to meet Buchanan. Had to straighten things out with New York's Finest.

Either I would walk away tonight, or a few days later a paramedic would carry me out in a body bag.

Nothing I could do about it.

I had to end this. One way or another.

67
Angel

Angel held the crosshairs on Flynn. His finger on the trigger, body perfectly still.

But Flynn wasn't taking any chances.

He had merged into a tight crowd as soon as he set foot out of the Aztek, and stayed in that crowd until he got inside the court building.

Frustrating, but there would be another chance. A better one.

When Flynn left the court building, he would be walking toward the line of fire. That's optimal shooting conditions. May as well be standing still, holding a target.

Angel waited.

He was good at waiting.

The hours ticked by and, on the hour, the clock tower bell rang. He was glad he'd brought the ear defenders. Without them his hearing would have suffered. If Flynn so happened to leave the court building on the hour, the chimes from the bell could be enough to put Angel off his shot.

Not with this head gear.

He drank water. Kept watch.

Waited.

His scope zeroed on the exit doors. A glass wall, with two doors in the center. He would need to wait until Flynn was out in the open.

Almost noon.

And there he was. Walking toward the exit.

Angel breathed slowly, bringing down his level of excitement. Settling his heart rate. He needed to be still for the shot.

Flynn stood in the lobby. It was definitely him.

Angel waited. No point releasing his shot now. Everything else was perfect. The sun was behind him. Raining down harsh light on the court building. It was like a spotlight on Flynn.

What was he doing? He was just standing there . . .

He resisted taking the shot. That was security glass. The bullet would likely penetrate it, but at this distance it would send the round tumbling. Maybe off course. Angel had seen that happen before. He couldn't risk missing his target.

Flynn walked toward the exit doors.

Angel touched the trigger.

Then Flynn took something from his mouth and put it on a piece of paper. He stuck the paper to the glass wall of the court building and walked back into the lobby away from the doors.

What the . . .

Angel focused his sight another one degree. Zeroed on the page. There was something written there.

LOOK BEHIND YOU.

YOU SONOFABITCH

Angel's heart seemed to stop.

Instinctively, his head swiveled around.

The curly-haired man in the wrinkled suit stood behind Angel. Five feet away. He wore ear defenders just like Angel. And just like Angel he had a weapon. A Glock pistol, pointed straight at Angel's head.

The Sako was all the way out of the window. He couldn't bring the weapon inside and swing it around. Not before the disheveled man pulled the trigger.

The man in the wrinkled suit said nothing.

The clock-tower bell rang.

The muzzle of the Glock flashed.

Angel suddenly couldn't see, but he was aware that his body was falling to the floor. His vision cleared, but only just.

Blood in his eyes.

He was on the floor. Looking at his ear defenders, which had rolled off his head. He could see the man's dirty shoes walk toward him and stop right in front of his face.

The muzzle flashed.

The bell rang.

Angel didn't hear it.

68

Eddie

I got the text from Jimmy with the meet location.

It was to be held in a garage on the corner of 43rd Street and Berrian Boulevard, in the Ditmars-Steinway neighborhood of Queens. I knew the area well. Any criminal defense attorney does.

Not far from 43rd Street is the visitors' center for Rikers Island, where you board a transport bus to take you across the Rikers Island Bridge over Bowery Bay to New York's largest jail. I'd visited clients there many times. It's the ass end of Ditmars-Steinway, a hip neighborhood that gave the world Steinway pianos and had been home to Telly Savalas and Tony Bennett.

The north part of the neighborhood, where I was headed, didn't have much in the way of culture apart from the old piano factory and the Steinway mansion, which was now an arts center on 41st Street. The garage faced the Bowery Bay Wastewater Treatment plant. There were a lot of commercial buildings here – construction-vehicle hire, iron-works and garages.

It was almost ten p.m. when I pulled in at the side of the curb. The garage roller doors were open and I could see light spilling onto the sidewalk. No one was around. You didn't walk these streets at night. The nearest living soul was probably three blocks away.

A quiet place for a meeting.

I got out of the car and picked up the two envelopes from the passenger seat and took them with me. I stood outside the garage, taking time to make sure I was seen. Buchanan and the rest of New York's Finest would be on edge and I didn't need to give them any more of an excuse to pull a trigger in my face.

A tall, thin man in a denim jacket came to the entrance and beckoned me to come inside. Before I could walk underneath the roller doors, he put his hand out to indicate I should stop. He reached behind his back, and I tensed. He had a long black device in his hand, which he switched on. A hand-held metal detector. He ran it over me and I held my arms out. The device beeped as it passed over my jacket. He felt the inside pocket where the device had registered my phone. He took the phone, made sure it was turned off and left it on a small table just inside the entrance. The metal detector wasn't just to sweep for guns or knives. They weren't worried about that. They were worried in case I was wearing a wire. He continued to move the metal detector over me. It beeped over my chest, in the exact place someone would wear a mic. I didn't move.

'Unbutton your shirt,' he said, stepping back. This time, he dropped the metal detector, hitched up his jacket to hold the .22 revolver he had tucked into the waistband of his pants. With one hand, I unbuttoned my shirt to reveal the Saint Christopher's medal I wore every day. He swiped the medal, it beeped. He let go of the gun. Ran the detector over the envelopes I'd brought. Satisfied, he nodded and gestured I should go on inside.

I left my phone on the table, and walked into the garage. Soon as I stepped inside, the thin man hit a button on the wall and the roller doors began to come down. As they rattled closed, I felt the sudden urge to duck and run back out before they clattered shut.

Instead, I got a hold of myself and studied the garage. It was a large rectangular space, lit only by a single bulb in the center of the room. Racks of tools on the wall to the right. The other three walls held steel racks of tires. There were two inspection pits cut into the concrete and they had been covered with steel plates. Some jacking equipment and car lifts stood on the left side of the space.

An aluminum table had been placed below the single bulb and a very large man sat on one side of it. A metal folding chair faced him. I'd never met Buchanan, but knew him by reputation. He had been a brutal patrol cop, with a string of excessive-force complaints. Of course, he was much loved by his fellow officers so none of those complaints ever went anywhere. His head was big and square, his body too. A nose spread over his face and put his thin lips into shadow.

'Sit down, Eddie,' he said.

I put my envelopes on the table and took a seat. The rest of the garage was in darkness. There could have been twenty guys in there that I couldn't see. I guessed there were more than just the man on the front door.

'Nice night,' I said.

He laughed, easily, leaned forward and placed his huge arms on the table, causing the legs to squeak with the weight.

'You got some balls – I'll give you that. What I want to know is how you think you can resolve this. You come after one of my guys, you threaten to expose my operation . . . none of these things are healthy choices for you.'

'I know how this city runs. Lots of people do. Greenbacks and kickbacks. Here's the thing: I did threaten to expose Ben Gray, but that's all I did. I just threatened him. Here . . .' I picked up the large brown envelope, tossed it across the table at Buchanan. 'That's all that I have on Ben Gray and the towing operation.'

He picked up the thick envelope, opened it, reached inside and pulled out the contents, set it on the table. He stared at it.

'This is the TV guide.'

I nodded, said, 'I had it Xeroxed so it looked like a thick pile of important documents I could wave around in court. I don't have any evidence against Sergeant Gray.'

'What about the four guys from the other towing companies that you brought to court?'

'One of them is a former client. He mostly sleeps in the homeless shelter in Tribeca – the Bowery Mission. The other three guys are his friends. I bought them overalls, my secretary sewed some badges onto them – not very well, I might add – and they sat in the gallery and put the shits up Sergeant Gray. Like they were supposed to. After court, I paid them a hundred bucks each and let them keep the overalls.'

'You're shittin' me,' he said.

'Before I was a lawyer, I was a conman. The two jobs aren't that different. Listen, I'm not your problem, Buchanan. Ben Gray, he's your problem. This whole pile of shit started because he got played, then he got scared. Cops do stupid things when they get scared. You know that.'

He leaned back in his seat. I could see the cogs working in his brain.

'I came here to make you an offer so all of this can go away,' I said.

He said nothing for a moment. He was re-assessing Gray in his mind. Whatever Gray had told him, Buchanan was now looking at him in a different light.

'How much are you willing to pay?' he asked.

'Nothing,' I said.

Buchanan stared at me, hard. His jaw set.

'But I can give you this . . . call it a gift,' and I slid the small envelope across the table.

He stared at it for a moment. Then looked at me. The envelope looked like something from a kid's stationery set in his huge hands. He ripped it open. Five photographs fell out.

Picking them up, one by one, he stared at them. As a cop and now a mob boss, Buchanan had to have a poker face for situations like this. But there was no way he could keep his feelings in check as he looked at those photographs. His eyes widened, lips parted. Like I'd just shown him a photo of his house in flames.

'Where did you get these?'

'I kept an eye on Ben Gray, like you should have done.'

His left arm slammed the table, the photographs jumped and I saw a large dent where his fist connected. He started swearing. I didn't blame him.

The photographs were taken at different angles in the All American Diner. The place was busier than normal, with almost every available seat taken up by the voluminous number of junior associates in the employ of Al Parish. They had taken the photos for me. When I said they took up almost all of the seats, they did leave one free.

The seat at the counter, beside Sergeant Ben Gray. The photos had been taken last night, at seven in the evening. When I was supposed to meet District Attorney Castro to discuss a plea deal for John Jackson. I didn't show. But Castro took the only available seat while he waited for me. That was the seat at the counter beside Sergeant Ben Gray. Castro is effectively his boss, and no way was Castro going to sit beside a cop and not at least say hello. They had some small talk while Castro waited for me.

Perfectly innocent.

Perfectly arranged and executed by Al's associates, who had no idea of the significance of the meeting.

'I take it that you didn't know that Ben Gray was talking to the district attorney?' I asked.

Buchanan rubbed his forehead, closed his eyes. Swore again.

'You know Castro wears that white suit for a reason. He's the anti-corruption DA. When my people showed me these photographs, I had them watch Gray's house. He's scared, Buchanan. He's making a deal with the DA and then he's going into witness protection. He's got his traveling money all ready to—'

'Traveling money?' asked Buchanan.

'If you go to his house now, you'll find a blue gym bag with about two hundred grand in it. We saw him bring it into the house. I'd check the garage first. Cops are no good at hiding money. I'm guessing you didn't know about this extra cash?'

Buchanan shook his head.

I didn't tell him that my friend Bugs had broken into Gray's house and left the gym bag behind some old cardboard boxes. Bugs had split the other fifty grand we'd taken from Mr. Christmas with his pals and right now they were on a Greyhound bound for Atlantic City.

I said, 'I'm guessing this is money he skimmed off the top of the tow trucks and God knows what else. But it's money that should have been split with you in the first place. Gray is getting ready to run. And he's running straight into the arms of the white knight DA. If you don't believe me, go over there right now and ask him about the gym bag. I bet he pretends he doesn't know anything about it.'

The big man rolled his head back, rubbed his eyes, then sat forward and gathered up the photographs.

'Like I told you,' I said. 'I'm not your problem. Ben Gray is your problem.'

Buchanan stood, said, 'How do I know you're not going to come after me or my people?'

I sat forward, said, 'First, I don't have any evidence against you. Second, like I said, I know how this town works. I can't change that. I represent people who are falsely accused. Sometimes, I represent people who have made a mistake and got themselves in trouble. If they hold up their hands and plead guilty, I'll help them change their lives. Everyone makes mistakes. *You* made a mistake by coming after me. If you call off the hit, I'm willing to give you a second chance, but with certain conditions.'

Buchanan studied me for a time. Like he was trying to read me. He had expected me to come in here and beg for my life, to cry for mercy and offer to pay him thousands of dollars to take the contract off my head. Now, he was in a totally different position. I was telling him I would *allow* him to call off the hit, but he had to do something for me first.

'What conditions?'

'I'm willing to accept a truce with one condition. If you come after me, or any of my people again, I'll kill you. Is that fair enough?'

I thought I detected a slight shiver of fear. A flash that came over his eyes. He looked over at the thin man, said, 'Call off the hit on Flynn. Then get the car. We're going to see Ben.'

'Call the Christmas guy,' I said. 'Tell him the contract is off.'

'He's first on the list,' said Buchanan as he got up, gathered the photographs and walked toward the exit. I could hear the mechanism for the roller doors activating.

'You don't want the TV guide?' I asked.

There was no reply. He had already ducked under the doors.

I leaned back in the chair and let out my breath, unclenched my fists. That was damn close. Too close.

I rolled my shoulders to relieve the tension. Got up.

It was finally over.

I was wrong.

69

Eddie

Footsteps behind me.

I turned.

Four men walked under the roller shutter doors into the garage. Black T-shirts. Jeans. Boots. Khaki combat pants. Tactical vests.

One of them stepped into the light and I saw a snake tattoo curling up both arms, its body twisting into a figure eight.

The 88s.

The figure in front had a pistol on his hip. He had long hair tied up in a ponytail. I took him for the leader.

'Buchanan called off the hit,' I said.

'We guessed as much, seeing as how they left you breathin',' said the leader. 'This ain't about business. This is all pleasure.'

One of the men hit the control button on the doors. They stopped going up.

Started coming down.

I stood away from the desk, put my hands in my jacket pockets.

'I'm armed. You should leave,' I said.

The leader laughed, said, 'You're not armed, conman. I saw Buchanan's guy scan you from head to toe. Your people put two of our friends away – Grady Banks and Butch.'

'I have no idea what you're talking about.'

'Sure you do. And we lost a good man outside the Cardozo Hotel. One of your people damn near cut his leg off and he bled out. So this isn't about collecting a paycheck, Fly Man. This is about what's right.'

They advanced. The leader first.

My phone was all the way behind me, on the table. Switched off.

No one else knew I was here. That's the way I'd wanted it. I'd played the odds of talking my way out of the hit with Buchanan. This was unexpected.

Two of the men behind the leader drew knives from their tactical vests.

The doors were halfway closed. No way to get around them and out onto the street. One of them would grab me and take me down.

There are no retired conmen. Sooner or later, this game catches up to everyone. That's why I'd gotten out of the life and chosen a new one – a lawyer. Trouble was I couldn't leave my past behind. I was still the hustler. Still playing long cons and short cons.

And this is what happens to every conman sometime down the line. I was still Eddie Fly.

Right now, that was a good thing.

The leader bunched his hands, put his right foot forward and started inhaling through his nose. Chin down. He bounced on his feet. Loosened his arms. Ready to charge in with a big right hand.

The good thing about ceramic knuckles is that not only are they lighter than brass, they don't show up on metal detectors.

The leader sprang forward.

I slid all four fingers of both hands into the knuckles and pulled them out of my jacket.

The leader was fast, powerful, but not skilled.

I dropped into a boxing stance, punched from the hip with my right.

I hit him on the left side of his nose. Felt the bones break. He dropped, instantly.

The other three took a second. Stood there.

I can take my chances one on one. Not three on one. Not when two of them have knives.

This was it. Stabbed to death in a dirty garage in northern Queens.

I couldn't win. But I could hurt a couple of them while they took me down.

Two figures rolled underneath the shutter doors.

And I dropped to the floor and covered my head.

Gunfire. One weapon had quick, cracking shots. The other boomed like a goddamn cannon. I could smell the gun smoke, but I dared not look up. I covered my head and lay flat until I heard the last body drop.

I looked up.

Bloch and Lake, their weapons drawn, were checking the bodies. Making sure the 88s were down and that they stayed down.

I got to my feet, saw the leader rolling on the floor, his hands over his face, blood gushing through his fingers.

Lake stood over him, pointed the weapon and fired once.

The man without much of a nose became the man without a face.

I put away the ceramic knuckles.

'How did you know I was here?'

Bloch said, 'When I checked your car for explosives, I put a GPS tracker under the wheel arch. Somebody has to look after you. We need to get out of here.'

I thanked them both, and we hustled out of the garage. I stopped outside, ran back in and picked up the TV guide and my phone.

On the street, I switched my phone back on.

One missed call. One voicemail message.

I hit play.

'Mr. Flynn, this is Chantelle at Mount Sinai. I'm sorry to bother you at this hour, but I see you are the next-of-kin contact for Harry Ford. I'm so sorry . . . You need to get to the hospital as soon as you can . . .'

70

Eddie

I can drive. I mean, I can *really* drive.

But I had nothing compared to Bloch.

She tore through Queens, onto the Robert F. Kennedy Bridge over the East River and onto Randalls and Wards Islands and hit one hundred miles an hour over the Harlem River. I could see Lake holding on to the handle above the passenger door, his body being thrown around as Bloch cornered coming off the bridge and onto FDR Drive.

It was all I could do to stay a hundred yards behind her. I could hardly breathe, and I had to slow down twice to wipe the tears out of my eyes.

I called Kate and Denise from the car, told them to get to the hospital right away.

Told them I'd got the call.

The call we had all dreaded for so long. That nurse in the hospital I'd spoken to before – she had been trying to prepare me for the worst.

And now the worst was happening.

Denise and Kate were closer, and they said they would meet us there.

Traffic on the FDR caused Bloch to weave in and out of lanes and I lost her twice.

By the time we pulled onto Madison Avenue, it had been ten minutes since I'd seen Bloch's Jeep.

But I saw it double-parked outside the hospital and I pulled up behind it.

As I ran inside the hospital, I tried to remember if I had even closed the door to the Mustang, never mind locked it. I had the keys in my hands.

I couldn't think.

It didn't matter.

All that mattered was Harry.

All that mattered was that I made it in time to say goodbye.

I hadn't been there when my father died. I was in the hospital with him and my mom for days. She sent me out of his room to get something from the vending machines. When I came back in, he was gone. My mom knew he was going, and didn't want me to have to watch his last few minutes. She was trying to save me pain, and I didn't blame her for that. But I wished I had been there for him.

I wished I could have held his hand.

I wanted more than anything to hold Harry's hand right then.

There were people waiting at the elevators, and I ran right past, burst open the stairwell doors and started climbing, taking the stairs two at a time, three at a time, grabbing the rail on the landings and hurling my body around them, up more flights, my heart pounding, gasping for air, up again, counting off the floors in my mind. I couldn't speak, no air, sweat and tears streaming down my face as I burst through the doors of Harry's floor and sprinted down the corridor, my shoes sliding on the polished tiles. The door to his room was open and nurses were surrounding the bed. Lake stood outside and I rushed past him.

Bloch stood at the back of the room. There were four nurses around Harry's bed, hovering over him. Kate was among them. She was crying.

I couldn't speak. I had no air.

'Can you believe they won't let me have one glass of bourbon in this goddamn hospital?' said Harry.

Two of the nurses stepped away from the bed.

Harry was sitting up. Eyes open, wide awake.

One of the nurses turned to me and said, 'I'm Chantelle. Sorry, I was talking to your partner Kate – I think maybe you misinterpreted my message. I'm really sorry. He woke up shouting for you and for a drink. He hasn't been rude to the staff at all – he's just really disturbing the other patients and we thought you could calm him down. I think it's the drugs that's making him react this way . . .'

It was only then I noticed Kate was smiling as the tears fell over her cheeks.

I still couldn't speak. I had no breath, but even if I could have talked I had no idea what I'd say. The nurses moved away from the bed and gently I put my head on Harry's shoulder. He put his arms around me.

'I love you too, kid,' he said.

Something sharp drove into the small of my back. I didn't care. Then something wet licked my face.

'Clarence, my boy,' said Harry, as the dog licked his face too and I heard Denise screaming with sheer joy.

'Could I ask you all to be quiet,' said Chantelle.

'I'll get him some bourbon,' said Bloch.

'It's not allowed in the hospital,' said Chantelle.

'Lady, either you owe us all about a thousand dollars in speeding tickets, or you can let her go get this man a drink so we can shut him the hell up,' said Kate.

Chantelle apologized again, said one small drink wouldn't hurt, and left the room.

I closed my eyes.

And held my friend.

Epilogue
The Man

The man slipped on a new T-shirt, stepped into his khaki shorts and worked his feet into his flip-flops as the coffee machine in the kitchen began to gurgle.

He poured himself a cup and took it to the work station. He picked up his Bluetooth headphones, and his phone, and moved onto the balcony with his coffee. This was the last condo in the development to sell, because it was the most expensive. Partly you were paying for the view – an unobstructed one-eighty vista of Miami Beach and the vast Atlantic Ocean.

Life was good for the man.

He sipped his coffee and smelled the sand and the sea.

His phone rang.

Caller display read *Bedford Hills Correctional Facility.*

He stared at the number for a moment, perplexed. Bedford Hills was a women's prison. He answered.

'Hello, can I help you?' he said.

The voice on the other line was female.

'Hi, I'd like to talk to someone about movies,' she said.

'May I have your name, please?' said the man.

'Ruby,' she said.

'Any particular actors you're interested in?'

'Marlon Brando,' she said. 'Two movies in particular. *The Chase* and *One-Eyed Jacks.*'

The man hesitated, said, 'We should discuss a rental fee for those titles. They can be expensive.'

'I don't have any money. Tell him Ruby called,' and she hung up.

The man thought for a moment. He didn't work for free. However, his colleague might be irritated if he didn't pass the message along.

The man dialed a secure number, rerouted many times through a sophisticated cell network to ensure that no one could possibly eavesdrop on their conversation. He took another drink of coffee.

'Good morning, Mr. Christmas speaking . . .'

'Good morning to you,' said the man. 'Just got a call from a woman named Ruby. I imagine she used the payphone in Bedford Hills Correctional.'

'What did she say?'

'She said she didn't have any money. I think that's most important.'

'She is a friend,' said Mr. Christmas.

'Is this the same Ruby you were supposed to deal with in New York?' asked the man.

'The very same. We became acquainted. That was an enlightening project. A lot of our competition retired. And Flynn and his team did most of the work for us. Ruby was the highlight of my trip, by far. She's now serving life in Bedford Hills, New York, for multiple murder. She pleaded guilty. I imagine she struck a deal in exchange for her mother's immunity.'

'She killed people with her mom?'

'Just one. Ruby and her mother killed her father, Josef, and hid his body in the house. Afterwards, they never spoke of it. Her mother insisted that the father had left home and run away to Kansas. I think something broke inside Ruby when she killed her father. Fascinating young woman. Ruby loves her mother, in her own way. She was protecting her. The *whole thing* was about Ruby protecting her mother. What else did she say?'

'She said she was interested in two Brando pictures. *The Chase* and *One-Eyed Jacks.*'

The line fell silent.

The man gazed out at the ocean.

'Does that mean anything to you?' asked the man.

'Those movies have a number of things in common. Brando stars in both. And both have a prison break as a key element of the plot.'

'We're breaking people out of prison now? For free?' asked the man.

'Money isn't everything,' said Mr. Christmas.

'Money helps. And we're not prison breakers. We operate a niche business here, need I remind you, we're professional hitmen.'

'I suppose I could always kill a few correctional officers while I'm there if that would make you feel any better . . .'

'That's not the point. It's a huge risk.'

'Let me think on it,' said Mr. Christmas. 'While I'm thinking, if you would be so kind, please book me a flight to New York City.'

Mr. Christmas hung up.

The man took off his earpiece, drank his coffee and smiled as he stared out at the blue horizon.

Acknowledgements

Thank you to my amazing wife, Tracy, who is my first reader, first editor, and saves me every time. I could not do this without Tracy. She is my heart and soul. To Chloe, Noah, my Dad, Tom and Marie, and of course Lolly and Muffin.

To the wonderful minds belonging to Toby Jones, Sean DeLone and Jon Wood, for all of their insightful thoughts and notes which have helped this novel along.

At Headline, to Toby, Joe, Lucy, Patrick, Becky, Isabel, Jennifer and Mari, and everyone who works on my books, thank you so much. It is a joy to work with you all. I am delighted that Eddie Flynn has a new home at Headline Books. He is in good hands.

At Atria Books, Sean, Alison, Maudee and the whole team – thank you! It has been a wonderful experience at Atria and I am excited and glad to be working with you all!

At RCW Literary agency, Jon, Safae, Sam, Tristan, Katharina, Stephen, Chris, Sampurna, and all who represent my books and sell them so well and with such care and dedication. God Bless all at RCW.

To John 'The Debacle' Mackell, Alan 'Ace' Wilson, Matt 'The Man' McKee and 'Sparky' Mark O'Connor. And to Mrs. Sally Rodgers, John's mother-in-law, an apology on behalf of your barrister son-in-law.

My final thanks is once again to *you*, dear reader.

Thank you for reading this book.

I really mean that.

If this is your first time reading one of my novels, then I sincerely hope you enjoyed yourself, and you check out some of the other Eddie Flynn novels or some of my standalone works. If you are a dedicated fan of my work, then God Bless you. I hope this was just as entertaining as the first book of mine you picked up off the shelf. Thank you so much. I hope you are enjoying Eddie's adventures.

This book is about family. There are many characters in series fiction that I have read over many years and in some weird way I have come to think of them as family. If you are a fan of my books, then you are also part of a family of readers, and part of Eddie's family too. Eddie Flynn belongs as much to you, as he does to me. I hope you have many happy years of reading ahead, and again, if this is your first time reading my books – welcome to the family.

I hope, dear reader, you are well and in good spirits.

My heartfelt thanks to you for supporting me.

With my very best wishes,

Steve Cavanagh.

8/5/24 — 8-18-24